MAGIC BREAKS

ACE BOOKS BY ILONA ANDREWS

The Kate Daniels Novels

MAGIC BITES
MAGIC BURNS
MAGIC STRIKES
MAGIC BLEEDS
MAGIC SLAYS
MAGIC RISES
MAGIC BREAKS

The World of Kate Daniels

GUNMETAL MAGIC

The Edge Novels

ON THE EDGE
BAYOU MOON
FATE'S EDGE
STEEL'S EDGE

Specials

MAGIC MOURNS
MAGIC DREAMS

MAGIC
BREAKS

Ilona Andrews

ACE BOOKS, NEW YORK

THE BERKLEY PUBLISHING GROUP
Published by the Penguin Group
Penguin Group (USA) LLC
375 Hudson Street, New York, New York 10014

USA • Canada • UK • Ireland • Australia • New Zealand • India • South Africa • China

penguin.com

A Penguin Random House Company

This book is an original publication of The Berkley Publishing Group.

Ace Books are published by The Berkley Publishing Group.
ACE and the "A" design are trademarks of Penguin Group (USA) LLC.

Library of Congress Cataloging-in-Publication Data

Andrews, Ilona.
Magic breaks / Ilona Andrews.
pages cm. — (A Kate Daniels novel ; 7)
ISBN 978-0-425-25622-0 (hardback)
1. Daniels, Kate (Fictitious character)—Fiction.   2. Shapeshifting—Fiction.   3. Magic—Fiction.
4. Atlanta (Ga.)—Fiction.   5. Fantasy fiction.   I. Title.
PS3601.N5526625M34 2014
813'.6—dc23
2014009023

FIRST EDITION: August 2014

PRINTED IN THE UNITED STATES OF AMERICA

10   9   8   7   6   5   4   3   2   1

Cover art by Juliana Kolesova.
Cover design by Jason Gill.
Interior text design by Tiffany Estreicher.
Map by Julie Krick.

"Magic Tests" was previously published in the anthology *An Apple for the Creature*.

To Anastasia and Helen

Dear Readers,

Thank you so much for reading Kate's adventures for these seven years. We appreciate your support. Your enthusiasm for the series keeps us going.

Some really big things happen in this book. It reads like the final book in the series, but it's not. As we write this, we are under contract for three additional books. Magic Breaks *might finish the story arc, but it doesn't finish the story. For those of you who are just coming to the series, we've included a list of characters and "From the Journal of Barabas Gilliam," a series summary written from the point of view of one of the series' most popular side characters. If you are a long-standing fan of the series, the information in those two sections will probably sound redundant, and if you choose to skip them, you won't lose anything.*

Some stories are big in scope, where the future of the world seems to hang in the balance, and some stories are small but no less important. Because Magic Breaks *is one of those large-scope stories, we thought you would enjoy a smaller story as well, so we offer you "Magic Tests," a short story about Julie's adventures in a new school. The fate of the world might not be in jeopardy, but the life of a child is, and we hope you will like the contrast between the two stories.*

As always, we would like to thank the people who helped us bring this story to you. Our wonderful editor, Anne Sowards, and our agent, Nancy Yost, who both strive to keep us in line. The senior production editor, Michelle Kasper, and the assistant production editor, Julia Quinlan. Judith Lagerman, the art director; Juliana Kolesova, the artist responsible for the image on the cover; and Jason Gill, the cover designer.

We would like to thank Jonathon Frisby, attorney-at-law, and his wife; Veronique Cantrell-Avloes, attorney-at-law; Noel Goudreau, attorney-at-law, and her husband; Sarah Javaheri, attorney-at-law; Carol Najera, attorney-at-law; Tiffany Murphy, attorney-at-law; Nina Javan, attorney-at-law; and others for their incredible generosity and knowledge and willingness to entertain hypothetical criminal scenarios involving a weremongoose lawyer. We are deeply grateful. Any errors of fact or law are our own.

We would also like to thank our beta readers, who kindly donate their time and skills to help us make the book the best it could be. They are, in no particular order: Ying Dallimore, Carrie Wassenaar, Omar Jimenez, William Stonier, Stella Won, Julie Heckert, Laura Hobbs, Antoinette Hodges, Nichole Walford, Michelle Kubecka, Melody LeBaron, Wendy Baceski, Shannon Daigle, Cathy Thilmany, Jeanine Rachau, Michelle Kraut, and others.

Finally, thank you once again to you, our wonderful readers.

CHARACTER LIST

The Pack

KATE DANIELS: Main character. Female, approximately twenty-seven at the time of the book. Former mercenary, former member of the Order, currently Consort to Curran, Beast Lord of the Free People, and female alpha of the shapeshifter Pack. Carries a sword named Slayer. Daughter of Roland, from whom she has been hiding all of her life, and raised by his renegade warlord Voron. Kate owns Cutting Edge, a small investigative agency bankrolled by the Pack.

CURRAN LENNART: Beast Lord. Alpha and leader of Atlanta's shapeshifters. Male, about thirty-three. Has been Beast Lord since he was fifteen. Turns into a North American gray lion. Blond, gray-eyed, approximately 5'10" with the build of a longtime weight lifter. In human form, prefers hand-to-hand combat with a concentration on grappling, which utilizes his training in judo, wrestling, and jujitsu.

JIM SHRAPSHIRE: Werejaguar and alpha of Clan Cat. Male, age thirty-five; 6'2" and built like a middleweight boxer. Dark skin, brown eyes. Jim moves with an easy athletic gait that belies the pent-up energy and violence waiting just under the surface. Jim is the Pack's head of security. He is a paranoid micromanager who sees threats to the Pack around every corner and in every shadow. Has a history with Kate Daniels (nonromantic) going back to their service together in the Mercenary Guild.

BARABAS GILLIAM: Weremongoose but member of the bouda (werehyena) clan; 5'9" and slender. Appearing to be in his late twenties, Barabas is very pale-skinned with a shock of bright red hair, usually gelled and spiked atop his head. He has the lean build of a fencer or dancer. Barabas is the Pack's lead legal counsel and one of Kate's "babysitters" appointed by Aunt B prior to her death in *Magic Rises*. Barabas is a skilled knife fighter with an encyclopedic knowledge of laws both human and Pack.

ANDREA NASH: Female, 5'2", blond. Andrea is Kate's best friend. Former knight of the Order and expert marksman. Andrea is beastkin, meaning she is the extremely rare offspring of a female bouda and a hyenawere, a hyena who could shapeshift into a human. In many shapeshifter packs, beastkin are at best tolerated but mistreated, at worst seen as abominations and killed at birth. Andrea and her mother suffered unspeakable abuse and cruelty at the hands of her birth pack. As a teen, Andrea escaped and, disguising herself as human, joined and graduated with honors from the Order's Academy for knights. After the events of *Magic Bleeds*, Andrea was exposed as a shapeshifter and forcefully retired from the Order; she subsequently joined Kate in the detective agency Cutting Edge. Andrea is engaged to Raphael, alpha male of Clan Bouda, and together they now run the clan after Aunt B's death.

RAPHAEL MEDRANO: Scion and alpha of Clan Bouda, late twenties and around 6'3". Only surviving son of Aunt B and her late husband. Raphael is a right sexy bastard, tall, dark, and extremely handsome with a devilish smile that hints at exciting sex. Like the majority of Clan Bouda, Raphael is romantically experienced with a long list of partners but fell in love with Andrea Nash at first sight and pursued her relentlessly until, despite her better judgment, she accepted his advances. Curran has a grudging respect for Raphael but until recently viewed him as spoiled and vain, despite his status as arguably the best knife fighter in the Pack.

DEREK GAUNT: Werewolf and protégé of both Jim and Curran. Introduced in *Magic Bites* as a teen, Derek is now a young adult, about nineteen and an experienced fighter. Once almost pretty, Derek was irreparably disfigured during the events of *Magic Strikes*. His vocal cords were also damaged in the attack, leaving him with a permanently low and menacing voice. Kate often refers to Derek as "boy wonder" and his devotion to her is almost fanatical, second only to his admiration and loyalty to Curran. Derek, like Curran, has a profound hatred and disdain for loups, shapeshifters gone feral.

ASCANIO FERARA: Teenage bouda, age sixteen. Basically a younger version of Raphael, but even more incorrigible. Introduced in *Magic Slays*, Ascanio is a young bouda raised until recently in a religious compound and sheltered from the outside world. He's determined to make up for lost time and sometimes his behavior is extreme, even by bouda standards. His antics often bring unwanted attention to Clan Bouda and the Pack. He is seen by Derek in somewhat the same light that Curran views Raphael, wild and undisciplined. At the time of the book, Ascanio is an unpaid intern at Cutting Edge where Kate and Andrea can keep an eye on him.

DESANDRA: Female, late twenties, werewolf. Introduced in *Magic Rises*, Desandra is an enigma. Her father was one of the most ruthless and sadistic alphas among the Mediterranean shapeshifter packs. The only one of his children to live to adulthood, Desandra survived by pretending to be vain and stupid. Brought back to Atlanta with her twin infant sons, she has quickly risen through the ranks of Clan Wolf to become beta, second only to Jennifer. Beneath her outwardly crude and shockingly blunt exterior, she is her father's daughter, cunning, smart, and capable of sudden shocking violence.

DR. DOOLITTLE: The Pack's premier medmage, Doolittle is an African American male appearing to be in his midfifties, with short graying hair, wire-rimmed glasses, and a stocky, powerful build. An extremely talented physician and medical mage, Doolittle tends to devote his time to science and the treatment of the Pack, but much like his honey badger alter ego, he is fearless and willing to stand up to anyone, up to and including Curran and Kate. Doolittle was severely injured in *Magic Rises*, which resulted in him using a wheelchair.

JULIE: Teenage female referred to by Curran as "Kate's cub." Blond, petite, and pretty, Julie is being raised by Kate after losing her mother in *Magic Burns*. Like Kate, she is a human with magic living among and under the protection of the Pack. Julie has the unique ability to see magic; she is a human m-scanner and her powers are still developing. She has a crush on Derek, who sees her as a little sister, and an adversarial relationship with Ascanio, who views her as a rival and potential romantic conquest. During *Magic Slays*, Julie had been infected with

Lyc-V, the shapeshifter virus, and was going loup. Kate used one of her father's rituals to save Julie's life by washing her blood with her own, which bound Julie to her. Julie is unable to refuse Kate's direct order, a fact that Kate and Curran hide from her.

JENNIFER: Female alpha of Clan Wolf and widow of Daniel, who died in *Magic Slays*. Jennifer still holds a grudge against Kate for killing her sister and hates her even more now for bringing Desandra back to Atlanta. Jennifer knows she is weak and it is only a matter of time before her new beta makes her move. She fears for herself and her child.

ROBERT AND THOMAS LONESCO: Married alphas of Clan Rat. Second only to the wolves in numbers, the rats are excellent scouts and spies. The Lonescos feel undervalued and distrusted by Jim, the Pack's head of security.

CHRISTOPHER: Once a favorite in Roland's court, Christopher was given to Hugh d'Ambray, who punished him for some unknown transgression by slowly starving him to near death. By the time Kate rescues him in *Magic Rises*, months of being kept captive in a cage by Hugh d'Ambray have left Christopher a shattered shell of his former self. Christopher seems to have a tenuous grasp on reality and sometimes believes he can fly but has simply forgotten how to do so. He is utterly devoted to Kate for freeing him and believes Barabas, his de facto handler, to be an angel.

The Order

TED MOYNOHAN: Caucasian male, late fifties. Heavily built like an aging boxer or football player, Ted is 5'10" and weighs well over two hundred pounds. As knight-protector, Ted oversees Atlanta's chapter of the Order of Merciful Aid, and as such, he's also Kate and Andrea's old boss. Ted is a fanatic who distrusts and despises the shapeshifters and the People equally. He was once seen as a major player within the Order, but his star was tarnished when the Order's offices were attacked and burned by one of Kate's late aunt Erra's henchmen; Ted's plan to stop Erra backfired and resulted in dozens of civilian casualties (see *Magic Bleeds*). His subsequent handling of the Andrea Nash situation further damaged his reputation. He is now seen as more of an aging embarrassment, but because of his long service the Order is unable to force him into retirement unless he makes a colossal mistake. Ted is determined to go out with a bang, not a whimper.

MAXINE: Powerful telepath and longtime secretary and gatekeeper of the Order. A noncombatant, Maxine refers to everyone as "Dear." She is fond of Kate in spite of Ted's animosity toward her.

MAURO: Hulking Samoan knight of the Order, Mauro is the last of Ted's old guard, the rest having transferred after or perished during the attack on the Order in *Magic Bleeds*. Mauro is a gentle giant, intelligent and slow to anger with a massive 6'8" three-hundred-plus-pound frame and is covered in tattoos that glow when he is using his power to redirect fire.

The People (Pilots of the Undead)

GHASTEK: Thin and dark, age undetermined, could be late thirties or early forties. A powerful Master of the Dead, Ghastek is locked in a power struggle with Mulradin Grant to fill the power vacuum left by the recent and unexplained disappearance of Nataraja, Atlanta's former head necromancer. Ghastek senses that there is more to Kate than meets the eye and wants to know who she really is. He is very intelligent and gifted, and he knows it, which occasionally causes him to make mistakes out of arrogance.

MULRADIN GRANT: Ghastek's main rival for power in Atlanta's chapter of the People. The Pack knows little of Mulradin beyond his reputation as a solid family man.

The Bad Guys

HUGH D'AMBRAY: Roland's warlord; he hunted down and killed Voron nearly a decade ago. He discovered Kate's identity and is determined to present her to her father. Kate presents an irresistible prize for him: she's the daughter of Roland and she had been trained by Voron, just like Hugh himself. His hatred for Curran is matched only by his determination to overcome Kate's resistance. He's determined to make her submit to his will even if he has to burn Atlanta to the ground or drown it in shapeshifter blood. He doesn't really care if she comes to him of her own free will or is dragged to him in chains. Hugh is a superb strategist and an exceptional medmage. He is also the preceptor of the Order of Iron Dogs, the elite unit of the military arm of Roland's forces.

HIBLA: Female, origin unknown. Hibla is one of Hugh's Iron Dogs. A shape-shifter and expert with a blade, Hibla is directly responsible for the death of Aunt B, and Kate has been looking for some payback since the end of *Magic Rises*.

ROLAND: Kate's father is a mythical figure whose origins lie somewhere between fact and fable. He is the Builder of Towers. He slept for centuries but now the reemergence of magic has ended his long absence from the world of man. Roland possesses a nearly godlike power.

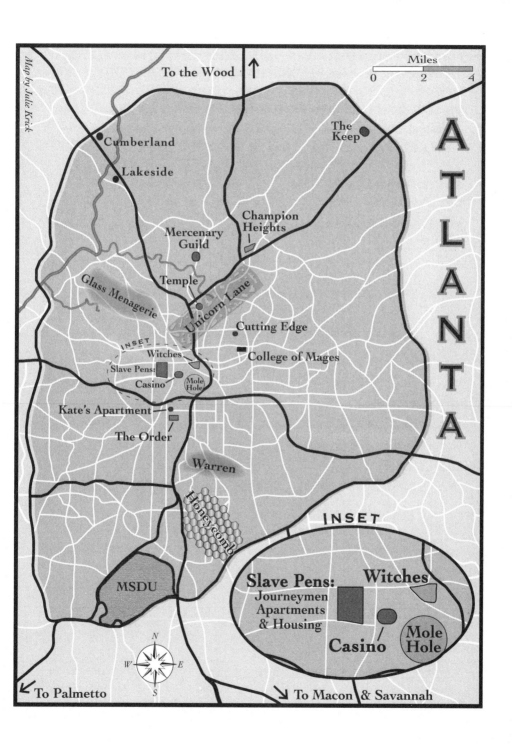

MAGIC BREAKS

FROM THE JOURNAL OF BARABAS GILLIAM

M Y NAME IS Barabas. I was named that because my mother was ambitious. It could be worse. One of my cousins is named Lucifer. I once
asked my aunt why and she said, "Because I wanted him to be beautiful and
to think for himself." Boudas, or werehyenas as most people know us, have
an interesting perspective on the world. Technically, I'm not a bouda. I'm a
weremongoose, but my mother is a bouda and I grew up among them.

At the time of writing this, I'm twenty-nine years old. I have a law
degree from the University of Virginia and I currently reside in Atlanta. I'm
employed as a Pack lawyer, which is to say I'm a member of the largest
shapeshifter organization in the South and second largest on the continent
of North America. I also work for the Consort of the Pack as a special advi-
sor. The Consort refers to me as her nanny occasionally, and I find that term
uniquely accurate. I would put one of those hideous child leashes on her if
I could, except I'm reasonably sure she would cut my arm off.

I find myself in a strange moment in time. Something momentous is taking place right in front of me, something that I suspect will drastically alter
the future of not just the Pack, not just my generation, but generations to come.
I have a front-row seat. I'm in the middle of it. Yet nobody around me seems
to realize that years from now our descendants will look back on this moment
and wonder how it all happened. Someone must document it. After all, history
is written by and for the survivors, and right now I'm not sure who those sur-

vivors will be. Don't take me wrong, I don't intend to roll over and fade into the night. I will rage with the best of them, just like Dylan Thomas's poem advises. But on the off chance we don't prevail, there must be a record of how hard we fought. It looks like I'll be the one making that record, since nobody else can be bothered. Funny how it always turns out that way.

So, I suppose, I'll begin at the beginning. The world has suffered a magic apocalypse. As expected, it was completely our own damn fault.

In ancient times, technology and magic existed in perfect balance, but then came the human race. They built a civilization based on magic. Creatures of terror and beauty roamed the land. Wizards with godlike power built entire cities overnight and rained winged snakes and molten metal on their enemies. (As an aside, that age must've been a nightmare. Concentrating that much power in the hands of individual human beings? Why, that could never go wrong or lead to horrible atrocities. Just read the Bible.) Finally the balance between magic and technology became so disrupted that magic receded. The cities wrought by magic crumbled, their wonders turned to dust, and their beasts became myth.

Fast-forward five thousand years. It's the early twenty-first century and we've created a civilization based on technology. Once again, we upset the balance and magic returned with a vengeance to slap us upside the head. It floods the planet in waves. One moment technology rules, internal combustion engines work, guns fire, and electricity keeps the monsters away. The next an invisible magic wave drowns the area, choking guns and spawning creatures with nightmarish teeth and robust appetites. Then, without warning, the magic wanes and SWAT's mages stop spitting fire and switch back to rifles.

This apocalypse is called the Shift. The Shift destroyed the technological civilization. Air travel is no longer possible, because planes fall out of the sky when the magic hits. The Internet is all but dead, because half of the time we have no electricity and magic chomps computer parts into dust. Cell phones do not work, unless you're in the military and have really good clearance. The high-rises and skyscrapers have fallen, gnawed to nubs by magic's teeth, but life goes on and people survive. And in the new post-Shift Atlanta, new factions and powers came into play.

First, there is the Pack. As mentioned, I am a shapeshifter and I work for the Pack, so I have a vested interest in explaining exactly who we are and what we do. The Pack is the second-largest shapeshifter organization in the country and has over fifteen hundred members. It's segregated into seven clans, according to the species of their beast, so boudas, wolves, and so on. Each clan is led by a pair of alphas. Together the alphas make up the Pack Council. But as Disney taught us, there must be a king, and our king is known as the Beast Lord, because we, as red-blooded Americans, have an issue with monarchy. His name is Curran Lennart. Curran took charge of the Pack when he was fifteen by defeating a mad werebear nobody could touch. He unified us. He persuaded the alphas to collectively purchase land and he built the Keep, our fortress, giving us a safe place to be ourselves. He imposed rules and laws and taught us that abuse won't be tolerated. Because of him, we live together in relative prosperity. When Curran says jump, we jump so hard, the ground shakes. Which isn't to say that he doesn't have bouts of assholeness, but all things considered, they are forgivable. He's also a really scary bastard who is fond of "my way or the highway" style of governance. More on that later.

We, the shapeshifters, are viewed with open suspicion by the rest of Atlanta. Our existence is the result of the Lyc-V virus, and sometimes the virus overwhelms our bodies, turning us into loups. Loups are vicious, insane, cannibalistic murderers. There is no cure for loupism, which is why we all practice strict discipline and undergo extensive mental conditioning to keep our emotions in check. When everything fails, there is panacea, an herbal concoction cooked with magic. It won't cure loupism, but about thirty percent of the time, it will reverse the transformation in progress. More on that later, also. In the eyes of the general public, every shapeshifter is a potential loup and "werewolf" is still a dirty word.

Next up we have the People. They are a nationwide organization, with offices in every major city. The People pilot the undead, specifically vampires, for fun and profit, but if you ask them, they do it for some dubious scientific purposes. Vampires have no minds of their own. The Immortuus pathogen, which leads to the death and subsequent reanimation of its victims, cleanses their bodies of everything it doesn't require, including internal organs, hair, genitalia, and consciousness. A vampire is a feeding machine, consumed by a never-ending hunger. They don't speak; they don't think; they kill anything with a pulse, and stopping one requires a heavy-duty antipersonnel howitzer or decapitation. Mincing them into small pieces has also been known to work, as the Consort has proven on many occasions. A single vampire on the loose in the city results in the immediate evacuation of a ten-block radius and the dispatch of several emergency police units, because a single SWAT team will run out of ammo before they take it down.

The necromancers—they prefer to be called navigators—telepathically grab hold of a vampire's empty mind, imposing their will on that blank canvas. This is called piloting. The navigators pilot the vampires like remote-controlled cars. They see what the undead sees, they hear what he hears, and when a vampire speaks, the navigator's voice comes out of his mouth. They can send the vampire into danger while sipping coffee in the armored bowels of the Casino. The best navigators call themselves Masters of the Dead, because modesty is clearly their most prized virtue.

The People make their headquarters in the Casino, while our HQ is in the Keep. The People are the Pack's biggest competition within the city. When we butt heads, people die; so a while ago, in an effort to cut down on possible bloodshed, we nominally divided the city into their "territory" and ours. It's a bit complicated with specific streets and areas, but for simplicity's sake, north and northeast are ours and south and southwest are theirs. When you hear one of us say "city territory," that's what we mean. We don't own property in each other's specific areas, and we patrol our imaginary borders.

Right now the People are embroiled in an inner power struggle. The head of the Atlanta office retired—or perhaps they killed him off, nobody knows—and two of the Masters of the Dead are maneuvering their way to the top spot. One is Ghastek, who is quite brilliant, competent, extremely dangerous, and wrapped in a protective shell of world-weary arrogance. Basically a know-it-all with the expertise and a pack of vampires to back it up. The other is Mulradin, of whom we know little except that he is a family man and he becomes perturbed when people say harmless things, such as "Holy shit!" in the earshot of his wife, who mustn't be sullied by being exposed to such coarseness. Bite me.

Here's the kicker: most people don't know it but the entirety of the People answer to one man. Remember the Age of Magic and wizards with godlike powers? Turns out that when magic began to disappear from the world, not all of those wizards died. Some of them went into hibernation. Thousands of years later, the Shift woke one of them up. Think about it. Here's a man unconstrained by ethics and morals. A man who used to rule an empire. A wizard-king, a law unto himself, who has lived for thousands of years with the power to crush thousands of lives with one single push of magic. A walking nuclear bomb. A man so powerful, he doesn't need a name; he has phrases attached to him starting in all capitals. The Father of Undeath. The Builder of Towers.

He calls himself Roland now. I asked the Consort why and she showed me the *Song of Roland*. It's a twelfth-century ballad about a knight who is ambushed because of treachery and refuses to blow his horn out of pride until all of his soldiers are dead and he finally blows so hard, his temples burst and he dies a martyr. Make of it what you will.

Thousands of years ago, Roland created vampires and now he runs the People from his territory in the Midwest. There are stories and myths of him scattered throughout folklore, the Torah, the Bible, and other holy books under different names. Apparently, Roland has two compulsions. First, he is a social engineer. He builds empires. He can't help himself. He knows that the only way we can achieve enlightenment is under his rule. Democracy isn't a concept he considers relevant, which is really bad news for us. Second, he falls in love. He falls in love a lot and makes children, and sooner or later, these über-powerful children turn on him and he has to kill them. For example, Abraham was one of his; they had some sort of a spat, and Roland exiled him until Abraham finally died later in poverty. Not exactly the way the Bible tells it, but there you go.

Before Roland went into hibernation, he apparently swore off procreation. But after he woke up during the Shift, he must've been overcome by the euphoria of being alive. Same reason why people have sex after funerals. Roland fell in love with a woman called Kalina. She wanted to have children and he apparently was cool with it, until a child was conceived, a daughter, and then Roland decided to pull the plug and to kill her in the womb. Kalina had her own magic, the magic of compulsion, and she was desperate to save her baby. She bewitched Roland's warlord, Voron, and magicked him into thinking he was in love with her. Together they ran away. Kalina gave birth, but Roland eventually caught up with them. Kalina realized that of the two of them, Voron had the better chance of surviving and raising the baby, so she told him to run and stayed behind to confront Roland. She stabbed him through the eye and he killed her.

Not a happy story.

So here is Voron, a cold ruthless bastard, a really talented fighter who was supposed to lead Roland's armies when he got around to taking over our continent, a guy who probably killed hundreds of people to get that good, and now he is alone with this baby. His brain is permanently cooked by Kalina's magic. So he looks at this tiny cooing magical baby, the daughter of probably the only woman he ever loved, and he doesn't say to himself, "At least I have something remaining of her. I'll raise this child and I'll do everything in my power to guard her, and protect, and love her, and make sure she has a happy life." No, he looks at her and he thinks, "I'm going to get even." Because he is that kind of a cold ruthless bastard.

He takes this baby and he hones her and shapes her, until she turns into a living weapon. She can kill you with her sword. She can kill you with a toothpick. She can kill you with her bare hands. I'm a weremongoose. I'm fucking fast. When I get bored, I play with my pet cobra, and I don't mean that figuratively. I never get bitten, because I'm fast enough to easily dodge a striking snake. Sometimes when Kate swings her sword, I can't see it. She's that fast.

So while this little girl is growing up, she and Voron roam all over the Americas. They never stay in one place for long; one month she's training with someone in Oklahoma, the next she's in a gladiator pit in Brazil. The entire time he's telling her how her father killed her mother and how he would kill her if she was ever discovered. All that is true. But Voron also tells her that the only way for her to survive is to kill Roland. She learns how to end human life before she reaches puberty. The damage that was done to her as a child is staggering. But that's not the worst thing.

Voron set out to make her into a perfect assassin, but he didn't teach her any magic. He wasn't a magic user himself, so she learned general magic skills, a little from the witches, a little from the mages, but she didn't practice the blood magic, the Roland brand of magic—first, because nobody could teach her and second, because Voron thought it would give her away. But there is a third reason. There was no need for it, because Voron knew what Roland was capable of. He knew that Kate's skill was sufficient for her to cut her way to Roland, but she would have no chance against her father. That was the crux of his revenge. He raised this child from the time she was a baby solely so one day he could watch Roland kill or be killed by his own flesh and blood. I'll let that sink in a little bit.

He didn't get a chance to see it for himself. Roland decided he needed a new warlord, so he took Voron's best pupil, the boy he raised like a son, and made him his warlord. His name is Hugh d'Ambray, or Sick Fuck, which is more fitting. Hugh d'Ambray had been hunting Voron since his betrayal. One day, when Kate was away from the house, Hugh found him and killed him. He claims to be somewhat broken up over it, but you can't trust a single word that comes out of that lying bastard's mouth.

With Voron dead, Kate was on her own. A knight of the Order of Merciful Aid temporarily assumed guardianship of her and tried to send her to the Order Academy, but she dropped out. The Order is a semiofficial law enforcement agency. Their legal status is murky, as I've pointed out a number of times to anyone who will listen. They are fanatics, they have a rigid mind-set, and they believe that any deviation from your average vanilla *Homo sapiens* makes you nonhuman.

You've read what I wrote. Do you think I'm human?

To these guys, Charles Manson and Jack the Ripper are more human than I am. If it weren't for the fact that our police force is overwhelmed, their presence wouldn't be tolerated. It shouldn't be tolerated anyway. But, as is typical, when someone comes to you and offers to remove that pesky griffin that's killing people in your neighborhood and to do it free of charge if you can't afford to pay, most people refuse to look a gift knight in the mouth.

So Kate decided the Order's brainwashing wasn't for her. She bummed around Georgia, dropping in and out of Atlanta. Worked for the Mercenary

Guild for a while. They're the guys you call if you have money and a monster in your backyard, and the cops are too busy with a poisonous flying jellyfish downtown. She tried to hide in plain sight. She might have succeeded except she ran into the Beast Lord. As I mentioned, he is a scary, bossy bastard. She hates all authority. He said, "Jump." She said, "Screw you." Of course, they would fall madly in love after that. And when I say madly, I mean it.

Kate never does things halfway. I'm certain that Voron attempted to create a psychopath but somehow he failed. Kate will put herself between danger and some idiot bystanders every single time. She found the half-starved child of an alcoholic on the street, almost died saving her from demons, and then adopted her. Julie is an exceptional child in every way, including the amount of trouble she can generate. She isn't easy to raise. I've never heard Kate complain.

Kate counts me as one of her friends. It is a privilege. It means when I'm several states away and I call her and say, "I'm in trouble," she will get her sword and come to get me, expecting nothing in return. That is a rare thing. Curran might be the Beast Lord and a stubborn one, but he knew what he had when he met her. That's why she's now the Consort of the Pack. We needed a Consort for a long time. Someone to balance out Curran. Then she came along and she is sensible and tries to be fair. Things were going so well for a while.

Remember I mentioned panacea, the herbal medicine that helps us to not go loup? Until recently we had no access to it. It was created somewhere in Europe and they wouldn't sell it to us at any price. Last summer suddenly the Beast Lord and his Consort got an invite to settle a shapeshifter family dispute in a small country on the Black Sea. They would be paid in panacea. We all knew it was a trap, and we all went to see who was holding the string of the trapdoor. It was Hugh d'Ambray. He'd followed the trail of bread crumbs and found Kate. Here is a woman who had been trained by the man he viewed as his father. She is better with a sword than he is. She is the daughter of the guy he worships. You see where I'm going with this? Hugh wants her and he doesn't understand "no." She hates him, because he's a sick fuck and he killed her sensei. It went weird really fast and ended up in a giant fight and a castle on fire.

So here we are. We didn't get the panacea, but we got Christopher, an insane mage Kate pulled out of a cage where Hugh was slowly starving him to death. Christopher isn't all there. Turns out he can make panacea, so now we have our own supply, but the price was high. We lost Aunt B, the alpha of Clan Bouda. The boudas are misfits. Other shapeshifters don't trust us. We don't do things by the book. Aunt B took care of us. Of me. Words can't describe what she meant to me. She is gone now. Kate watched her die. It eats at her. I can see it in her face. She visits Aunt B's grave more than her son does, and Raphael is over there every chance he gets.

So here we are, at a crossroads. We don't know if Hugh is alive or dead. Curran had broken Hugh's spine and hurled him into the fire, but Kate says she felt him teleport out. We know that the days of hiding are over. Roland will come for his daughter. He'd attacked the Pack before through his agents. He doesn't like us, because we are growing and gaining in strength. But now, whether Hugh survived or not, Roland is coming for sure. If Hugh is dead, Roland will come to see who killed him. If Hugh's alive, he will have told Roland about his daughter, and Roland will come to see her.

As I said, this is the moment when everything hangs in the balance. If Roland attacks us, we will fight, not just for the Consort, but for our lives, as overly dramatic as it sounds. Roland understands the concept of personal freedom. He just believes it's highly overrated. Freedom is everything to us. We won't be slaves. Kate is our best hope of stopping him, but—there is that pesky word again—she knows her magic can't match his. The Covens of Atlanta threw their lot in with her and are supplying her with undead blood so she can practice her father's blood magic. She's learning, but I'm afraid it's not fast enough. If Roland takes over Atlanta, other cities will follow. We, the Pack, have the best chance of fighting him off.

There is a storm gathering on our horizon. We will make a stand, but I wonder if it will matter in the end.

1

"**K**ATE, THIS IS really dangerous," Ascanio said.

Teenage shapeshifters have an interesting definition of "dangerous." Lyc-V, the virus responsible for their existence, regenerates their bodies at an accelerated rate, so getting stabbed means a nap followed by a really big dinner, and a broken leg would equal two weeks of taking it easy and then running a marathon with no problems. On top of being a shapeshifter, Ascanio was an adolescent male and a bouda, or werehyena, who were in a category all their own when it came to taking risks. Usually when a bouda said that something was dangerous, it meant it could instantly incinerate you and spread the ashes to the wind.

"Alright," I said. "Hold the rope."

"I really think it would be better if I went instead."

Ascanio gave me a dazzling smile. I let it bounce off me and fixed him with my hard stare. Five ten and still slender from growing too fast, Ascanio wasn't just handsome; he was beautiful: perfect lines, cut jaw, sculpted cheekbones, dark hair, and darker eyes. He had the kind of face that could only be described as angelic; however, one look at those big eyes and you realized that he'd never been to heaven, but somewhere in hell a couple of fallen angels were missing a sixteen-year-old. He realized the effect he had early in life, and he milked it for everything it was worth. In about five years, when that face matured, he would be devastating. If he lived that long. Which right now didn't seem likely, because I was mad at him.

"Hold the rope," I repeated, and took the first step.

"Don't look down," Ascanio said.

I looked down. I was standing on a metal beam about eighteen inches wide. Below me, the remains of the Georgian Terrace Hotel sagged sadly onto the ruined street. Magic hadn't been kind to the once-proud building. Its eighteen floors had collapsed in stages, creating a maze of passageways, sheer drops, and crumbling walls. The whole mess threatened to bite the dust any second, and I was on the very top of this heap of rubble. If I slipped, I would fall about a hundred feet to the pavement below. My imagination painted my head cracking like an egg dropped onto the sidewalk. Just what I needed. Because balancing on the iced-over beam wasn't hard enough.

"I said don't look down," Ascanio said helpfully. "Also, be careful, the ice is slippery."

"Thank you, Captain Obvious."

Below me, the graveyard of Atlanta's Downtown stretched into the distance. The massive buildings had toppled over decades ago, some shattering into gravel, some almost whole, sprawling on the ground with their beam work exposed, like rotting beached whales with their bones on display. Heaps of rubble choked the streets. Strange orange plants grew among the debris, each a thin stalk terminating in a single triangular leaf. In summer, sewage and rain overflow spilled into the open, but the harsh winter froze it, sheathing the ground with black ice.

The magic of Unicorn Lane swirled around me, dangerous and twisted. Magic flooded our world in waves, here one minute, gone the next, but Unicorn Lane, the lovely place that it was, retained its power even when the tech was at its strongest. It was the place where you came when life's troubles became too much for you. Things with glowing eyes bred here among fallen skyscrapers, and if you lingered in these ruins, one of them was guaranteed to cure all that ailed you.

Anyone with half a brain avoided Unicorn Lane, especially after dark. But when your business is floundering, you have to take whatever job comes along, especially if it starts with the chief editor of the *Atlanta Journal-*

Constitution crying in your office chair because her rare and expensive pet has gone missing. Since the magic killed the Internet and crippled TV, newspapers had once again become the primary source of news, and an endorsement from the largest newspaper in the region was worth its weight in gold. Also, she cried in my office. I took the job.

Being a Consort, I didn't have to work for my living. The Pack took care of the necessities, but I wanted Cutting Edge to succeed and I would do whatever it took to make it stand on its own two feet. Even if it involved tracking down escaped pets.

Unfortunately, the fluffy critter in question had made a beeline straight for Unicorn Lane, and so it took me a few hours to find it. And I let my sixteen-year-old bouda intern come with me, because he could track the beast by scent and I couldn't. Ascanio wasn't bad in a fight. He was physically powerful and fast, and he had a strong half-form, a meld between a human and animal that made the shapeshifters incredibly efficient killers. Raphael, the alpha of Clan Bouda, had been whittling Ascanio down into a decent fighter over the past months. Unfortunately all that training didn't do anything for his common sense.

I had finally cornered the small creature, hiding in a crevice. While I tiptoed toward it making quiet nonthreatening noises, Ascanio decided to help by snarling "to flush it out," which caused me to nearly fall into a hole in the floor and sent the panicked beast straight to the top of the precariously standing building. Which is how I ended up with a rope around my waist, trying to maneuver on a foot-and-a-half-wide beam protruding twenty feet over a sheer drop, while the exotic and rare pet shivered at the very end of it.

"Please let me do this," Ascanio said. "I want to help."

"You've helped enough, thank you." I took another step along the beam. If I fell, with his shapeshifter strength he would have no problems pulling me to safety. If he fell, getting him back up to the top of the building would be considerably harder for me. The deadweight of a human being was no joke.

"I'm sorry I scared it."

"When I grab it, you can apologize."

The small beast shivered and tiptoed toward the other end of the beam. Great.

Ascanio growled under his breath.

"I can hear you growling. If I can hear you growling, it can hear you, too. If you scare it into leaping to its death, I'll be really mad at you."

"I can't help it. It's an abomination."

The abomination stared at me with large green eyes.

I took another step. "It's not an abomination. It's a bunnycat."

The bunnycat scooted another inch toward the end of the beam. It resembled a criminally fluffy average-sized housecat. Its owner described the fur color as lilac, which to me looked like pale grayish-brown. It had a cute kitten face, framed by two long ears, as if someone had taken regular cat ears and stretched them out, enlarging them to bunny size. Its hind legs were all rabbit, powerful and muscled, while its front legs, much shorter than those of an average cat, looked completely feline. Its tail, a squirrel-like length of fluff, shook in alarm. The first bunnycats were the result of some sort of botched magical experiment at the veterinary school of the University of California. They were sold off to private breeders and since they were rare and cute, they became the latest rage in hideously expensive household pets.

The wind buffeted me. I fought a shiver. "What's your problem with it anyway?"

"It's wrong and unnatural," Ascanio said.

"And turning into a hyena is natural?"

"A cat is a predator. A rabbit is prey. It's a rodent. They took a cat and mixed it with a rodent. It doesn't smell right."

I took a couple more steps. Damn, this beam was high.

"I mean, how would it feed itself?" Ascanio asked. "If it doesn't hunt, it can't survive on its own and it's something that shouldn't exist. If it does hunt, it will probably catch mice, the only thing small enough besides birds, which means it would be feeding on its relatives. It's a cannibal rodent. It sounds like a bad movie."

"Rodents are already cannibals. Ask Clan Rat, they'll tell you." The Pack consisted of seven clans, segregated by the species of the animal, and members of Clan Rat were rather pragmatic about their natural counterparts' habits.

"What do they feed it anyway?" Ascanio asked.

"Bacon and strawberries."

There was an outraged silence behind me.

"Bacon?" he managed finally.

"Yep." I moved forward another six inches. Easy does it.

"Because that's what it would catch in the wild, a boar, right? I can't wait to see a pack of bunnycats take down a wild hog with those short tiny legs. Wouldn't the boar be surprised?"

Everybody was a comedian.

"Maybe if I oink loud enough, it'll leap across the beam and try to devour me."

A gust of cold wind slammed against me, biting straight through three layers of clothes into my bones. My teeth chattered. "Ascanio . . ."

"Yes, Consort?"

"I think you misunderstand the whole nature of what it means to be an employee. We have a job to do; we are doing it. Or I'm doing it, and you're making it more difficult."

"I'm not an employee. I'm an intern."

"Try to be a silent intern."

I crouched on the beam. The bunnycat shivered less than a foot away. "Here . . ." Bunny? Kitty? "Here, cute creature thing . . . Don't be scared."

The bunnycat squeezed itself into a tiny ball, looking sweet and innocent. I'd seen that look on feral cats before. That look meant they would turn into a tornado of razor claws as soon as you were within striking distance.

I scooped it up, bracing myself to be clawed bloody.

The bunnycat looked at me with its round green eyes and purred.

I rose and turned. "Got it."

The beam collapsed under my feet and we plunged down. My stomach tried to jump out of my mouth. The rope jerked, burning my ribs, and I hung suspended over the sheer drop, the bunnycat snuggled in my arms. The beam crashed to the ground with a loud clang, gouging the crumbling pavement.

The rope rotated slightly. The bunnycat purred, oblivious. Across the ruined city, the sun was rolling toward the horizon, turning the sky orange in its wake. I was alive. How about that? Now I just had to stay that way.

"Okay, pull me up."

The rope didn't move.

"Ascanio?" What was it now? Did he see a butterfly and get distracted?

The rope slid up, as fast as if wound by a winch. I shot upward. What the . . . ?

I cleared the edge and found myself face to face with Curran.

Oh boy.

He held the rope up with one hand, muscles bulging on his arm under his sweatshirt. No strain showed on Curran's face. It's good to be the baddest shapeshifter in the city. Behind him Ascanio stood very still, pretending to be invisible.

Curran's gray eyes laughed at me. The Beast Lord reached out and touched my nose with his finger. "Boop."

"Very funny," I told him. "Could you put me down?"

"What are you doing in Unicorn Lane after dark?"

"Apprehending a bunnycat. What are *you* doing in Unicorn Lane after dark?"

"Looking for you. I got worried when you didn't come home for dinner. Looks like I found you just in time. Again." He lowered me onto the ruined roof.

"I had it under control."

"Mm-hm." He leaned over the bunnycat and kissed me. He tasted just like I remembered, and the feel of his mouth on mine was like coming home out of a dark cold night to a bright warm house.

I put the bunnycat into the pet carrier and we hightailed it off the roof.

I HOPPED OVER a metal beam covered in pink slime that steamed despite freezing temperatures. The cold wind licked my back through my jacket.

Ahead of me, Curran leaped onto a concrete boulder. For a large man, he was remarkably graceful. "I parked on Fourteenth."

Mmm, car. Warm nice car. We had come on foot, and right now the car heater sounded heavenly.

Curran stopped. I landed next to him. "What's up?"

"Remember this?"

I looked over Unicorn Lane. In front of me an old apartment building sagged to the street, its weight too much for its magic-weakened steel bones. To the right, frost turned a twisted heap of concrete debris and wire into a labyrinth of white lattice. Looked familiar . . . Ah.

"What is it?" Ascanio asked.

I pointed at the half-crumbled apartment building, where a dark gap offered a way inside. "This is where we first met."

I had been investigating the death of my guardian and discovered that the Pack was involved. At the time I was doing my best to lie low, which made me an unknown, so Curran invited me for a face-to-face meeting in that apartment building. He'd wanted to see if I'd brave Unicorn Lane at night. I did.

It seemed so long ago now.

Curran put his arm around me. "Here, kitty, kitty, kitty?"

"I had to say something to make you come out of the dark."

"There?" Ascanio asked. "You met in that dark hole?"

"Yes," I said.

"Why would anyone want to meet in Unicorn Lane? Something bad could've happened. Why not a nice restaurant? Women like restaurants."

I cracked up. Curran flashed a grin and we climbed off the concrete into the alley.

Curran had parked his Pack Jeep on the corner of the alley and Fourteenth Street. Three thugs, two men and a woman, were trying to pop the lock open. Oy. Thanks, Atlanta.

The would-be carjackers saw us. The man in a blue jacket swung around and leveled a gun in our general direction. Big barrel, small brain. *Hey, here are some guys walking out of Unicorn Lane at night. They're in good shape and look like they could kick my ass. I think I'm going to try to take their car at gunpoint. Sheer brilliance. Yep, this will totally work.*

Without breaking his stride, Curran moved slightly in front of me. I had no doubt that if the thug fired, His Furriness would block it rather than letting the bullet hit me. He'd pulled this maneuver before a couple of times. I still wasn't sure how I felt about it. I really didn't want him getting shot on my account.

"Give me the keys!" Blue Jacket said, his voice raspy.

Curran's eyes went gold. His voice dropped into a rough growl. "If you're going to shoot, make sure to empty the clip, because after you're done, I'll shove that gun up your ass sideways."

Blue Jacket blinked.

"Can you even do that?" I asked.

"Let's find out." Curran stared at the thug. "Well? Shoot, so we can start this experiment."

Blue Jacket stuck the gun into his pocket and fled. His buddies dashed after him down the street.

Curran shook his head, got the keys out, and opened the hatch. We packed the crate with the bunnycat inside, Curran slid into the driver's seat and started the engine, and we were off, heading through the city toward the northeast, where the shapeshifter Pack made its lair in the Keep.

The car heater kicked in. My teeth stopped chattering.

"I'm so hungry," Ascanio said. "What's for dinner in the Keep?"

"We are going to the Keep," Curran said. "You're going to your mother's house."

Ascanio bristled. "Why?"

"Because you haven't been there in the past three days and she would like to see your face. And because she would like to discuss your latest report card."

Damn it. Him and Julie both. My fifteen-year-old ward had failed algebra in a spectacular fashion. First, she tried to convince me that the teacher lost her homework, all four different assignments of it. Then she ranted for a while about how school was hard and we were placing unreasonable demands on her, and then, for a big finish, she informed us that she would rather drop out and be homeless. Curran and I slow-clapped for a whole minute.

"What did you fail this time?"

"I failed nothing. I'm passing all my classes."

"He has a forty in algebra," Curran said.

Algebra again.

I turned around in my seat so I could see Ascanio. "How the hell did you get a forty?"

"I don't know."

"He isn't turning his homework in. He spends half of his time with Raphael and the rest with you at Cutting Edge."

"School is overrated," Ascanio said. "I don't like it and I have no interest in it. I just want to work for the Pack."

"Let me burst that bubble for you," Curran said. "The Pack requires educated people. If you want to climb up the food chain, you need to know what you're doing. Most alphas have advanced college degrees. In fact, most people you know have degrees."

"Like who?" Ascanio asked.

"Raphael has an MBA. Barabas has a Juris Doctor. Andrea has completed the Order's Academy. Doolittle completed medical school. Mahon has a doctorate in medieval history."

That explained some things. Mahon ran Clan Heavy and I always thought his reasoning was on the medieval side. Oooh, I should tell him that sometime. He would like that. Just not while he was in his bear form. I could run really well for a human, but I had a feeling an enraged Kodiak would be faster.

"Aunt B didn't have a degree," Ascanio volunteered.

"Yes, she did," Curran said. "She went to Agnes Scott and majored in psychology."

Ascanio stared out the window.

"What's the plan?" Curran asked. "You're sixteen; you have to have a plan. Or are you going to let your mother pay your bills for the rest of your life?"

"No." Ascanio bit off the word.

"Then I suggest you rethink algebra," Curran said.

WE DROPPED ASCANIO off, delivered the bunnycat, got paid, and Curran drove toward the Keep. I snuggled up in my seat. All was well that ended well. I didn't die; I'd earned my money, I was finally warm, and now, after a long day at work, I'd get to go home and take a nice shower.

"You watch him a lot," Curran said. "Like you're expecting he'll break. He's a sturdy kid. He can hold his own and I know you know that, so what's the deal?"

That was a loaded question. "I had a dream last night. I was trapped on the castle tower. The roof was on fire. There were flames all around me and they burned off my feet." In real life, the castle had been consumed by magical flame, but it had never gotten to that particular tower. It was too high. "In the courtyard Hibla was killing Aunt B."

That part of the dream was born from my memories, so vivid they hurt. When we had gone to the Black Sea to get the panacea, we found Hugh d'Ambray, my father's warlord and preceptor of the Order of Iron Dogs. Hibla was his second-in-command. When the castle caught fire, I ended up trapped on top of the tower. I saw our people try to get out of the castle, chased by Hugh's Iron Dogs, and Aunt B had sacrificed herself. She knew the Iron Dogs would kill her before they would move on. They had a mage with them. I could see it in my mind, the silver chains whipping from the mage and pinning Aunt B in place, the hail of arrows that pierced her body, and finally Hibla, walking to her, sword in hand.

"I was trying to help her," I said. "In my dream. I was trying to help her, but I had no feet."

Curran reached over. His warm fingers closed over my hand. He squeezed my fingers gently.

"I remember the way Aunt B snarled just before Hibla took her head off. I can replay that snarl in my head over and over. I was a hundred and fifty feet above them. I couldn't have heard it."

"Is that the first time you had the dream?"

"No. I should've done . . . more."

"I love you," he said. "But even if I didn't, I would still tell you the same thing. There was nothing you could've done. Does it help?"

"No."

"I'm sorry."

"Thank you."

"Did you talk to anybody besides me?"

"No."

"You should talk to someone. The Pack has twelve therapists on our payroll."

Right. "I'm fine," I told him. "I just don't want any of them to die."

"Any of whom?"

"Clan Bouda."

He squeezed my fingers again. "Baby, you can't wrap them in bubble wrap. They'd rip through it and go for your throat. They're their own people. Ascanio has two alphas and two betas, and a mother, who is, by the way, a licensed Pack therapist. Talk to Martina. It will help. Talking about it always helps."

"I'll think about it."

He kissed my fingers. "If Derek came to you with this, what would you say?"

"I'd tell him to talk to someone and that the Pack has twelve licensed therapists on the payroll."

I knew exactly what would help. I needed to kill Hibla. After the castle, when we had boarded our ship, half-dead and barely standing, I was too tired to see anything. But Derek had watched the pier and he saw Hibla run up it, her sword bare. She had survived and she watched us leave. Killing her wouldn't bring Aunt B back, but it needed to be done. I wanted to send a message. If you killed someone I cared about, I would find you and make you pay for it. It didn't matter where you ran or how well you hid, I would punish you and I would make it so brutal that nobody else would dare to hurt anyone close to me again. I made Jim look for Hibla, but so far we had nothing. For all I knew, she had stayed back in Europe and I would never see her again.

"You don't have to go alone," he said. "If you decide to go and you need me, I'll come with you. I'll go in with you or I'll wait by the door until you're done."

"Thank you," I told him, and meant it.

We fell quiet.

"I have to leave in the morning," Curran said.

He said "I," not "we." "Why?"

"Do you remember Gene Monroe?"

I nodded. Gene Monroe's family owned the Silver Mountain Mine, near Nantahala Gorge. It was one of the primary sources of silver for the southeast. Gene claimed that his family traced its roots all the way to the Melungeons, Spanish Moors who had settled in the area centuries ago trying to escape the persecution of the Spanish Inquisition. Given that some members of his family turned into Iberian wolves, his claim had some credit. Gene was isolationist by nature and difficult to deal with. He ran a small shapeshifter group and although his neighbors had joined the Pack a long time ago, Gene had held out.

"Is he giving us trouble?"

"Not exactly. Apparently once a year the men of their pack gather together and go off into the mountains on a hog hunt. Family and close friends only."

"You're been invited?" I guessed.

"Yep."

"Do they know you hate hunts?"

"I might have neglected to mention it." Curran turned the wheel to the right, avoiding a pothole the size of a tire filled with luminescent purple goo of unknown origin. "He wants the panacea."

I hadn't quite appreciated the extent of Curran's diplomatic scheming until I watched him work with panacea. The first thing he did upon arriving home from that trip was to pass a law that no shapeshifter at risk of loupism would be denied panacea within the Pack's territory. As a result, shapeshifter families from all over the country began settling on the border of the Pack's territory, forming a buffer between us and the outside world. Some waited for formal admission to the Pack. Some simply wanted a short trip across the border if their child began showing signs of loupism. If trouble came, they would fight for the Pack, because we were their only hope. Meanwhile Curran used panacea as both a club and a carrot, plotting, bribing, and dealing to stabilize the Pack and strengthen our defenses. A war was coming and we were doing all we could to prepare.

Thinking about the panacea and the war made me think of my father. I stomped on that thought before it ruined my evening. "So Gene wants the panacea. What do you want?"

"I want him to be choosier about the buyers for his silver. He's been trading with the Midwest."

"Roland?" My father's name rolled off my tongue. So much for not thinking about the bastard.

"His agents."

Silver was poison to shapeshifters. If my father started buying it in large quantities, he was coming our way and he wouldn't be bearing gifts. He viewed shapeshifters as a threat. Me, he hated. He'd tried to kill me in the womb, but my mother ran away and sacrificed herself so I could live. My stepfather hid me and over the years honed me into a weapon against my father. I was raised for one purpose: to murder Roland. Unfortunately, my father was a living legend and killing him would be difficult. I'd need a few armored divisions and nuclear support.

Curran grimaced. "Gene won't like me dictating his business. But I know for a fact that two of his grandchildren went loup at birth, so he will want to deal. That's what the invitation is about."

He had to go. Anything that weakened Roland was good for us. Still, I felt uneasy. Ever since the overseas trip, I'd been acutely aware that we'd been living on borrowed time. We didn't know if Hugh d'Ambray was dead or alive. Personally, dead worked for me, but either way my days of hiding in plain sight were over. Roland would come to investigate who nuked his warlord, sooner rather than later. Every day without him was a gift.

"How long will you be gone?" I asked.

"A day to get there, two days for the hunt, and a day back. I'll be back by Friday."

I did some quick calculations. Besides the Pack, Atlanta housed several supernatural factions, of which the People were the most dangerous to us. The People answered to Roland, which was why I'd been doing my best to avoid them. In the past, the Pack and the People nearly drowned Atlanta in a supernatural war over a misunderstanding. Now we met every month at a local restaurant to resolve our conflicts before they spiraled out of control, a meeting imaginatively titled "the Conclave." Because simply calling it a "monthly get-together" didn't make everybody feel special enough.

"Leaving tomorrow and coming back on Friday means you'll be missing the Conclave this Wednesday." And that meant as the Beast Lord's Consort, I'd have to lead the Pack's side of the discussion. I'd rather stab myself with a rusty fork.

He looked at me. "Really? Is the Conclave this week? That's crazy how it worked out."

I rolled my eyes.

Curran grinned. He liked sitting through the Conclave meetings about as much as I did.

"It's been quiet," he said.

He was right. Today was December third. This was the time the individual clans of the Pack had their year-end meetings. The hunting season was still in full swing and most of the younger, excitable shapeshifters were out of the city chasing after deer and feral hogs and having fun rather than picking fights with the People's journeymen.

"Jim says over a third of our people are out," I said. "It's making him paranoid."

Curran looked at me. "Making?"

"More than usual."

Jim was always paranoid, but on our trip to get the panacea, Hugh d'Ambray let it slip that he had a mole on the Pack's Council. Since that moment Jim's paranoia level had shot into the stratosphere. He swept the entire Keep for bugs. His people sniffed every square inch of the Council room. He interviewed everyone over and over, until the alphas threatened violence to get it to stop, and when he couldn't interview them anymore, he tried to have them followed. We almost had a riot. Each individual clan had its own meeting place, and Jim would've liked nothing more than to turn them inside out, but nobody would let him in. It was almost Christmas and we still had no idea who was feeding Hugh d'Ambray information. Jim took it personally and it was driving him up the wall.

"When everyone goes hunting, Jim complains about reduced strength," Curran said. "When everyone comes back for Christmas dinner, he'll complain that there are too many people and he has to have extra manpower to keep track of them."

"True."

Curran shrugged. "The holidays are coming. Nobody wants to fight before Christmas. The People will bitch and moan at us about some minor stuff, then we will bitch and moan at them about some minor stuff, then everybody will eat, drink, and go home. Just don't kick any of the Masters of the Dead in the face and we'll be fine."

"Don't worry, Your Furriness. I can hold the fort until Friday."

He paused. A serious note slipped into his voice. "Just stay safe."

"What could happen to me? With you gone, Jim will go into overdrive, which means I'll be surrounded by trigger-happy spree killers and guarded like the Hope Diamond. You're the one leaving to go into the woods with some people we barely know. Are you taking anyone with you?"

"Mahon, Raphael, and Colin Mather," Curran said.

Alphas of Clan Heavy, Clan Bouda, and Clan Jackal. Nice.

"I'll be back before you know it."

With that backup, he could wipe out a small army. "Give my best to Gene. And please let him know that if you don't come back to me safe and sound, I have no problems mobilizing our shapeshifter horde and invading North Carolina." And if Gene did anything to hurt him, he would live just long enough to deeply regret it.

The Beast Lord grinned at me. "I doubt it will come to that."

We drove in silence. I liked sitting next to him. The night outside the car was vast and cold, and he sat warm next to me. If something nasty crossed our path, he'd get out of the car and take it apart. Not that I couldn't do it myself, but knowing he would be there with me made all the difference in the world. Three years ago, on a night like this I would have been driving my old car home alone, praying it didn't die a noble death in some snow drift. When I rolled up to the house, it would be dark. My heat would be off to save money, my bed would be cold, and if I wanted to tell someone about my day, I'd have to talk to my sword and pretend it listened. Slayer was an excellent weapon, but it never laughed at my jokes.

"You still haven't told me what you want for Christmas," Curran said.

"Time," I said. "For you and me." I was so tired living in the glass bowl of the Keep.

"Check the glove compartment?" he asked.

I opened it and pulled out a piece of paper. *Cordially invited . . . thank you for your reservation . . .* "Is this . . . ?"

"The Black Bear Lodge," he said.

Two weeks earlier we'd had to go to Jackson County, North Carolina, to remove a loose troll from campus. The Appalachians had a large shape-shifter population and many of their kids went to Western Carolina University. We had stayed at Black Bear Lodge, a newly built timber lodge with good food and cozy rooms with huge fireplaces. We'd spent two glorious days there, hunting the troll, drinking wine in the evening, and making love in a giant soft bed. I wanted to stay so much it almost hurt.

He got this reservation for me. A warm happy feeling spread through my chest.

"How long?" I asked.

"Two weeks. We could leave as soon as I get back and stay until Christmas. We'd have to come back for the holidays or the Pack will scream and howl, but with the ley line it's only a two-day drive."

Two weeks. Holy crap. "What about the petition hearing?"

"I handled it," he said. "Remember that emergency session that ate up last Thursday? I cleared everything."

"The Gardner lawsuit?"

"Handled it, too." Curran leaned over and looked at me. His gray eyes glowed with tiny golden sparks. He slowly furrowed his blond eyebrows and moved them up and down.

"Is that your smoldering look?"

"Yes. I'm trying to communicate the promise of nights of ecstasy."

I laughed. "Did you read that pirate book Andrea left for me?"

"I might have leafed through it. So how about it? Will you do me the honor of accompanying me to the Black Bear Lodge, so we can lie in bed all day, get drunk and fat, and not have to think about anything related to Atlanta for the entire time?"

"Will I get nights of ecstasy?"

"And days. Ecstasy all the time."

Two weeks, just Curran and me. It sounded heavenly. I would've killed to be able to go and I meant it literally.

"Deal, Your Majesty."

≡ CHAPTER ≡

2

I STOOD IN a small concrete room and watched the undead blood lying in a placid puddle at my feet. The magic in it called to me, eager and encouraging, whispering a soft seductive song.

Sometimes the Universe smiled. Mostly she kicked me in the face, stomped on my ribs once I fell down, and laughed at my pain, but once in a while she smiled. It was Wednesday. I had gone through the entire stack of activity reports for the Conclave detailing all incidents and conflicts between us and the People that could possibly cause us trouble. No murders, no assaults, no heated exchanges of words. Nobody had stolen anybody's property. Nobody had gotten drunk and hit on someone's boyfriend. Hallelujah.

My work done, I locked myself in here, in a small rectangular room of stained sealed concrete. It used to be a storage room for Curran's gym equipment, but he moved it out and gave the room to me. Nothing interrupted the light brown concrete except for the drain on the floor. Most days I didn't need the drain.

My magic streamed out of me, like vapor from a boiling pot thrust outside into the cold. If it glowed, I'd look like I was on fire. Most of the time I kept the magic hidden inside me. Leaving it on display was extremely unwise for someone of my lineage.

I beckoned the blood with my magic. A faint tremor troubled the puddle of blood on the floor, as if something moved under the surface.

Voron, my adoptive father, always taught me that suppressing the power of my blood was the best strategy. Keep quiet. Keep hidden. Don't practice magic that could give you away. That was no longer an option. I needed this magic. I had to be good at it. Nobody could teach me, so I taught myself. I practiced and practiced and practiced. Some of the blood came from Jim. He bought it for me on the black market. Some undead blood came from Rowena, a Master of the Dead who owed the local witches a favor. The witches knew who I was and backed me up. They saw the writing on the wall: when Roland came, I was the only thing standing between them and my father, so they made Rowena supply me with vampire blood. She had no clue what it was for. I had practiced every day the magic was up.

My progress was slow, so slow, I gritted my teeth when I thought about it. I was beginning to hate this room. It reminded me of a tomb. Maybe I should add some graffiti to spice it up. *For a good time call the Consort. Beast Lord eats your food and turns into a lion in his sleep. Mahon has hemorrhoids. Boudas do it better. Warning: paranoid attack jaguar on the prowl . . .*

A quiet knock echoed through the room. I jumped a little.

"Yes?"

"It's me," Barabas said.

I unlocked the door. "Come in."

He sauntered in, moving with casual elegance. No matter what he wore, Barabas always managed to project an air of urbane, civilized polish that came with a sharp edge. Tall, lean, and pale, he had fire-bright red hair that stuck out from his head like a forest of aggressive spikes. If he ever frosted his hair blue, he'd look like a gas burner. And if someone looked at me the wrong way, he'd rip right through his civilized veneer and become a manic tornado of razor claws and dagger fangs. One messed with a weremongoose at one's peril.

"If it's bad, I don't want to hear it."

Barabas was one of the Pack's lawyers, and he did his best to navigate me through the treacherous mire of shapeshifter politics and laws.

"It's not bad." Barabas sat on the floor, throwing one long lean leg over the other and grimaced. "Well, I take it back. It might be."

"Will it freak you out if I finish this? I already poured blood on the floor."

"No, no. Why let good undead blood go to waste?"

I pricked my forearm with a needle and let a single drop of blood fall into the puddle. Magic shot through the undead blood like lightning. The blood slid upward in a graceful crimson arch.

"Whoa," Barabas murmured.

The blood touched my fingers and wound around them, gliding over my skin, elastic and pliant. A blood gauntlet sheathed my hand. It wasn't pretty but it was functional. I pulled a knife from my belt and sliced across the gauntlet.

Barabas made a sympathetic sucking noise.

No blood. I felt the pressure of the blade but it didn't penetrate. I bent my fingers, trying to make a fist. I made it about two-thirds of the way. About a year ago my aunt Erra had come to Atlanta intending to wreck it. I killed her. It was the hardest thing I'd done in my life. She was wearing blood armor when she died. It fit her like spandex. She had run and twisted in it, and she had no problem swinging an axe fast enough to counter me. I tried the gauntlet again. The blood refused to bend. I was clearly doing something wrong. This wouldn't work. If I couldn't hold a sword, I might as well sign my own death warrant.

I concentrated on thinning the blood, turning it into segments that sat on top of each other like the plates of armadillo armor. "So what's up?"

"Two things. First, Christopher wants to talk to you."

Speaking with Christopher was like playing Russian roulette: sometimes you got brilliance so bright it hurt and sometimes you got complete nonsense. We had rescued him from Hugh d'Ambray. He must've been exceptionally smart at some point and he definitely had knowledge of advanced magic, but either Hugh or my father had broken his mind. Christopher's hold on reality frequently slipped, and once in a while we had to drop everything and run out on the parapets to convince him that no, he could not fly. I could usually talk him down, but if he was really far gone it took Barabas to make him stop.

"He's been agitated for the last two days," Barabas said. "I have no idea if he's even coherent."

"Where is he now?"

"Hiding in the library."

Not a good sign. The library was Christopher's refuge. Books were precious to him. He treated them like treasure and hid among them when the world became too much for him. Something must've really gotten under his skin.

"Did he say what it was about?"

"Just that it was important. You don't have to talk to him," Barabas said.

"That's okay. I'll speak to him after the Conclave." I tested the gauntlet. Like having a can wrapped around my fingers. Ugh. What was I doing wrong? What? "What was the second thing?"

"Jim has assembled the Praetorian Guard and is waiting for your inspection."

Oh joy. Jim must've pulled together a cutthroat crew of shapeshifters ready to protect me at the Conclave. "As I recall, the Praetorian Guard killed the Roman emperors as often as it protected them. Should I be worried?"

"Are you planning on setting the Keep on fire while playing thrilling melodies on a fiddle?"

"No."

Barabas flashed me a quick smile, showing sharp teeth. "Then probably not."

"Anything else?"

Barabas looked at me carefully. "Clan Nimble inquires if the wedding date has been set."

"Again?"

"Yes. They want to prepare and choose the appropriate present. You're really throwing them off their game by refusing to set the date."

I never pictured myself getting married. I never picked out my future gown or looked at a bridal magazine. That wasn't my future. My future was surviving until I was strong enough to kill my father. But then Curran threw a wrench into those plans and asked me, and I said yes, because I loved him and I wanted to marry him. My future had made a one-hundred-eighty-degree turn. Now I had to think about the details. I wanted a small ceremony with as little ceremony in it as possible. Quiet, private, maybe a few friends.

As soon as the engagement was announced, the Pack Clans converged and shot the idea of a quiet ceremony out of the water and then kept firing at it until it stopped convulsing and died. They wanted the whole Pack to be there. They wanted presents and rituals and a giant feast. They wanted a Wedding, with a capital W. Clan Heavy and Clan Rat both owned bakeries, and the bakers almost came to blows over who would be doing the cake. Should it be a winter wedding or a spring wedding? Who would make my gown and what should it look like? Was it appropriate for me to wear white or should it be gray, the official color of the Pack? Argh.

Every moment Curran and I spent together was ours. Just ours. And so we kept putting off the wedding. We never conspired to do it. We both were just too busy to get married and when we did have a few free hours, we hoarded them to spend with each other and Julie.

"I have had it up to here with my wedding," I said. "The other day Andrea tried to explain to me that apparently I am supposed to have a new thing, an old thing, a blue thing, and something stolen."

"Borrowed, Kate," Barabas murmured.

"Who the hell even makes up those rules?"

"It's tradition," he said.

"Even Julie talked to me about it the other day."

"What did she say?" Barabas asked.

"She thinks I should wear black."

Barabas sighed. "The clans will have a collective heart attack."

The gauntlet still refused to bend. Screw it. I yanked my magic out. The blood armor turned dark brown and crumbled into powder. "I'm done with them hounding me about it. I'd rather be shot."

"I understand. However, if you want them off your back, I have to give them something."

I growled in his general direction. Sadly, growling worked much better when you were a werelion.

"Could you narrow it down to the season?" Barabas asked.

"Spring," I said. Why not. We could always put it off later.

Barabas sighed. "I will let them know."

CONTRARY TO POPULAR opinion, most shapeshifters weren't hardened killers hungry for blood. They were normal people—teachers, masons, human resources specialists—who just happened to practice strict mental discipline and turn furry once in a while. Some of them learned enough control to maintain a warrior form, a meld of human and animal frighteningly efficient at killing. Of those, even fewer became full-time soldiers of the Pack. The best of the best among the soldiers became renders. Renders were weapons of mass destruction and they loved their job.

To get more than five combat-grade operatives in one room was rare. Unless we were about to battle an army, which so far had happened only once, one or two soldiers were sufficient. I was looking at twelve of them. Ten combat operatives, two renders, plus Barabas and Jim. Six feet two inches tall, one hundred ninety pounds of steel-hard muscle, Jim wore black accented with the kind of stare that made people run for cover. His skin was dark, his black hair was cut short, and he was built like he could go through solid walls. You knew that if he punched you, something inside you would break. Being a werejaguar on top of all that was just a bonus.

"What, no Rambo?"

Jim scowled at me. Usually when he scowled at people, they made a small squeaky noise and tried to look small and nonthreatening. Fortunately, I managed to scrape together enough valor and not faint.

"You keep doing that, your face will get stuck that way."

"Will you take this seriously?" he growled.

"Okay." I surveyed the crew of vicious killers. "Let me guess: an elite unit of commandos from some evil empire invaded Bernard's Restaurant and fortified it. Now it's trying to secede from Atlanta and the city asked us to take it back?"

Nobody laughed. I must be getting rusty.

Jim scowled harder. Wow. I didn't think that was possible. Showed what I knew.

"Don't you think this is overkill?" I asked.

"No."

Ask a stupid question . . . "Jim, there is enough manpower here to destroy a small country."

He waited.

"Don't you think it will communicate that we're scared of the People?"

"It will communicate that if they even think about starting some shit, we'll rip them into bite-sized pieces."

I looked at the red-haired render in the front. His name was Myles Kingsbury and he was built to break bones: broad shoulders, hard chest, lean waist, and a calm look in his eyes. Myles was my age and the few times we spoke, he struck me as competent and sensible.

"Mr. Kingsbury, what do you think?"

The render opened his mouth and said in a deep voice, "I think it communicates that we won't hesitate to take the initiative to be decisively aggressive."

I closed my eyes for a second and exhaled. "Jim, if I were Curran, would you saddle me with this many bodyguards?"

"No."

Well, at least I could still count on the no-bullshit answer from him. "So you agree that being heavily guarded is making me appear weak?"

"Yes. However, it makes the Pack appear strong. I'm not inclined to gamble with your safety. And"—he held up his hand—"I'd make Curran have a guard as well, if that stubborn bastard wouldn't overrule me."

I looked at Barabas. "Do I have the power to overrule him?"

"Yep," Barabas said.

Jim gave Barabas his hard stare.

Barabas shrugged. "Do you want me to lie?"

Jim turned to me. "If I could have a moment of your time, Consort?"

Oh, it's "Consort" now, huh. "Sure, Chief of Security. I'd be delighted."

Normally walking a few feet was sufficient to get out of earshot, but everyone in the Keep enjoyed the awesome benefits of enhanced hearing. Jim and I marched fifty yards down the hallway.

"We're at less than half of our normal strength," Jim said. "Curran is away from the Keep. Whether accurate or not, you are viewed as much less of a threat than he is. If I were planning something, I'd hit us now and I'd hit us where it hurt."

I kept my voice low. "This spy-on-the-Council thing is really getting under your skin."

He inhaled slowly and looked at me. "Are you trying to say I've lost my perspective?"

"Maybe a little."

He bent closer to me. His voice shook slightly, not with fear but with controlled concentrated anger. "Three months. Sixteen of my best people. Over a thousand hours of surveillance. I have nothing to show for it. Nothing. We have a mole and I have no idea who it is."

Curran was so much better at this shit than I was. "Do you remember the hydra?"

Jim grimaced.

It happened years ago, in my first year in the Guild. We'd had a hell of a winter, and while I was trying to figure out how to stay warm in my old house, a coven of amateur witches near Franklin was throwing odd things into a giant pot. I didn't know what the hell they had been hoping to cook up, but what came out of the pot became known as the Franklin Hydra. It wasn't a classic dragon with many heads. It was something tentacled, with spikes and mouths with shark teeth in places mouths shouldn't be. It ate the witches and slipped into the frozen depths of Lake Emory. Under the ice, it turned the lake into sludge and ate anything that came close. The town asked for assistance and allocated some funds. Two weeks later twenty mercs and a National Guard unit walked out onto the ice. It broke under us. Four people survived.

I shouldn't have been one of those four. I fell through the ice into the sludge up to my chest and kept sinking while spiked tentacles slithered around me. I knew I was done, and then some merc I didn't know slid across the ice to me and tossed a belt my way. It fell out of my reach.

If I thrashed, the tentacles would tighten and pull me under. So I inched forward, one painful centimeter every few seconds.

"Do you remember what you said to me?" I asked.

He shrugged.

"You said, 'Don't tense up. No sudden movements. Take it nice and slow.'"

He looked at me without any expression. Bull's-eye. Score one for me.

"Bernard's is neutral territory where no weapons are permitted, including vampires." And my sword, about which I wasn't happy. "The People will come to this meeting unarmed. Our people are always armed, because they can turn at a moment's notice. Bringing this many combat-trained shapeshifters could be perceived as a threat. With the alphas from the other Clans, we will outnumber the People two to one."

I nodded at the posse of biological weapons arranged for my inspection. "This is a sudden move. You're escalating things. The People will feel pressure to retaliate. It will make diplomatic relations a lot harder."

Jim chewed it over. "Fair enough. However . . ."

I was beginning to really hate that word.

"I have intelligence that indicates that the People bought one of the buildings next to Bernard's and set up a command center inside. Tonight it will hold several journeymen and at least six vampires. You know what six vampires can do."

Six vampires could depopulate Atlanta in a week. Six vampires piloted by navigators would do it in three days. A vampire telepathically guided by the navigator was a precision instrument with the destruction potential of a small nuclear bomb.

"It's a precaution," I said. "Ghastek isn't about to jeopardize his rise to the top."

The most skilled navigators were known as Masters of the Dead. There were seven of them in Atlanta, and two of them, Ghastek and Mulradin Grant, were currently scheming and plotting, trying to gain control of the chapter. My money was on Ghastek. We had cooperated before out of necessity. He was smart, calculating, and ruthless, but he was also reasonable. It was his turn to attend the Conclave.

"Maybe a war with the Pack is exactly what he wants," Jim said. "I don't want to take chances. Hold on." He peered at the far end of the hallway.

A man with pure-white hair turned the corner and sped toward us. Stick-thin, he moved at a near run, holding a stack of books to his chest. His jeans sagged on him, and his turtleneck, which would've been tight on most people, had a lot of spare fabric. Christopher occasionally forgot to eat. Sooner or later Barabas caught it and made him consume three meals a day, but Christopher never seemed to put any meat on his bones.

Jim turned and watched him close in. No love lost there. Jim viewed Christopher as a puzzle box. It could open to reveal a treasure or a bomb, and Jim didn't like not knowing which it was.

"Remember all those bodyguarding jobs we used to run?" Jim asked.

"I remember. Are you trying to tell me I'm being a difficult body to guard?"

"Something like that."

Christopher reached us. His blue eyes were opened wide. Some days they were like a clear summer sky, not a thought in sight, but right now they were focused with a single-mindedness bordering on obsession. Some idea had grabbed hold of him and driven him off a cliff. He probably didn't even know he was carrying books.

"Mistress!"

I had given up on telling him to call me Kate. He always ignored it. "Yes?"

"You can't go!"

Jim's eyebrows came together.

"Go where, Christopher?" I asked.

"To that place." Words came tumbling out of him. "I've been trying to be in my right mind."

"Aha." When in doubt, stick to simple words.

"I know what I used to be, but I cannot be that anymore. I try. I try so hard. But my mind is unraveled and the threads, they're too tangled. There are pieces of me floating. I'm shattered. He broke me."

"Who broke you?" Jim asked.

Christopher looked at him. His voice was a mere whisper. "The Builder."

My father. The Builder of Towers. Anger spiked inside me. I wished I could reach across time and space and punch Roland in the face.

Christopher turned to me. "If I had known what it was like to be shattered, I would've rather died."

Oy. "Don't say that," I said.

"It's the truth."

"Christopher, you matter to me. Shattered or not. You are my friend."

Christopher opened his arms. The books fell to the floor. He clutched at me, long fingers gripping my shoulders. "Don't go. Don't go to that terrible place, or he will shatter you and then you'll be alone. You will be like me. Don't go, Mistress."

Jim moved, but I shook my head.

"What terrible place?" I asked, keeping my voice soothing.

He shook his head and whispered, "Don't go . . . Don't leave."

"I won't," I promised him. "I won't go, but you have to tell me the name of the place."

"You don't understand." Christopher looked at me, and in his blue eyes I saw pure panic. "You don't understand. I'll follow you to the ends of the earth, but not there. I cannot go there again."

I wouldn't go there either, if I knew where "there" was. "It's okay. Just tell me . . ."

He shook his head. "No. No. It's not."

"It will be okay."

He reached out, touched the strand of my hair that had slipped out of my braid, and yanked it, ripping some hair out.

Ow.

Jim lunged at Christopher, knocking him back. The thin man fell on the floor. I rammed Jim with my shoulder. "No!"

Christopher scrambled to his feet, wild-eyed, a few strands of my hair in his hand. "Don't trust the wolf!"

He turned and fled down the hallway.

"What the hell?" Jim growled. "I'm going to have him sedated."

"He knows something," I told him. "I don't know if he had a vision or someone told him something, but it freaked him out and he can't explain it. Let's see what he does with the hair. I might be able to figure it out from there."

Hair, like body fluids, retained the magic of its owner once removed from the body. A year ago I would've killed Christopher to retrieve the hair, because studying it would reveal all my secrets. But my secrets were about to burst into the open anyway. Hugh knew the truth, Roland probably knew as well, and sooner or later everyone would know. I had come to terms with it.

"If someone told him something, it has to be either someone in the Pack or divination magic," I thought out loud.

Even now the Keep held at least two hundred shapeshifters, and strangers weren't welcome. Christopher never left the Keep and the grounds.

Jim growled. "I'll put a guard on him. Someone discreet. If he's getting his information from some apparition that manifests in his bedroom at night, I don't want him sharing your hair with it."

I looked at him. "What wolf do you think Christopher was talking about?"

"Beats me."

There were more than six hundred of them and I didn't have many fans among them.

"And you say I'm paranoid." Jim pointed in the direction of Christopher's escape. "What about him?"

"He's shattered. What's your excuse?"

"I have to work with your ass. You've driven me crazy."

I sighed. I could overrule Jim and go to the Conclave on my terms. But Jim and I had to work together. I could tell by the line of his jaw that he would die on this bridge if he had to. Going along with him cost me nothing, except a small chunk of pride, and pride was one of the things I didn't mind sacrificing.

"What if we compromise?" I asked.

Jim looked at me for a long second. "They're going to need sweaters in hell."

Because me trying to be the voice of reason froze hell over. "Har har. You said they had vampires for backup. Let's split our people in two. One group comes with us, the other waits as a backup. Put someone solid in charge of it, whoever you want, and have them wait nearby. Within running distance."

Jim pondered that. "I pick both crews."

I spread my arms. "Fine."

"I can live with that. I'll prepare a couple of exit strategies for you in case shit hits the fan. If I'm wrong, we lose nothing. If I'm right . . ."

"I hope you're wrong."

"I hope I'm wrong, too," he said.

"Good. Then we're done here." I walked away from him, conquered the hallway, and started up the stairs. That was enough excitement for the day. If nobody did anything crazy, I could hide in our rooms and read . . .

Hannah, one of my and Curran's guards, ran down the stairs.

Please don't be for me, please don't be for me . . .

"Consort!"

Damn it. "Yes."

"There is a knight of the Order here to see you."

What now? The Order of Merciful Aid served as a semiofficial law enforcement agency. Competent and efficient, but rigid in their thinking, they helped private citizens deal with their magic hazmat problems. Unfortunately, once you asked them for help they did it their way and not everyone liked it. I used to work for the Order. They decided shapeshifters weren't people, I decided they were, and we went our separate ways. Ted Moynohan, the knight in charge, was still pissy about it.

"He has Ascanio and Julie with him. He says no charges will be filed."

Why me?

I WALKED INTO the conference room ready to do battle. Ascanio sat in one chair, looking suitably guilty and regretful, and if I hadn't worked with him for the last few months, I would even believe it. Julie sat across from him, slender, blond, and defiant. She had mostly passed through her Goth phase, but black was still her favorite color and I was treated to a lovely ensemble of black jeans, charcoal turtleneck, and piercing stare.

A huge man took up the only other occupied chair. Massive, slabbed with muscle and covered in elaborate tattoos, he had the bold handsome features, dark skin, and dark eyes of a Pacific Islander.

"Mauro!" Of all the knights of the Order I liked him the most.

"Hello, Consort," Mauro boomed. He got to his feet, spread his arms, and curtsied.

Ascanio clamped his hand over his mouth.

"I see you still think you're funny."

"Damn right." His face split in a happy grin.

I turned to Hannah. "Could you bring us some hot tea?"

"Sure."

Mauro nodded at my ward and Ascanio. "I brought these two miscreants to you."

"What happened?"

"I was on an unrelated call in the Shiver Oaks, when a woman ran out from the house across the street and asked me if I could help her with some burglars her dog cornered."

I turned to Ascanio and Julie. The look on my face must've been scary, because they flinched in unison. Ha! Still got it.

"Burglary?" I asked quietly. The Pack took a dim view of any criminal activity. We had enough trouble as it was.

Ascanio sighed, clearly resigned to his fate. "She wanted to see the bunnycat kittens. It was the breeder's house. We found the ad in the newspaper. The woman wouldn't let us in unless we showed her money, so we scaled the fence when she went out. I could've dealt with the Rottweiler. I just didn't want to hurt him."

Of course, Julie would want to see bunnycat kittens. Hell, I wanted to see the bunnycat kittens. And of course, he took her. The problem was, they got caught.

"We weren't going to steal them," Julie said. "We just petted them."

"Is she pressing charges?" I asked Mauro.

"I convinced her it wouldn't be a good idea."

"Thank you."

"Any time," he said.

I looked at the kids. "Scram! I'll talk to you later."

They scurried out, nearly knocking Hannah and her platter of tea off her feet. She bared her teeth at them.

"Thank you." I took the platter. Hannah stepped out and closed the door. I served tea to Mauro. "How's it going?"

Mauro took his cup and blew on it. "Thank you." He swallowed a little. "God, that's good. I was about frozen solid. Damn weather. Things are . . . going. Selena still thinks I work too much."

"How is your wife?"

"She's good, thank you." He hesitated. "I'm thinking of transferring."

That was news. Atlanta was considered one of the more important Order chapters in the South. Not only that, but knights didn't like changing duty stations. Once they were assigned to a chapter, they developed street contacts and professional relationships. Most of them would do just about anything to avoid starting over. "Transferring where?"

"Somewhere. Charleston. Orlando."

Odd. I added more tea to his cup. I've learned that if you just stay quiet, people will say more to fill the silence.

"Thank you." Mauro sighed. "This post used to be the place you went because it would be good for your career. You know, high-speed post. Where things were happening."

"Things are still happening."

"Not the right kind of things." Mauro set the cup down. "Did you know Ted Moynohan was one of the original Ninety-Eight?"

Twenty-three years ago the original Ninety-Eight, drawn from different law enforcement agencies, formed the core of the Order of Merciful Aid. They were dramatically knighted in a single ceremony in front of the Washington Monument. The Order had wanted to make a statement.

"That makes Ted a knight-founder," I said.

Mauro nodded. "We've had three hundred fifty percent turnover in personnel in the past three years. Typical for a chapter is about twenty percent."

That made sense. Knights died, but they died occasionally. They were really well trained and difficult to kill. "Atlanta also had a hard three years."

"People up the chain of command noticed. A three-knight investigative team came down from Wolf Trap. There was a hearing. A question was raised about some of the turnover. You came up."

"Me?" I was never a knight, more like an off-the-books employee.

"You were seen as an asset, and then you became a Consort, and the question was asked why that bridge wasn't mended. Andrea came up. They spent a long time on that one."

Damn right they did. I was never a knight, but Andrea was a decorated veteran and a master-at-arms, which was nothing to sneeze at, and they tossed her out like garbage when they found out she was a shapeshifter.

"The Order can't afford to bleed masters-at-arms," Mauro said. "It never sat right with me the way that was handled. It shouldn't have ever come to that. There was no need to put her back against the wall the way Ted did. I respect her and her skills."

Hard not to respect someone who can shoot you in the eye from a mile away. "She knows you had her back."

"How is she doing?"

"She's running Clan Bouda with Raphael. She has her hands full." And Aunt B's big shoes to fill, which wasn't a job I'd wish on anybody.

"Good to know." The big knight shifted in his chair. "After they got through with Andrea, they went straight to Shane Andersen and the Lighthouse Keepers."

There was no way for Ted to come out smelling like roses on that one. One of his knights had proven to be a terrorist. If Ted knew, he was as guilty as Shane. If he didn't, he was incompetent. "So what happened?"

"That's the bad part. Nothing. They conducted their hearings and went back to HQ. Then came the time to rebuild the chapter with new personnel. We got completely new people in. The only ones left of the old crew, besides Ted, are me, Richter, and Maxine."

Mauro was a good knight and Maxine, the Order's telepathic secretary, was the backbone of the Atlanta chapter, but Richter was psychotic and a liability.

"That's it?" I asked.

"Mm-hm. The rest are . . . new."

"Don't like the new people?"

Mauro grimaced. "We are being staffed with people who are on their second or third chapter. Their command made no effort to keep them, because they didn't distinguish themselves. Most of them made some mistakes. Some made a lot of mistakes."

The light dawned. Since Ted was a knight-founder, well connected and probably vigorously defended, the Order's High Command couldn't force him out without some glaring evidence of his incompetence, so they staffed him with rejects. Either he would see the writing on the wall and retire or his new people would screw up so badly, it would give them grounds to remove him. Mauro didn't want to be part of the screwup squad.

"Mauro, you're a good knight. Any chapter would fight to get you."

"Yeah. I like the city. It's home. But yeah. Time to go." He rose. "Thank you for the tea."

"Thank you for saving the kids from trouble."

"Any time." He grinned. "Any time."

I walked him out. It was almost five. I would lay into Julie and Ascanio after the Conclave. For now I had to get dressed, get my sword, and go make polite noises at the Masters of the Dead.

THE PACK JEEP rolled through the dusk-soaked streets. The other car, carrying my murder-prone honor guard, followed us. Jim drove. Barabas sat in the backseat.

Post-Shift Atlanta had many neighborhoods, some old, some new, born from the magic age. There was Honeycomb to the southwest, a place where "solid wall" was a relative term. In the southeast was the Warren, a rough dirt-poor neighborhood, policed by roving gangs preying on each other. And then there was Northside, where Atlanta's wealthy used their money to hold the chaos of the ravaged city at bay.

Magic liked to nibble on the asphalt, but here the pavement felt smooth, the clean streets a far cry from the refuse and garbage-choked pathways of the Warren. Large houses, each sitting on its own acre-sized plot, stared at us with barred windows from behind iron fences topped with coils of barbed wire. Most houses were built post-Shift, no more than three stories tall, with thick walls, reinforced doors, and barred windows. Money bought security, land, and good masons.

The sun had set, and the moon claimed the sky, a huge, deep orange as if dipped in blood. The magic was down, but the city still held its breath, apprehensive and watchful. It was the kind of night when monsters came out to play.

Slayer, my saber, lay on my lap. I stroked the sheath. The saber went where I went, but tonight I would have to leave it behind. Bernard's had a strict no-weapons policy. Without it, I felt naked.

"Who else is coming?" I asked. The Pack's protocol called for the representatives of at least three clans to be present at each Conclave meeting. In the beginning, every alpha wanted to be included, but now we had trouble getting three to come. Jim served as the alpha of Clan Cat, so he counted as one. That left two more.

"Robert Lonesco and Jennifer," Barabas said.

Robert Lonesco was married to Thomas, and together they ran Clan Rat. Jennifer headed Clan Wolf. She and I didn't see eye to eye. First, I had to kill her sister after she had been driven loup by my aunt's magic. Then her husband sacrificed himself to prevent a magic catastrophe, about which we had learned through my office. Jennifer blamed me for both. We had struck an uneasy truce, because we had to work together, but not killing each other was as pleasant as it got. Christopher's warning popped up from my memory. When it came to the wolves I shouldn't be trusting, she was definitely at the top of the list.

"Any challenges?" I asked. Jennifer had given birth over a month ago and her thirty-day reprieve from being challenged had run out last Wednesday.

"No," Jim said.

Odd. "I thought Desandra would've gone after her by now."

"So did I," Jim said.

Like Christopher, Desandra was a rescue from our trip overseas. She was the daughter of the most powerful alpha in the Carpathian Mountains. He was a psychotic, cruel egomaniac, who built his pack out of nothing and ruled the entire region with steel claws, terrorizing his enemies, foreign and domestic. He had eleven children. Desandra was the only one who lived to adulthood and she did this by pretending to be a spoiled, petulant idiot. Her father was obsessed with finding an heir who'd measure up to his standards. He had no idea she was right under his nose, and when she broke through his rib cage and ripped out his heart moments before giving birth to twins, he was terribly surprised.

Desandra ended up coming with us to Atlanta. She was smart, cunning, and ruthless. When we returned, Jennifer was still pregnant and couldn't be challenged. Desandra also had two weeks of maternity leave left, but she didn't use it. She made her first kill within forty-eight hours of swearing loyalty to the Pack and began climbing up the food chain. Now she held the beta spot in Clan Wolf and Jennifer was sleeping with her eyes open.

"Did Jennifer and Desandra strike a deal or something?" I asked.

"Not that I know of," Jim said. "Jennifer hates her even more than she hates you. If Desandra were on fire, Jennifer wouldn't piss on her to put her out."

"Then what's the holdup?"

Jim shrugged. I glanced at Barabas. Barabas shrugged, too. Neither of them had heard anything. That was rare.

"She would make a better alpha," Jim said. "She's stronger."

Despite Jennifer's impression, I never had a problem with her. She'd start a fight and I'd hit back hard, but I never went after her. Still, I had to admit Desandra would be a hell of an alpha. That didn't mean I was eager to deal with her.

"Looking forward to sitting next to Desandra at the Pack Council?" I asked.

Jim gave me a look of pure hate.

Barabas laughed.

Jim permitted himself a small half-smile without showing his teeth. He very rarely smiled—it conflicted with his badass image. In all the years I'd known him, I only saw him bare his teeth to three people, and two of them were dead. The third would be dead, except for the technicality of him being a Friend of the Pack.

"They need to sort this mess out and soon," Jim said. "There are six hundred wolves and they're all holding their breath. Rumor says Desandra went to Orhan and Fatima to ask for their blessing."

Orhan and Fatima had run Clan Wolf before Daniel had taken over. They had trained him as their successor, stepped down, and retired from Pack politics. They lived on an orchard not far from the Keep and stayed strictly neutral. So far, I had seen them exactly twice, at a Thanksgiving dinner and at a wedding, and they both struck me as the kind of people I didn't want to screw with.

"What do you mean, she went to ask their blessing?" I asked.

"It's a Pack term," Barabas said. "An alpha can either be killed in a challenge or choose to step down. When an alpha steps down, he gives his successor his blessing to take up where he left off. This pretty much guarantees that the old alpha's supporters will support the new alpha out of respect, at least for a time. It's the passing of the keys to the kingdom, which is why Daniel wasn't challenged until almost six months into being an alpha. If Desandra had gone to Orhan and Fatima, it was in poor taste. They made it clear they don't want to be bothered."

The road turned. I remembered taking this turn about a year ago going really fast in the opposite direction. It's amazing how precisely you can steer when a pissed-off Beast Lord is chasing you.

Bernard's swung into view. In a city proud of its Southern heritage, the restaurant stood out like an English lord among the cowboys. Broad, two stories tall, and built with red brick, it resembled the Georgian-style British mansions sometimes featured in the old movies, except that Bernard's owners gave up on the whole symmetrical thing in favor of ornate balconies. Long dense strands of kudzu climbed up its walls, their edges frosted by the encroaching cold. Warm yellow light filtered through the barred windows.

We parked in the reserved spot in the first row. Four people stood by the door. The lights of the car caught them and their eyes flashed with the familiar shapeshifter glow. Three men and a tall woman. The woman watched us, distaste obvious on her face. Jennifer. Always tall and spare, with the physique of a long-distance runner, she looked even thinner now. Most women put on weight during pregnancy, but if Jennifer had picked up some extra pounds, they were gone now. She wore a jacket edged with rabbit fur and skintight black pants. The long, lean muscles of her legs and her knobby knees stood out through the fabric. I worked out every day, because I had a dangerous job and when the time came, I'd have to fight to stay alive, but my legs were thicker than that. It was like she had purged every hint of softness from her frame. This wasn't simply dedication. This was panic.

Jim shut off the engine. He and Barabas got out and stood for a second, their faces raised, sampling the scents in the air. And sitting in the car while they did this didn't make me feel like an idiot. Not at all. I sighed and slid Slayer off my lap. I had agreed not to be the difficult client. Now I had to live with it.

A foul patina washed over my mind, like the decomposition fluid from a rotting corpse. Vampires. I concentrated. Six. Not in the buildings nearby, though—these were closer. Right above us, on the roof. I shouldn't have been able to feel them so clearly with the magic down. My sensitivity must've increased. It made me feel like even more of an abomination. To fight my father, I had to practice my magic, and the more I practiced, the more like him I became. One hell of a slippery slope.

"Jim."

Jim opened the driver's door. The cold exhaled into my face, biting at my skin.

"Six vampires on the roof," I told him quietly.

He looked up. "Either Bernard's is in on it, or they don't know they have extra guests."

"Either way, by the time we get to the roof, they'll be gone," Barabas said.

And we would look like scared idiots. "Warn our people," I murmured to Barabas. He nodded.

"If we're separated . . ." Jim said.

"Mt. Paran Bridge. I remember." That was where he'd stashed our backup.

Barabas tapped on my window. I rolled it down.

"Now remember, Kate." Barabas leaned over to me, grinning. "You are the Consort. Be the Consort." He stretched "be" into a three-syllable word. "Think like a—"

"Open the door or I'll punch you right in the face," I growled.

Barabas chuckled and opened my door. Ice crunched under my feet. Next to us the second Jeep disgorged five of my bodyguards, including the two renders, Myles Kingsbury and Sage Rome. I circled the Jeep and met Jennifer's gaze. She stared at me for a long second and looked past me to my right. Her face jerked.

I glanced to the side. Another car had pulled up next to our two. The door swung open and Desandra jumped out. She wore a sheepskin jacket with a hood. Her hair, a long blond plait, spilled out over her shoulder. The cold turned her cheeks pink. Her eyes shone shapeshifter orange. She waved at me and headed my way.

Jennifer's face went hard, as if chiseled from stone.

"My favorite alpha." Desandra gave me a big brilliant smile.

My, my, what big teeth you have. "Desandra," I said.

Jennifer looked hard and gaunt, like a half-starved wolf who had been driven into a corner and was now baring her teeth. Desandra was a picture of health, curvy, smiling, her eyes bright. Jennifer oozed anxiety; Desandra projected confidence. It was impossible not to compare the two. But I didn't trust Desandra further than I could throw her either.

Jennifer needed to step down. I'd seen Desandra fight. I wouldn't go up against her unless I absolutely had to. Jennifer was decent in a fight, but she was predictable and when her shit didn't work, she lost her temper. Her anxiety clearly ate at her, gnawing her down to nothing.

"Should you be so friendly with me? I'm not exactly popular with the wolves."

Desandra smiled wider, her green eyes sly. "Yes, isn't it distressing how the spirit of cooperation has suffered in the past oh, nine months or so? Somehow we've managed to alienate all other clans. Some even suggest it might be due to a failure in leadership."

We, huh? "Perish the thought."

"And to think that Clan Wolf is missing out on all of the perks and benefits a good relationship with the Beast Lord and Consort could bring. A shame." Desandra sighed and winked at me. "But have no worries. I, unlike some, am a team player. I have no problems being friendly and even humble if my clan can benefit from it."

Aha. And she was rubbing Jennifer's nose in it in front of witnesses. "You are the devil."

"Thank you, Consort. You say the nicest things." Desandra lowered her voice to a murmur. "Is she watching?"

"She's watching."

"See those three guys with her? They're her bodyguards." Desandra sneered. "She has to have *bodyguards*, Kate. I can smell the fear." She waved her hand in front of her face, as if fanning an aroma to her nose. "Mmm, delicious."

I nodded at Jim and the small crowd of fighters who maintained the great distance of a whole ten feet around me.

"That's different," Desandra said. "You're the Consort and a human, and this shindig is all about ceremony. We are supposed to defend you to the death. But an alpha of a clan should never require bodyguards."

Jennifer turned sharply and went inside. The three men followed her. She had to have heard that.

"I thought you'd challenge her by now," Jim said. "What are you waiting for?"

"Do I have the Beast Lord and Consort's approval?" Desandra asked.

Her questions weren't questions, they were bear traps ready to be sprung. "The leadership of Clan Wolf is a private matter to be decided within the clan. We do not interfere. I won't speak for the Beast Lord, but I will tell you that I prefer a peaceful solution."

"That was very diplomatic," Desandra said. "Not very clear. Also, since when do you prefer peaceful solutions?"

"Since I don't want to deal with a bloodbath for Christmas. She's the widow of a man who sacrificed himself for the Pack. If you murder her in cold blood and leave her daughter an orphan, I'll make things harder for you. So will the other wolves. Handle it like the alpha you want to be."

Desandra grimaced. "I'm not about to make her a martyr. And I don't want to leave her daughter an orphan. There's no need for tragedies. It's not time anyway. The clan isn't completely mine yet, but I'm getting there. Jennifer knows I'm watching for her to stumble, so she hesitates. She puts off important decisions and gets defensive when people question her, which makes her look weak and timid. Meanwhile I sit in the shadows and bide my time, converting the clan one by one. The wolves require a strong leader and the longer Jennifer teeters on the edge, the louder they rumble. Soon they will come to me. They'll say that it's regrettable, but the clan has had enough of Jennifer's leadership. I will be hesitant and humble. I'll need to be convinced that this is the right thing, the noble thing to do. It will take some doing to convince me, and when I force her out, the entirety of the clan will be overjoyed."

Desandra grinned at us. "So you don't have to worry. I won't kill her in the middle of some formal dinner. I'm not my father, after all. Enjoy your meal." She winked, turned, and walked away.

Wow.

"This is going to turn into a giant pain in the ass, isn't it?" Barabas said.

"Yes, it will." Suddenly I missed my apartment. It was small and cramped and located in a rough part of town, but it had been all mine, before my aunt had demolished it. It was a ruin now, but I really wanted to go home, close the door, and not have to deal with any of this bullshit.

A dark SUV turned the corner. Another followed, then another. The People were incoming.

"Showtime," Jim said.

Black Bear Lodge. If I got through this, I'd get two weeks with Curran at Black Bear Lodge. I put my business face on and marched into Bernard's with ten shapeshifters at my heels.

"WE ARE NOT saying that the Pack can't buy a building on the border of our city territory." Ryan Kelly tapped the table with his index finger. "We're saying that when they do, we notice."

I killed a yawn before it started. Most Masters of the Dead maintained a strict corporate uniform that would've made them at home in any high-pressure boardroom. Ryan sounded the part and looked the part as far as his dress was concerned. His navy suit was obviously custom tailored, his square chin clean shaven, and his cologne expensive. He also had a huge purple Mohawk. The Mohawk was currently lying down, draped over the left side of his skull, and he kept tossing his head back, because the hair kept getting into his eyes. The flip of the purple hair turned out to be strangely hypnotic and I had to force myself to listen to what he said instead of waiting for another head toss.

"It's not that we object to the purchase of that particular building." Flip. "It's the principle . . ."

Bernard's had put us into a private dining room with one long table. We sat on one side, the People sat on the other. To the right of me Jim surveyed the room, periodically glancing at the door. To the left of me Robert Lonesco played with his fork, his handsome face lost in thought. Ryan's journey-woman, whose name was Meghan and who stood behind her boss's chair, was discreetly checking him out. Robert turned heads. He had the kind of quiet beauty that with the right photographer and a big billboard would stop traffic. His skin was a light even bronze, his hair soft and so dark it was almost blue-black, and his eyes, serious and large, seemed bottomless.

To the right of Ryan, Ghastek watched Meghan's pining with neutral curiosity. Thin to the point of being gaunt, he was somewhere on the crossroads of thirty and forty, his short brown hair still untouched by gray, and he wore "smart" like it was a perfume. Where Ryan Kelly looked like a businessman who somehow sprouted a Mohawk, Ghastek looked more like a scientist who accidentally found himself invited to a formal party where everyone was dumber than him and was now spinning his wheels, trying to make his brain acclimate.

Mulradin Grant himself was MIA, since it was Ghastek's turn to participate in the Conclave, but his wife, Claire, was in attendance. She was in her late thirties, blond, well-groomed, with an average build and a toned figure. Her pantsuit looked expensive and her hair spoke of pampering and many salon visits.

Ryan droned on. He supported Mulradin and he would've loved nothing more than to create some sort of problem between the Pack and the People and then dump it in Ghastek's lap. Unfortunately for him, nothing potentially problematic had happened, and so he was forced to make a mountain out of a molehill. He knew it, everyone else knew it, and now we were all collectively bored to death by it. Out of convenience, the People and the Pack had divided the city into imaginary territories, with each party patrolling their own imaginary borders, and Raphael's reclamation business happened to have bought a building on the border.

Claire tugged at the metal bracelet on her wrist. All of the People wore one today, and knowing them, the new jewelry was a corporate fashion statement.

". . . we object to the Pack's continued disregard for . . ."

The double doors separating the private dining room from the rest of

Bernard's swung open. A tall broad-shouldered body filled the doorway. Hugh d'Ambray strode into the room.

For a moment my mind struggled to digest the fact that Hugh was there, and then every cell in my body went on full alert, as if someone had dumped a bucket of ice water on me and then shocked me with a live wire.

My memory shot me back to last summer. I heard the crunch of his back snapping as Curran broke his body over the stone parapet. I smelled the smoke of the stone-melting conjured fire that devoured Castle Mego-bari and watched Hugh fall into the flames down below. Yet here he was, wearing jeans and a leather jacket over a black T-shirt. He seemed no worse for wear, the bastard. No limp. No stiffness. Even his hair, dark, almost black, was the same length, falling to his shoulders. Same fist-breaking chin, same hard, square jaw, same stubble. Over six feet tall, he was corded with hard, supple muscle and he moved with a swordsman's grace, perfectly balanced, sure, and adroit in his control.

How could this be?

He was broken. He was broken, damn it. His bones had been crushed. His face had been battered. Curran had snapped his spine like a toothpick, and here he was casually strolling in, like it was nothing. His face showed no signs of the broken bones. His skin had no burn marks. The scar on his cheek was missing. He looked . . . younger. Less carved up by fighting. Maybe it wasn't him. Maybe it was Saiman wearing Hugh's skin, or . . .

Hugh met my gaze. Icy blue eyes laughed at me.

The hair on the back of my neck rose. It was him. Hugh was in those eyes and I would know him anywhere.

I had no idea what my father had done, but he had somehow fixed his favorite human wrecking ball. Dear God, how much magic did it take? How . . . ?

It meant Roland knew. I'd been trying to pretend that Hugh had died and I'd almost managed to convince myself that Roland didn't know about me, but Hugh's continued existence just ripped right through my denial. Roland had healed him. They had talked. My father *knew*. My father was coming for me.

Fuck.

Jim smiled, showing his teeth. Next to him, Barabas froze.

A small hysterical voice inside my head screamed, *Run! Run!*

I quashed it. I had no sword. None of us had any weapons. Now wasn't the time to panic.

We were on the third floor. There were only two exits, the front door leading out and the back door, which wasn't an exit but an entrance to a narrow hallway that led to a sunroom. I would have to go through Hugh to get to the front door. Hugh outweighed me by sixty-five pounds and I had experienced what his body could do. I wouldn't get past him without a sword. The back door was our only option for retreating with minimal casualties. I had to get my people out of here in one piece. I could freak out about all of this later.

The journeymen gaped at Hugh. Most of them probably didn't recognize him. Ghastek's face went white. So did Ryan's. They knew exactly who he was and what he was capable of.

Ghastek recovered first and stood up. "We didn't expect you, Commander."

Translation: *What the hell are you doing here?*

Hugh moved to stand next to Ghastek. Ghastek was tall. Hugh dwarfed him. "My fault. I should've called ahead."

Hugh smiled. He was wearing his affable, pleasant disguise. *No need to bother, I'm just one of the guys. I topple governments, reap a harvest of death, and revel in violence, but please don't get up on my account.*

This would end badly.

Hugh waited. Ghastek woke up and stepped aside. "Please sit down."

"You should introduce me," Hugh told him and took a seat.

Ghastek chewed on that for a second. *This is my colleague, a nearly immortal psychotic warlord . . .*

"Please welcome Hugh d'Ambray," Ghastek said. "He is a representative of our main office and he has sweeping executive powers."

"Let's not be so formal," Hugh said. "Please carry on with your business. I'll just sit here quietly and observe."

Ghastek and I looked at each other.

"Please," Hugh invited. "I believe there was something about a building?"

Ryan Kelly's mouth remained firmly shut. Everyone looked at me. Apparently I was supposed to say something.

"The building in question is a ruin that Medrano Reclamations is going to pull apart. They'll salvage the materials, sell them off, and move on."

"I'm aware of how the reclamation process works," Ryan said, his voice carefully neutral. "The reclamation isn't the issue. It's the location of the building. We object to the Pack playing fast and loose with our city border."

Fast and loose? Somebody had renewed his subscription to *Catchphrase Monthly.* "Are you aware of where the border lies?"

"Of course I'm aware."

"Then you do acknowledge that the building is on our side of it?"

"Yes, but the building, as you yourself have indicated, is a ruin. It is partially on our side and according to our agreement, the Pack can't purchase property within our territory."

"You're right." I raised my hand and Barabas put a paper into it. "An independent appraisal done by the city shows approximately four hundred fifty-five cubic yards of debris on your side of the border, of which seventy-five percent is defined as loose concrete and magic-reduced powder, fifteen percent as wood, and ten percent as assorted metal, all of it valued at approximately fifteen hundred dollars. Which is why we have prepared this grant. As a show of good faith toward the continued cooperation and friendly relations between our two factions, the Pack hereby gifts the value of said debris to the People to do with as they please."

I held the paper out. Ryan took it and paused, unsure. "Commander, would you like to . . . ?"

Hugh shook his head.

Why are you here? What are you planning?

Ryan read the paper. "Looks right."

"The People thank the Pack for their generous gift," Ghastek said.

"The Pack thanks the People for their continued cooperation." Good, great, let's get the hell out of here.

Hugh leaned forward, looked at me, and said in a quiet conversational tone, "Do you ever just get bored at these things and want to punch someone?"

"Punch any of mine, and I'll break your arm off and beat you to death with it."

"Kate." Ghastek's voice vibrated with a warning. "I don't think you quite grasp the situation."

Hugh grinned. "That's my girl."

Ghastek blinked.

Jim bared all his teeth in a feral snarl.

"Do the People have any other issues?" I asked.

"Not at this time," Ghastek said, his gaze fixed on me and Hugh.

"Fantastic. The Pack has no further issues either."

Hugh cleared his throat.

The doors burst open and four people I'd never seen before hauled in a tarp.

I got the hell out of my chair and backed away. My people backed away with me.

The four dropped the tarp on the table with a thud. The plates and cups went flying. The bloody, ripped-up body of a man splayed out in front of us, his clothes shredded and stained with sticky redness. The thick metallic stench of blood hit me.

The two renders behind me went furry in a whirl of twisting flesh.

The corpse's stomach had been sliced open, the edges carved with the telltale marks of shapeshifter claws. His intestines bulged out in thick clumps. His face was a bloodstained mess, but I recognized him instantly.

Claire screamed. The journeymen shied back from the table. Everyone said something at once.

"Your people murdered Mulradin Grant," Hugh said, his voice drowning out the others.

"Let's not lose our heads," Ghastek warned.

"Show me proof!" Jim snarled.

"Look at the body." Hugh pointed to the corpse. "He's all the proof anyone will need."

Even the greenest recruit fresh out of the police academy would instantly identify these wounds. The spread of the gashes, the pattern, the size of the gouges, all of it was unmistakable. Mulradin had been murdered by a shapeshifter.

"There is no proof that this was done by a member of the Pack," I barked. "You employ shapeshifters in your goon squad."

Claire rocked back and forth. "Oh my God, oh my God, oh my God."

"Let's not jump to conclusions," Ghastek said.

Hugh pointed at him. "You—be quiet. The Pack claims dominion over all shapeshifters in the state. They bear full responsibility."

"Don't bring my people into it," I said. "I'll make you regret it."

"I love it when you make threats," Hugh said.

"You'll love what follows even more."

Ghastek kept looking at Hugh, then at me, at Hugh, then at me.

"I can't wait, baby," Hugh said.

Only Curran called me baby. He was goading me.

"You killed him!" Claire screamed, her voice shrill. "You killed my husband!"

Hugh stepped to her. His voice turned gentle. "They did. Look. Look at him. Your husband suffered before he died. Don't you want to do something about it? Don't you want to make the animals pay?"

Claire's face went white. She grabbed at the metal bracelet on her arm.

"Stop!" Ghastek's voice snapped like a whip.

Hugh spun to him. "It's *his* will. Let it happen."

Ghastek took a step back. "It's our city. I have discretion."

"Not anymore," Hugh said, met my eyes, and winked.

You sonovabitch. This was exactly what he wanted: a big ugly public incident from which there was no return. We could come back from killing vampires—they were property. But we were already accused of murder. If we took down any of the People now, with Mulradin's body on the table and his grieving widow out of her mind, the entire city would turn against us. They didn't love the People any more than they loved us, but if Atlanta had a chance to be rid of either one, the city would take it. Hugh would have an excuse to declare a war against the Pack and be celebrated for it.

Claire ripped the bracelet off. It pulsed with red, and the ceiling burst.

Six vampires dropped into the room. For a fraction of a moment they froze, three perched on the table, three on the floor, their eyes glowing pools of scarlet hunger. Emaciated, hairless skeletons wrapped in hard ropes of muscle and clothed in rubbery skin, no longer human, no longer sane, and always hungry.

Ryan shot forward, his arms opened wide. The vampire eyes dimmed. His face shook with strain. He was trying to hold them and his hold was slipping.

"Retreat!" I barked.

The shapeshifters on both sides of me streamed to the back door, all except for two renders. A thud announced the door flying off its hinges as someone kicked it free.

Hugh spun around and hammered a punch to Ryan's jaw. The big man's eyes rolled back into his skull, his face went slack, and he crashed down.

The vampires shot forward like rabid dogs with snapped chains. One—large, female, and recently turned—lunged at Hugh. Five came sailing through the air at us, their eyes bright ravenous red, free of any navigator's restraint, their minds like open sores, oozing undeath. Five. Too many.

The People fled through the front door. Ghastek stopped, his face twisted.

I grabbed the five vampires with my mind. It was easy. So shockingly easy. The undead went limp in midleap, falling rather than jumping.

Behind the table one of Hugh's men stepped forward, fit, his hair a short dark stubble, two guns in his hands, and fired point-blank into the female vampire's face. The bullets tore into the undead, chewing through the dried flesh.

My renders moved as one. Sage on my right yanked a vampire out of the air, before it could even hit the ground, and twisted its head off with her huge monster hand armed with leopard claws. The werewolf to my left disemboweled the second bloodsucker. I pulled the next pair to them.

The female vampire kept pushing forward, against the stream of gunfire. The man kept firing, his carved profile cold. Bright puffs of red mist shot out of the back of the vampire's head as bullets tore through the brain and muscle. The top of its skull disintegrated. The undead paused, turned slightly, unsteady on its feet, and I saw the wall through the gaping hole where its brain used to be. The vampire took another halting step and sank down, limp, its limbs twitching.

Hugh laughed.

Yeah, yeah, your flunky knows how to squeeze the trigger. Bite me. I pulled the last undead toward the renders. A single person sprinted from behind me to the table. She leaped over the vampire corpses and landed by Mulradin's body. Desandra. Damn it.

The renders tore into the last vampire.

The man with the guns turned and I saw his face. His stare punched me. Nick. Dear God.

"Desandra!" I snarled.

Nick sighted Desandra and fired. The guns roared, spitting bullets in quick one-two bursts. Desandra jerked, spun around, and ran straight for me.

The renders dropped the last two vampires to the floor. Desandra shot past me into the doorway. The renders closed in, blocking me from the People's view with their bodies. I turned and sprinted out into the hallway. The last thing I saw was Ghastek's face from the other doorway. He looked like a man who had just witnessed the start of a war.

The hallway was deserted. Twenty yards away, at the end of the hallway, the moon shone through the shattered windows of the sunroom. Jim stood to the side, snarling as the shapeshifters leaped out the windows one by one. I jogged to him, the two renders covering my exit.

"Run!" Hugh thundered, his voice chasing us. "Run to your pathetic castle! You have until noon tomorrow to give me the murderer or I'll end you! If I see you in our territory, I'll kill you!"

I wanted to turn around and break every bone in his body before I cut his head off. He'd killed my stepfather, destroyed Aunt B, and broken Curran's legs. He would pay. I turned back toward the room. If I just killed him . . .

"Consort!" Jim called.

If I killed him, the shapeshifters would pay for it for years. And I had no sword. Argh.

I forced my way through the fog of blinding rage and ran to the shattered windows. Hugh expected me to enter the People's side of the city. This wasn't a warning, it was a dare.

The broken sunroom windows loomed before me. Three stories, a big fall.

Jim grabbed me and leaped through the broken window. My stomach jumped into my throat. We landed on the ground and he dropped me on the pavement. I hit the ground running and jogged to our cars.

Jim thrust the key into the car door.

A vampire plunged from above and landed on the Jeep's roof. The insane red eyes glared at me. I grabbed its mind with mine.

Before I could do anything else, a weremongoose shot into view, red fur standing on end, the pink eyes with horizontal pupils looking demonic. Claws flashed. The vamp's head went flying one way, its corpse the other. I jerked the door open and slid into the passenger's seat. Jim shoved the key into the ignition, and Barabas dropped into the seat behind me. The engine purred.

The magic wave hit. Wards ignited on the walls of Bernard's, glowing pale green. The engine sputtered and died.

Damn it all to hell and back.

Jim swore.

It would take fifteen minutes of chanting to warm up the car and start the engine that ran on enchanted water. Every second we delayed, the People's reinforcements would be getting closer. We had to get the hell out of here and get to Mt. Paran Bridge before this incident grew any bigger.

I JUMPED OUT of the vehicle and slid Slayer into the sheath on my back. "We go on foot." I turned and ran, not looking back. A moment and the two renders drew even with me. Behind me Jim called, "Form a line. Sarah, point. Rodriguez, rear guard."

We ran out of the parking lot.

"I can carry you!" Demon-Barabas offered from behind me.

"I'm good." As long as they didn't run at full speed, I could keep up. I wouldn't be able to do it for very long, but I wouldn't have to. Mt. Paran Road was a mile and a half away. That was where Jim's backup waited. We would regroup and then I'd make Hugh regret ever finding Atlanta on a map.

THE COLD AIR burned my lungs. Around me trees crowded the road. Plants loved magic; it spurred their growth like supercharged Miracle-Gro, and the trees around us looked decades old, their limbs braiding into a single mass of branches.

My muscles felt warm and loose under my clothes. We'd been running for nine minutes and the shapeshifters on all sides of me seemed no worse for wear. For them, this was jogging pace. For me it was a fast run.

In my mind I killed Hugh d'Ambray for the fourth time. Fantasy wasn't as satisfying as the real thing, but thinking about sliding Slayer into his chest made me run faster.

The timing couldn't have been worse. We were at less than half strength and Curran was gone. Hugh was a planner. He never left things to chance. Either he had a really good intelligence source within the Pack, which would be in line with his highly placed mole on the Pack Council, or he'd engineered this whole thing, which meant Gene and his Iberian wolves were in Hugh's pocket and Curran had walked into a trap. Fear squirmed through me. I picked up speed. The shapeshifters accelerated with me.

Curran could handle himself. He wasn't exactly a shrinking violet. If they were dumb enough to try to trap him, he'd come home to me covered in their blood.

Behind me an undead mind flickered into range. This one wasn't loose.

Someone was piloting it. Another vampiric mind joined the first. Then another. An escort to the border. How thoughtful of the People.

The vampires drew closer. I glanced over my shoulder and saw them, three nightmarish shapes, loping in a jerky but fast gait down the road.

I sprinted, squeezing every drop of speed out of my legs. The road turned and I saw the Mt. Paran Sinkhole, a football-field-sized gap like a giant's mouth half-open in the ground. The sinkhole had been born during a strong magic wave, and Northside's wealth made sure that a single-lane bridge had been built over it almost overnight. The moonlight bathed the stone railing and the six shapeshifters waiting on the bridge with three familiar-looking Jeeps.

One shapeshifter stood in front of the others. His jacket was off. He leaned forward, his dark eyes fixed on the vampires behind us with a cold predatory expression, his muscular body coiled like a compressed spring. I used to call Derek "boy wonder," but "boy" no longer fit. He was nothing but hard muscle wrapping bones connected with sinew. His body might have been nineteen, but his eyes under the dark eyebrows were thirty-five. Well, I did tell Jim to put someone solid in charge of the backup unit.

A second shapeshifter perched on the bridge's stone railing to the right of Derek. The light of the moon slid over his face. The bane of my existence. Figured.

Derek and Ascanio. As long as they were separated by the length of a football field, they got along just fine. Getting them into close proximity to each other was like bringing a lit match into a house full of gas fumes. It's a wonder the bridge didn't explode under the pressure.

The distance between us and the vampires shrank. The undead were gaining. The air turned to fire inside my throat. A moment and we pounded onto the bridge. A white line drawn in chalk crossed the stone—the border. We cleared it.

The leading bloodsucker was so close, if we stopped it would be on us. Derek shot past us like a bullet out of a gun.

I glanced over my shoulder. The vamp stepped over the chalk line. Derek leaped and kicked the undead. His foot connected with the vampire's head. The impact knocked the abomination back twenty feet. It fell, sprang back up, froze, and trotted back to the rest of the living corpses waiting for it on the sidewalk.

I kept moving past the line of shapeshifters, slowing to a walk. I really wanted to bend over but I was on display, so I forced my body to remain upright. Breathing is like riding a bicycle. You never forget how to do it, and eventually my body remembered that it too could breathe instead of biting the air and swallowing it down in great big gulps. I walked on, past vehicles, until the bulk of the Jeeps hid us from the bloodsuckers' view. The rest of the group followed me.

My mind finally processed what had happened at the Conclave. Hugh d'Ambray had come for me. Everyone associated with me had just acquired a big target on their chest. He would kill them one by one or a dozen at a time, whatever it took. My memory replayed Hugh's voice. "It's his will. Let it happen." My father had targeted the shapeshifters before, but never so openly. Roland knew I was here, and he'd sent Hugh to break the Pack's back and pry me loose while he was at it. The thing I'd been dreading had come to pass. My friends would die because of me.

Acknowledging it was like dunking my head into a bucket of cold water.

It wasn't supposed to be this way. In my plans Curran was always with me. In my plans we stood together, we fought together, and we did it on our terms. Instead Curran had disappeared into some Appalachian wilderness, and I was stuck here, with a murder on my hands and fifteen hundred people to keep alive. I was the Consort. I had a job to do. I had to quash this war.

I would have to take it one step at a time. Step one: find the killer.

Jim matched his stride to mine. "What the hell was that back there? You almost let him goad you into walking right back to him."

"I need you to find Curran. Hugh hates him and he likely knows exactly where Curran is. Best-case scenario, Gene is keeping him away from here. Worst case, it's a trap."

Jim bent toward me. His gaze met mine. "Hey. Look at me."

I looked.

"Curran will be fine. He's got this. They would have to have sent an army to North Carolina in order to bring him down. I have people watching Gene's territory. Nobody came in or out."

That's right. Jim would have someone watching them.

"Hugh will try to fuck with your head. Don't let him. Do your job. You've got fifteen hundred people depending on you."

"Awesome pep talk."

"If you want a pep talk, get yourself a cheerleader. Did you recognize the crusader with Hugh?"

"Yes." I'd recognized Nick, alright. I saw him shoot Desandra.

"Why did we run?" a man demanded behind me.

I stopped and pivoted on my foot to face him.

It was one of Jennifer's bodyguards. In his early twenties, he was large, with a head of wild blond hair, athletic. His eyes shone yellow, catching the moonlight. His lips trembled, baring his teeth. Right, all the lights are on and he's exhaling aggression with every breath. Adrenaline junkie. Bad choice for a bodyguard.

"We had the numbers on them. We could've taken them."

"Make him sit," I told Jennifer. "Or I will and he won't like it."

Jennifer's expression was blank.

"We look like fucking cowards," the blond snarled. "We should've . . ."

Desandra shot forward, grabbed the blond by his throat, and slammed him on the stone surface of the bridge. His back slapped the rock. Desandra's voice was a ragged snarl. "Do not question the Consort! Do not shame your clan in front of your alpha!"

The blond gasped, trying to breathe.

One does nothing, the other does double. I didn't know who was worse.

Desandra pulled the blond up to his feet and stared in his eyes, her face an inch from his. "Look at *me*."

The man stared at her, his face shocked.

"Jennifer is lenient. Search my face; do you think I'm lenient?"

The blond swallowed. "No, Beta."

"Do you want me to demonstrate that I'm not lenient?"

"No, Beta."

"When you earn the right to question the Consort, you can speak. Until then, when she gives you an order, you shut your mouth and obey, or I'll rip out your tongue. I had it done to me once and it takes six months to grow back. Are we clear?"

The blond nodded.

"Enough," Jennifer said.

Desandra opened her hand and ducked her head at me. "Our apologies, Consort."

"I don't need you to apologize for me," Jennifer said. "Watch yourself."

Desandra's spine went rigid for half a breath, then relaxed so fast I would've missed it if I wasn't looking for it. She shrugged, looked down, and purred. "I'm sorry, Alpha."

I didn't have time for their games. "We have less than eighteen hours until Hugh d'Ambray and the People attack the Keep. Once war starts, it will be difficult to stop."

The People and the Pack had never seen eye to eye, and both sides had plenty of idiots who thought they had something to prove.

Desandra shrugged off her jacket and turned her back to a male wolf. He pulled a knife out and sliced her back open. She bared her teeth for a tiny second. The bullet was probably still in her body.

"We have to prevent the war," I said. "Mulradin's body, thoughts?"

"The killer's a shapeshifter," Jim said. "Not a bear. They tend to crush. The body had punctures consistent with canine or feline teeth."

"I agree." I looked at Jennifer. I needed a consensus, because none of them would like what I was about to say. "What do you think?"

"It's possible that it was a shapeshifter," Jennifer said. "Someone outside the Pack. I can't imagine any of our people doing it."

"I got a good whiff of the body. It's a wolf," Desandra said. "One of ours."

"You're lying!" Jennifer spat.

Desandra shrugged. "Why would I lie? I recognize the scent. I smelled it before a couple of times, at the Keep and at the clan house. It's not someone who is at the Keep often, but I know the scent and it's one of ours."

Anger and hate clawed at each other on Jennifer's face. "Why are you doing this? What could you possibly gain from this?"

"I'm telling the truth," Desandra said.

"This is one of your schemes, isn't it? Not this time."

The three wolves escorting Jennifer and the wolf render next to me simultaneously decided to look everywhere except at the two women. Behind them, Derek also pretended that nothing was happening. Ascanio rolled his eyes.

"Not this bloody time, do you hear me?" Jennifer's voice spiked, picking up notes of hysteria. "No more plots, Desandra. No more *Desandra Show*."

And Jennifer had just lost it in public. Awesome. Because that was what we really needed, to have this pissing match right this second in front of witnesses.

"Table it," I said. "Back to Mulradin's body."

"Desandra's right," Robert said, his voice cold and precise.

We all turned to the alpha of the rats. He'd been so quiet, I had forgotten he was there.

"It's a wolf," he said. "I didn't get a scent because the odor of blood was too thick, but I was close enough to see the wounds in detail. Mulradin had fought back. He must've grabbed at his attacker, because I saw fur stuck to his bloody hands. Wolf fur."

Jennifer glared at him. It was like flicking a match at a glacier. Robert remained unperturbed.

"We need to find the killer before the deadline is up," I said before she could freak out again. If we had the killer in custody, there was still a chance to defuse the situation.

"If he or she still lives," Jim said.

Good point. If I were Hugh, I'd kill this wolf to make sure we couldn't turn him or her over.

"And should we find this person, what will happen?" Robert said.

The question was asked in a mild tone, but I got the feeling a lot rode on how I answered.

"If the killer is apprehended, an investigation will be conducted within the Pack," I said.

"And if found guilty?" Robert persisted.

"Robert, what are you really asking?"

Robert paused. "I'm asking about custody."

"I have no intention of giving the People one of our Pack members for their burn-a-shapeshifter-alive party," I said. "We don't roll over when they stomp their feet. But we need to find whoever is responsible. We can't act until we know what happened."

"We need to examine the crime scene," Jim said. "The body didn't smell of wolfsbane."

Wolfsbane was used to obscure the scent trail. Once a shapeshifter smelled it, even the best tracker would dissolve into sneezing fits. No wolfsbane meant a slight possibility that somewhere an intact crime scene waited for us and shapeshifters could read its scents like an open book.

"We don't even know a crime scene exists," Robert said. "They could've set it on fire."

"No, it exists," Barabas said.

"D'Ambray likes games," Derek said. "He wants us to play."

If there was a crime scene, where could it be? The blood on Mulradin's body was fresh. "Desandra? Did you get an idea of how long he's been dead?"

"I'd say less than two hours," she said.

Jim nodded. "That sounds about right, but it would put Mulradin in the Casino at the time of death."

My nose had six million olfactory receptors. A wolf's nose had two hundred and eighty million. If Desandra said he had been dead a couple of hours, I was inclined to believe her, but there was no way a shapeshifter had walked into the Casino, murdered Mulradin, and walked out. I turned to Jim. "Are you sure he was in the Casino?"

"Yes," Jim said. "Ghastek and Mulradin switch off supervising, so that one of them is at the Casino at all times. Ghastek was at the Conclave, so Mulradin had the evening shift. He wouldn't have left the Casino."

"Not necessarily," Robert said quietly.

Jim turned to him.

"Two weeks ago I got a report that one of my people saw him outside when he was supposed to be on call," the wererat said.

"Where?" I asked.

"The Warren," Robert said. "My scout saw Mulradin go into a building, but was unable to follow up because he had a different objective that night."

"And were you planning on sharing that with the class?" Jim asked.

"There are a number of things the class chose not to share with us," Robert said.

Clearly there was some tension there. "Which building in the Warren?" I asked.

"The scout didn't specify."

That narrowed it down about as much as pointing out which of the haystacks had the needle hidden in it. When magic wrecked Atlanta, it had stomped on the Warren, crushing entire streets. Anyone who could have moved, did. Now the Warren consisted of slums, populated by the destitute, criminals, and street kids, and it was huge.

"Can we ask the scout to narrow it down?" I asked.

Robert looked slightly uncomfortable. "Yes. But he's at an observation post."

"Where?" Please don't say in the People's territory.

"The People's territory."

This was not my night.

"Phone line?" I asked.

Robert shook his head.

Of course. The phone probably wouldn't have worked with the magic up anyway. "I'll need a small strike team to go in with me to find the observation post."

"No," Jim said. "You can't go."

"Overruled," I told him.

"Kate!"

"Last time I checked I was in charge. Would you like to challenge me to settle this?"

Jim scowled at me.

"Very scary, but I'm still in charge. Robert, where is the observation post?"

"On Centennial Drive."

You've got to be kidding me. "On Centennial Drive? Across from the Casino?"

Robert nodded.

Great. Sneak into the People's territory, while Hugh has every vampire in Atlanta looking for anything with a tail or a saber, find a wererat who wanted to stay hidden, which was pretty much impossible, and then high-tail it over to the Warren. Piece of cake. Let me just get my invisibility cloak and a teleportation device . . .

"With all due respect, Consort, you'll never find the observation post," Robert said. "And even if you did, my scout won't speak to you."

"Will you come with me?"

Robert nodded. "Yes."

"We have enough people to get you there," Barabas said. "We could go in force."

"No. The idea is to sneak in and out. If we go in with a large group, we'll fail. First, we'll be more conspicuous. We might as well hook ourselves up with a neon sign that says 'Target here. Bite to kill.' Second, if we bring the numbers, they'll view it as an invasion of their territory. Third, if we do encounter any vampires, the plan will be to run and hide to minimize any damage, not fight them off. No, we go in with a small group and whoever comes with us will keep their human skins on."

"That bastard planned this whole thing," Jim said. "He was gloating. There will be a trap at the crime scene."

"Most likely. Which is why I have to go." Of all of us, I had the best chances of surviving a meeting with Hugh and getting our people away alive.

"You seem very sure of that," Jennifer said. "Maybe this whole thing was a coincidence. This d'Ambray came down to inspect the People, looked for the man in charge, couldn't find him, and discovered the murder."

Oh shut up. "Whatever his motivations are, we must get to the crime scene. This matter isn't up for discussion." I raised my foot and deliberately stomped on the bridge. "This is my foot. I put it down. Deal with it."

They all looked at me.

"No more objections. Just help me get there and get out alive."

"I'll come," Jim said.

"I need you to initiate the siege protocol." Under siege protocol, every shapeshifter in the city would be pulled into the Keep. Those in the nearest towns would be advised to evacuate to the Wood, a huge forest up north.

"Barabas can do it."

Curran was gone, I was gone, and now Jim would be gone. How about no? How about for once in their lives, the Pack just did what I told it to do? "The Pack Council might need someone with direct knowledge of the incident and experience with running things." And I didn't want Jennifer to be the sole voice reporting what had happened.

Jim looked at me. I knew exactly what he was thinking. He would've loved nothing more than to drag me back to the Keep and surround me with rings of combat shapeshifters, but Hugh changed everything. I was the Pack's best hope against Hugh. He was an enemy I was uniquely equipped to fight. Curran had put his life on the line for the Pack dozens of times. It was my turn. If I didn't come back, someone had to hold the Pack together. Jim would be that someone, because he was the best man for the job and he was pissed as hell because of it.

"You're taking Robert," he said, his voice very calm. "Take Derek with you, too."

I opened my mouth to say no and stopped. I had no clue where Robert's loyalties lay, but Derek would die for me. He was almost twenty, he'd had combat training since he was sixteen, and he'd been through more shit than most people could handle in their lifetime. Objecting to him because I still thought of him as a kid and didn't want to see him hurt would just humiliate both of us.

"Are you in?" I asked.

Derek looked mildly offended.

Right. How dare I ask? Teenage werewolves and their touchy feelings.

I turned to the rest of them. "We need one more."

There was a reason why everyone from SWAT to the Marines and SEALs used four-man fire teams. They were fast, maneuverable, they let you cover all four sides, and in our case, having four people would make sneaking into the People's territory much easier. We could break into pairs. A couple walking at night in Atlanta wouldn't immediately attract attention. Three or four people together would draw the eye.

Myles, the wolf render, stepped forward. Perfect.

"No." Jennifer narrowed her eyes. "Take Desandra with you."

Seriously? She wasn't even trying now. I was an amateur when it came to Pack politics, but this was just blatantly obvious. If I insisted on Myles, I'd insult Desandra. If Desandra backed out, she'd lose face.

Jim and Robert looked at each other.

"This is a dangerous mission and Clan Wolf wants to assist the Consort," Jennifer said. "We're still the largest in the Pack, and as the alpha present at the Conclave I feel our clan must do everything in its power to help. Desandra knows the scent and she's an excellent fighter."

"You're sending her off hoping she'll die and for what, so you can clutch onto power for a couple of extra days?" Jim said.

Jennifer raised her chin. "You have something to say, cat, say it."

"I just did," Jim told her.

If I didn't cut this off right now, they would bicker all night. "Enough. Desandra, are you up to it?"

Desandra looked like she'd rather suck on some rotten lemons. "I'd be honored, Consort."

"Great." Now I had two wolves in my fun party. My wolf avoidance strategy had so far proved to be an epic fail. "We'll take the northern evacuation route."

We'd planned both north and south escape routes, but the northern one ran right past a stable. I'd need a horse to keep up with the shapeshifters. Good that I had already rented one.

"Remember the way d'Ambray was howling about killing anyone caught in the People's territory?" Jim asked. "For this shit to happen, d'Ambray must've made arrangements with the cops. I don't know if he bribed them, blackmailed them, or what, but he's done something. Steer clear of the Paranormal Activity Division."

"Will do," I said.

"Who's got the treasure chest?" Desandra asked.

Sage, the other render, went to the left Jeep and popped the hatchback. An assortment of weapons looked back at us: swords, knives, and batons. Nothing elaborate, just simple, functional tools to speed the journey to the afterlife. Derek looked at the smorgasbord for a long moment and fished out a tactical tomahawk. Solid black and about eighteen inches long, it had a six-inch blade on one side of the axe head and a sharp spike on the other. Desandra pulled out a two-foot-long solid metal mace. Its weighted head sported eight sharp flanges. I glanced at Robert.

He smiled. "I'm good. I retrieved my toys from my Jeep before we left."

I turned to Barabas. "Can I have a word before we go?"

"Of course." He walked off with me. I put a hundred yards between us and the rest of the shapeshifters, made sure my back was to them, and said, "Barabas, before you leave the city, I need you to stop at a courier and send a few messages. Call in every favor we have with the city and whatever goodwill we have with law enforcement. Use anything we've been saving for a rainy day, because the hurricane is here. Please call Evdokia or one of her kids. Tell her what happened."

Evdokia was one of the prominent witches in the Atlanta Covens and one of the few people who knew my background. The Covens would fight Roland to the end, and letting them know Hugh was on the warpath would buy them time to prepare.

"Will do."

"As soon as you get to the Keep, please put together a combat team and send it into North Carolina to find Curran. Keep it quiet. We don't need a panic."

Barabas nodded.

"Jim will want to send one, but I want you to oversee it. Use renders, use combat people, the best you can get without leaving us too vulnerable. I don't care if they have to take the mountains apart rock by rock. They need to find the Beast Lord and they need to do it fast."

"I understand. What about the Pack Council?"

"They are Jim's problem. If you can, try to stall them. Delay any decision making until tomorrow. We should be back by morning. If I don't check in by noon, I am dead and you're on your own."

"Understood."

"*Find him*, Barabas."

"Kate, I will. I promise you, I will."

"Also, please tell Jezebel to take Julie out of the city. She'll need backup, because Julie is good at escaping. If Hugh takes Atlanta, Julie can't be here. He will use her and make her into something terrible."

"He won't take Atlanta," Barabas said.

"I know. Please do this for me."

"Of course. Good luck."

"Thank you. We'll need it."

We went back to the cars. Jim's face looked grim. "For the record, I'm sick of being left behind," he said.

"For the record, I'm sick of Hugh being alive."

The weremongoose was waving at our people. "We're moving out."

Jim paused. "Don't get yourself killed and don't make me come and rescue your ass."

"Thanks, Mom. I love you, too."

Jim growled under his breath and went to the Jeep.

"Jim!" I called, too loud.

He turned.

I waited a second to make sure I had everyone's attention. "If I'm not back by tomorrow evening and the Beast Lord is still gone, you have my blessing."

Jim blinked. His mouth opened. "Understood, Alpha."

Someone would have to run the Pack. He had done it before and if I didn't come back, he would do it again, and now I had a dozen witnesses who would support his right to do it.

Jennifer shook her head. She and her bodyguards got into their vehicle. The dark-haired man who had cut Desandra's back open lingered. Desandra stepped close to him. "Go with our alpha. When you get to the Keep, send someone to Orhan and Fatima. And if Jennifer tries to do something stupid, delay her as much as you can. Get George to help you."

So she had gone to see the retired alpha couple.

The man nodded and took off.

We turned and trotted down the bridge, hidden from the vampires' view by the cars. The shapeshifters began to chant, cajoling the Jeeps' enchanted water engines into life.

"Orhan and Fatima?" Robert asked.

"Mm-hm," Desandra said. "I have their blessing to take over the clan. Can you believe that bitch threw me under the bus?"

WE FINISHED CROSSING the bridge and jogged another quarter mile along the forested road, then turned off the barely visible trail to the left. Trees choked the path, their roots thrusting across the dirt, all but invisible in the night shadows. Perfect. Maybe I'd trip, break my neck, and save Hugh the trouble of hunting me down.

"It's not that Jennifer shoved me off the cliff," Desandra said. "I understand. It's that she was so ham-fisted about it. The woman has been an alpha now for what, six months on her own? It's fair to expect some subtlety."

"When did you go to see Orhan and Fatima?" Robert asked.

"A few days ago," Desandra said.

"They don't want to be involved in the Pack's operations," Robert said. "They've made it abundantly clear. An alpha who steps down surrenders all right to meddle with their clan. You've put them into a difficult position."

"They invited me to meet with them. I didn't ask. You want to know why Orhan and Fatima sent for me?" Desandra pointed at me, then at Robert in turn. "Alpha, alpha . . ." She pointed at herself with her thumb. "Beta. One of these things is not like the other. Jennifer should be here instead of riding with her bodyguards in a comfy car. That's why."

"I'm not an alpha," Derek said.

"You're like Curran's baby brother." Desandra waved her hand. "You don't count. So no, I didn't break the rules and go and bother Orhan and Fatima on my own. Give me some credit."

Robert tried his best to look quietly unapproachable. His best was pretty good, but it didn't stop me.

"So, Robert, how does that foot taste?"

Robert looked at me, clearly unsure how to react.

"Oh, and one more thing," Desandra said. "About Hugh having planned all this. You're right."

She shrugged the jacket off her shoulder and turned her back to us. A bright red bullet wound, still wet, marked the skin above her shoulder blade.

The bullet must've penetrated from the front and torn straight through the top of her chest to the back. A dark gray stain bordered the wound. She'd been shot with a silver round. As the toxic bullet passed through the body, the Lyc-V in the surrounding tissues died. When the other wolf had cut her back, she must've bled gray.

Nobody carried around silver bullets unless they meant to fight shape-shifters. Silver was too expensive and there were better and more accurate rounds available.

The eardrum-bursting roar of enchanted water engines announced the Pack vehicles passing along the road behind us. We kept moving.

The last echoes of the engines faded.

"Where are we going?" Desandra asked.

"We're going to Blue Ribbon Stables," I said. "It's the closest place to rent a horse."

"Why?" Desandra asked.

"Because I can't keep up with you on foot," I said.

"And she runs like a rhino," Derek added. "You can hear her a mile away."

Traitor. "I thought you had my back?"

"I do," Derek said. "The rhino running is nice. Makes it easy to keep track of you. If I ever lose you, I just have to listen and there you are."

"Yes," Desandra agreed. "It's convenient."

I laughed.

"Are you always this casual?" Robert asked.

"Derek and I worked together for a long time," I told him. "He's allowed some leeway."

"What about Desandra?"

"She only bothers with protocol when she wants something. The rest of the time it's lewd jokes and descriptions of plums."

Desandra snickered.

Robert's eyebrows crept up. "Plums?"

I waved my hand. "Don't ask."

Ten minutes later the wooded path spat us out into Troll's Ferry Road, and fifteen minutes later we stopped next to the fence near the gate leading to Blue Ribbon Stables. Half an hour gone. We didn't have much time.

"You better go in by yourself," Desandra said. "Or they might get scared that Derek and I intend to blow their house down."

"If there is an issue," Robert said, "we're only a few feet away."

I heard a low guttural sound and I realized it was Derek laughing. Well, at least his sense of humor was coming back. Thank the Universe for small favors.

I jogged to the door and knocked. The door swung open and an elderly black man leveled a crossbow at me. I held up my hands. "Mr. Walton? I need a horse. I called you yesterday and asked you to hold one for me."

Mr. Walton squinted at me. "About that . . ."

"Yes?"

"I've done rented them all."

You've got to be kidding me. "You said you had one and would hold it for me. I sent one of my people here and he told me you took the money."

"I did say that and I did take it. But you know. Money is a funny thing. The more of it, the prettier it looks. You said you might need a horse and it wasn't a sure thing."

Argh.

"You want a refund?"

"I want a horse."

"I'm all out of horses for this week, but I've got a mammoth jenny."

"A what?"

"Come, I'll show you."

He led me to the stable. Inside in the third stall something large moved. It looked like a horse, about sixteen hands or so tall. The man raised a fey-lantern. A long face with two-foot-long ears looked at me with big blue eyes. A donkey, except it stood about eight feet tall, hoof to ear. Big white spots painted its black shaggy hide.

"What is this?"

"That right there is a mammoth jenny. A female American Mammoth donkey."

"Is she magic?"

"Nahh. They developed them in the early twentieth century, primarily for mule breeding. She's a good mount. Good on a trail. She'll give you a twenty-mile-per-hour gallop in a pinch, but not for long. One thing, though. Most of her kind are sweet. She's what we call in the business a freak of nature. Smart, stubborn, and ornery."

"What's her name?"

"Cuddles."

Perfect. "I'll take her."

The moment I walked Cuddles out of her stall, she turned to face me, stood erect, and put her ears forward. Okay. When a horse was ready to be aggressive, she typically put her ears back. This, I didn't know. Donkeys were a new territory for me.

"What do the ears mean?"

Mr. Walton shrugged. "Means she isn't sure about you. Donkeys are stoic animals. They're not horses with long ears, you know."

Okay. If Cuddles were a horse, I'd wave the lead at her to make her take a step back. In horse dominance games, whoever moved first lost face. Something told me it wouldn't work here. "Do you have any carrots?"

Mr. Walton crossed the stable to the front and brought me a large carrot.

"Thanks." I took one, bit into the top, and made loud chewing noises. "Mmm, yummy carrot."

Cuddles opened her eyes a little wider.

"Mmm, delicious."

Cuddles took a step forward. I turned sideways and tried to chew louder. Cuddles clopped toward me and nudged my shoulder with her nose. I held the carrot in front of her and petted her cheek. She ate the carrot and looked at me.

"Very nice," Mr. Walton approved. "You're a donkey whisperer."

"You got more carrots?"

Two minutes later I packed three pounds of carrots into Cuddles's saddlebags. He let me have them for free "on account of Cuddles isn't a horse and I did rent your mare out from under you." If a herd of giant donkeys crossed our path and needed to be subdued, I had it covered.

I rode out of the stables on top of an eight-foot-tall donkey that looked like she had robbed a Holstein cow and was now wearing the stolen clothes.

Robert gaped at me. Desandra made a weird face: her right eyebrow crept up, her left went down, and her mouth got stuck somewhere between surprise and the beginning of the word "what." Derek's mouth opened and didn't close until we came to a halt next to him.

"What the hell is this?" Desandra asked.

"This is Cuddles. She's a mammoth donkey."

Derek grinned, leaning on the fence. "Do you have any self-respect left?"

"Nope."

"I think she's cute." Desandra reached out.

Cuddles promptly tried to bite her. Desandra jerked her hand away and bared her teeth. "Donkey, you don't know who you're messing with. I'll eat you for breakfast."

"Where to now?" I asked.

"Hold on," Robert said. "I'm still . . . coming to terms with your mode of transportation."

"Take your time." I nudged Cuddles, turning her to give him a better view. Cuddles flicked her ears, lifted her feet, and pranced. Oh dear God.

Derek put his head down on the fence and made a moaning noise. Desandra chortled.

"Okay," Robert said. "I think I've absorbed. I am ready for strategy planning now. Could you please stop prancing?"

"She isn't done."

It took another thirty seconds and a carrot to get Cuddles under control.

"How do we get into the territory without being killed?" I asked.

"We can try the northwest approach," Robert said. "It's more lightly patrolled. But with the current state of things, they likely doubled the security. They'll be looking for us."

That was the understatement of the century.

"I could go alone," Robert offered.

"If they find you, we'll never find your scout or the crime scene," Desandra said.

He spared her a look. "They *won't* find me."

Sure, they won't. Pointing out that his pride was getting the better of him wouldn't be politic. I had to say something neutral.

"Accidents happen." Kate Daniels, Master of Diplomacy.

"We can come in on one of their usual patrol routes," Derek said. We turned to him.

"They know our patrol routes," the boy wonder said. "So we shift them when there's an emergency. They'll likely do the same, leaving the original route open."

"Likely?" Desandra shook her head.

"Likely is what we have," Robert said.

"I don't like it," Desandra said. "I don't know about you, but I have two babies to go home to. We could be walking right into their patrol."

"We won't," I said.

"What makes you so sure?" Robert asked.

"We have a real-life vampire detector with us," Derek said.

It was my turn to be looked at.

"You keep staring, I'll have to do a dance or something."

"You can sense vampires?" Robert asked.

"Yes."

"From how far away?" the alpha rat asked.

"From far enough to give us time to hide."

"Okay," Robert said. "Then I vote for the patrol route."

Desandra surveyed me as if she had met me for the first time. "What other fun things can you do?"

I winked at her. "Stick with me and you might find out."

"We can go through the quarantine zone," Derek said. "Even bloodsuckers stay out of there."

"There's probably a reason for that," Desandra said.

"Fortune favors the brave," I told her. It also kills the stupid, but I decided to keep that fact to myself. "Come on. We need to hurry."

NIGHT DRENCHED ATLANTA'S streets, blue-black and viscous like ink. It slid down the ruined buildings, gathering in the empty holes of the windows, and dripped into the rubble-choked alleys. Cuddles clopped down the street, the sounds of her hoofbeats sinking into the darkness. Robert and Desandra moved with me on my left, Derek on my right. Robert didn't jog; he glided completely silently, his movements small and fast. Desandra and Derek had dropped into that long-legged wolf stride that would let them go for miles and miles. Derek's face had gone flat, neither brooding nor hard, just ready.

I didn't brood either. I had a target. I would take care of it. The trick was not to think of everything I would lose if I failed.

I should've made more time for me and Curran. I should've . . .

I slammed that door shut. Fix this mess first. Guilt, regret, and moaning later.

Our people would find Curran and if they failed, I would find him. He was okay. We would be together again. I'd bury Hugh's head next to Hibla's grave. I already had a spot picked out for her. Right next to Aunt B. Maybe my nightmares would stop then.

Derek stopped and pivoted on his heel, looking behind us. He tilted his head down, his expression predatory, his unblinking eyes staring at a fixed point in the distance, where ravaged houses cast deep night shadows onto the street. His muscles tensed and his mouth opened slightly, betraying just a hint of his teeth, as if he were a wolf frozen in the moment before a strike.

I reached for my sword. Robert put his hand inside his jacket. Desandra smiled.

"Come out," Derek said. "You're busted."

A shadow separated from the deeper night shadows and stepped into the street. An angelic face looked at us with devil eyes.

Damn it all. "Ascanio!"

The bouda sauntered forward, a picture of pure innocence on his face.

"What the hell are you doing?" I growled.

He pulled on a disarming smile like a shield. "Following you."

"Why?"

"Because."

So help me God, I would brain him with something heavy in a minute. "Because why?"

"I wanted to come. It's too dangerous for you and I'm concerned."

Derek snarled quietly under his breath.

"You can't blame me," Ascanio said. "Anybody in my place would be concerned. You don't even have a proper horse. You're riding a mutant equine of unknown origin."

"Don't disrespect my donkey. If you wanted to come, why didn't you say so?"

Ascanio gazed at me, broadcasting sincerity. "Because you would say no. And I would never disobey you, Alpha."

Argh. "Did you tell Jim where you were going?"

He looked taken aback. "Of course not!"

"Why not?"

He spread his arms. "Because he would say no."

I put my hand over my face.

"Technically, I haven't disobeyed any orders," Ascanio said.

I pointed at him.

"Okay." Ascanio took a step back. "I understand you need a moment."

"Would you like me to beat him?" Derek asked.

"Personally, I don't think this is a good time to be fighting among ourselves," Ascanio said. "But if Mr. McBroodypants would like to see how much I've learned in the past year, I'd be happy to show him. It would make a lot of noise and draw a lot of attention with all the blood flying around."

Mr. McBroodypants took a step forward.

"No," I said.

Derek growled quietly under his breath.

Ascanio shot me another brilliant smile. "I'm sorry for all this trouble. I honestly was just trying to help. But now that I'm here, I couldn't possibly go back all alone and defenseless. Unless you want to condemn me to certain death. Alone. In the night. In the freezing rain."

Desandra laughed.

"It's not raining," I told him.

"How old are you?" Robert asked.

"Sixteen," Ascanio said, suddenly dropping the plaintive tone. "Not old enough to drink or sign a contract, but old enough to be tried as an adult if I kill a human. Also old enough to fight for the Pack."

Robert's eyebrows crept up. "Old enough to accept the consequences of your decisions?"

"Yes," Ascanio said.

Robert glanced at me.

That was exactly what I needed. A hundred forty pounds of teenage crazy in a pressure cooker. "Fine."

Derek glanced at me. "Really?"

"Yes."

He stared at me, incredulous. "So he gets what he wants?"

"Yes. We're too close to the People's territory. If we chase him off, he'll just keep following us and walk himself into something he wouldn't get out of. And if the People get hold of him, they'll use him as leverage against us."

Ascanio beamed.

"Look at me," I squeezed through my teeth. "You will obey me. If I say 'stop,' you stop. If I say 'jump,' you jump. If I say 'hold your breath,' you'd better pass out before you start breathing again."

"Yes, Alpha."

"This isn't over. If we survive this and get back to the Keep, I'll have a talk with your alphas. You think the Beast Lord is scary, wait until we get back to the Keep. I promise you, after I am through with you, you'll regret this."

"I'm regretting it already," he promised.

I turned Cuddles. Ascanio trotted over next to Derek. Derek snapped his teeth. Ascanio winked at him. "You know you missed me."

We turned up the street.

Now I had two of my personal bodyguards. Too bad their average age was seventeen and a half. That reminded me . . . "Desandra?"

"Hmm?"

"The blond curly-haired guy with Jennifer. What's his story?"

Desandra sighed. "Brandon. He just turned twenty a month ago. A classic case of second child syndrome: he has an older brother who is better than him at everything and he's pissed off at his parents, because they mostly ignore him. Jennifer is really good at making him feel special. That's her secret talent. She picked up on his insecurities and made him feel like he's her hero. From what I found out, that's how she got Daniel, too. He must've had some inner demons that needed soothing. The woman is very good at it, I'll give her that."

"How loyal is Brandon?"

Desandra shrugged. "Jennifer is older, attractive, more sexually experienced, and higher up on the food chain. Brandon is dying to be appreciated and praised for the special treasure that he is. Plus, I'm pretty sure she's playing that whole forbidden-sex card. 'I want you but we can't. It would be so wrong.' I know they haven't slept together yet, but she must've dropped hints, because she's got a leash around his dick and when she tugs, he comes running. He would throw himself off a cliff for her. That put-down I did on the bridge wasn't for his benefit. It was for the others, in case they get any wrong ideas, because let me tell you, Kate, if Jennifer tells him to stab you in the back, Brandon will do it."

Nice to know. Yet another wolf to beware of.

"Derek?" Desandra looked at him.

"Yes?" he said.

"Let's say I do make a bid for the alpha spot. What will it take to earn your support?"

He shrugged. "I'm just another wolf."

"We both know that's bullshit," Desandra said. "You're a member of Curran's inner circle. You're practically family. You have a lot of pull in the clan. What will it take? Would you like the beta spot?"

Derek smiled. "No."

"Aiming higher?" Desandra raised her eyebrows.

"No. I watch them." Derek nodded at me. "I can see how happy the alpha spot makes them."

"The sarcasm, it burns," I said.

"Why do you want it?" Derek asked.

"I can make things better," Desandra said. "I can make the clan run smoother. I can make the people feel safer and happier. And one of my children is a monster."

If the younger of Desandra's twins ever tasted human flesh, he would become lamassu like his father. He'd grow wings and huge teeth. We weren't exactly sure what else he was capable of.

"What does that have to do with anything?" Ascanio asked.

Desandra smiled at him. "Jennifer will never let him grow up in the Pack. She all but said so."

Jennifer, you dumbass.

"I've spent my life under an abusive alpha," Desandra said. "I know what it's like to be at someone's mercy. My children won't grow up persecuted. If I have to take the alpha spot and hold it to make sure they have a happy childhood, I'll do it."

A deserted building sat on our left, sagging to the street, thin streaks of graffiti staining its walls like tears. Robert squinted at it. "One moment."

He took a running start, jumped, and ran up the near-vertical wall. His fingers fastened over the third floor's windowsill and he dived into the window. Desandra whistled quietly.

"You know he's married, right?" I asked.

"I can still enjoy looking at his ass."

Her eyes lit up.

Oh no.

"It's like two . . ."

"No."

Desandra giggled.

That was a close one.

"You know, if you have certain frustrations," Ascanio said, "I would be happy to help you work them out."

Derek looked at me, pointed at Ascanio, and punched his left palm with his right fist a few times. I shook my head. *No, you can't pummel him.*

Desandra laughed. "Maybe in twenty years. When I have, what is it called? Midlife conflict?"

"Midlife crisis," I supplied.

"Yes. That. Assuming you live that long."

"That's a big 'if,'" Derek said.

Robert reappeared carrying a small dirty sack, leaped down, and jogged over to us.

"What's this?" I asked.

"It's a rat stash," Derek said. "They hide them all over the city."

Robert reached into the sack, pulled out a large roll of duct tape and a bundle of canvas rags, and smiled.

"What's this for?" Desandra asked.

"You'll see," I told her.

We headed down the street.

Desandra shrugged her shoulders. "Hey, Kate? Have you thought of walking up to Hugh and telling him that he's got the biggest dick ever?" She spread her arms to the size of a baseball bat.

"No, you think it would work?" I asked.

"It's worth a try. Maybe he'll be so happy you noticed his pork sword, he'll forget all about trying to kill us."

Pork sword. Kill me now. "I'll think about it."

Ascanio began patting his clothes.

"What?" Derek growled.

"Looking for something to take notes with."

Robert gave no indication he heard us but I knew he was listening. Any idiot could figure out that Hugh and I had a history, and Robert was far from being an idiot. Soon questions would be coming, I could feel it.

Ascanio gave up on patting and gazed at Desandra with something akin to admiration. Found himself a role model, had he? Because he wasn't trouble enough already.

"What is it, child?" Desandra asked.

"Did you really have your tongue cut out?" Ascanio asked.

Desandra's eyes narrowed. "When I was twelve, my father didn't like what I was saying, so he took a knife and sliced my tongue off. It took six months to grow back and as soon as I could speak, I told him to fuck off. I decided then that nobody would ever make me shut up. I won't hold my tongue. I won't shut my mouth."

"Neither will I," Ascanio said.

"If the two of you don't knock it off right now, I'll turn this car right around and send you both home," I told them.

They clamped their mouths shut.

The street narrowed. A thick wooden pole thrust straight into the middle of the pavement supported a quarantine sign. Thick black letters on a white background read:

IM-1: Infectious Magic Area
Do Not Enter
Authorized Personnel Only

Under the sign, someone had drawn a skull with horns, just to hammer home the point.

We stopped at the sign. The street rolled on, the pavement puckering here and there. Chunks of glass thrust through the crumbling asphalt, some blue, some green, others translucent white, like the tips of subterranean icebergs. In the distance spires and sheets of glass jutted upward, enclosing what was once Inman Yard, Norfolk Southern's train yard, into a massive glass glacier. Once we crossed the glass labyrinth, we'd officially be in the People's territory.

"You have the freakiest shit in Atlanta," Desandra said. "How did this happen?"

I dismounted. "It used to be a massive train yard, over sixty tracks. The city built a huge new train station just before the Shift, all glass and steel beams, very modern. When the magic hit, the trains collided and the station collapsed. Mounds of glass spilled everywhere, and then people started noticing it was fusing and growing, until over the years this happened."

"It's called the Glass Menagerie," Robert said, and passed me the duct tape and the rags. I wrapped Cuddles's front left hoof with a rag and duct-taped the whole thing.

"Is it dangerous?" she asked.

"Oh yeah," Ascanio said. "I killed a monster in there with Andrea. It was bigger than a house."

Derek rolled his eyes.

"There's shit in there nobody knows how to classify," I said. "The College of Mages has been studying it for years, and they're still not sure how the glass grows or spreads. That's why the duct tape and the rags. Once we go through, we'll dump them so we're not dragging contamination all over the city."

I finished taping Cuddles's hooves, fixed the rags over my boots with tape, and passed the roll to Robert. He duct-taped his feet, and then the roll made its way to Desandra and to Derek and Ascanio.

Robert shifted from foot to foot.

"Are you okay?" I asked.

"I don't like having things on my feet." He shrugged.

"You're wearing shoes," Desandra pointed out.

"Yes, but I'm used to the way they look." Robert stared at the wraps and sighed.

"*Still time to turn back,*" Voron said quietly inside my head.

"*Not happening.*" I thought I had banished his ghost.

"*This is dangerous. Don't do this. Walk away.*"

"*This is what you've trained me for. Let me be what you've designed me to be.*"

I waited for an answer, but my memories remained silent.

"Kate?" Derek asked quietly.

I nudged Cuddles and we headed into the Glass Menagerie.

THE MOONLIGHT FILTERED through the glass iceberg, diffused and fractured, until it seemed to come from everywhere at once, bathing the interior of the glacier in a soft ghostly glow. Solid sheets of glass covered the ground. I led Cuddles, moving as fast as I could without sliding. I had no watch but it had to be past midnight.

"Any vampires?" Robert asked.

"No."

"How long have you had the ability to sense vampires?" Robert asked.

Here we go. "Why the sudden interest?" I asked.

"We hear things," Robert said. "Rumors."

"What kind of rumors?" I asked.

"Disturbing rumors," Robert said. "We are dissatisfied with the current level of disclosure. We are concerned."

We. We as in Clan Rat. The alphas of the clans intensely disliked being kept out of the loop, and Jim was always walking a fine line between endangering Pack security by saying too much and pissing off the Pack Council by saying too little. Lucky for me, I wasn't in charge of security.

"If you have concerns, you should address them to Jim," I said.

The alpha of the rats nodded. "Because he will cover for you by stalling and not answering any of the questions we pose?"

I gave Robert my best hard stare. "Cover for me?"

The wererat held my gaze. "Yes."

"He doesn't seem to be scared. You need to work on your alpha glowering," Derek observed. He was watching Robert with a calm, relaxed expression, one I knew very well. If the alpha rat as much as sneezed in my direction, Derek would try to rip his throat out and Ascanio would help. "Maybe you should pick an easier target to practice on, like a small fluffy bunny."

Ascanio clamped his hand to his chest and staggered closer to Robert. "I think McBroody just made a joke. I . . . I don't know what to do. Nothing makes sense anymore."

They were setting him up. If Robert moved toward me, Derek would hit him head-on and Ascanio would rip into him from the side. Desandra's eyes narrowed. She saw it, too.

Derek pretended to study Ascanio and glanced at me. "Would you like me to pull his legs out?" His eyes were completely serious. He was asking if I wanted Robert jumped.

"No, I want the two of you to hang back about fifty yards, so Robert and I can have a conversation."

"But . . ." Ascanio began.

"Hang back," I told him, sinking an order into my voice.

"You heard her," Derek said.

"I'm going," Ascanio said.

They went back a few feet. We resumed our trot through the glass labyrinth.

Desandra laughed under her breath. "So this is what a boy bouda is like."

"Usually they're worse," Robert said. "I've known Raphael since he was six and I was eleven. He was insufferable as a teenager. Beautiful, but so high maintenance. Ascanio is typical."

"The boudas feel like outsiders," I said for Desandra's benefit. "There aren't that many of them and the chance of loupism runs high within their clan, so every child is a precious gift spoiled rotten. But Ascanio is in a class by himself. It's a long story."

"Back to my questions," Robert said. "How long have you had the ability to sense vampires?"

"You can't compel me to answer, Robert."

"No, I can't," he said. "However, I can explain my reasons for asking. Wererats have certain advantages when it comes to covert work."

The wererats were quiet and stealthy, and they could dislocate their bones in a pinch, which let them hide in very small places. A lot of Jim's surveillance people came from Clan Rat.

When not sure which way the conversation was going, say something vague and flattering. "Clan Rat is well-known for its uncanny stealth." So help me, I sounded like Curran. The Pack had slowly driven me out of my mind.

The anxiety stabbed me like a knife.

Curran was okay. Worrying about him wouldn't help him be okay, it would just make me distracted. I had to disconnect from it.

"We also have our own network of information gatherers," Robert said. "We get our information from two channels: official briefings from Jim and from our own people. There was always a gap between the information coming to us from Jim and through our own channels. Since you moved into the Keep, that gap substantially widened."

Robert waited.

I didn't say anything. My patience was wearing thin. I could just imagine Barabas's voice in my mind. Alienating Clan Rat was not a good idea. They were the second-largest clan . . .

"Consort?" Robert asked.

Oh, so we're back to "Consort" now. "So you're upset, because you feel Jim is holding back information?"

"I have proof he is."

I would have to word this carefully. Diplomacy wasn't my strongest suit, but I had a good memory and I'd read the Pack's code of laws cover-to-cover several times. "Has his withholding of information impeded your ability to effectively govern your clan or compromised the safety of your clan's members?"

"If you're quoting Article Six . . ." Robert began.

I was quoting Article Six. It outlined the duties of the Pack's chief of security. "Please answer my question."

"Not yet," Robert said. "However, we're concerned it might."

"Until it does, as Consort, I'm not obligated to take any action."

"She's right," Desandra said.

Robert glanced at her.

She shrugged. "I've read the book."

Robert's eyes narrowed. "I can take my concerns to the Council and make it very difficult for you to avoid questions."

The best defense is a good offense. "We both know that doing so will predispose Curran and me against Clan Rat."

"We're already marginalized!" Robert said.

"How are you marginalized?" Desandra gaped at him. "You're the second-largest clan in the Pack!"

"Yes, we are, but when it was time to go retrieve the panacea, our clan wasn't represented." He raised his hand and began counting on fingers. "The delegation included Clan Heavy, Clan Bouda, Clan Nimble, Clan Wolf, Clan Cat . . ."

Oh my God. "The jackals didn't go either."

"The jackals didn't ask to go. We specifically requested a place and we were cut from the list."

"It wasn't a plot against you. You were cut from the list because I was under pressure from Aunt B and I asked Curran to make space for her."

"That's precisely my point! You're biased against our clan, because we voted against you when Curran fell into a coma."

I couldn't believe it. "Are you serious?"

"Yes!"

"This is ridiculous."

Robert shook his head. "No, it's not at all ridiculous. When Jim provided us with the report of your trip to the Black Sea, it didn't contain three things. One, it said nothing about your prior relationship with Hugh d'Ambray, which obviously existed. Two, it didn't include the fact that you and Hugh d'Ambray had dinner in private. Three, it completely omitted the vision everyone experienced at the final dinner."

"What vision?" Desandra asked. "The one where you hacked people to pieces?"

I glared at her. "Thank you for confirming his paranoia."

"You're welcome," she said. "I do what I can."

Robert must've been holding back for a while, and now he kept going like a runaway train. "I have a responsibility to my clan. These are my people. Nothing will deter me from advocating on their behalf. This lack of disclosure combined with your personal bias—"

"I don't have a personal bias, but you are working on it."

"—with your personal bias is dangerous for my clan. I want to know the nature of your relationship with Hugh d'Ambray . . ."

"He wants to screw her, because she beat the shit out of him and they both have daddy issues over the same guy," Desandra said.

Robert froze midword, blinked, and looked at me. "Hugh d'Ambray is your brother and the two of you are sexually involved?"

Why me, why? "Desandra, you know what, don't help me anymore."

"I got tired of listening to him," she said.

"Will one of you explain this to me?" Robert demanded.

I had enough. "You really want an honest explanation?"

He faced me. "Yes."

"Okay. Hugh serves Roland, who is the leader of the People."

"I know who Roland is," Robert said.

"Good, then this will be easier. Roland wants to rule. He is five thousand years old, he possesses godlike magic power, and he doesn't believe the word 'no' applies to him. Hugh is his warlord. Think of him as a huge unstoppable wrecking ball. Where Roland points, Hugh smashes. Right now Roland is pointing at the Pack. He has fought shapeshifters in the past and they kicked his ass, so he wants to nip you in the bud. Hugh is here to smash you. Would you like to know exactly what Hugh thinks of you? He thinks you're dogs."

Robert bared his teeth.

"If he can't make you sit, he has no use for you. He will put you down—child, elderly, pregnant, doesn't matter—and treat himself to an extra beer at dinner to celebrate a job well done. He can't be bribed, he can't be reasoned with, and he is damn near impossible to kill. Curran broke his back and threw him into a fire that had melted solid stone. But here he is."

I paused to grab a breath. "Hugh and I were trained by the same person. I'm better than he is. In a one-on-one fight, I'll kill him and he knows it. He wants me, my sword, and my magic. While we were at the Black Sea, he showed me a room full of shapeshifters and told me he would slaughter every single one of them for a chance to have dinner with me."

Desandra shrugged. "That's kind of hot. In a sick way."

I ignored her. "Jim, who saddled me with a squad of bodyguards to go to the Conclave, didn't put up much of a fight when I decided to go off on this fun adventure. He knows that when I became Curran's mate, I promised to put myself between the Pack and Hugh. He expects me to do my job. I'm here doing it. I'm your best defense. So if we come across him and Hugh takes me down, you need to run."

The two of them looked at me.

"I mean it. If I'm out of the picture, you need to go and you'll need to drag Derek and Ascanio out of there, because they won't leave me. Do not stay. Do not fight. Just grab the two kids and go. That's as much information as I'm going to share with you. I have to stop this war from happening. Let me do my job and if you would like to be upset about how I went about it, you can address your grievances to my grave or to me in person at the next Council. Until then, I don't want to deal with any more politics. It's making my job more difficult and it's hard enough as is. That's an order."

"Yes, Alpha," Desandra said.

"Very well. I will—" Robert stopped and wrinkled his nose. Desandra inhaled sharply. Something clearly didn't smell right.

I glanced back. Ascanio and Derek sped up, closing in. Robert had a look of intense concentration on his face. I felt it too, that alarming feeling of something behind you watching closely, waiting for you to stumble so it can leap on your back and sink its sharp, cold teeth into the nape of your neck. I could feel the gaze on my back and I knew if I turned around, I'd see nothing, just the shadows between the glass cliffs. But something watched me. Something was there.

Derek fell in next to me and turned around. I followed his gaze. Four eyes ignited in the shadows, one pair right inside the other, bright, electric turquoise about four feet off the ground. The eyes shone once and vanished behind the slanted glass iceberg.

We slowed down to a walk, falling into formation: Derek and I in front, Robert and Ascanio on the sides, and Desandra guarding the rear. If you ran, predators would chase. We wouldn't be running.

Another set of four eyes flashed at us from the left, reflecting in the glass for half a second before melting into nothing.

"They're herding us," Desandra said.

Ahead three sets of twin pairs of eyes materialized from the gloom. They were trying to make us turn right. I pulled Slayer from the sheath.

Three squat, wide-chested shapes congealed from the gloom and moved into the light, step by step. About the size of a small calf, they stood on six muscled limbs. Their limbs ended in handlike paws with agile fingers, each tipped by a short curved claw. Pale hide sheathed their bodies, except for their spine and chest, where bony plates formed a protective carapace. Their jaws were massive, their teeth sharp, and they looked at the world with four eyes, nestled in two rows on their heads.

"I fought these before with Andrea," Ascanio reported. "These are just pups. Their mother was huge."

Awesome. "Can any of you see the tails? Are they segmented like that of a scorpion?" Six legs was a dead giveaway. Not that many creatures had six limbs, but I wanted to be sure.

"Yes," Robert confirmed from the side.

"It's a tarasque. It comes from the south of France, grows to an enormous size, and it's supposed to breathe fire."

Also according to the legends, a tarasque was a dragon. These guys looked more like cats who'd somehow sprouted rhino-like armor, but who was I to complain?

"How did the French kill it?" Derek asked.

"They sent a Christian virgin out, and she bound it with her hair and led it back into the city, where the citizens slaughtered it. We don't have a virgin handy."

"No shit," Desandra said.

The central monster bared her teeth. They were thick, sharp, and crooked.

"Quick, Derek, it's your chance to shine," Ascanio said.

Derek gave him a withering look.

"Desandra is a mother, Robert is married, Kate's affianced, and I'm an old soul. You're the closest thing to a virgin we've got. Get on with growing some flowing locks."

Robert laughed. The sound was so unexpected, I almost jumped. In all the time I'd interacted with him, a careful smile was as far as he got.

"I'm going to hurt you after this," Derek promised.

Ascanio grinned. "Hey, I just assumed you were saving yourself for marriage, my mistake."

Robert pulled two sets of steel knuckles from the inside of his suit. A long curved blade ran the length of the knuckles. Nice. On my right, Ascanio tossed his hair back and retrieved a short sword from his leather jacket. The blade was fifteen inches long and at least two and a half inches wide, single-edge, with a profile that looked almost like an overgrown kitchen knife but with a simple, saber-style cross guard. Ascanio reached for the hilt with his left hand and plucked another sword from the first. Baat Jaam Do. Butterfly swords. Handling two swords took a lot of practice. Well. Interesting.

Three tarasques emerged from the left, two from the right.

"We have two behind us," Desandra reported.

We were surrounded.

The thick front limbs of the tarasques tensed. Nostrils flared, sending clouds of vapor into the cold night. The tails curved upward, flapping back and forth.

I turned my sword, warming up my wrist.

Monstrous lips stretched. Wicked teeth bit the air.

"Let's go!" I barked. "I'm bored."

The beasts scuttled forward like giant cockroaches, moving with an odd gait, lifting the front and back leg on one side and the middle one on the other. The largest of the three beasts hooted like an owl. He was almost to me. In my mind I stepped to the side, swung, and sliced across its neck in a classic diagonal blow. The saber glanced off the carapace. No good.

Ten feet. Stand still.

Five . . .

The beast lunged at me. I dodged left. Wicked teeth snapped half an inch from my arm and I stabbed Slayer into the creature's pale side. My enchanted blade ripped through flesh and sinew. Dark rust-colored blood spilled out from the wound and washed over the beast's gray side.

To the left, Derek yanked a tarasque out of the air, flipped it on its back, and chopped its throat with his axe. To the right Ascanio spun in place, slicing at the beasts, his swords spinning in a familiar horizontal figure eight pattern . . . He was trying to use my butterfly technique. It was not awful. His feet were off, and he was leaning forward too much, but it wasn't awful. I had no idea where he'd learned it.

If we lived through this little adventure from hell, I'd have to correct his form before it was too late.

A familiar sickening magic washed over my mind. Just what we needed. "Vampires. Incoming."

The tarasque lunged at me and I sliced across its nose.

"How many?" Robert asked.

My tarasque screamed and fled.

"Two. They're heading this way, fast."

We had to finish the fight now. If we bled, it would be all over. A vampire was like a shark—a single drop of human blood would pull it from a mile away like a magnet.

The second beast attacked me from the right. I slashed the side of its throat. It crashed down and I stabbed Slayer into its left top eye socket.

Desandra spat some word I didn't understand. A pale body flew above us through the air, crashed against a glass iceberg with a sickening crunch, slid down, and lay still, its six legs limp. Wow. Behind me a wet hacking noise announced someone cleaving through flesh.

The two revolting sparks of undead minds drew closer.

"A thousand feet," I whispered. "Coming on the left. They'll see us."

A tarasque the size of a horse shot out of the darkness and leaped at us, six legs in the air. I stepped aside. That's the problem with jumping. Once you went airborne, there wasn't much you could do about changing where you landed. The beast fell right between us. I lunged on top of it and sank my sword between its ribs. The claws raked my steel-toed boot, ripping through duct tape and gouging the reinforced leather.

Derek cleaved the beast's skull with his tomahawk, grabbed the twitching body, and hurled it to my right, into the shadows. Desandra grabbed another and threw it into the dark. Bodies flew around me. A moment and all corpses were gone.

"Five hundred feet," I whispered.

Robert turned. A streak of red slid down his fingers from a small cut on his hand. Shit.

The vamps accelerated.

He stuck his fingers in his mouth. The cut on his hand knitted closed—Lyc-V scrambling to make repairs.

Turquoise eyes ignited on both sides of the road. How many of the damn things were there?

Desandra pointed up. Thirty feet above us a glass iceberg thrust to form an almost horizontal ledge. Derek grabbed me and hurled me up. I caught the ledge and pulled myself on it. He took a running start and jumped at the lowest part of the ledge. Desandra followed, slipped, and Derek caught her hand and muscled her up. Ascanio jumped straight up, like he had springs, and hoisted himself on the glass next to me.

Less than a hundred feet until the vamps reached us.

Robert ran to the nearly sheer glass wall, scrambled up, quick and silent, as if his hands had glue on them, and slid in place next to us. We lay flat on the glass, just close enough to the edge to look down. If the bloodsuckers looked up, they would see the outlines of our bodies through the glass.

Two emaciated, hard creatures loped into view directly below us. A man and a woman in their former life. The male still retained some semblance of humanity in his face and his body didn't seem as dry, but the female was older. She must've been dark-skinned in life, and undeath gave her skin an unnatural bluish tint. She crouched on her haunches and raised her head, looking around. The Immortuus pathogen leached all fat and softness from its victims, atrophying their internal organs. Her breasts hung on her chest like two empty pockets of skin. Cords of muscle stood out on her neck.

"It was here," a young male voice said from the female vampire's mouth. I could identify all of the Masters of the Dead in Atlanta by sound. I didn't recognize him, so he had to be a journeyman or someone new. Perhaps one of Hugh's imports.

"There's nothing here," another male voice answered.

That's right, there is nothing here. Move along, because we don't have time for this. We had to get to Robert's scout and the clock was ticking.

"I'm telling you, I felt a blood vector," the first navigator said.

The male bloodsucker raised his arms. "Where is it, Jeff? I don't feel anything."

Nope. Definitely journeymen. Not highly ranked either.

The female vamp moved around and slid on the damp patch of dark blood. "Look. What the hell is this?"

"Whatever it is, it has no hemoglobin in it, because my boy isn't pulling at his leash. Maybe it's vomit. Maybe one of those twisted things that lives here came over and puked all over the glass and now you're sliding around in it. Do you want me to call down and get some sawdust for you to deodorize her with when we bring them back?"

Journeymen. Always a pleasure.

The female vamp twisted its face, trying to mimic Jeff's expression. "Very funny, Leonard. You're a fucking comedian."

"We had a route mapped out, but no, you had to go off the reservation because you smelled some phantom blood somewhere."

"We're supposed to patrol. I'm patrolling because it's our job, Leonard. If you don't want to patrol, you can go up to that bigwig and tell him that. Just let me know in advance so I can take pictures when he tears off your nuts and makes you eat them."

"Alright, alright, calm down." The male vamp peered into the gloom. "Suppose we do find the shapeshifters. Do we go to Ghastek or do we go to d'Ambray with it?"

"To Ghastek," Jeff said.

"Yeah, but d'Ambray is higher on the food chain. You can tell Ghastek's pissed, but he keeps his mouth shut. You know. We could get ahead."

"And what happens when d'Ambray leaves and Ghastek's back in charge?" Jeff said.

Get out of here. Go on. Shoo.

"No guts, no glory." Leonard must've shrugged, because his vampire raised his shoulders in a jerky movement.

"We cover our asses and follow the chain of command. Nobody ever went wrong by following the chain of command," Jeff said.

Something clopped in the shadows. Oh no.

The vamps tensed, like two mutated cats getting ready to pounce.

Cuddles emerged into the open. I had completely forgotten she was there. Robert put his hand over his face. Desandra rolled her eyes.

"What the hell is that?" Jeff said.

Why me? Why?

"It's a horse," Leonard said.

"Are you blind? How is that thing a horse? Its ears are two feet tall."

"Then it's a mule."

"It's not a mule. The neck's wrong and the tail . . ."

"What about the tail?"

"Mules have horse tails. He's got a donkey tail. Like a cow. It looks like a donkey, but the damn thing is at least sixteen hands tall. I've never seen anything like it."

"It's a mule. It's got a saddle on it, so someone was riding it."

The male vamp moved forward.

"Where are you going?"

"I'm going to catch it and see who it belongs to."

Argh.

Cuddles put her ears forward.

"It doesn't look friendly," Jeff observed.

"It's fine. If she had her ears back, you'd have to watch out. It's all in the voice. Watch and learn. Come 'ere, girl. Come 'ere . . . Who is a good freaky mule? You are."

The male vamp inched forward. Cuddles stood just a little bit straighter.

"That's a good girl."

The vamp reached for the reins. Its fingers fastened about the leather.

Cuddles screamed. It wasn't a braying noise, it was an ear-slapping shriek of pure donkey outrage, like someone got hold of a foghorn and tried to strangle it.

"Whoa . . ." Leonard started.

Cuddles reared and tossed her head. The vamp slid on the glass and she dragged him left.

"Whoa . . ."

She dragged him right.

"Come on!"

Cuddles kept turning and rearing, her huge body going up and down, jerking the undead to and fro like a cheerleader with a pompom.

"Oh, you idiot," the female vamp snickered in Jeff's voice.

I saw the precise moment Cuddles realized that something was behind her and that something was the same unnatural thing that clung to her reins. Her eyes went big, and she planted her front legs down and kicked. The female vampire flew about twenty feet and smashed into a glass iceberg. Ouch.

The male vamp finally let go, fell, and slid down the glass. Cuddles backed up and braced herself. The male vamp rolled to his feet and gathered itself for a leap.

"Stop!" Jeff moved the female vampire between Leonard's undead and the donkey.

"I'm going to kill that dumb animal."

If he touched my donkey, I'd take his vamp apart.

"No, you're not. It belongs to someone and if you harm it, we'll have to pay restitution. I don't feel like having my paycheck docked."

"The bitch kicked us!" Leonard snarled.

"You put your hands on her. She was defending herself. Come on, the damage is minor. We'll feed them tonight and nobody will be the wiser. But if some hick shows up claiming we injured his donkey, there will be an inquiry. Ghastek's walking around like he's ready to explode. I don't want to be in his blast area."

Leonard's vamp twisted his face into a horrifying grimace.

"We need to move on anyway," Jeff said. "In five minutes Rowena's going to come down that hallway for check-in. I don't want to explain to her that we've been playing with what may or may not be a giant donkey instead of sweeping the perimeter."

The male vamp shook its head and circled around Cuddles, and the two undead took off into the glass labyrinth. We lay still for another five minutes, until they were a mile and a half away.

"I take back what I said about the donkey," Ascanio said. "She's awesome."

I wished Curran could've seen this. He'd die laughing.

My heart stuttered for a beat. I slid down the glass, caught myself with my feet, and went to give Cuddles a carrot.

6

B efore the Shift, Centennial Park occupied twenty-one acres inside Atlanta, a cheery space filled with engraved bricks, lawns, and beautiful fountains. After the magic hit and the buildings around the park took a dive, it stood abandoned for a few years. Eventually, Atlanta's witch covens banded together and purchased it from the city along with the nearby ruins. Shortly after they took over, the vegetation within the park rioted. Trees grew, sending thick roots through the neighborhood and spreading massive canopies, as if they had been growing here for hundreds of years. The park tripled in size. Now a dense wall of greenery bordered it, an impenetrable barrier of oaks, evergreen shrubs, blackberry that somehow resisted the frost, and thorns. In the defense department, the witches would make Sleeping Beauty's evil witch weep with jealousy.

I rode Cuddles next to that green barrier now, heading down Centennial Drive toward the Casino. The shapeshifters flanked me. I kept an eye on the greenery. The witches professed to be friendly to me. Evdokia, one of the three witches of the Oracle, even claimed we were distantly related. But their help was always conditional and right now I didn't trust anyone.

The bushes ahead of us rustled.

I halted Cuddles and reached for Slayer.

A brown bunny hopped out onto the sidewalk and looked at me.

"Snack," Desandra said.

The bunny pondered me with tiny eyes and turned toward the shrubs. Right.

"It's a bunny only part of the time," I said. "Sometimes it's a duck. Also, it can be a kitten."

Robert raised his eyebrows at me.

"We're being invited to visit the Witch Oracle." I dismounted and followed the bunny.

"Not again," Derek growled.

"Why, what's so bad about the witches?" Ascanio asked.

Derek's eyebrows crept together. "You'll see."

The bunny hopped into the shrubs. The greenery split and pulled to the side, revealing a narrow path.

"Do we have a choice?" Robert said.

"Not really."

I stepped onto the path. We were short on time, but pissing off witches ranked right between sticking your hand into a hornet's nest and telling Curran I'd made broccoli for dinner. By now, they had to know that Hugh was in town. If they wanted to see me, it had to be something important.

We passed through the thick barrier of green and emerged into a pine forest. Snow sheathed the ground in a dense blanket. Tall pine trunks towered on both sides of us, as if a Spanish armada were sailing under the snow and only its masts were visible. Past the pines a glade stretched, silver with moonlight. Behind it the translucent walls of a greenhouse rose into the night, sheltering rows of herbs. Centennial Park served as the hub for most of the Atlanta covens and they liked to have herbs in ready supply.

The bunny hopped between the trees. We followed it. Snow crunched under my feet. We really didn't have time for this. Unfortunately, I needed the Oracle. If Hugh and Roland intended to assault Atlanta, I would need their help and their magic. And I couldn't afford to ignore their advice. If I refused to see them and they had a magic self-guided missile that could take Hugh out, I would be kicking myself for years.

Derek wrinkled his nose. "Here it is."

I pulled a strip of gauze out of my pocket and passed it to him.

"What is that smell?" Desandra wrinkled her nose.

Derek ripped the gauze in half and handed her a piece.

The trees fell back and we came to a hill sitting in the middle of a large clearing. Perfectly spherical and smooth, it protruded from the snow, like the cupola of a submerged cathedral. I remembered it as being dark gray with flecks of gold and swirls of green, but the moonlight turned it glossy indigo.

The bunny stopped.

The ground under our feet rumbled. Derek sneezed. Desandra clamped the gauze to her nose. The hill shuddered and slid upward, the snow sliding off its top.

Robert jumped back ten feet. Ascanio just stared, wide-eyed.

A giant head broke free of the snow, its neck a brown mass of wrinkled folds. *Hey, pretty girl. Long time, no see.* The colossal tortoise stared at me with dinner-plate-sized irises and opened its gargantuan mouth.

Right. The full treatment. Just once, would it kill them to meet me in a gazebo someplace or in a fried chicken joint?

Derek and Desandra doubled over in a fit of sneezing.

The bunny's fur crawled, boiled, and stretched into the shape of a small black cat. The cat leaped into the tortoise's mouth.

"Wow," Ascanio said. "That's brutal."

I filed the new item of teenage slang away for future reference.

Desandra pointed at the open mouth, her other hand pinching her nose closed. "In dere?"

"Mm-hm," I said.

"Fuck dis! I'm stayin' here."

"I'm a rat," Robert said. "I'm not going into a reptile's mouth."

Oh boy. Fine time to develop phobias. "It's fine," I told them. "They'll probably cut you off from the conversation anyway."

"I'm coming," Ascanio declared.

Derek nodded, holding the rag over his nose, and came to stand with me.

I stepped into the tortoise's mouth.

.   .   .

THE THICK SPONGY tongue gave a little under my feet. I went forward, past the roof of the mouth, into the throat, draped with garlands of frozen algae and icicles. Ahead dark ice slicked the floor of the throat tunnel. Last time I came through here, I had taken a bath in what I strongly suspected was tortoise spit. I stepped onto the ice. It held. Score one for me.

"This is awesome," Ascanio volunteered behind me.

Someone was having entirely too much fun.

The throat tunnel ended and I walked out onto an iced-over pond in the middle of a colossal dome. The walls, dark at eye level, curved up, lightening until they grew transparent at the top. The night sky, studded with stars, spilled moonlight onto clusters of blue icicles suspended from the ceiling. The icicles glowed with soft blue light, illuminating the outlines of rectangular crypts within the walls, each marked by a glowing gold glyph.

In front of me on a rectangular platform waited three women. The first had seen seventy. Life had whittled her down, turning her body skeletal and her face sharp and predatory. She perched in a large black chair like a bird of prey. Maria, the Crone. Next to her a young woman sat in a comfortable chair. Slender, with pale blond hair down to her shoulders, she looked young, barely out of her teens, and delicate. Her power was anything but. Sienna, the Maiden. I had saved her life during the last flare. To the right, in a rocking chair, sat Evdokia, the Mother. Plump, with a heavy braid of reddish-brown hair, she rocked back and forth knitting a sweater out of gray wool. It looked almost done.

The black cat ran to her and rubbed against her feet.

Behind them a large mural showed their goddess, a tall, regal woman standing behind a cauldron that sat at the intersection of three roads. The woman's three arms held a knife, a torch, and a chalice. A black cat, a toad, a broom, and a key completed the picture. She had many names: the Queen of the Night, the Mother of All Witches, Hekate. Her power was vast and terrible and I was disinclined to disrespect her.

Evdokia pointed to Derek and Ascanio. "You! Wait there."

A wall of ice surged around the two shapeshifters, locking them into an icy ring.

Sienna turned to me. "Your father is coming."

THE UNIVERSE JUST kept dumping buckets of icy water on my head. "When?"

"Soon," Evdokia said, her needles clicking.

"He's coming to claim the city," Sienna said. "We have foreseen it."

Maria raised her bony hand and pointed at Sienna. "Show her."

Sienna stood up. The mural behind her faded, dissolving into a view of a city street. To the left typical old buildings bordered the street, one of dark brick with boarded-up windows, the other covered in beige stucco and in better condition. To the right a big, sand-colored building of Roman brick and granite took up most of the block. Its lower half, a typical rectangular structure, stood about four tall floors high. On top of it a hundred-fifty-foot tower stretched to the sky. I could see all the way down the street, past the streetlights, to the distant steeple of some church.

The sky above the city churned with storm clouds, furious and dark. Wind blew trash down the street in powerful short gusts. The air vibrated with tension and magic, as if charged and just waiting for a strike of lightning. The hair on the back of my neck rose. Something dangerous rode in that storm. Something powerful and frightening.

A man rounded the corner. He wore a white robe. The wind blew his long blond hair over his face.

"Uther Stone," Maria said.

"The name sounds familiar," I said.

"The Gypsy massacre," Evdokia told me, looking up from her knitting. "You're looking at Sioux City."

Ah. Now I remembered. Uther Stone was a really powerful zapper, an elemental mage who dealt in electricity. He came to prominence defending the city from a monstrous giant buffalo. They elected him mayor and he started making laws about what kind of people weren't welcome in Sioux

City. Then a group of Romani disappeared. Their bodies were found in a communal grave and Uther Stone had to answer some questions, except he never got the chance.

In the vision, other people trailed Stone, some in modern clothes, some wearing robes. Eight total. Stone threw open the door of the building and dashed inside. His posse followed.

The viewing angle of the vision slid up, showing the building in greater detail. A carving of a muscular bearded man flanked on both sides by six smaller figures decorated the space above the doors. Above it words spelled out in capital letters, JUSTICE AND PEACE HATH MET TOGETHER. TRUTH HATH SPRUNG OUT OF THE EARTH.

The view kept rising, higher and higher, to the top of the tower until we saw the flat roof and a small entrance, barred by a green metal door. The door thrust open and Stone emerged, the wind pulling at his robe. His people followed, forming a circle. A woman with purple hair pulled a jug of red liquid from her backpack and began throwing handfuls of it back and forth, her lips moving in a chant.

"A local coven," Evdokia said. "All he could muster. They're about to feed their magic into him."

The thunderhead above the building turned black. The sky boiled. The magic clamped the city into an invisible fist and squeezed. The pressure ground on my chest. Suddenly it was hard to breathe. Inside me my magic reared in response. If it had been an animal, it would've snarled. This was a challenge.

The purple-haired woman emptied the jug on Stone's feet. Stone thrust his arms out, gripping a staff in his right fist. The people surrounding him snapped rigid, their bodies unnaturally still.

The thunderhead split. Magic crackled. A spear, glowing as if made of molten gold, struck at Stone. He jerked his staff up, blocking it, and I almost moved with him. He wouldn't be enough.

The tip of the spearhead touched the staff's shaft. Power thundered through the air, shaking the city. Breath caught in my throat. My heart hammered in my chest, too fast. So much power . . .

The wood disintegrated.

For a second Stone stood still, the outline of his body glowing with violent red, and then he fell apart, a man made of ash. The spear buried itself in the roof. Its tip shone with brilliant light and a blast wave rolled through the city in a huge circle, sweeping the ash that used to be the coven off the roof.

I braced myself, expecting the impact, but the magic fell short of me. The spear turned dull.

A man landed on the roof, coalescing out of thin air. He was wrapped in a simple gray cloak, worn, with a ragged hem and a deep hood that hid his face. If I had seen him on the street, I wouldn't have given him a second glance.

"I want to see his face." I needed to see him. I wanted to see my father.

"I can't," Sienna's voice whispered. "He won't let me."

The man grasped the spear and pulled it out. He looked over the city, turned, and slowly, unhurriedly made his way to the door.

The vision faded. I gulped the air. Sienna sank back onto her seat. Sweat beaded on her face.

"The magic pulse, what was that?" I asked.

"The claiming," Maria said. "He has made the land his."

"Each land has a people," Sienna said. "Those who settle on it, those who are born and die on it, their bloodlines bonded to it for generations. Their bodies are buried within the soil, nourishing it. Their magic becomes rooted in it and grows from the land like a forest."

"Think of it like farming," Evdokia said. "Before a farmer can use the land, he must clear the trees, remove their roots, dig out the boulders, and pull out the weeds. Very hard to do if the forest is old and strong and the trees have been growing for thousands of years."

Maria stirred. "But here, we've done the farmer's job for him. We killed the Native people of this land. There is no forest anymore. There are just saplings, families of settlers and immigrants, the oldest from the seventeenth century, but most even younger. Their bond to the land is weak. What you do to others always comes back to you and the balance is always restored. We committed genocide. We destroyed a people and now we have to pay the price for the terrible crimes we perpetrated. The land lies fallow without defenses. All your father has to do is claim it."

So this was why he came here. I always wondered why he had left the Middle East and traveled to North America. Now I knew. He came here because there was no Native power to oppose him. The land was fallow and was ripe for the taking. "What happens when he claims something?"

"He reaps a harvest," Evdokia said. "The magic of the land nourishes him and makes him stronger."

"And protects him," Maria put in. "He's much harder to fight on his territory. The longer he keeps it, the stronger is his bond, the more difficult it is to remove him." She turned to me, her piercing gaze stabbing at me. "He is coming. What are you planning to do about it?"

"If he comes, I'll try to kill him." What else was there?

Maria spun in her chair to face Evdokia and jabbed at me with a bony finger. "She's a moron! I told you! I told you, but no, you said—"

"Will you stop badgering her for a moment?" Evdokia snapped. She leaned forward, looking at me. "If you fight your father directly, you will die. You're not old enough, strong enough, or educated enough."

"Thank you for the vote of confidence."

Evdokia grimaced. "If all of the covens, and all of the pagans, and all of the magic users of Atlanta got together and channeled their power, we could probably block your father, but we can't exactly get everyone together in time. We don't know how to put all of our power together. We don't know when the claiming happens. We don't know where."

It would be on some tower. That was what my father did. He built towers. They were the nexus of his power and now I knew why. The taller the tower, the more he could claim with one pulse.

"You are our best chance," Evdokia said. "There are things we can teach you, but this will take time. You have to buy us this time. You have to prevent the claiming."

"How?"

"We don't know," Sienna said.

"We supported you," Maria said. "We helped you and supplied you with undead blood. We didn't do all this so you can go and sacrifice yourself like a dimwit."

I always knew the witches didn't help me out of the goodness of their hearts. They wanted a return on their investment. "He killed my mother."

"*Obnyat e pluhkuht,*" Evdokia sighed.

To hug and cry. That was what exasperated Russians said when there was nothing left to do.

"Your mother gave her life so you could live," Evdokia said. "Your dying dramatically isn't going to help anyone. It won't honor her memory and it won't protect any of us. There are people in this city who depend on you. Do whatever you have to do, but you must prevent the claiming."

I spread my arms. "What do you want me to do? Should I go up to Roland and ask him nicely to please not claim the city as a favor to me?"

"If that's what it takes, yes!" Maria snapped.

This was a ridiculous conversation. "You do realize he'll try to kill me the moment he sees me?"

"That's not certain," Sienna said. "For almost six months now I've done nothing but look into your future. I've seen you die in dozens of ways and I have seen you survive. But I have never seen him die."

Awesome. Just awesome. "Thanks. This is really helpful. Is there anything else?"

Evdokia bit a thread off her knitting and tossed the sweater at me. I caught it.

"Pure wool," she said. "Will keep you warm even when wet. Put it on and don't take this off for the next twenty-four hours."

I shrugged off my jacket, pulled off my sweater, and slipped into the woolen one. "You know something I don't?"

Evdokia sighed. "Honey, we can fill this place with what we know and you don't."

Ask a stupid question. "If I can find a way to resolve this Hugh d'Ambray dilemma, I may need witnesses for my negotiations with the People. Will the covens act as my witnesses?"

"Yes," Sienna said. "We'll send representatives to the Keep."

I turned around and headed out. Behind me the ice cracked, releasing Ascanio and Derek.

Outside Robert and Desandra waited.

"How did it go?" Robert asked.

"Roland is coming to claim the city. They want me to stop this from happening."

"How?" Desandra asked.

"They don't know. They have no instructions. Their helpful suggestion is to 'just do it.'" I growled and headed out of the forest. So far this had been one hell of a day.

I CROUCHED IN the shadow of an apartment building. Desandra, Derek, and Ascanio leaned next to me, while Robert took a running start and ran up a seemingly sheer wall. We'd left Cuddles tied to an oak in Centennial Park. Nobody in their right mind would steal an animal belonging to the witches. If vampires sighted her, they would let her alone.

We were on the edge of the Slave Pens, a housing development next to the Casino reserved for Casino employees and journeymen, who'd given it its name. The original plan called for going down Centennial Drive but the vampires were too thick. We had to turn around, loop north and west, and approach the Casino from the Slave Pens. It cost us a precious half hour and if I thought about it longer than a second, it made me grind my teeth.

From my vantage point I could see Undead Alley, a four-lane street that now lay deserted. Past it, a vast paved lot stretched out, large enough to accommodate hundreds of cars. In its center, the Casino rose, glowing like a mirage born from cold air and asphalt desert. The huge dome of the main cupola shone with the pale bluish glow of feylanterns, surrounded by slim minarets and tall textured walls of white stone. On a good day, the sight would take your breath away, and then you noticed vampires crawling on it like fleas on a white cat.

The main entrance to the parking lot that surrounded the Casino lay to the west. We were at the southwest corner.

A pair of vampires trotted along the edge of the parking lot. I held my breath. They passed out of sight. They were the third pair I'd seen in the last five minutes. The People were on high alert. I could feel eight vampires patrolling the parking lot and three more stationed at random points, one to the north and the other two to the west and south of us.

Robert slid down and landed next to me without making a sound.

"Where is the observation post?" I whispered.

"There." He pointed to the east at the crumbling remains of the Centennial Drive overpass jutting against the night sky. At some point three overpasses had crossed there, one above the other, but now the top two had collapsed onto the lowest one. Frost had slicked the concrete and parts of the overpass, and enameled in silvery moonlight, they almost glowed. The whole thing didn't look particularly stable.

"There are two entrances," Robert breathed into my ear. "One in the east and one in the south. The southern entrance is there." He pointed to a pile of rubble across the street on our left. A vampire sat on top of it.

"How far is the east one?"

"On Marietta."

A mile away, half of it in plain view of the Casino. If we doubled back to draw a wider circle around it, we'd have to go around the wreckage of Phillips Arena, which would cost us another half an hour or more. Getting this far unnoticed was a miracle. Trying to circle the Casino with that many patrols out would be impossible.

I turned to the vamp perched on the rubble. Even if we managed to take it by surprise, this close to the Casino it would do us no good. When a vampire died suddenly, its navigator usually went catatonic or panicked, because his mind, still connected to the undead, became convinced that it was the navigator who had died. Experienced Masters of the Dead honed their reflexes enough to disengage in time and some navigators survived the sudden death, but most ended up as vegetables. The moment we killed that vampire, one of the navigators inside the Casino would either scream in panic or start drooling, and the Casino would vomit enough vampires to turn us into jerky.

"We need a diversion," Robert murmured.

If we backtracked, we could possibly set something on fire, but it wouldn't guarantee that the vampires would move from their posts. More likely they would send a recon team. We were stuck.

Think. Think, think, think . . .

Desandra ducked her head. "Where are we going after this?"

"Centennial," I whispered. "If we make it, we'll need to pick up my donkey."

"See you there."

"Don't!" I reached for her. My fingers missed her by a hair. She darted out and sprinted across the street. Damn it.

Desandra cleared half of the road. The vamp spun around to face her. She swung her mace and brained it. The vamp fell on the pavement, jerking, half of his skull caved in. Desandra kicked it. "Eat shit and die!"

She was officially insane and she had decided to do Jennifer a favor and kick the bucket.

Four lean shadows shot out across the parking lot, heading for her, two from the north and the two by the overpass. Desandra spun and sprinted away, running east, long legs moving fast, feet pounding the pavement.

I dropped to the ground, by the wall. Robert flattened himself next to me. Behind us Ascanio and Derek froze, trying to blend in with the rocks.

Four vampires tore past us, eyes glowing, talons scraping the pavement.

We had mere seconds before reinforcements arrived.

In the distance Desandra's throaty laugh echoed from the ruins. Apparently she was having fun.

I jumped to my feet and sprinted like my life depended on it. Robert and the kids shot by me like three bullets out of a gun. The apartment building flashed by. Sidewalk . . . street . . . I just had to get behind the pile of rubble. Circles swam in front of my eyes.

The door of the nearest minaret opened and vampires spilled onto the wall, scrambling over it like pallid lizards.

I dove behind the rubble, slid on icy dirt, and nearly collided with Robert leaning against a huge chunk of concrete. A dark hole gaped under it. Robert jabbed at the hole with his hand. I leaped into it, fell about twelve feet, and landed on hard ground in a shaft about six feet wide. The impact punched my feet.

In my head I could feel six undead moving toward us, their minds spreading wider apart as they fanned through the parking lot in our direction.

Ascanio jumped into the hole. I shied back against the wall and his feet missed me by half a second. Derek was next.

One of the vampires headed straight for us.

Robert leaped into the hole and yanked a metal lever in the wall. Above us, a metal platform moved, carrying the concrete boulder with it. The platform slid into place, plunging us into complete darkness.

We stood completely still.

The vampire mind was right on top of us.

My body screamed for air, starved of oxygen after the run. I opened my mouth and concentrated on breathing slow and quiet. Inhale. Exhale. Quiet.

A faint scrape came from above, claws sliding on concrete. The undead was sitting right on the boulder.

My lungs were on fire.

Go away.

A minute dragged by. Another.

"Team Two Leader to Mother," a muffled female voice said above. "Home envelope sealed, no pulse, no bogey, repeat no bogey, advise?"

Go home, I willed. *Go home.*

"Roger. Team Two, sweep complete, bingo to Mother."

The vampiric mind turned and fled, heading toward the Casino.

Everything went quiet. I remembered how to breathe properly.

"Go forward," Robert whispered to me. I put my hands out around me. My fingers found stone walls on either side. The opening between them was barely wide enough to pass through. Dark, cramped, and scary. My favorite.

I squeezed into the narrow hallway and blundered forward. The walls narrowed even further. My shoulders scraped the rock. *You've got to be kidding me.* When I got out of here, I'd kill Hugh for this. Slowly. With something dull.

The hallway needed to end. The walls were closing in on me.

What if the ceiling collapsed? I didn't even know what the hell was above me. I'd just end up buried here, under tons of dirt and rubble.

Any time now with the ending.

Now would be good.

How long did this place go on?

Suddenly the walls parted. I froze. With my luck, taking a step would land me into a pit of rabid vipers or molten lava. No wait, lava would be good. At least I'd be able to see something.

"Reach forward," Robert murmured behind me.

I groped blindly and touched something metal. A ladder. *Okay. Now we're in business.* I grabbed onto it and climbed upward in total darkness. Robert was right. I wouldn't have found this place in a million years.

My head connected with something hard. Ow.

The ceiling above me moved, letting in a pale glow. A hand with long clawed fingers grabbed my wrist and yanked me up. A horrifying face swung into view, illuminated by the faint blue light of a feylantern: pale, with patchy fur and a pink nose at the end of a tear-shaped muzzle. Long stiff whiskers fanned from a mouth studded with finger-long incisors. Dark, disturbingly human eyes stared at me.

My mind cycled through a chain of thoughts in a space of half a second. *Kill. Wait. Wererat in a warrior form = friend. Stop.*

I stopped the throwing knife a quarter of an inch before stabbing it into the wererat's windpipe. It's good that I had fast reflexes.

"Conssshort," the nightmarish creature said. "What are you doing here?"

I made my mouth move. "Looking for you."

The wererat smiled. My body flinched and tried to run away out of sheer self-preservation, and if I hadn't been hanging suspended over a dark hole, it would've succeeded.

"You found me!" the wererat announced. "I alwayshh wanted to meet you. I am sshhho ffflatterred."

Robert's head poked out of the hole. "Jardin, put the Consort down before you dislocate her shoulder."

"Alpha!" Jardin deposited me to the side. "Itshh shhuch an honor."

Robert pulled himself up into the room. Derek and Ascanio followed. I looked around. We were in a narrow, rectangular space about as wide as an average van. Three walls looked like concrete; the fourth was covered by a dark curtain.

"Any activity?" Robert asked.

"Not in the lasssht ten minutesh. Before that, very exshiting. I shaw Wolf Beta run by. There were vampiresh chassing her. She was yelling, 'Bill me, bloodshuckers!'"

Yep, that's the wolf beta, alright.

"I think I'm in love," Ascanio said.

Derek smacked the back of the bouda's head. Ascanio snapped his teeth at him.

"Stop it," I growled under my breath.

Jardin tossed a rag over the lantern. Darkness drowned the room. The curtain whispered as he moved it aside, revealing a long narrow space, filled with moonlight. Jardin hunched over, bending his six-and-a-half-foot body, and slipped through the opening. Robert followed and I did, too. My eyes acclimated to darkness and I saw Robert and Jardin leaning against the wall by a narrow gap in the concrete. The space was barely large enough for the five of us.

I crouched next to them and glanced through the gap. A hundred yards to the left the Casino glowed. Vampires scoured the walls, crawling on the textured parapets. We were inside the overpass.

"How did you even find this place?"

"By accident," Robert said so quietly, I barely heard it. "Before the overpasses collapsed, they crossed in this spot. This is a reinforced section, designed to hold the weight of all three in case a collapse occurred. When the top overpasses crashed, the magic began eating them from the inside, and eventually the three sections of the road fused, forming this hole."

"To what to I owe zhe pleashure?" Jardin asked.

"We're at war," Robert told him. "Someone in the Pack killed Mulradin."

The wererat blinked. "Oh. I ssshaw him leave the Casino tonight."

"How long ago?" Derek asked.

"Five houuursh."

Mulradin must've bailed right after Ghastek left for the Conclave. What could've been so urgent?

"You said you saw him in the Warren before as well," Robert said. "Where?"

"Corrrner of Marsharet and Joneshhboro."

Robert's eyebrows crept up. "The Fox Den?"

"Yessh."

"Did you see with whom?" Robert asked.

Jardin shook his head. "But I sshaw him there twice." He raised two long fingers.

"The Fox Den is a hit-'n'-split," Robert said to me.

A hit-'n'-split was a lovely post-Shift euphemism. It wasn't exactly a whorehouse and it wasn't exactly a hotel. Most of the hit-'n'-splits were run out of converted apartment buildings. If you wanted to have sex with something that grew fur, scales, or feathers and you wanted to do it privately, you went to a hit-'n'-split, worked your kinks out of your system, and left with your humanity mostly intact. Nobody would be the wiser.

I'd run across a couple of hit-'n'-splits in my time with the Guild and the Order. Most operated under the radar. A prospective client somehow got hold of a phone number, called the management, stated their preferences, and paid the quoted price. In return he would receive a key in the mail. At designated times he'd show up at the apartments, use the key, get his freak on, then leave. It was an "at your own risk" kind of venture. No security, no front desk, no witnesses. The management charged both parties a flat fee, but there was no pimp and no madam. Everyone operated independently. If Mulradin frequented a hit-'n'-split, he had a fetish and he wanted to keep it hidden.

"Red brick building," Jardin said. "Second one from the easht."

"We need to get back to Centennial Park first," I told him. I wouldn't leave Desandra stranded. Not after what she did. As far as I was concerned, she'd earned whatever support she wanted from me.

"You can ushe the other tunnel, but you can't leave now. The sshift change is in ten minutessh and they will do a shweep right past the entranshe."

"How long?" I asked.

"Sssshoould be clear in forty minutessh."

"We wait, then." I curled against the concrete.

Ascanio landed next to me. "Are you still mad at me for coming with?"

"Yes."

"It will be okay," he told me.

Derek sat down across from us.

"Did you know about Ascanio's master plan?" I asked.

"No," Derek said. "But I saw him walk off into the woods while everyone was talking."

"I don't know Desandra," Ascanio said. "I don't know Robert either."

"I do know Desandra," Derek said. "Ascanio's annoying, but extra backup is always nice."

Robert chuckled quietly. "You two were planning to fight me?"

"Not planning," Ascanio said. "Just ready. In case."

Teenage bodyguards. I closed my eyes. It would be a long night and I needed every drop of sleep I could get. I let myself drift, as Robert's and Jardin's soft voices receded into drowsiness.

"Thank you, Jardin. This will help us tremendously."

"Happy to hhhear it, Alpha."

"Once we are gone, I need you to return to Rat House."

"I have ennough food for two weekssh," Jardin said. "I could be ussheful."

"No," Robert said. "You're too valuable to us and this post is too dangerous. Your life isn't worth the risk . . ."

Sleep cushioned me, like a blanket wrapped around my body.

THE SEA WAS smooth, like the surface of a coin. I was lying in the sand next to Curran. My cheek rested on his chest, his skin heated by the sun. My hand was on his stomach, the ridges of hard muscle hot under my fingertips. His right arm was around me and he was playing with a strand of my hair. Lazy waves splashed against our feet, warm and soothing.

"We have to get up, baby," he said.

"No."

"We have to get up. Tide is coming in."

"Let it come," I murmured. "I just want to have more time. There's never enough time . . ."

"Kate . . ."

I hugged him to me.

"Kate."

Something touched me. I moved. My eyes snapped open. I was sitting on top of Jardin, holding my sword to his throat.

It was a dream. It wasn't real. Curran was still gone. I wanted to howl like an animal.

It wasn't real.

Losing him hurt like a punch to the gut. I was awake and back to my nightmare.

"Ssshecond time," Jardin smiled.

"Sorry." I got off of Jardin.

"Pay up," Derek said to Jardin.

The wererat rolled to his feet and dropped a dollar into Ascanio's palm.

"Did the two of you bet him I'd do this?"

Derek's eyebrows rose. "We can neither confirm nor deny that a bet took place."

"But we have seen you wake up when you're stressed out." Ascanio winked.

"I can't wait to get back to the Keep," I growled.

"So the two of them would start bickering again?" Robert asked.

"Exactly." This united Derek and Ascanio team was getting on my nerves.

Robert rolled to his feet. "Thank you again, Jardin."

"I could ssshtay," the wererat offered.

"No." Robert said. "You're going home. Your job is done. Now it's time for us to do ours."

He was right. Time to get it done and get out of here.

≈ CHAPTER ≈
7

W̲E FOUND DESANDRA sitting in a tree above Cuddles. Her clothes were splattered with blood. She grinned at us.

"Lovely perfume," Robert noted.

"Glad you like it." She hopped off the branch. "I call it Dead Vampire."

"How did you get away?" Ascanio asked.

"Please." She gave him a look. "I'm a werewolf raised in the Carpathian Mountains and they can't smell or track for shit. I can outrun them in my sleep."

I mounted and we headed east. Twenty minutes later we turned south and made our way into the dense tangle of streets that was the Warren.

I rode Cuddles. Derek pulled ahead to scout; Ascanio ran on my left, Desandra and Robert on my right. The Warren peered at us with the black eyes of broken windows: mean, suspicious, and predatory, like a thug who'd gotten his face bashed in and was looking to get even. Jonesboro, the most direct route, was out of the question—too obvious and too well patrolled—so we wove our way through the twisted back streets. Long scars gouged the walls of the run-down houses, as if a tornado of steel blades had brushed by them. On Harpy's Drive we passed a row of trees, each one with its trunk unnaturally bloated and covered with black fuzz. I had no idea what the fuzz did, but we steered clear of it. The law of navigating post-Shift Atlanta was simple: if you don't know what it is, don't touch it.

The moon was rolling down. It had to be around three in the morning. The winter night had caught the city between its teeth and bit down hard. Here and there an ancient vehicle hunkered down. The tips of my fingers had turned to painful icicles. Any colder, and I'd have to dismount and walk next to Cuddles just to warm up.

I wanted Curran back here with me. It was a completely selfish need, as urgent as breathing. I wanted to know that he was fine. I missed him. If I concentrated enough, I could conjure his voice in my head. Funny, yesterday I couldn't wait to escape the Keep with him and run away to Black Bear Lodge. Now I would happily sit through a hundred Council meetings back to back for a ten-second phone call from him letting me know he was okay.

In the distance something screeched. It was the triumphant violent shriek of a predator that'd connected with its prey. The Warren was in its usual form tonight. Come to think of it, that was the first sound I'd heard in a while. It was too deserted and too quiet. The cold or the People must've driven the Warren's scavengers indoors.

I could feel two vampire minds behind us. They were about a mile and a half back and not moving. Most likely an observation post that got staffed after we passed through.

We passed a rusted wreck of a truck. Ice slicked the road. Probably an overflowing sewer or a busted waterline that spilled water over the street before it had frozen solid. Up ahead a hole gaped in the pavement, about five and a half feet wide. A manhole cover lay frozen in the ice. Looked like something tore out of the sewers and pulled a good deal of soil with it. If some mysterious mole people cornered us, I'd point them toward the Casino and tell them that's where our leader lives.

A man in dark clothes walked out into the middle of the road and blocked our way. He was lean, with short dark hair. He raised his head and looked at me. I developed a sudden urge to check for the quickest exit.

"That's the bastard who shot me. Well!" Desandra cracked her knuckles. "Let me just take care of this . . ."

"Wait," I told her.

"What? Why?"

"Yes, why?" Robert asked.

"Do you remember the Red Stalker thing? The serial killer who collected and tortured women and ate vampires?"

"Yes," Robert said.

"He ate vampires?" Ascanio asked.

"Before your time," Derek told him.

The Red Stalker also killed Greg Feldman, my legal guardian and the knight of the Order who took care of me after Voron died. It was my first time interacting with the Pack, my first time meeting Derek, and the first time, but not the last, I had felt an irresistible need to punch Curran in the arm. "During the investigation, the Pack captured a crusader."

"I remember," Robert said. "He smelled like rotting food. I think we had to dip him. He had lice."

I nodded toward the man. "That's him."

Robert squinted. "It can't be."

Back then Nick looked like a hobo. He wore a filthy coat smeared with trash and old food, had greasy hair down to his shoulders, and cultivated the kind of hygiene that guaranteed him loads of personal space from anyone with a nose or a pair of eyes. Cleaned up, he looked fit and athletic, but average. The man in front of us now looked hard and mean, stripped of all softness. His hair was cut so short, it was almost stubble. His triangular jaw was clean shaven. He looked like a soldier or a fighter, clean, spare, and hard.

"It's him," I said. "I've seen him before with Hugh at the Midnight Games."

So this was Hugh's game plan. He wanted to separate me from the Pack. When we had talked during the Black Sea trip, he'd said that prying me from the Keep would be too difficult. He dangled the crime scene in front of me like bait, stationed his people along the approaching routes, and waited. Nick wasn't here to kill me. He was here to delay me. He probably sent a signal to Hugh, letting him know he'd sighted me, and now he would do everything he could to stall until Hugh got here.

Derek stared at him. Their expressions were almost identical, flat, carrying an awareness of how vicious life could be and knowing they would never forget it.

"He looks like he's been through some shit," Derek said.

You'd know.

"What's a crusader?" Desandra asked.

"Crusaders are knights of the Order," Robert said.

"Aw crap," Desandra growled.

The knights of the Order were strictly off-limits for the Pack. You might as well walk into a police station and shoot a cop.

"They're not assigned to any chapter," I said. "They go where needed and they bend the rules. They're like janitors. Got a nasty problem, throw a crusader at it. He'll cut it to pieces and leave town."

"But he shot me! Doesn't that count for something? What the hell is he doing with d'Ambray anyway? If he switched sides, I can kill him."

"Crusaders are fanatics," Derek said. "It's not likely he switched sides. Jim thinks he's undercover."

"Even if he is, it doesn't matter," I said. "He made the decision to block us. But running up to him and trying to punch him is a bad idea. We don't know what he's capable of."

We had to get past Nick. We had vampires behind us and taking a different route would take too long. We were committed now. We had to go forward.

"We don't want to fight," Robert called out. "We know who you are. We have no reason to kill you."

Nick pulled off his gloves and dropped them on the ice.

"Perhaps you should negotiate?" Robert glanced at me.

Sure. I cleared my throat. "Move or I'll cut your head off."

Nick took off his leather jacket and tossed it aside.

"He has no weapons," Derek said.

Robert grimaced.

No weapons meant magic, and whatever he had would be nasty, because there were five of us and one of him and he didn't look worried. The Nick I knew had very specific powers. He could tell how much magic you had by touching you and he had uncanny hand-eye coordination, which made him very accurate with guns and knives. If he had combat magic, he didn't use it even when fighting for his life, which probably meant he didn't have it at the time. But he'd been hanging out with Hugh for over a year, probably more. Now Nick was a jack-in-the-box. There was no telling what fun surprises would pop out when you wound him up.

Nick pulled off his sweater. His arms weren't just defined, they were carved, as if someone had cut him out of a slab of stone with a sharp knife. His neck was thick, his shoulders broad, and his gray T-shirt, tight across his shoulders, was loose over his middle. That body was the result of hours and hours at the gym, spent not bulking up by lifting heavier and heavier weights, but by kicking, punching, grappling, and running. He wasn't shredded, he was just hard, conditioned to throw a devastating blow and to take one and keep going. He looked like you could punch him for hours and it would just make him madder.

His T-shirt followed. Yep. Just like I thought.

"Before you start dancing, we don't have any cash!" I called.

"Woo!" Desandra waved her arms. "Take it off!"

"How do you want to go about this?" Robert asked me quietly.

"I can give it a shot," Ascanio offered.

"Sit your ass down, Don Juanabe," Derek said.

"Don Juanabe?" Ascanio pulled out his swords.

"Don Juan Wannabe," Derek explained. "See, I shortened it. If you still don't get it, I'll write it down for you after the fight."

"You've maxed out your wit quota for the night," Ascanio said.

"I'm just getting started."

"Be careful, you might sprain something in your brain."

"Quiet," I growled.

I knew why Nick joined Hugh. The Order hated Roland. He was their public enemy number one. It made sense for him to go undercover with Roland's warlord. If Hugh had turned him to his side, then there was nothing I could do. But if he hadn't, imagining the things Nick had to have endured to survive his time with Hugh turned my stomach. It would've been hell for him. Somehow Nick had done it and I didn't want to end his sacrifice here.

"Let's try to keep him alive if we can," I said. "If we have to kill him, we will, but only as a last resort. If we do kill him, it's on my authority. You'll bear no responsibility for it."

Nick flexed, warming up.

I slid off Cuddles and unsheathed Slayer. We needed to know what we were up against. "Desandra, want to go knock on his door?"

"Oh yes." She bared her teeth.

"He's really fast. Don't get killed. Just tap him enough for him to open up and show us what he's got." I glanced at Derek. "Back her up."

Desandra stalked forward, pulling off her woolen gloves one finger at a time. Nick watched her.

"Remember me?" She took off her jacket and tossed her long blond braid back. "You shot me."

He rolled his head from side to side, stretching his neck. Derek followed Desandra, hanging about twenty feet back.

Desandra lunged forward, as if for a kick. Her leg went forward, then back. She leaped and hammered a blur-fast cross-punch at Nick's head. He dodged, just barely, and struck at the back of her head with his left hand. She blocked with her left arm. Nick turned and sank a vicious hook to her ribs, while she punched his jaw with a hard right. The blow knocked Nick back. He dropped and rolled to his feet. Desandra staggered back, favoring her left side. Cracked or broken ribs.

Nick shook his head. I've been punched by a shapeshifter before. Not fun.

They circled each other. Desandra closed in, arms up, hands open, and launched a low kick. Her foot connected to Nick's leg. Just barely too high, or she would've taken out the knee. He staggered back, his arms up, and she pounded a flurry of punches at his guard. He ducked, taking it on his arms, and snapped a front kick with his injured leg right into her stomach. His foot had shot out like a hammer. There was no deflecting that. Desandra staggered back. Her clothes burst. Bone surged upward, tendons and muscle spiraled over it, dark skin sheathed the new body, and fur sprouted from the pores. A seven-foot-tall werewolf snapped savage teeth.

Two olive vines shot out of Nick's chest, spiraling over his arms, and clamped Desandra, winding about her like twin whips.

What the hell was that?

I started forward. Robert and Ascanio followed me. An eerie giggle broke free from Ascanio.

"Not yet," I told him.

Desandra flexed, trying to break free, but the vines gripped her. Flexible, about an inch thick and at least twenty feet long. I'd never seen anything like it.

Derek sprinted forward and grabbed the vines, raising his tomahawk to chop them. Thorns burst from the twin shoots, biting into Desandra's and Derek's skin.

Oh no you don't. I sprinted.

Bloody thorn tips emerged from the back of Derek's hand. The skin around the punctures turned gray. Poison. Shit.

Desandra screamed. Derek chopped the vines and tore his hand free. The ends of the vines snapped back to Nick. The vise of vines around Desandra cracked and dried in an instant, turning into hard wood.

"This isn't better!" Desandra snarled.

I lunged between them and Nick. Robert landed next to me.

Derek chopped at the wood with his tomahawk. The petrified vines held. The shapeshifters had resistance to diseases, but toxins could do them in.

Nick focused on us and began to spin the vines, faster and faster. I'd seen the technique before. Chinese chain whip, made of metal rods joined by rings. It was considered a soft weapon, but there was nothing soft about it and it took a hell of a lot of concentration to keep it going.

"Ascanio, run around him and throw rocks."

The bouda dashed to the side.

"Divide and conquer," Robert murmured.

"Let's do that."

We spread out. Nick kept spinning the whips. They encased him, a weapon and a shield at once.

I feinted forward. The whip sliced my boot, ripping it, but not cutting through.

"Get me out!" Desandra roared.

"I'm trying," Derek snarled, hacking at the vines.

I hurled a throwing knife. It glanced off the vine whips. I could use a power word, but it would both drain me and announce to Hugh our exact location. Power words had a lot of magic echo.

A rock smacked against Nick's back. Ascanio ran around us in a circle, hurling chunks of ice and concrete at him.

Robert attacked, zigzagging and twisting like a dervish. Nick snapped the vines at him. Robert dodged. His knuckle knives sliced at the whips. The left vine slid off onto the ice and instantly dried. Nick spun toward Robert. I dove into the opening, sliding on the ice, and buried my sword in his side.

He twisted and kicked me, ramming his knee into my ribs just as I straightened. My bones screamed, cracking. Robert jumped and kicked at Nick's head. Nick dodged. The whip coiled around me and I sliced at it before it caught me. Nick leaped backward like an acrobat, once, twice, and landed twenty feet away. Two new vine whips slid from his chest.

I flicked the blood off my sword. Robert straightened. My ribs were on fire. A dark red wound marked Nick's right side. Blood slid from it, wetting his skin. I hadn't hit anything vital. He'd live, especially with Hugh around to heal him.

Nick dodged a chunk of dirty ice flying at his head. Ascanio hurled another, and Nick spun his new vines, knocking it aside. We just had to keep Nick moving. The more he spun his whips, the more he would bleed.

"How far will you go?" I asked. "What won't you do for him? Would you kill us for him?"

Nick looked at me, his eyes cold. "Whatever it takes."

I had my answer. He wouldn't break his cover. Fine. We'd bleed him out, nice and slow.

Nick charged me. The vines smashed all around me, scouring the ice with their thorns. I dodged and ducked on instinct. Left, right, left, left. We danced across the ice. My feet slipped. Thorns scratched my arms like stinging bees. I wasn't fast enough.

Robert lunged from my right. The vine took him straight across the chest. Clothes ripped and a wererat in a half-form dropped to the ground. One vine whistled over his head. He lunged under it, snarled, and kicked Nick's feet from under him with one devastating sweep.

Wow.

Nick stumbled. Desandra, huge and shaggy, leaped over my head and smashed into the crusader. Derek must've finally cut her out. Nick slid across the ice into the hole gaping in the pavement. His vines shot out and caught the ice with their thorns. I dashed forward, slid on my knees, and sliced across the vines. Slayer's blade sliced through the shoots. Nick dropped down into the hole.

"Move," Derek roared behind me.

I rolled to the side. A rusted truck blocked the sky. Derek turned it and hurled it into the hole, hood first. The vehicle slid in a couple of feet and stopped, wedged. A frantic scratching sliced against the truck—Nick's vines scouring the metal.

I exhaled. My ribs hurt. Small cuts on my shoulders and sides stung as if burned.

"And stay there!" Desandra snarled.

I turned to Derek. "Let me see your hand."

He thrust his left hand at me. The cuts from the thorns hadn't closed. The skin around them turned dark. Blood streaked with gray oozed from the wounds. The toxin was killing the Lyc-V inside his body. The scratches on Desandra's furry arms were still bleeding, too.

"I'm fine," Derek said.

"Yes. We're fine," Desandra added.

There was nothing to be done. The best we could do was to get through to the crime scene and get back to the Keep, where Doolittle could treat them.

Ascanio sniffed at Derek's hand. "Smells wrong. I think we should chop it off. Here, hold it steady."

Derek pantomimed squeezing Ascanio's throat with his other hand.

In the distance the two vampire minds stopped pacing and moved toward us. Shit.

"We have to go." I jumped to my feet. "Now!"

. . .

CUDDLES GALLOPED THROUGH the streets. No need or time for stealth now. We had to get to the crime scene and get the hell out.

We swung onto Jonesboro and Cuddles pounded down the street. The Fox Den loomed before us, alternating apartment buildings of red brick and yellow stucco fused together into one giant complex. Finally.

The stucco had seen better days. Graffiti marked the crumbling walls. Trash sat in piles in the corners. If you saw the place in daylight, you'd steer clear of it. The night made it even grimmer. It looked like the kind of place that would shelter a rough crowd, driven to desperation by human predators and poverty. The type of people who'd see you being stabbed to death on the landing and shut their doors while you screamed for help.

"I smell Mulradin." Robert turned right and sprinted toward the entrance to one of the brick buildings. I jumped off Cuddles, tossed her reins over a hook driven into the wall for that purpose, and followed Robert up the stairs. In his warrior form, he didn't just run, he scurried, so fast, his paws might as well have been greased. I pushed myself to keep up.

One flight. Two, three.

Blood on the stairs. Faint smudges, getting bigger as we moved higher.

A door swung open above us.

I ran across the landing and up just in time to see Robert tear a crossbow out of a man's hands. He looked about my age, Hispanic, and rough.

"Go inside," Robert told him.

The man ducked into the apartment. The deadbolt clicked, sliding in place. Robert charged up the stairs and I followed. We cleared the third floor, another landing . . .

Robert stopped. I almost collided with his tail.

"A ward," he said and stepped aside.

I walked up to the door. An invisible wall of magic enveloped the door.

"Can we get in from the outside?" Derek asked behind me. Next to him Ascanio and Desandra moved to watch the stairs.

I shook my head. Hugh would've warded the windows as well.

I pulled Slayer out of the sheath and tested the ward. Magic nipped at the saber's point and the sword stopped, unable to go any farther. Usually wards had an elastic resistance, like trying to puncture a basketball that had gone a little soft. This ward was completely solid. I'd come across only one type of ward that was both invisible and solid like this.

I crouched and leaned forward, searching the grimy floor. There it was, a barely noticeable dark smudge. Hugh had sealed the place with his own blood.

"It's a blood ward." I straightened.

"Can you break it?" Robert asked.

When Julie had caught Lyc-V months ago, I had performed a ritual to cleanse her blood with mine. She retained some of my magic as a result. My father had used the same ritual or one very much like it to bind Hugh to him. My father's blood was in that ward, which would make breaking it easier for me. But the power of Hugh's own magic was in it too, and Hugh had a crapload of magic.

"If I break this, the backlash will be a bitch. I'll be out of commission for a while." And while I was trying not to pass out, whatever was inside the apartment would grab me. Nicely played, Hugh. One trap after another.

"For how long?" Derek asked.

"I don't know. Could be seconds, could be minutes. Can you smell anything from here? Anyone inside?"

The four of them stood very still.

"No," Robert said. "It's like a wall."

"That's some messed-up crap," Desandra said.

I knelt on the floor and examined the door. Several scratches marked the lock, all old. It had probably been picked, and more than once. Expected, considering the location of the door. The door itself didn't look forced. Not much to go on. For all I knew, the apartment behind the door lay empty or it contained a giant fire-breathing terrestrial octopus in a bad mood. No way to tell. I had to break the ward.

"Hugh likes magic and traps. Once we're in, don't touch anything. Get ready to defend my deadweight."

"Go for it," Derek said.

I pulled my left sleeve up and sliced Slayer across my skin, just enough to draw blood. Curls of vapor slithered from the opaque saber. I turned the blade upside down, letting the blood wash over it, raised it, bracing myself, and pushed it into the ward.

The magic buckled, kicking at the blade like a wild horse.

I leaned into it. Slow and steady. My blood hissed on the blade, boiling. I fed my magic into the blade.

The ward didn't budge.

Come on. I pushed harder.

Slayer stopped as if I were trying to thrust it into solid rock. If I pushed any more, the blade might snap. If I'd had time, I would have just sat there for the next fifteen minutes, keeping constant pressure on the sword, until the ward gave. But we had no time.

"Not working?" Robert asked.

"It's a game to him." I pulled Slayer free and slipped it into my left hand. The best way to break a ward was to slowly, methodically push through it. Slowly and methodically had failed, which left me with brute force. If it broke too quick, the repercussion from the magic would be very sharp and severe. This wasn't my brightest move, but we had to get into the apartment and time was short. "Okay, fine. I'll play. Stand back a bit. This could go really wrong."

I squeezed the cut on my left arm, smearing the blood over my fingers, and thrust my hand into the ward. The magic snapped taut, trapping my hand. A hundred tiny needles of magic pierced my skin, tasted my blood, and recoiled. Bright red cracks split the empty air, radiating from my hand.

I pushed.

Thunder cracked in my head, slapping my brain. The ward broke and fluttered to the ground, melting as it fell. The world swam around me, the edges turning fuzzy. I shook my head, fighting to keep upright.

Robert pushed the door open and slipped in. Desandra followed. Derek and Ascanio hovered next to me.

I should probably go in. If I could only stop my ears from ringing . . .

"Clear," Robert called.

I shook my head. Ow. That only made the pain worse. The doorway wavered in front of me. I had to get into the apartment. Okay, the door had to be at least three feet wide. If I just aimed myself in the right direction, I'd get through. I clenched my teeth. Step. Step. Another step. I was in. Kick-ass. Now I just had to remain conscious and not fall down on my face.

I squinted: an old couch, a threadbare rug, and a stripper pole. A long trail of blood led from the living room through the narrow hallway. Some-one had dragged a bleeding body out.

"Oh, this is rich." Robert laughed, his voice dry.

Derek grimaced.

"Yeah." Ascanio rolled his eyes.

"Clue the human in," I said.

"Dorie Davis," Derek said. "Otherwise known as Double D."

"Her scent is all over this apartment." Robert went down the hallway.

"Oh!" Desandra snapped her fingers. "So that's who it is."

I followed them down the hallway to the bedroom. The stench of blood clogged my nose, so strong I almost choked on it. A giant bed occupied most of the bedroom, equipped with a padded bench at the foot of the bed and a steel rack above it with several metal rings attached to the wall. The red sheet lay crumpled in a knot, drenched in darker red, the same red that stained the exposed mattress. Mulradin was killed here, no doubt about it. A human body had only so much blood, and most of it had remained in this room.

Derek turned right. Robert turned left. Desandra inhaled deeply, mak-ing a slow circle around the bed. They stalked through the room, pausing by objects at random, sampling the scents. Ascanio paused at the entrance to the room, so he could see the front door. "Ripe."

My legs decided to take a vacation and the room crawled sideways. I really needed a wall to prop myself up on, but touching anything here wasn't a good idea. "Double D, is that supposed to tell me something?"

"She's a sofie," Derek said, the same way one would say *She's a child molester.*

"I can tell by your voice it's bad, but I have no idea what it is."

"Most shapeshifters don't have sex in animal form," he said.

"That's not strictly true," Robert said. "Most shapeshifters have sex in animal form, but only once. It's not that great. It doesn't last long, it's awkward, and there's no communication. Let's just say, you don't appreciate having hands until they're gone."

"No shit," Desandra volunteered.

"The exception being the boudas," Derek said.

Ascanio raised his eyebrows. If looks were knives, Derek would be bleeding.

"The Repressed One is trying to tell you that some people like to screw shapeshifters in animal form while they themselves stay human," Ascanio said. "They're called sofies. Skin on fur."

Robert rolled his eyes and dropped down to the floor to smell the carpet.

"Okay," I said. "I wish I didn't know that."

"Welcome to the Pack," Robert said. "This is one of those gray areas. Technically, it's not forbidden. What two consenting adults do on their own time is their business."

"But it's bestiality," I said.

"Yes," Robert said. "Which is why it's strongly discouraged."

Desandra leaned over the bed and swallowed. "The smells here are giving me a sour stomach."

"Not just you," Derek said.

"And for the record, I like women," Ascanio said. "Maybe some wolves out there get turned on by the fur, but I like skin."

"Oh, will you two quit it," Desandra said. "It's kinky forbidden sex. Some wolves do it, some boudas do it, some humans do it. Everybody's equally fucked up."

"We get enough flack from normal humans as it is," Robert said. "Three years ago there was a campaign to ban wererats from restaurants because we're disease-ridden rodents. The petition had three thousand signatures before we killed it. A year before, Clan Wolf was sued by a farming cooperative who claimed they would be hunting their livestock. The chief argument was that wolves can't fight their natural urge to hunt and run prey to ground. If this stuff got out, there would be no end of public outcry. We don't want to be accused of running a petting zoo for perverts."

"Dorie is a pay-to-play sofie," Derek said. "She charges for her services."

"She doesn't have to prostitute herself," Robert said. "She's an accountant with a decent salary. She does it because she's decided that it's an easy way to earn money on the side and because she's got some sort of itch and this scratches it for her. When Jennifer's husband was alive, he made a couple of attempts to get her into counseling, but she never went. She is a consenting adult and how she has sex is her own business."

"She's one of the only two shapeshifters to date who managed to catch an STD," Ascanio said. "The other one was a male panther she was with. They caught it together at a, ahem, group event."

Okay, that would take some doing. Lyc-V exterminated all invaders into its territory with extreme prejudice.

Derek winced. "An STD?"

"Oh, you didn't hear about that?" Ascanio asked. "They got some kind of magical rabies."

Derek opened his mouth and closed it. "How did they . . . ? Never mind, I don't want to know."

"I don't either." It was best to put that out there before they decided to enlighten me.

"We're broadening your horizons, Consort." Desandra grinned.

"My horizons are broad enough, thanks." Now if only they would stop wobbling, I'd be all set. "I get how Robert and Desandra know about Double D. I want to know how the two of you know."

Derek and Ascanio made valiant attempts to look casual.

"Everybody knows," Ascanio said.

"Then why didn't Desandra identify the scent?"

"When Double D showed up in Doolittle's medward with the STD, he read her the riot act about safe sexual practices," Robert said. "She didn't like it, so she avoids him like the plague. Which is ironic, really, because the plague is exactly what she didn't avoid."

"I didn't quite get that," Desandra said. "Was it supposed to be funny?"

Robert frowned. "Never mind. I was going somewhere clever with that, but I managed to bungle it up. The point is, Double D doesn't feel exactly welcome at the Keep."

"She isn't often at Wolf House either," Desandra said. "I've seen her once, I think. Jennifer hates her guts. The last time her name came up, our illustrious alpha called her a 'filthy immoral creature.'"

"In front of witnesses?" Robert asked.

"A room full of people," Desandra said.

Great. There was a hierarchy of insults you could level at a shapeshifter. Telling them they smelled bad was probably one of the worst. But calling one of them "a creature" took it to another level. It implied a shapeshifter wasn't human. A loup was a creature. Jennifer should never have said that, not about one of her own people.

Robert's lips rose, wrinkling his muzzle and baring sharp teeth. He made a short angry noise, halfway between a deep growl and a grunt.

"I know, I know . . ." Desandra said.

"We may not approve," Robert said, his voice precise and cold. "We may find it revolting and we may roar and snarl at our people in private, but we may not single out our people and make them an object of public shaming. It just isn't done. Jennifer made her a target. Now anyone within the Clan Wolf who shows a drop of kindness to Dorie does so against their alpha's wishes."

"I agree," I told him. "We can deal with it later. We're short on time. We have to move on."

"There are no other shapeshifter smells in the room," Robert said. "Only Double D and humans."

"I got Mulradin, Double D, Hugh, and a few others who are probably Hugh's people," Derek confirmed.

I tried to concentrate. It was proving tricky. My magic-stunned brain still wanted to float off into the shocked haze. "Can you tell what happened?"

"Dorie came in first," Robert said. "Mulradin arrived about half an hour later. They had sex, once on the bench, once in the corner over there." He pointed to the left of the bed, where a chain fell to the floor. One end of it was attached to the ring in the wall, the other to a spiked collar.

"Then Dorie killed Mulradin on the bed," Desandra said.

Shit. "Are you sure?"

Derek nodded. "Once you get accustomed to the smell of blood, it's very clear. Her scent is on the bed and the linens, and her fur is stuck to Mulradin's blood. No other scents on the bed."

"D'Ambray came in at some point, with five other people. They entered as a group," Derek said. "Also someone fired a shotgun slug into that wall." He nodded at the opposite wall.

"Before or after the murder?"

He shook his head. "No way to tell. It's fresh."

Ascanio nodded at the hallway. "Dorie left after the murder. Her scent trail is separate from the others, tainted with blood, and older. You can see her bloody tracks." He pointed to the side. "She ran out of here."

A member of the Pack had murdered a Master of the Dead. A small part of me had been hoping that Hugh's accusation wasn't true, and now that hope died a sad death.

I tried to make sense of it. "So she killed Mulradin for some reason. Either it was some sort of accident or she did it on purpose. If it was an accident, how did Hugh get involved? If it was a premeditated murder, Hugh either hired her to do it, forced her to do it, or happened to somehow be watching the apartment when she did it." That last one didn't seem likely. "Would she kill for money?"

"I doubt it," Derek said. "She isn't violent. I wouldn't call her a nice person, but she wouldn't kill someone on her own."

Why did Hugh let Dorie go? I rubbed my face. It didn't make me any smarter. If I were Hugh, what would I do with Dorie? How could I use her? If Dorie was dead, the Pack couldn't turn her over in time for the deadline, which would guarantee a war. We could still produce her corpse or acknowledge that she was the killer and offer to pay restitution. But if Dorie was alive, things would get really complicated. If we did turn her over, we would look weak. If we didn't, we would look like we thought we were above the law. There was no good way to resolve this situation, and the responsibility for it would land on my shoulders. Whichever decision I made, the Pack would detest me for it.

No, Hugh wouldn't kill her. Why, when he could kill a whole flock of birds with one stone? "Dorie is still alive."

Ascanio raised his eyebrows at me.

"The question isn't why Dorie killed Mulradin, it's what we do about Dorie. We have to get out of here."

"We have company," Robert announced, looking out the window.

I willed my legs to move and crossed the room. My head was still swimming. Riders flooded the street, one, two . . . twelve. The leader rode a familiar dark horse. Hugh.

We'd been in the apartment about six minutes, and here he was.

Desandra leaned out to glance past Robert. Her clawed fingers grazed the wall.

Magic pulsed through the window in a flash of dark green. Desandra jerked her hand-paw away and cursed. "I know, I know. I touched something. My fault."

Tiny runes ignited in the paint of the windowsill, pulsed, and vanished, as a ward snapped closed.

I spun around. "Door?"

Ascanio was already checking. "Warded," he called out a second later.

We were trapped. Great. I moved to the window and pushed against the ward with my palm. It nipped at me with magic teeth. Not a blood ward. This was incantation-based and someone had sunk a wallop of power into it. Shit.

Ascanio returned.

"Is it breakable?" Robert asked me.

"Sure. Give me an hour to figure out how it was made."

Derek swore.

I dropped on my knees by the window and slid my hand against the ward, trying to trace its boundaries. Magic scraped at my skin with pale green lightning. Ouch. If Hugh had warded the whole building, we'd be in trouble.

At the street, the riders dismounted.

I found an edge of the ward. Another edge. "He didn't ward the entire building. He just warded the openings, the windows and the door."

Derek bared his teeth. "Ceiling or floor?"

"Ceiling," Robert said.

It would take them at least a few minutes to break through the ceiling onto the roof. A few minutes, and nothing between us and Hugh except for a busted door. I ran to the door.

"Where are you going?" Ascanio called.

"To buy us some time. Stay in the bedroom out of sight."

"Ask him about the cops!" Robert called.

Good point. If Hugh had bought the Atlanta PAD, we needed to know.

The front door stood ajar, just as we had left it. The sound of people running up the stairs floated up.

I couldn't break this ward, but I had enough magic left to make one of my own. I dipped my fingers in my blood and touched the bottom corner of the door frame on my side.

The pounding steps drew closer.

I concentrated. The magic rushed out from me, twisted into an invisible current, kissed the empty air of the doorway, and snapped like a broken rubber band. The pain lanced my mind and for a second the world teetered in a red haze. Ow. I forced myself upright. *Breach that, you sonovabitch.*

The steps reached the landing just below us.

I leaned against the wall and tried to look casual. All this practicing must be paying off, because a couple of years ago I couldn't have broken the ward and put up one of my own in the space of fifteen minutes. It still hurt, but at least I wouldn't give Hugh the satisfaction of passing out in front of him.

Hugh conquered the last few steps and halted by the door. He still wore jeans tucked into tall riding boots, a black wool sweater, and a plain cloak, splattered with mud and melting snow. Gloves shielded his hands. His height and broad shoulders guaranteed that people would maintain their distance, but if he pulled the hood over his face, he wouldn't stand out too much. Hugh in his inconspicuous mode.

The hood was down now. I scrutinized Hugh's face, looking for any sign of the wounds Curran and I had left on him. I knew they weren't there, but my brain refused to acknowledge it. I just couldn't help myself. No old scars on the square chin or the cut jaw. No hint of crushed cartilage in the nose. I looked higher and ran straight into his eyes. They brimmed with arrogance, power, and humor. Hugh was having fun.

I took a rag out of my pocket and began cleaning Slayer, drawing the cloth along the pale blade.

Nick followed Hugh to the door. He was wearing clothes and seemed no worse for wear. A woman walked with him, at least fifty, but strong and fit, built like she could punch a tank out. Bright red paint crossed her left cheek, an upside-down T, smudged, probably drawn with a finger. It stood for Uath, the sixth letter of the Ogham alphabet used by the ancient Celts. It meant horror or fear, and according to Voron, Uath had earned her name. My adopted father had found her years ago. She was one of his elite soldiers who later formed the backbone of the Order of Iron Dogs. Hugh must've inherited her. I had no idea she was still alive. Voron knew how to pick them.

Hugh flicked his fingers. Nick and Uath backed off, took a couple of steps down the stairs, and waited.

Hugh pulled a glove off his hand and reached for the doorway. His defensive spell flashed green and drained down. His fingers touched the invisible wall of my blood ward. He pushed.

I kept cleaning my sword.

"Clever girl," Hugh said.

"Learning as I go."

He reached into his cloak and pulled out a small white bottle.

"What is it?"

"Ibuprofen," he said. "For your headache. I know you have one."

Hugh, a benign and considerate mass murderer. Always thinking ahead.

Hugh shook the bottle at me.

"No, thanks. I've had my daily dose of poison already."

Hugh smiled.

"Something funny?"

"The more you struggle, Kate, the more I learn about you."

"Learn anything interesting?"

He moved, stalking around the landing. He seemed to have gotten bigger somehow since our encounter in the Black Sea. Taller, broader, stronger. Maybe it was my memory playing tricks, or maybe it was the cloak.

"You can break my ward. This morning I knew of eleven people in the world who could. Now there are twelve."

"Whoop-de-doo."

Hugh shrugged his shoulders. "You know what I hate about the winter in this city?"

The longer we kept talking, the more time I would buy for Derek, Ascanio, and Robert to take the ceiling apart. I raised one eyebrow. "Mmm?"

"It's so damn cold, I wouldn't let a dog out, but there's no snow. There's just this crud. It's not rain, it's not snow, it's like freezing mud falling from the sky." He rested one hand on the wall next to the side of the door. "I say we call it quits. The new Four Seasons has VIP suites. I stayed there on my last trip here. We'll have them build us a nice fire and hide in the room, hot, dry, and cozy. We'll order some food, some decent wine, and talk."

"What would we talk about?"

"About the future."

I pretended to think about it. "Pass."

Hugh flashed his teeth in a narrow smile. Before a hungry tiger pounced on its prey, he would smile just like that.

"Where is Hibla?"

"Hibla has been reassigned."

"Where?"

"Let it go," he said, in that good-natured way as if we were sitting somewhere in a bar, sharing a drink, and I were venting to him about a co-worker who annoyed me. "She's hard to kill and not worth the time."

"When you see her, let her know I have a grave picked out for her. With a headstone and everything."

"How about this: if you come with me, I'll deliver her to you. You can play with her as long as you want. I'll even heal you if she rips you up."

"Still a pass."

"You should reconsider. Just some friendly advice."

"I don't think so."

Hugh leaned forward, his eyes amused, and looked me over, slowly, head to toe. "You look good."

Spare me. "Nice touch letting Dorie go. If I don't turn her over, you'll start a bloodbath and I and the alphas will be blamed for it. If we do turn her over, we look weak and our own people will lose confidence in our leadership. Either way the Pack is destabilized and I'm the bad guy."

"You're beginning to catch on to how the game is played," Hugh said.

"There's a third possibility. I could kill Dorie and dump her dead body on your lap."

"I don't think so."

He said it with absolute surety. Not a moment's hesitation. *Note to self: bluffing—learn to do it better.*

"Why not?"

"Because it sends the wrong message. If you kill Dorie, every shape-shifter who has ever broken the law will wonder if they're next on your hit list. If you go that route, nobody will follow you. I'm a bastard but even I don't kill my own people, unless it's absolutely necessary."

"No, you just put them in cages and let them slowly starve to death."

He rolled his eyes. "Of course, there is a fourth option."

"And what's that?"

"You come with me now," he said. "And this whole ugly mess goes away."

"I don't believe you." The words had come out almost on their own. But a look into his eyes told me he wasn't lying. Shit. He really had come here for me. I was the sole reason Mulradin was dead and the Pack was now evacuating. Well, that was one mystery solved.

I didn't need that kind of pressure. I had plenty to drag me down as it was.

Hugh shifted his weight, reached over, and drew a doodle on my ward. The magic nipped at his finger. It must've hurt. "I meant what I told you before. Their lives don't matter to me. If I have to crush the coal to get to the diamond, I'll do it."

"Aha. And I'm the diamond?"

"You cut like one."

Ha! "Flattery, really? Subtle like a hammer."

He shrugged. "Why not? Do the shapeshifters take time to flatter you? Do they tell you how grateful they are for you sticking your neck out for their sake?" He touched the blood ward again. "Do they beg your forgiveness every time this precious blood is spilled?"

No, they generally didn't. They mostly complained at me, but I wasn't going to tell him that. "The answer is no."

"No, they don't flatter you?"

"No, I'm not leaving with you."

"I suppose I'll have to come and get you then."

"Knock yourself out. I've got a sword I'm dying to introduce to your blood." Wait. *Knock yourself out.* Funny I said that. An idea began to form in my head.

Out of the corner of my eye I saw Robert leaning into the hallway. He was watching. He'd probably heard every word. Great. I could look forward to more questions I didn't want to answer.

"Come with me," Hugh said. "Let me show you the kind of power you're missing. Nobody else has to die. He's waiting for you."

Every nerve in me came to attention. "Don't see how he has the time for me, preparing for the claiming and all."

Hugh's eyebrows rose a quarter-inch.

I laughed quietly. "I see he doesn't tell you everything. I think I'll stay right here."

He shook his head. "Seriously, what the fuck are you doing, Kate? Running around the frozen city in the night like some filthy bottom-feeder playing queen of the shapeshifters? Come to me. I'll give you the city on a silver platter. A gift."

"If I wanted the city, I would've taken it."

"I love that snarl in your voice," he said. "Sexy."

I rolled my eyes.

"I like that, too," he said.

"Just out of curiosity," I asked. "Last time I checked, the cops frowned on the random murder of civilians. Do you think Atlanta's Paranormal Activity Division will just let you blunder about hunting shapeshifters?"

Hugh pretended to ponder it for a long moment. "Let me think. Yes."

Jim was right. He had made an arrangement with someone high in the police food chain. "Aren't you smug?"

"That's what happens when you play in the big leagues."

"Big leagues, huh?"

"That's right." He winked at me. "Stick around, I'll show you how we do it."

"No need. I've already had the proper instructions from my aunt." Big leagues, I'll show you the big leagues. It was a gamble, but if it worked, it would buy us enough time to get the hell out of here. "Curran broke Erra's ward, by the way."

Hugh's eyes narrowed. "It's adorable when you try to manipulate me. I find it charming."

"I'm not manipulating you. I'm stating a fact. The man I'm sleeping with broke Erra's blood ward." I indicated the ward. "Mine is still standing."

In the bedroom Robert leaned out for a second to catch my eye. *Yes, yes, I know what I'm doing.*

"I've been waiting for you to break mine. I have to say, your technique is really different. Curran hammered at the spell until it broke. You just talk. Help me out here, what's the strategy? Are you hoping the ward will get tired and kill itself so it won't have to listen to you anymore?"

Hugh's eyes turned dark.

I yawned. "I don't know about the ward, but I'm done talking. I'm going to go and take a nap."

"Last chance," Hugh said. His voice lost all of its amusement. "Come with me, and I'll spare your precious Pack. All your pets will go to bed safe and won't have to worry about fighting for their lives in the morning. Or they can wake up to a slaughter and blame you when their kids and lovers start dying."

I slid Slayer into its sheath on my back and crossed my arms. "Time for talking is over. Come on, Preceptor. The man I sleep with broke the City Eater's ward. You just have to break one of mine. Do it, Hugh. Show me something."

"Remember, you wanted this," he warned.

I dug into my memory and pulled out the worst rebuke Voron ever used. He said it to me and he had said it to Hugh, because Hugh threw it in my face the last time we met.

"If you're too scared to try, just say you're scared, Hugh."

Nothing was worse than not being brave enough to try.

Hugh pulled a knife out, sliced his forearm, and dropped the blade on the floor. Show-off. Why not use the knife?

He squeezed his forearm. Blood swelled, bright sharp crimson. Slowly he rubbed it all over his hands. His stare locked on me. Wow. Hugh was pissed.

I raised my eyebrow at him.

He leaned forward, his feet shoulder width apart, his arms bent at the elbows, fingers apart, pointing up. His whole body tensed, gathering together as if before a great jump. Muscles bulged on his legs. His biceps strained the sleeves of his sweater. His abdomen hardened. Thin streaks of blue vapor slithered from him, growing stronger and stronger, until pale blue smoke emanated from his whole body. I'd seen it before when he pulled Doolittle from the brink of death. The ward blocked me from feeling it, but I remembered the magnitude of that power.

Maybe this wasn't such a good idea.

On the stairs Nick crouched. Uath gripped the guardrail. Out of the corner of my eye I saw Robert, standing in plain view in a hallway.

Hugh's eyes turned bright electric blue. Indigo radiance coated his hands.

"Today," I called out.

He lunged forward with both hands. His fingers pierced the ward like talons.

The blood ward flashed with brilliant red light, the magic crackling like thunder. Hugh flew back ten feet and hit the stairway leading to the upper floor. The back of his head bounced off the steps. He slid down and didn't move.

Ha! Serves you right!

Behind me Robert said, his voice completely deadpan, "Oh my."

A wall of translucent red pulsed in the doorway and turned transparent. My spell was still up. I laughed.

Nick and Uath charged up the stairs to Hugh's prone body. I turned around and hurried to the bedroom.

A hole gaped in the ceiling next to the bed. Derek waited by it. Ascanio swung down out of the hole and offered me his hand. I grabbed it and he pulled me up until I could grasp onto some wooden beams. Ascanio let go and climbed up, and I crawled up after him. My cracked rib was screaming. Derek followed me into the ceiling structure. Beams, broken brick, insulation, and more beams.

A cold drop fell on my head. I looked up and saw Ascanio's feet disappear, replaced by the night sky. My fingers caught cold metal and I pulled myself outside onto the roof. Frozen rain sifted from the gray sky. In the distance Desandra in a warrior form crouched on the edge of the roof, like a sleek monstrous gargoyle.

"Did you know that would happen?" Robert emerged from the hole.

"I hoped it would."

"And if he broke through?"

"Then we'd have to run away very fast." Well, we still had to run away really fast. Hugh's people wouldn't move until he came to, but that head was really hard. He'd bounce back soon.

The roof, slicked by frost, sloped down at a sharp angle. The ground looked very far down below.

Ascanio ran across the slippery roof toward the wererat. My head swam. The roof teetered before me.

Don't think about it. Just do it. I sprinted. My stomach lurched. Tiny black dots swam in front of my eyes. Okay, running might have been too ambitious.

The roof ended. A twenty-foot gap separated us from the next building. Far below, hard pavement promised a painful landing.

Robert leaped across the gap and scurried on.

Twenty feet was so beyond me, it wasn't even funny. Well rested, on solid ground, and with some training, I could possibly come close, but right now, on a slippery roof, it might as well have been a hundred feet. I had to get off the roof. When Hugh finally managed to deal with my ward, the backlash would be a bitch. I needed distance, but I was stuck.

"Kate." Derek grabbed me and leaped. The ground yawned at me and then we landed on the other roof.

Robert cleared the roof and jumped down, right over the edge. I followed and nearly slid off the icy shingles. A fire escape, ten feet below.

I jumped down, landed with a thud, and slid down the fire escape, trying not to trip over my own clumsy feet. Wind whistled around me and then we were on the ground and next to Robert, who held Cuddles's reins.

I swung into the saddle and gave her a squeeze. We had to hurry.

Cuddles didn't move.

"Come on!" I kicked her sides. "Now isn't the time to be an ass!"

Cuddles planted herself. *Not now, you stupid donkey.*

Ascanio snarled and smacked her butt. Cuddles shot into a gallop, thudding down the street.

8

T HE WARREN FLEW by. We made another right and burst onto Garbage Road. Trash and refuse lay piled in huge heaps against the walls of abandoned buildings, forming a twenty-foot-deep canyon of garbage. If we made it through, we'd reach White Street.

Cuddles began to slow. I let her drop to a canter. A mile of gallop over rough terrain was all I could ask, even with Hugh behind us. It was that or, in another mile, she'd quit on me.

Small scavenger beasts with long tails scampered back and forth on the hills of trash, their eyes pinpoints of yellow against the darkness. The shapeshifters ran on both sides of me, leaping over hazards on the garbage slopes. Garbage Road had come about because of the Phantom River. It flowed through the Warren, invisible to the eye, picked up trash and loose refuse, and dragged it here, to Garbage Road. The Phantom River terminated when it reached White Street, which had its own brand of screwed-up magic. People said that the river's "waters" pooled here, held back by White Street like a dam, before they deposited all of its stolen treasures and disappeared.

The road widened and we emerged into what must've been a roundabout at some point. Now with the side streets choked by debris, it was just a trash bottleneck: one way in, one way out.

Ahead Derek stumbled.

I pulled on the reins, trying to get Cuddles to stop.

Derek tried to keep running, but he stumbled again and rolled down the garbage slope right under the donkey. Cuddles's hoof missed his head by a hair. She finally stopped, and I jumped to the ground.

Derek rolled up clumsily to all fours and vomited a torrent of gray on the ground. A putrid sour reek hit me. It smelled like someone had sliced open a cow carcass that had been baking in the sun for days. I gagged and knelt by him. The vomit was filled with dark gray slime, streaked with black and red.

Ascanio and Robert dropped down next to me. Desandra landed next to us, shivered, and vomited to the side, the same torrent of slime and blood. Something was horribly wrong with them.

"I'm okay." Derek coughed.

"Are you still bleeding?"

He didn't answer.

I grabbed his hand. Blisters bulged on his skin where the thorns had punctured it. The wounds still wept gray blood. The toxins from Nick's magic were eating them from the inside out.

Desandra turned to me. Open gashes weeping gray blood marked her furry arms.

Behind us something screeched. The long ululating cry rose above the rooftops and hung somewhere between the sky and the city, braided from hunger, predatory glee, and mourning, as if the thing that made it knew exactly how horrible it was. Only a human being could be so self-aware. It chilled every bone in my body.

Ascanio whipped around. "What the hell is that?"

That was the sixty-four-thousand-dollar question.

"Can you walk?" Robert asked.

Derek staggered up and swayed on his feet.

I grabbed Cuddles's reins and walked her over. "On the donkey."

"I can walk."

"Don't be ridiculous," Robert snapped.

"Get on the donkey. We don't have the time for this shit." I glared at Desandra. "You, too."

Desandra vomited again. The stench hit me. My stomach tried its hardest to empty itself. I choked down the bile. "Obey me, damn it. Now!"

Desandra staggered to Cuddles and climbed into the saddle. Robert picked Derek up as if the seven-foot werewolf in warrior form weighed nothing and lifted him into the saddle like he was a child. Cuddles flicked her ears, unperturbed by two werewolves on her back.

Behind us, the howl rose again: heart-wrenching, hungry, filled with despair. Closer this time.

The trash on both sides of us moved. Dozens of small creatures dashed past us, their glowing eyes wide. Oh crap.

Cuddles brayed and dashed up the street, carrying the two werewolves with her. Robert, Ascanio, and I chased her. Pain stabbed my side with each step, as if my cracked ribs had turned into spikes and pierced my insides. I clenched my teeth. Fuck it. I'd beaten a lot of pain before; I would beat this one, too.

Behind us, a forlorn cry shook the night. I turned to look over my shoulder.

A colossal creature moved through the trash canyon. It towered even with the garbage walls: giant, white, with fringes of coarse pale hair along the back of its enormous arms. Its pelvis sat low to the ground, its arms disproportionately long and armed with long, garden-shears-sized claws. Its bones pushed against its skin, its stomach so sunken in that if I had seen it in the wild, I'd think it was sick and starving. Its head was round and pale, sitting on a short neck. Its face might have had a distinct bone structure at some point, but all of its bones seemed to have melted into the skull to make room for its wide mouth. Its lips were missing and the rows of long sharp teeth in its mouth jutted, exposed. Its nose was little more than a bump with two holes, but its eyes, three inches wide and sunken into their orbits, looked completely human.

The moon broke through the clouds, its light illuminating the abomination. The creature's white flesh glowed, translucent, and within it I saw its pale lungs and pink stomach, and, in the middle of this mess, cradled in the cage of its ribs, a darker, humanlike shape, as if the beast had swallowed a person whole and the corpse became its heart.

Goose pimples ran up my arms. I had seen one before in photographs but never in real life.

Ascanio shivered and shifted shape, so fast he was a blur.

"A wendigo," Robert whispered next to me.

"Run!" I sprinted. "Ruuuun!"

We charged down the street. My cracked ribs set my side on fire. Speed was our best chance. There was no place to hide on Garbage Road. We didn't have the numbers or the means to kill it, and every second we spent fighting would cost us time we didn't have.

Legends said that wendigos haunted the winters on the Atlantic seaboard in the States and Canada, feeding on the Algonquian tribes. According to the Native American myths, those who reverted to cannibalism eventually transformed into a wendigo, doomed to a never-ending hunger for human flesh. I had never fought one, but I'd talked to a man who had. The wendigo couldn't be reasoned with. Their hunger overrode all else. They would devour their prey even as they themselves were being cut apart, and the only way to kill one was to dismember it and burn the pieces. If you didn't, it would regenerate in minutes, knitted together by magic.

A wendigo wouldn't just show up in Atlanta on its own. We were too far south, and even if it had somehow arrived, once it turned, it would have gone on long eating sprees. We would've heard about it. This was Hugh's import. A special present just for the Pack.

"Faster, faster!" Robert snarled.

I couldn't go any faster. I glanced over my shoulder. The wendigo was closing the gap.

Ahead Cuddles stopped and brayed.

Ascanio dashed forward and whipped around. "It's blocked!"

A massive industrial Dumpster lay on its side, blocking the path. At least eighteen feet long and filled to the brim with bricks and concrete. One of the Warren's gangs must've set it here to trap passersby so it would be easier to rob them. We had to go around.

The wendigo opened its jaws and let out another scream. It was barely two hundred yards away.

I grabbed Cuddles's reins and pulled her, trying to get her up the trash slope. Cuddles brayed and stopped dead.

Robert grabbed the reins next to me and pulled. "Come on."

Derek slid off the saddle and screamed, "Stop, you moron!"

I whipped around.

Ascanio was running toward the wendigo, his knives out.

No, no, no, you stupid idiot!

My body had moved before my mind realized I was running after him.

The wendigo paused, scooped something from the trash, and shoveled it into its mouth. The huge teeth scissored and a piece of a wooden beam fell from its mouth, sheared clean.

Ascanio leaped and carved at the wendigo's legs, his knives a whirl-wind. The creature howled.

I sprinted so fast, I was almost flying.

Ascanio whirled around the wendigo's legs like a dervish, slicing and cutting. Pink blood sprayed the trash piles. The wendigo's left ankle gave out and he dropped to one knee.

Run faster, damn it, I had to run faster.

Ascanio backed up toward me to avoid being crushed. The wendigo's hand snapped, shockingly fast, and closed about the boy. He jerked him up and smashed the bouda against the ground.

Oh no.

Robert shot past me and leaped onto the wendigo's face, his claws slicing.

The wendigo jerked Ascanio up, oblivious to the wererat clawing its face, and smashed him against the ground again. Bone crunched. The wendigo raised its hand. It was blood-red. The claws raked Ascanio's prone body. If I didn't stop it now, it would kill him.

I stopped to inhale some air.

The creature bent down . . .

"*Aarh!*" Stop.

The power word tore from me in a rush of agony. The wendigo froze. Robert froze too, the claws of his left hand buried in the wendigo's face, his right arm raised to claw at the creature's human eye.

Four seconds. That was how long the spell would hold them.

A furry shape leaped from the right above me, sailing through the air, arms raised, a tomahawk in his right hand. Derek landed on the wendigo's face and carved at its neck with his axe.

I shot forward and sliced the tendons on both hind legs.

Desandra swept Ascanio up and staggered back, stumbling.

The wendigo shook. Derek chopped into it again and again, casting off a pink mist of blood.

The spell broke. The wendigo crashed down and I carved its side open, thrusting through the ribs into the spongy lungs within. *Regenerate that, you sonovabitch.* Slayer thrust through thick muscle, and a wet pop announced the stomach rupturing. The reek of acid and sulfur washed over me. Blood wet my hands, gushing down the wendigo's side.

The massive creature shuddered, trying to rise.

Robert cut and gouged his way to the wendigo's back. Bright human blood stained his fur. The alpha of the wererats sliced the translucent flesh, planted his feet, bent down, locked his fingers on an exposed rib, and pulled. Bone broke. He tossed the rib out, shoved his hand into the hole, pulled a handful of organ tissue out, and hurled it into the night.

I scrambled the wendigo's human-looking heart with my blade. I minced its liver. I hacked its lungs into bloody paste. I severed its arteries. Pink, almost transparent blood sprayed me again and again, its taste burning on my lips. Above me Robert threw intestines onto garbage. I caught a glimpse of Desandra ripping into the wendigo's body next to me.

Suddenly the massive horrifying head sagged over, hanging from the stump of the neck by a thin thread of flesh. With one final blow, Derek sliced through it, and the head fell to the ground. Derek landed next to it, kicked the skull, sending it rolling down the trash-choked street, and fell like a chopped-down tree.

His body shivered and shrank back to human.

A few yards away Ascanio cried out on the ground, naked, human, and bloody. Everything inside me went cold. Their injuries were so bad, the Lyc-V had shifted them back to human as it strained to heal them.

I knelt by Derek and pulled his head up. He was out, but he was breathing. The wounds on his hands had stopped bleeding and I couldn't tell if it was good or bad.

"Kate!" Desandra called, her voice shaking.

I ran to her.

Long gashes carved Ascanio's chest and stomach. Wet intestines gaped through the gashes, weeping blood. His skin split where shards of broken ribs had punctured it. His face was bloody. He breathed in short sharp gasps. Oh God.

"Fix him!" Desandra looked at me.

I couldn't. He was gone too far. We had to get a medmage. We had to get one now.

Ascanio's gaze fastened on me. "So . . . sorry."

"Don't talk now." We couldn't load him onto the donkey. There was no room.

"I . . ." Ascanio swallowed and coughed out blood. He looked so young. "I don't . . . Want to die. Please."

"You're not going to die." I was getting much better at lying.

"Sorry," Ascanio whispered. "Sorry."

"Yes, you are. When we get to the Keep, you'll be even sorrier. What the fuck were you thinking?"

He tried to smile, his teeth bloody. ". . . buy Broody . . . some time."

Oh, you young fool.

A loud howl came from behind the wendigo, a wild human shriek. Hugh's Iron Dogs were hunting us down.

Desandra vomited again.

My guts turned into a cold twisted clump. Three people down. I couldn't let them die. They had come to protect me. I had to find a medmage even if I had to conjure one out of thin air. Derek would not die on my watch. Ascanio and Desandra would not die. I wouldn't stand before Aunt B's grave and tell her I let one of her bouda kids throw his life away. I wouldn't tell Curran that I got the boy wonder killed.

I pictured the area in my head. I knew this part of the city well. I'd covered just about every square inch of it during my tenure with the Order.

The Order.

This was nuts. But then beggars couldn't be choosers.

"Robert, can you carry him?

"Yes. Where are we going?" Robert asked.

"The Order."

"But they hate us," Desandra forced through her teeth.

"The Order has a medmage on staff and the kind of wards it would take an army to breach. They'll help anyone in need. We're in need. They hate Hugh d'Ambray more than they hate us."

At least I hoped they did. As much as Ted Moynohan despised me, he was still a knight-protector. He wouldn't let my people die on the street in front of his chapter. And I was betting three lives on that.

THE ULULATING HOWLS of the Iron Dogs floated behind us, constant now, like an eerie, bone-chilling din. As soon as one ended, another started. How they could run and howl at the same time was beyond me. They had to be riding and they were getting closer. We had lost two precious minutes coaxing Cuddles to climb the trash around the Dumpster and we weren't moving fast.

Desandra held Derek in the saddle in front of her. He'd gone completely limp. Her eyes were wild and she shivered as she rode. She wouldn't last much longer. Next to me Robert ran silently, carrying Ascanio in his arms.

The streets crawled by, painfully slow. My side hurt so much now, I didn't even anticipate the pain anymore. I just kept going.

A familiar storefront slid by. We had to be in range now.

I strained, trying to send a focused thought out into the world. *"Maxine?"*

The Order's telepathic secretary didn't answer.

"Maxine!" I whispered. Vocalizing helped sometimes. *"Maxine!"*

A familiar dry voice sounded in my head. *"Hello, Kate."*

"I'm on New Peachtree, being pursued by supernatural creatures. I request protection for five people."

Maxine paused. *"Kate, the Order isn't the safest place for you. Moynohan doesn't view you as an upstanding citizen."*

Moynohan can bite me. *"I have two injured teenagers, and one is dying. Tell Ted I'm running from Hugh d'Ambray."*

"Please stand by."

We made a sharp left. The howls chased us, louder and louder. The street rolled out in front of us, completely empty. Ten more blocks to the Order. To my knowledge the Order's wards had been breached only once and it took my aunt to do it. We had to make it behind those wards.

Hoofbeats. I turned.

Hugh rounded the corner. He was riding a huge black horse. A dozen men and women rode with him.

"Protection granted," Maxine said in my head. *"Please proceed to the Order chapterhouse."*

We wouldn't make it. I stopped and turned to face the Iron Dogs, unsheathing my sword. Hugh wanted me. Hugh would get me. Be careful what you wish for.

"Down!" Mauro boomed behind me.

I dropped to the ground. The air whined as half a dozen arrows flew above my head and bit into the asphalt, falling feet short of Hugh's horse.

The bolts pulsed once with bright blue. The night exploded. I caught a glimpse of Hugh's giant black horse rearing.

I jumped to my feet and turned. Four knights of the Order walked toward us: Mauro, Richter, another man I didn't know, and a redheaded woman with a buzz cut. They carried crossbows. *Hello, cavalry.* Behind them Robert was running full speed to the Order.

"Go, Kate!" Mauro waved at me.

The knights were reloading. I ran to the chapter.

The Order's nondescript building loomed before me. Robert ducked through the doors. I squeezed one last burst of speed, dashed through the doors, and almost ran into two knights pointing loaded crossbows at me.

"Give me your sword," the taller one said.

"I don't think so."

"I would do what he says, dear," Maxine said in my head. *"They're under orders to shoot you if you don't."*

══ CHAPTER ══

9

THE ORDER HAD remodeled the Vault after my aunt scorched the place. The massive door was gone. Shields and weapons still hung on three walls, but the fourth was now lined with loup cages, the bars made of silver and steel alloy two inches thick. The Order had spared no expense and I was getting a lovely view of the bars from the wrong side.

I paced back and forth, while Robert lay next to me, stretched out on the floor of the cage, resting to let his body heal. If he overextended himself, the Lyc-V would shut him down for repairs and he wanted to stay conscious.

My side still hurt, and my ribs reminded me once in a while that they were there.

To the right, separated from my and Robert's cell by bars, Derek and Desandra sprawled in their own cage asleep under blankets. The Order's medmage, a tall man with a long braid of brown hair who went by Steinlein, had examined them and declared there was nothing he could do. The toxin was working its way through their systems and they would bounce back or they wouldn't. He seemed to think they would, because once they had turned human, their wounds had closed, which was a good sign.

Through the bars, I could see Ascanio. He lay limp on a table in the open. They had chained his ankles and his wrists. The chains weren't silver, but they were thick enough to hold him. Steinlein chanted over him, rocking back and forth. I couldn't tell if his chanting was doing anything. The boy didn't look any better.

I felt so hollow, as if someone had gutted me. I didn't know about whom to worry more, Ascanio dying or Derek and Desandra barely breathing.

The redheaded female knight with the buzz cut—Steinlein had called her Diana—watched us. Next to her a lean, muscular knight in his late twenties was giving me his version of a hard stare. He was carrying a tactical sword. A long scar crossed his face from his short blond hair to his chin. They both seemed convinced that if one of them looked away for a second, I'd escape from the locked cage and explode the Order.

"You keep staring, you'll set me on fire," I told them.

Neither of them answered. Great.

Mauro stepped into the vault.

"Did you call the Pack?" I asked him

"The phones are out," he said.

Can I just fucking catch a break?

"But I sent a courier to Atlanta Medical, asking for assistance," Mauro said. "They've got a new satellite office about four miles from here."

"Thank you," I said.

"It won't help," Steinlein said. "His chest and everything inside it is crushed. If he were weaker, he would be dead already. I'm only delaying the inevitable."

Ascanio trusted me. He trusted me and I had let him come with me. He had no fear, because he was young and he thought he was immortal and because he counted on me keeping him alive. I couldn't lose him. "If you're done, chain me next to him, and I'll keep chanting."

The medmage turned to me. "I didn't say I was giving up. I'm just telling you that there's no light at the end of this tunnel. You have a couple of hours to come to terms with it."

Doolittle would've ripped a new hole somewhere in him for his bedside manner. If he hadn't been holding Ascanio's life in his hands, I'd have told him exactly what I thought about it.

"We don't have a couple of hours," Robert said, his eyes still closed. "D'Ambray is coming."

And soon, too. We'd been inside the chapterhouse for about fifteen minutes. Everything I had read about the wendigo said they regenerated in anywhere from five minutes to half an hour, depending on the magnitude of the magic wave. We hadn't had the time to cut it into little pieces and then burn them. As soon as his wendigo got on its feet, Hugh would come. I had taunted him, and my ward had kicked his ass. He wouldn't let it go.

"D'Ambray would be an idiot to attack the Order," Diana said.

"We've got backup coming in," Mauro said. "I've talked to the knight-protector. Ted reached out to the Paranormal Activity Division and the National Guard."

Neither the PAD nor the National Guard would get here in time.

"We've fought one of them before," Mauro said. "It was me, Kate, and Nash, and we all lived through it."

We had lived through it, because I *was* one of "them." Pointing that out wasn't in my best interests. "Let me out. I'll fight with you."

"Sorry, Kate." Mauro grimaced. "Orders are orders."

"Kate," Maxine's voice said in my head.

"Yes?"

"I'm being evacuated out of the office. I'm instructed to stay within my range so I can make a full report of what happens."

Ted was expecting trouble.

"Thank you for your help," I whispered. *"I truly appreciate it."*

"I know, dear. I'm very sorry you left. It hasn't been the same without you and Andrea."

Heavy steps came down the stairs and Ted Moynohan walked into the room. The knight-protector had aged since I last saw him. He'd been in his early fifties when we met. Now he seemed closer to sixty. He was built thick and had gotten thicker. The layer of fat was deceiving—there was hard, powerful muscle underneath—and Ted didn't look soft. He looked like a heavyweight fighter who had let himself go a bit. He wore blue jeans, a gray shirt, cowboy boots, and a belt with a buckle that had illusions of grandeur. A black cowboy hat sat on his head, and if it got real hot, he could shelter a gaggle of street orphans in its shade.

Ted stopped by my cage and peered at me, his square jaw locked. I looked back. He would do me no favors and I expected none.

"Here you are in a cage, Daniels. I always knew you'd end up in one."

I didn't answer. If he got it all off his chest, I'd have a better chance of making him understand what was coming.

"You put the Consort of the Pack in a cage," Robert said.

"I don't see a consort. I see the same smart-mouthed merc with a sharp sword, except she's dressed better now. Mercs have no loyalty and this one has no brains. She'll get you killed just like that kid over there. You should've found yourself someone smarter to follow."

"D'Ambray is coming," I said. "He has a detachment of Iron Dogs and at least one wendigo with him. He also has access to the entirety of the People's stable of vampires. He wants to bring down the Pack and he has decided that killing me is the way to do it." It wasn't the complete truth, but close enough. "He's pissed off. If you let me go, d'Ambray will follow me."

"Mm-hm," Ted said.

"He has superior numbers and he's very determined. You don't have the manpower to oppose him. Let me out." I just needed them to keep Ascanio, Derek, and Desandra safe. That's all. Robert and I could go and draw Hugh off with us.

Ted shook his head. "No. This is a human fight and you've picked the wrong side. Live with your choices."

Stubborn bastard. "You have no authority to detain me."

"Yes, I do. When you petitioned the Order for protection, they gave us sweeping power to guard you in the way we see fit. Enjoy being guarded, Daniels."

Argh. *Listen to me, you dense asshole.* "They will breach your defenses. You're throwing your people away. Hugh isn't some Joe Blow off the street, he's the preceptor of the Order of Iron Dogs. He has Uath with him. She likes to skin people alive."

Ted smiled.

He wanted it.

The crazy sonovabitch actually wanted a shot at Hugh d'Ambray. As long as the Order held us, there was a chance that Hugh would pick a fight, and everything I had just said only confirmed Ted's decision to keep us here. My mind wrestled with it and I clamped my mouth shut.

Why? What could he possibly gain by this? My aunt had left this building a smoking wreck, and she hadn't even done it in person. She'd used a flesh golem to do it. Ted was a bigot, but he wasn't an idiot. He had to know there was a chance Hugh would break through the Order's defenses. The Iron Dogs were the elite of the elite, and according to Mauro, his knights, who'd be outnumbered two to one, weren't exactly the Order's cream of the crop.

Why risk his people? Was it some sort of last-minute attempt at some glory before he died?

I had to change my strategy and fast. I scraped my brain for the contents of the Order's Charter. I learned slowly, but once I managed to chisel infor-mation into my brain, it stayed there.

"Under article one point seven, a petition is valid only when it's been signed by the petitioner after the terms and conditions of the petition have been explained to said petitioner. Show me that signature."

Ted took a paper off the desk and raised it. *Robert Lonesco.* Got you.

Robert shrugged. "It was that or they wouldn't let us in."

"Article one point twelve, a group petition may be filed by an individual, provided said individual has been selected by the group to act as its repre-sentative. Robert, have you been selected to act as our representative?"

The alpha rat smiled. "No."

The knight with the scar raised his eyebrows. He knew where I was going with this and he knew I was right.

"To the best of your knowledge, who has the right to represent our group?"

"You do, Consort," Robert said.

I looked at Ted. "This petition is invalid. You are detaining us illegally. Release us now."

Magic crackled through the building, followed by a hair-raising desper-ate wail. Hugh's wendigo had just tested the strength of the wards.

"She's right," the knight with the scar said. "We have no right to hold them."

Ted looked at him. "This is D-day, Towers. This is what you've trained for." His voice rose. "This is what we all trained for. This is important. We make a stand today. Can I count on you?"

Muscles played on Towers's jaw. "Yes."

"Good. We'll continue this talk after we're done." Ted moved to the weapon rack and picked up a mace. Diana began to chant under her breath.

"Let us out!" I snarled.

Ted ignored me. "Diana, Towers, Mauro, with me." He pointed at the medmage. "Steinlein, back us up."

"Ted, listen to me, you stupid sonovabitch! Maybe you want to go out in a blaze of glory, but—"

They moved out. Steinlein, the medmage with the long braid, followed them. "Sorry."

No. No, damn it. "Wait! The boy will die!"

"I'm sorry, but he's dead anyway." The knight left the room.

The wendigo's enraged howl erupted. The building shook.

I TOUCHED THE bars. Magic surged through me in a flash of agony. Warded. Ascanio was dying, Hugh was breaking in, and we were trapped in a cage. Like sitting ducks. Well, this was going well.

I had a lock pick on my belt, but the knights had taken my belt, my jacket, and my sword.

Above us something shuddered with rhythmic, loud thuds, as if someone were hitting the building with an enormous hammer.

Robert rolled to his feet, hunched over by the lock, and tried to pass his hand between the bars. Magic nipped at his claws. He grimaced, baring vicious teeth, and tried to touch the lock. His forearm grazed the bars. He jerked his arm back. A gray scar crossed his skin, where the silver had killed Lyc-V.

Robert clawed at the floor of the cage, pried a board open, and dropped it back down. "Silver and steel."

Same with the ceiling. We weren't going anywhere. If I used a power word, it would bounce off the defensive spell protecting the bars and backfire at me. I had tried it in a warded cell under other circumstances and the pain left me crippled for an hour.

The pounding was getting louder.

I turned to Robert. "If Hugh gets through and you get a chance to run, I need you to leave us and run. Somebody has to tell the Pack what happened."

Robert gave me a small smile. "If Hugh gets through, it's unlikely I'll survive."

Magic slapped me with an invisible hand. I reeled.

"What?" Robert asked.

"Someone just broke the Order's main ward."

Something tore down the stairs and Hugh burst into the room. Blood slicked his clothes and cloak, but they were intact. None of it was his own. Too bad. A woman could hope.

He saw me and paused. "In a cage."

Yeah, yeah.

Hugh shook his head. "How the fuck did you let yourself be put in a cage?"

He sounded offended on my behalf. Well, wasn't that sweet? "I'm sorry, I can't hear you. My ears are still ringing from that big boom your head made when it hit the stairs. Is your brain okay? Because your skull sounded hollow."

Behind him Nick walked through the door. The crusader stared at each of us in turn, his eyes cold. Maybe I was wrong. Maybe Hugh had turned him.

Hugh strolled around the room, paused by Ascanio's prone body, and grimaced. "I hate amateurs."

I wanted to snap at him to leave the kid alone and caught myself. Anything I prized and anyone I cared about, Hugh would use against me. He was savoring the moment.

Hugh walked to the back of the room, with Nick at his heels, turned, and faced the entrance. "Don't interfere."

Nick nodded and leaned against the far wall.

Diana burst into the room, her face and arms smudged with soot. Towers, the one with the scar, was only a step behind. A gash tore his chest from left to right. Bloody but shallow.

"Is this it?" Hugh asked.

The two knights stared at Hugh.

Towers jerked a crossbow up.

Hugh said something. Magic popped like a huge balloon exploding. A power word. The cages shook. Pieces of the crossbow clattered on the stone floor.

"You have a problem." Hugh shrugged off his cloak and hung it on a weapon hook in the wall. "You know who I am. You know what I can do. I'm here for her." He nodded at me. "I won't leave without her. I won't let you shoot me. You could try locking me in, but your walls can't hold me. And containment isn't really what you had in mind, is it?"

Hugh unsheathed a gladius. A simple, ancient sword, with a straight double-edged blade, twenty-five and a quarter inches long, two and a quarter inches wide, weighing barely two pounds. Simple and brutal. The sword that carved the Roman Empire out of Europe.

Diana hunched her shoulders, whispering under her breath. Towers eyed him warily.

Above us the wendigo screamed again. Something thumped, followed by hoarse human cries.

Hugh hefted the gladius and turned the blade, warming up his wrist. Towers's eyes narrowed. Hugh held the sword as if it were an extension of him, as if it had no weight. He was intimately familiar with it. He must've used it so much for so long that if he closed his eyes, he could probably reach out and touch its tip, because he knew exactly where the blade ended. I knew he could, because even in absolute darkness I knew exactly how long Slayer's blade was.

"Get me out of this cage," I growled.

"Shhh," Hugh said. His eyes were hard. "Just watch."

He shrugged, stretching, and nodded to the knights. "If you want me, you'll have to come and get me."

"Don't," I said. "He'll kill you."

Diana pulled a slender saber out. She held it like she knew what she was doing, but Hugh was in a class of his own. Fire dashed from Diana's hand onto the blade, coating the saber in flames.

"A flaming sword." Hugh shook his head. "Come on. Let's do this."

"Wait," Towers said.

Diana shot forward, bringing her saber up for a thrust. It was a good thrust, well aimed and fast. Hugh met her halfway. His gladius slipped into her side almost on its own. He spun her about, clamped her to him, her back against his chest, and held the blade covered with her blood to her throat. It took less than a second.

Argh. I grabbed the bars. Magic burned me and I let go.

"Tell me, Kate," he said, his voice casual. "When Lennart is on top of you and you're waiting for him to finish, do you ever think of me? Just to spice things up."

Diana rasped, gasping for breath. Her side bled as her body pumped her lifeblood out of the wound.

"No," I ground through my teeth. "But when I feel down, I picture killing you and it cheers me right up. It makes me giggle."

Hugh laughed and jerked Diana up, her temple pressed against his cheek. "See that woman you put in the cage?"

Diana's breath came out in hoarse gasps.

"Ask her for your life," Hugh said.

"You fucking bastard." When I got out of here, I would cut pieces off him until he stopped moving.

"Ask her nice," Hugh repeated. "If she gives you your life back, I'll let you go."

"You made your point. I don't want her to die," I said.

"Ask her," Hugh said.

Diana's lips moved. "Fuck you."

"Wrong answer." Hugh sliced her throat and stepped back. The female knight froze, upright, eyes opened wide. Dark blood gushed from her throat. Her eyes rolled up and she stumbled and fell. Her blood spread in a wide puddle on the floor.

Nick's eyes were empty. He looked at the blood, seemingly untroubled by it. He might as well have been dead.

"A waste." Hugh flicked the blood off his sword.

Towers moved forward, cautious. He moved like a spooked cat, light on his toes and jumpy.

Had everyone gone crazy today? "What are you doing? Just shoot this asshole! He can't keep using power words. He'll run out of juice before you run out of crossbow bolts."

"Swordsman, huh." Hugh put the gladius on the examination table behind him. "Look, Ma, no sword."

Towers darted at him and thrust, lightning-fast. Hugh leaned out of the way just enough for the blade to miss, grabbed Towers's wrist, leaned back, and hammered a side kick into the knight's ribs, just above his right hip. The kick didn't just land, it exploded. Towers stumbled back, bending over his injured side.

Hugh smiled and motioned him over. "Come on."

Towers darted in and slashed left to right, aiming for Hugh's throat. Too slow; I'd lean back.

Hugh leaned back and the blade grazed his left shoulder.

Towers reversed his swing and tried to smash the pommel of the sword into Hugh's face, leaving his midsection wide open. You could drive a bloody cart through that opening.

Hugh dodged, grabbed his gladius from the exam table, and cut at Towers. The first blow opened the knight's stomach. Before he had a chance to reel, Hugh sank a sharp precise thrust to the knight's side, right between the ribs into the liver.

Towers dropped to his knees, cradling his guts. Hugh grabbed his hair. "Ask her for your life."

"I want him to live," I ground out.

"He has to ask," Hugh told me.

Towers jerked a knife from his belt and buried it in Hugh's thigh.

"I guess we've got ourselves a no." Hugh stabbed his gladius into the knight's chest.

Towers gurgled and sagged to the floor.

I spun in the cage, helpless. He kept killing them and they kept dying and I could only watch. Rage boiled inside me. "Why are you doing this?"

Hugh flicked the blood off his sword. "You wanted me to show you something."

"Well, so far all I've seen is you killing the Order's second-best. Pick on someone your own size."

"All in good time." Hugh smiled at me, his eyes cold.

Where the hell were the PAD and the National Guard? How long did it take them to mobilize?

"Like it or not," he said, "you're still his daughter. Run from it, spit on it, that's your choice. Those of the blood can insult the blood. Nobody else. I won't allow it."

I finally understood. This wasn't just about me; this was about the Order dragging my name through the mud after I left and then caging me here now. This wasn't just elimination. This was punishment. He would kill every knight in the chapter but not before he made all of them submit to me and beg me for their lives.

I had to do something.

The ward between the bars of the cage wasn't solid. It hurt like hell when I thrust my hand through it, but I could thrust it. I turned my back to Hugh and clawed the cut on my left forearm. Pain lanced me. Crimson washed my skin, the magic in it alive and ready. I pulled it, shaping it with my will into a five-inch-long spike. It was long and sharp and an eye was such a soft target, with the brain right behind it. I just had to get him close to the cage.

"You're going to want to see this next part," Hugh said. "I'm just getting started. Or is it too much for you?"

I turned to Hugh. "I keep thinking about the fire that destroyed your castle. Nobody could've lived through that. What if you aren't even you?"

Hugh stepped closer to the cage.

"What if my father has a closet full of Hughs, and every time Curran and I break one, he just pulls another copy out?"

Hugh stepped over Towers's body and slowly, deliberately, walked over to the bars. Just out of striking range. All I needed was another two or three inches.

"I once watched a movie where a man made clones of himself," I told him. "Each clone was dumber than the previous one. I think that actually might be true. You've attacked the Order. That's the stupidest thing I've seen you do yet."

Hugh leaned forward. His blue eyes fixed on me, hard and predatory. *That's right, show me how big and bad you are. Come on. Tell me all about it. Come closer. Closer.*

"Tell me, what's your number, clone-Hugh?"

"You want to know how I survived? He stole a phoenix egg and put me inside it. For two months I soaked in it, growing new skin and a new spine, and thought of what I would do to Lennart and you when I got out." Hugh leaned closer. Another inch and we'd be in business. "And let me tell you, the look on your face when you watch them die makes it all worth it."

The stairs shuddered under rapid steps. Hugh turned.

No! Argh, almost had him.

Four people charged into the room: a dark-haired female knight I didn't know, Ted Moynohan, the medmage Steinlein, and in front of them all, a slender man with a bald head and Celtic-blue war paint tattooed on his face. Richter. The Order's resident psychopath.

Great. More people for him to kill.

"The knight-protector." Hugh swung his sword in a lazy circle, warming up his wrist. "Finally. And here I thought you'd just let me wreck your house."

"Open the cage and I'll take him apart," I said. I had beaten him once. I could do it again.

Hugh chuckled. "Come on, Kate. Don't embarrass them. They're knights. Time someone tested them."

Ted looked at the two prone bodies on the floor around him and smiled. His people were dead and he smiled.

The realization hit me like a ton of bricks. Ted wanted a massacre. He was on his way out, either to be disgraced or to retire, and he must've wanted it to count. He must've decided to go out in a blaze of glory. But his death alone wouldn't be enough. If Hugh killed him, the Order might find a way to overlook it, but if Roland's warlord slaughtered the entire chapter, the knights would do everything in their power to hunt him down. It had to be brutal, and bloody, and vicious, so those who died wouldn't be just fallen knights or victims, they would become martyrs.

Hugh wanted to kill all of them. Ted wanted all of them to die. He wanted his own Alamo. The knights would give their lives, every single one of them, after a dramatic final standoff, and Maxine would bear witness to all of it. We were watching the start of the war between Roland and the Order.

Nothing I could do or say would make any difference. I sank to the floor next to Robert. Across the room Nick looked at me, his face pale like the snow outside. Our gazes met. He understood and he would watch it all just like me and Robert.

Ted pointed at Hugh. "Get him."

RICHTER PULLED OUT two short blades and blurred, splitting into three transparent versions of himself. Two were false and one was real. The triplets charged, launching a flurry of strikes at Hugh. The preceptor of the Order of Iron Dogs backed away under the barrage, blocked, and kicked, putting all of the power of his massive legs into it. The real Richter flew across the room and bounced off the wall.

The dark-haired woman lunged from the side and stabbed at Hugh, aiming between his left ribs, fast. Hugh leaned back, let the sword pass, and drove his left elbow into the female knight's face. She stumbled back. Richter dashed back and sliced at Hugh's right shoulder. Blood sprayed. Hugh backhanded Richter out of the way.

The woman charged in again and froze, caught on Hugh's blade like a fish on a hook. He thrust up into her chest, twisted, carving out the heart, and hurled her corpse at Richter. The smaller knight dodged and charged Hugh again in a frenzy. Hugh dropped back, blocking with the flat of his blade, his face calm and collected. His eyes turned calculating. It was like Voron had been resurrected and possessed Hugh, and I knew exactly what came next. He would cut Richter apart, slowly, methodically, using every opening. He would not lose his temper, because in this place, where the angle of the blade separated life from death, Hugh was impossible to rattle.

If a red-hot meteorite punched through the roof and exploded, he wouldn't blink an eye. I knew that place well. That was where I was at my best.

Richter drew blood again and again, each strike of his blades opening another minor wound. Hugh held back.

Then Richter swung his right arm a fraction too wide.

Hugh's sword sliced, precise and merciless. He stabbed Richter in the stomach, whirled, and kicked the knight's leg out from under him. As Richter dropped to his knees, Hugh stabbed him in the spot where the neck met the shoulder. Richter gasped. Hugh swung his sword and Richter's head rolled on the floor.

My chest hurt. I would remember this feeling for as long as I lived, this terrible feeling of being locked in a cage and being able to do nothing.

Ted Moynohan roared. A dark red outline flared around his body, sliding over his mace. Apparently the knight-protector had some magic of his own.

Hugh crouched and grabbed a second sword from Towers's body sprawled on the floor.

Ted charged. Hugh moved out of the way. Ted whipped the mace around as if it weighed nothing. Hugh blocked, letting the mace slide off Towers's sword, but his arm shook a little. He shifted his feet. That was a hell of a blow. If I were him, I'd try to avoid blocking.

"Did you know who she was when you decided to belittle her?" Hugh asked.

"I don't need you to fight my battles for me," I said.

"Someone has to do it, since you won't."

Ted spun the mace and swung at Hugh. Hugh blocked again and the mace head snapped the blade in half. Hugh slashed Ted's arm with the broken blade and jerked his hand away. The broken sword clattered to the floor. Whatever that red aura was, it hurt like a sonovabitch.

"Did you know who she was?" Hugh repeated.

Ted swung his mace again. Hugh ducked, leaped over Richter's corpse, and grabbed a shield off the wall.

"You didn't. You still don't, do you?"

Ted swung again and Hugh thrust the shield in his way. The mace connected. *Boom.* The shield rang like a gong.

"I would've thought your boys would have better intel."

Boom.

"At least do your damn homework. Sloppy, Moynohan. Very sloppy."

Boom. Hugh was waiting for Ted to fall into a pattern. Ted would hit harder and harder, trying to break through the shield with raw strength. Once an opponent fell into a pattern, they became predictable—and they could be defeated.

"When you get a power like that on your side, you move heaven and earth to hold on to it."

Boom.

"But you didn't, did you?"

Boom.

"Because you're a moron."

Ted swung, putting all his power into the blow, expecting to break through the shield. Hugh stepped right and turned. The mace whistled through the air a hair from his chest. Ted had put so much momentum into the blow, he couldn't stop. The weight of the mace drove him down and Hugh stabbed him in the chest. If he didn't hit the heart, he was damn close.

Blood surged. Ted's eyes bulged.

"No," Hugh said. "No, that was too easy."

What?

Ted struggled to raise the mace. The red aura around him died.

Hugh clamped his hand to Ted's chest. "Come back. You've got more in you."

A blue glow flared around Hugh's fingers. Something gurgled in Ted's throat. Red bubbles expanded out of his mouth.

He was healing him. This was torture. "Just let him die!"

"No, not yet." Hugh shook his head. "Come on. Come back to me."

Ted's arms shook. He sucked in a breath.

Hugh released him. The knight-protector stumbled back.

Hugh banged his gladius against the shield. "Come on, knight. Show me more."

The carmine aura flared around Ted once more. He charged forward and slammed his shoulder into Hugh. Hugh flew back and rolled to a crouch next to the medmage. Steinlein had stood so still, all of us had forgotten he was even there, pressed against the wall and holding a small axe. Before Hugh could rise, the medmage swung the axe. Hugh moved, but not fast enough. The axe sank into his left shoulder.

Hugh kicked out, sweeping the medmage's legs out from under him. Steinlein crashed down. Hugh buried his gladius in Steinlein's gut, casually, almost in passing, and rolled to the left just in time to avoid Ted's mace. The knight-protector chased him.

Steinlein shuddered on the floor. His legs shook. The gaping wound in his stomach gushed blood.

I had no feelings left anymore. Just cold quiet hate.

Hugh charged Ted like a cornered tiger. They clashed, mace to shield, muscling each other across the floor. Hugh dug his feet into the floor and pushed, knocking Ted back. The knight-protector spun his mace, aiming at Hugh's head. Hugh swung his shield to counter, putting all his enormous strength into the blow. The shield connected, knocking Ted's mace aside. For a fraction of a second, the knight-protector was wide open. Hugh swung and opened a second mouth in Ted's stomach. Ted sagged against the wall and slid down.

Mauro charged into the room, bloody and smeared with soot. Blood dripped from his short, wide sword. "I can't hold them. Pull the . . ." He saw the bodies. His eyes bulged. He dropped his sword.

"Don't!" I yelled.

Mauro bellowed and ripped off his shirt. Tattoos wound along his torso, dense swirls of dark ink in precise patterns. He clapped his hands together like a sumo wrestler. His skin turned black. The edges of his tattoos flared bright red, shifting slightly, as if his obsidian skin had cracked along their lines, revealing a glimpse of the lava underneath. Heat bathed me, rolling off him in waves.

Hugh shrugged his shoulders. "Come on, big man. Let's see what you've got."

Mauro charged. Hugh swung out of the way and sliced at Mauro's stomach with the gladius. The blade glanced off. Mauro drove his shoulder into Hugh. The preceptor flew a few feet and bounced off the wall. Mauro lunged at him, roaring. Hugh spun out of the way, avoiding being trapped.

Hugh was better with a sword, but I had once seen Mauro lift a car when a cat was trapped under it. *Do it, you can do it.*

Hugh stabbed the gladius at Mauro's side. The blade slid off. Hugh dropped the gladius and drove his fist into Mauro's throat. It was a hard, powerful punch. Hugh's skin sizzled. He stumbled back. *Hot enough for you, you asshole?*

Mauro locked his hands on Hugh's throat and drove him into the wall. Hugh's back slapped the stone with a satisfying thud. Mauro slammed him again and again.

"Snap his neck," I yelled.

Mauro smashed Hugh into the stone again, shaking him back and forth. He didn't hear me. He was too far gone.

Hugh thrust his arms upward, between Mauro's massive arms, trying to break his hold. The air smelled of singed flesh. Hugh jerked his arms up, Mauro's arms went wide, and the big knight headbutted Hugh in the face. Blood drenched Hugh's lips. Broken nose, for sure.

Mauro grabbed Hugh into a bear hug, lifting him off his feet. Bones groaned.

"Kate!" Robert pointed to the right. I glanced in that direction at the medmage lying in a pool of blood. Steinlein strained to say something and reached into his pocket.

Hugh jabbed his thumbs into Mauro's eyes. Mauro hurled him aside like Hugh weighed nothing.

Steinlein pulled out a bloody key ring.

Keys. Keys to the cage. I dropped on my knees by the bars. "Here." If I could get out of the cage, between Mauro and me Hugh was finished.

Mauro grabbed at Hugh, but the preceptor moved out of the way. Burns covered his arms. The flesh around Hugh's neck blistered.

Steinlein's hand shook. He crawled toward the cage, leaving a bloody smudge on the floor. *Hurry. Hurry.*

Mauro bellowed again.

Steinlein stretched his hand with the keys toward me. I reached for it. The tips of my fingers just brushed against the keys. Magic sawed through my arm with fiery teeth and I jerked my fingers back. Damn it.

Hugh darted behind Mauro, grabbed his right wrist with his left hand, planted his right hand on Mauro's shoulder, and swept his legs out from under him. The big man crashed down like a colossus on legs of sand. The room shook from the impact. Mauro's head bounced off the floor.

Steinlein pulled himself forward another foot and collapsed, his hand stretching to the bars. I thrust my arm through the ward. The magic burned me, so intense that tears slid from my eyes. I clenched my teeth and reached through the agony, stretching.

I couldn't let Mauro die, not big, kind, funny Mauro. He'd watched my back, he brought my dog treats, he helped people . . . I wanted him to live and be happy. I wanted him to go home to his wife. I wanted it so much. I didn't want him to die here.

Magic was ripping my arm off.

Mauro was my friend. I couldn't let him die here.

The world melted into pain. I screamed.

Something pulled me back. I blinked and realized Robert's arms gripped me. My fingers held the blood-slicked keys.

Hugh grabbed his sword with both hands, point down, and drove it into the big man's chest, sinking the entire weight and power of his body into it. The gladius sank in three inches. Mauro screamed.

I lunged to the door.

"No!" Robert clamped me down.

Hugh picked up Ted's mace and brought it down onto the gladius like a hammer. The sword slid into Mauro's chest.

Mauro gasped. His skin paled, his tattoos fading. His body shuddered. The massive knight drew a single hoarse breath and lay still.

He killed him. He killed Mauro. It felt like someone opened a big dark pit under me and I was falling into it screaming. I failed. I wasn't fast enough. My friend was dead and there was nothing I could do to bring him back. He was alive yesterday morning. He'd curtsied in my office.

He killed Mauro. I was right there and he . . .

I couldn't breathe. My rage and grief were choking me, trying to rip out of me.

Oh my God, what would I tell his wife?

Hugh straightened, groaning, spat blood to the side, and crouched by Ted. His face was a bloody mess. On the floor seven people lay dead or dying. In the corner Nick looked at all of it, impassive.

Hugh surveyed the scene and looked at the wound gaping across Ted's gut.

"I like this better—more satisfying all around. Gives us a few moments to bond before you pass on. I have a secret to tell you about one of your former employees." Hugh turned on his feet and put his arm around Ted, moving his face so he would see me. "That one. She really hates cages, by the way. You'll like this."

He leaned closer to Ted and whispered into his ear. Ted's eyes bulged.

"Life is full of surprises, isn't it?" Hugh smiled.

He straightened and closed his eyes. Magic condensed around him. A pale blue glow licked his shoulder. His wounds knitted closed. His nose reset itself. He shrugged and walked up to my cage, blood dripping from his sword.

"It never lasts. They die too quickly on me. Give me the keys, Kate. You fought a good fight, but it's over."

"No." Before I would've left the cage to fight him so I could save them. Now there was no need. Now they were dead. Mauro was dead.

"Was he a friend?" Hugh glanced at the big knight's body. "So sorry. Give me the keys."

"I'm going to kill you," I told him. "If I don't, Curran will."

"That's why I like you. It's always the hard way." Hugh turned on his foot, his boot sliding on the blood, and walked over to Ascanio. "What do we have here?"

I didn't think I had enough stamina left to be scared. I was wrong.

He glanced at Steinlein's corpse. "That would be his handiwork. I detest amateurs. The kid is a shapeshifter and a teenager. His regeneration factor is through the roof. I mean really, how difficult is it to heal this?"

Don't touch him. Don't . . .

Hugh held his hands out and began to chant under his breath. Magic moved, slow and sluggish at first, then faster and faster, winding around Hugh and raining on Ascanio's body. The crushed ribs crawled under the boy's skin, re-forming.

Hugh stopped chanting. The flow of magic stopped as if cut by a knife and I almost cried out.

Ascanio lay on the table, pale and smeared with blood. He looked so young. So young, just a child dying slowly on the metal table.

"So what will it be, Kate?"

Hugh held his hand out and Ascanio's wounds began to knit themselves closed. "Yes?" He closed his hand into a fist. The healing stopped. "Or no?"

"Don't." Robert's voice vibrated with urgency. "Don't take the bait."

"Yes?" Fractured shards of ribs slid into place.

Ascanio had trusted me to keep him safe. I had promised Aunt B. I'd promised her on her grave that I would look after her people.

"Or no?" The flesh stopped moving.

"Perhaps you'd like me to do it in reverse?" Hugh raised his eyebrows.

"No." The word escaped before I could catch it.

"Don't!" Robert's voice snapped like a whip.

Hugh grimaced, his face jerking with effort. Ascanio's bones crunched. Oh God.

"Make up your mind," Hugh said. "Because I'll splinter every bone in his body. He'll be soft like a rag doll by the time I'm done."

I couldn't let Ascanio die. It wasn't in me.

It felt like the words cut my mouth on their way out. "Heal him and I'll open the cage."

"This is a mistake," Robert said.

Hugh smiled.

I held up the keys. "You have my word. Heal the boy and I'll open the cage."

Hugh turned to Ascanio and raised his hand. Magic built around him like a wave about to break. A steady blue glow slowly flared around his body.

The magic plunged onto Ascanio's body in a deluge. He cried out.

Ted struggled to say something. His big body shook. The tough old bastard refused to die.

Hugh ignored him, his magic streaming from him into Ascanio.

Ted's voice was a hoarse rattle, as if an anvil rested on his chest and he couldn't draw enough air. "Your . . . mission . . ."

Ascanio's rib cage expanded back, the bones moving slowly back into his chest.

". . . is . . ."

Ted gasped. Blood poured from his mouth. "Aborted."

What?

"Effective immediately."

Ted's legs convulsed. He gripped the edge of the desk, holding himself upright by sheer will. "Central, acknowledge."

"Acknowledged," Maxine's voice said in my head. Robert looked around, startled. Hugh stopped and raised his head. Everyone in the room must've heard it. *"Knight-crusader Nikolas Feldman, you are hereby ordered to return to regular duties."*

I knew only one Feldman. Greg, my deceased guardian.

Ted's hand slipped. He sagged to the ground. Blood gushed out of his mouth.

Nick stepped forward. The twin thorn vines shot out of his body and punched Hugh in the chest, sweeping him off his feet. The preceptor of the Order of Iron Dogs flew and crashed to the floor outside the room. Nick ripped a green shield off the wall, revealing a switch and punching it. A metal portcullis slid in place, separating Hugh from the rest of us.

They had a portcullis! I almost choked. Okay, so I didn't know it was there; the other knights may not have known either. But Ted knew. He could've locked Hugh out at any time.

Hugh rolled to his feet and screamed, a howl of pure fury.

Uath ran down the stairs. "We have to go."

Hugh stabbed at the portcullis with his hand. "I want this broken."

"There's no time," she said.

He spun to her, his face contorted.

Uath shrank back. "A National Guard platoon is incoming. They're less than a mile out."

"How many?"

"Two squads. Eighteen soldiers and a mage unit. We can wipe them out but it will take too much time. By the time we're done, half of the city will be on us."

Hugh looked at the ceiling.

"Sir," Uath said. "Should I take up a defensive position?"

Hugh's anger imploded. His face slid into icy calm. "No. Move our people out."

Uath ran back up the stairs.

Hugh pointed through the bars at Nick. "Well played. You and I aren't done." He turned to me. "At noon, I'll be coming for you."

He turned and walked up the stairs.

I thrust my hand between the bars and unlocked the cage.

Nick walked over to Ted, crouched, and touched his neck. His voice shook with suppressed rage.

"Well, here we are. You're dead, you fucking dumb bastard. Two years of my life undercover. Do you have any idea what sort of shit I've seen? Do you know the things I had to do? The things they did to me? Two years of gathering information, waiting for a chance to make a difference. And you burned me. You threw it all away so you could have a witness to your holy war." Nick rose and kicked Ted in the head. "And now you're dead, you fucker, and I have to live with all of it."

I swung the door open and ran to Ascanio. He was breathing. The gashes were still open, but his chest was no longer a misshapen mess. I turned to Mauro and felt for a pulse. Please. Please, please, please . . .

No shiver. Not a hint. Mauro was dead. He was dead. How would I ever explain it to his wife? How . . . ? Who would look after all the dogs he raised . . . ? He was just alive, just a minute ago. He would never go home. He was just dead. I felt so hollow, so ragged, as if my soul had been shredded to pieces. It hurt. It just hurt so much.

When the National Guardsmen came to pry us out of the vault, I was sitting by Mauro's body, Robert was trying to call to the Pack from the Order's phone, and Nick was kicking Ted Moynohan's corpse and growling like a rabid animal.

≡ CHAPTER ≡

10

ONCE THE MSDU took over the scene, they found the Order's petition and released us. The last I saw of Nick Feldman, he was surrounded by soldiers. There was no getting to him. We had convinced the National Guard to give us a lift to one of the Pack offices. From there Robert and I had loaded Desandra, Derek, and Ascanio into a Pack vehicle and driven to the Keep. None of the three moved. They were still breathing, but we needed to get them to Doolittle.

I walked into the Keep two hours before dawn, covered in drying blood and limping. My face must've been terrible, because people moved out of my way.

The Keep was crowded. Every shapeshifter in the city who didn't evacuate had traveled here.

Barabas came running down the stairs.

"Curran?"

"No word yet."

"Julie?"

"Should be in Virginia by now."

I turned around. The Keep had gone quiet around me. People stood in the hallways and on the stairs, waiting. I was the Consort. I was their alpha.

My voice rang out in the sudden silence. "Bring me Dorie Davis! Bring her to me alive!"

Everyone moved. People dashed in all directions, some human, some furry. The Keep sprang to life.

Behind me Robert roared, "We need a medic!"

Jim appeared as if by magic.

"I need to tell you some things. Come upstairs."

I marched upstairs into one of the conference rooms and landed in a chair. Some time ago I had gone to a place where pain didn't matter, but now it was coming back again, gnawing at me. Everything hurt. Jim followed me.

Thirty minutes later I finished talking.

Jim leaned forward and flashed his teeth. "Hugh fucked up."

"Yes. He'd had the advantage, what with us being the guilty party, and he pissed it away by attacking the Order. He'll still bring the People here, but now the city won't help him."

"We can use this," Jim said. I could almost see the wheels in his head spinning.

"We need Dorie Davis."

"I'll find her," Jim promised. "We can work with this, Kate. The MSDU and PAD were staying neutral, but this just changed the game."

"Maxine called Nick the crusader Nikolas Feldman," I said.

"Interesting last name," Jim said.

"Is he related to Greg Feldman?"

"I don't know," Jim said.

"Nick showed up right after Greg was killed, he involved himself in the investigation, and he has the same last name. When this is over, I need you to find out if Greg Feldman had a younger brother or a son." Because that would just be the cherry on the bloody sundae of the past twenty-four hours.

"Likely a brother. Greg was about forty when he died," Jim said.

"No, Greg looked about forty. He looked like that for the last fifteen years I knew him. Who did you send to North Carolina?"

"A unit with three renders and our two best trackers. They'll find him, Kate. No worries."

If they didn't, I would. I would look for Curran and I would not stop.

"I've got this from here," Jim said. "Rest. I'll send Doolittle up."

Last time I checked, the good doctor was still in a wheelchair. It would be a lot easier for me to go down the stairs than for him to come up. "Not now. There are three sick people downstairs. He'll be busy for a bit anyway."

I still didn't know if they would live or die.

Jim rose and leaned on the table, closing the distance between me and him. "You look like hell."

"Thanks." I felt like hell. I felt like I had walked through it, wading through blood and dragging a giant rock behind me.

"Go upstairs, take a shower, and sleep. You pulled us out of the quicksand. We've got a fighting chance now. You earned an hour of sleep."

I forced the words out. My voice was hoarse. "A whole hour, oh boy!"

"An hour, then I'm sending Doolittle up. I need you to be at the top of your game. Go," Jim said. "I'll wake you up if the sky starts falling."

He left.

I sat alone in the chair. I felt completely empty, like someone had drained me of all anxiety, fear, and anger. It was still there, simmering under the surface, but fatigue had taken over.

I was so tired. My God, I was so, so tired.

I covered my face and waited for the tears. I'd brought this on us. It would've happened eventually. The Pack had grown and Roland wanted to limit its power. But my presence had accelerated the process. I had watched as the entire Atlanta chapter of the Order was slaughtered. I wanted to cry just to let the pain bleed out of me, but my eyes were dry.

I would've given anything to have Curran walk through the door behind me. I could imagine him doing it. He would walk in, put his arms around me, and it would all be better.

I stared at the door.

Please walk through it. Please.

The door remained shut.

This wasn't the way it was supposed to be. When we prepared to fight d'Ambray, we always assumed we'd be together. We would be a team. I hadn't realized how much stronger that belief had made me and how much I had leaned on it until he was gone. Now I felt like my crutch had been jerked out from under me. Well, fate had once again confirmed that when you assume, you make an ass of you and me.

I leaned back and rested my head on the chair's back. It'd been twenty-four hours since I slept. My side hurt. My left arm was going numb. Breaking Hugh's ward had cost me. My ribs hurt.

So tired . . .

The Keep would hold against anything Hugh would muster. Of course, it would hold. Even if Hugh had brought every vampire in the People's stable, it would hold.

I needed to drag myself up and go down to the third floor to see if Doolittle had an update. Just another minute to rest and I would get up . . .

THE PLAIN ROLLED out before me, far into the distance. It looked like some magical giant had cut the world in half: the bottom was a vast field, the blades of dried grass frosted white with snow, and above it, endless, painted with the pink and orange of sunrise, the sky soared. A colossal tower rose from the grass, silhouetted against the sky, impossibly tall.

The wind stirred my hair. It smelled of wheat.

The clouds churned above the tower.

Anxiety drowned me. I gritted my teeth.

A man strode toward me through the grass. He wore black pants and a fisherman's sweater of undyed gray wool. Ice crunched under his shoes. Magic shrouded his face. It emanated from him, controlled, but too powerful to be hidden, folded around him the way a condor might fold his wings when not in flight.

A voice rolled through the field, lifting the dead grass. "Child . . ."

I jerked upright.

The door of the room swung open and Doolittle rolled in. He looked the way he usually looked, a black man in his midfifties, his hair touched by gray, his eyes intelligent and kind.

"I told Jim not to bother you."

"First, it's not a bother, it's my job. And with you, young lady, it's also a challenge. Every time you return to the Keep I wonder what new and inventive way you've found to injure yourself." Doolittle looked at me. "Unless you're implying that my chair is somehow preventing me from doing my work. In that case, I can . . ."

"No, it's not what I meant. I just thought stairs would be inconvenient."

"That's why I have interns. They carried me up here. I thought of commissioning a palanquin. Something understated."

"With silk and crimson velvet?"

"And golden tassels." Doolittle rolled forward. "Then I could be transported in a manner appropriate to my vast experience and wisdom. Off with the shirt."

Arguing with Doolittle was like trying to block the tide from coming in. I pulled off the sweater the witches had given me. Ow. Ow. "It was the guards, wasn't it?"

"In all fairness, they let you sleep for two hours before they became concerned and called for help."

I stripped down to my sports bra.

Doolittle sighed.

I looked down. My entire left side had gone blue and purple. "I think I have a cracked rib."

He examined my side, whispering under his breath. "I think you have three."

Ow.

I couldn't avoid the question any longer. "How are they?"

"Derek and Desandra will live," Doolittle said. "They lost their teeth, nails, and hair and had to have several blood transfusions, but now the poison is out of their bodies. They're weak, but that's nothing a few good meals and some rest won't fix."

"Ascanio?"

"He's eating soup downstairs."

I blinked. "You're kidding me."

"No. And trust me, right now he has much bigger problems. His alpha and his mother are both in the Keep, so he's getting chewed out in stereo. It's quite frightening. No more questions until I'm done."

Doolittle put two fingers into his mouth and whistled. The door swung open and Agatha, one of Curran's and my guards, stuck her head into the room.

"Wheel my cart in, please. I need water, and the Consort needs a fresh change of clothes."

I PULLED ON my T-shirt. Agatha and I had a mild argument over Evdokia's sweater. I wanted to put it back on and she pointed out that it was filthy and smelled of unnatural and very noxious things. We reached a compromise. She would have it washed and dried to get the wendigo guts off it and then I would put it back on. The witches told me to wear it. I saw no reason not to. My side still hurt, but the pain had subsided to a dull ache. I sat next to Doolittle. Agatha had brought us some iced tea and honey. The guards had made the tea, so for once I was safe from falling asleep immediately after medical treatment. Doolittle had a bad habit of lacing his tea with sedatives. According to him, it saved him from arguing with hard cases about taking their prescribed rest.

We sipped our tea. This was the calm before the storm, and I welcomed it. It was selfish, but there was something about Doolittle's presence that steadied me.

"Who healed Ascanio?" Doolittle asked quietly.

"Hugh d'Ambray."

"The same man who healed me when my neck was broken?"

"Yes." The injury had left Doolittle's legs paralyzed, but without Hugh he would've died. I never knew why Hugh did it. He asked me if I wanted Doolittle to live, I said yes, and he pulled Doolittle back from the brink of death.

Doolittle frowned and drank his tea. "Ascanio is seven pounds lighter than his last weigh-in, which was less than a week ago. Hugh didn't just mend bones. He forced Ascanio's body to absorb the bone matrix and build entirely new tissue."

"Could you do that?"

"Yes, but it would take me hours. Possibly days. How long did you say he worked on him?"

"Maybe six or seven minutes."

Doolittle's face turned serious. "Let me show you something."

He looked down. I looked down too, at his feet in white socks.

Doolittle made fists with his toes. I blinked to make sure I wasn't seeing things. No, he was making fists with his toes.

"You're getting better." The relief washed over me. I was drowning in grief and I had no defenses against it.

"It appears to be so. It is possible that in a few years I may even walk again."

I hugged him.

He hugged me back gently.

Something hot and wet slid over my cheeks. I realized I was crying.

"Oh no," Doolittle murmured and patted my hair. "No, no, none of that now. If you do that, I'm going to tear up and I'm too old for that."

I let him go and sat down. He cleared his throat.

"This chair, Kate, it isn't a bad thing."

"But you can't walk."

He raised his hand. "Hear me out. Before this injury, I had never been seriously ill. I'm a physician who understood what it's like to be sick but had never personally felt the impact of a life-threatening disease or experienced a significant injury. This chair made me a better physician. It has given me a new perspective. Tell me, when you see me rolling toward you in the hall, do you see me or do you see the chair?"

"I see you." Of course I saw him. He was still Doolittle.

He smiled. "My point exactly. I've come to believe that the word 'disabled' is a misnomer. 'Disabled' implies that you are broken beyond use. No longer functional. I'm quite abled. I may no longer participate in field operations, but I'm a better teacher now. I require additional arrangements to negotiate a flight of stairs, but I stop to smell the proverbial roses more often. I'm fortunate to have bowel control, and while my bladder requires occasional use of a catheter, I refuse to be defined by which functions my body can or cannot perform well. Quite frankly, I'm more than the sum of my physical parts. I've come to terms with my new life and achieved personal happiness. Whether or not I will recover pales in comparison. Does that make sense?"

"It does."

I poured him more tea and poured myself some.

"I should've been dead," he said. "I have no prior experience with this specific injury on which to base my judgment, so I don't know if this partial recovery comes because Lyc-V is repairing my body or if this is the result of what Hugh did, an extended residual healing. I believe that every time the magic wave comes, it heals me a little more, but it's not something I can measure. Ascanio should be dead as well."

"But he isn't." I still couldn't quite believe it. As soon as I had a free minute, I'd go down to the med ward and beat the shit out of Ascanio for his wendigo heroics. Assuming there was anything left of him after Andrea and Martina were done with him.

Maybe I was dreaming. Maybe all this was just wishful thinking.

"He's remarkable," Doolittle said.

"Hugh?"

"Yes. I'm a powerful medmage, but he is truly gifted." Doolittle looked at me. "He's a miracle worker."

"Sometimes. Mostly he's a butcher."

"I'm trying to understand why."

I sighed. "Voron, my adoptive father, found Hugh on the street in England. Hugh was seven years old. His mother died when he was four and somehow he ended up begging instead of being sent through the system. The homeless fed him, because he could cure them. When Voron found him, he was borderline feral.

"Voron took the boy to Roland, who determined that Hugh had an enormous magic reservoir at his disposal. His raw power is staggering, and Roland saw an opportunity. At the time Voron served as Roland's warlord, but Roland knew he would need a replacement. Voron had no magic power. He was a supreme swordsman and strategist, but his time was at an end. Magic was growing stronger and stronger and Roland realized he would need someone who could use it. Hugh was in the right place at the right time. Roland gave him to Voron and my adoptive father forged him into a general the way one would forge a sword. He did an excellent job and that's how Hugh became the lovely psychopath we all know and want to kill."

Doolittle's eyes widened. "He could've been anything. He could've saved thousands over his lifetime. The amount of good he could've done. What kind of twisted mind would look at that miracle child and make him into a killer?"

"That's how Roland works. He sees the hidden potential in people."

Doolittle drew back. "That's not potential."

"Yes, it is. Hugh enjoys what he does. He's frighteningly good at it."

Doolittle shook his head.

I rose. "Look out the window."

Doolittle rolled his chair up to the window and looked down at the courtyard for a moment.

"What did you see?"

"People working."

I turned to the window, glanced down briefly, and then turned my back to it. "Left tower, four people, two men on top working on the scorpio, a woman in the second-floor window with a crossbow, a man on the balcony. Courtyard left to right: two women in the far left corner working on a Jeep; Jim, talking to Yolanda and Colin, who are his trackers; a man and two teenagers carrying beams, probably to reinforce the gate. The man has a knee injury and favors his left leg."

"Three teenagers," Doolittle said. "One caught up while you were talking."

"This is how I was trained. It's part of the skill set I needed to survive. This is what I do. If I had to, I could go through that courtyard with a sword and cut my way through them. It would cost me, but at the end I would kill or maim all of them and on some deep level I would enjoy it, because I would be doing what I'm good at, what I've been trained to do. Hugh is like me. You look at him and see the special child who was diverted from his path. I look at him and see a man who revels in what he does. Hugh could've healed thousands, but he would've never been as happy as when he slaughtered the Order's knights in their own chapterhouse."

"It's not always about one's personal happiness. Sometimes it has to be about the obligation we have to others. A duty to pay back for the gift you were given."

"Is that why you became a physician?"

Doolittle sighed. "I was already a physician, a very freshly minted one, but still a physician, when I realized I had medical magic. It came together with the shapeshifting. That last bit I had kept to myself. I wasn't sure what to think or how to handle it. At that point, medical magic was new, and to have someone with the capability who already had medical knowledge was very rare. I was one of two physicians with medmage abilities in our graduating class. Jim's father, Eric Shrapshire, was the other. We both found ourselves in a delicate position. There was a lot of pressure to go into research. We both received offers to go private, catering to a single family on an exclusive basis. A lot of the offers were very lucrative and I was seriously considering some of them."

"So why didn't you take them?"

"One night Eric called me and told me that he'd made up his mind. He'd watched a documentary on loupism. It affected him deeply and he realized this was his calling. In the chaos of post-Shift Atlanta, he realized that shapeshifters, with their regeneration and resistance to diseases, would be overlooked. The attention of the medical community would center on human diseases, because regular humans would be the most vulnerable. Normal people saw shapeshifters as monsters, and monsters would be the last on the list no matter how much they needed help. He felt he could make a real difference by working to aid shapeshifters." Doolittle looked up at me. "He didn't know I was one of the 'monsters.' He saw people in need being neglected and he chose to help them. He felt it was his duty, while I was selfishly trying to select the best combination of benefits and money. I decided then that I could do no less."

Jim's father had died for what he believed in. One day he was brought a child who'd gone loup and committed multiple murders. Despite this, he had hidden her rather than euthanizing her, as required by law. The crime was discovered, he was convicted, and in the first week of his jail sentence, another inmate stabbed him to death. Years later Jim had tracked down his father's killer and made him pay.

"I had joined the Pack," Doolittle said. "Took a new name. Beatrice, Aunt B, had vouched for me. She and my wife had been best friends."

"I didn't know you were married."

"She passed away a long time ago. In another life."

"If you hadn't become the monster doctor, would you still practice medicine?" I asked.

"Yes."

"Hugh and I would still practice murder. We're two sides of the same coin."

"Exactly," Doolittle said. "The opposite sides. Why did you choose to work for the Guild?"

"Partially because I was hiding in plain sight."

"And?"

It was my turn to sigh. "Because I wanted to be happy with what I did with my life. I had done some things when I was a child. I don't blame myself for them. I did them because the adult in my life directed me to do them and praised me when I succeeded. But when I grew up, looking back at what I had done became difficult. I wanted to help someone for a change. The Guild let me choose which jobs I took, and I got to be 'the good guy,' if only for a while."

"And that's the crucial difference between you and Hugh. He's an aggressor, and you're the protector." Doolittle leaned forward. "You could've been a hired killer or someone's private weapon. Instead you chose to protect everyone around you. It's as natural to you as breathing and I selfishly count myself to be very lucky to benefit from that, even if that urge sometimes takes you too far."

The way he said "too far" threw me right back to a few months ago, when he had come to after Hugh had healed him. I sat down so we would be on the same level. This had to be said. I just didn't know how to say it. I decided to just barrel right through it. "You don't have to worry. I know how you feel about my particular brand of magic. I hope it never comes to that, but if it does, I won't pull you back from death like I did Julie."

What I had done to Julie wasn't healing. She didn't know it, but it made her unable to refuse a direct order from me. I remembered the fear in Doolittle's eyes when he regained consciousness and thought I had taken away his free will with my magic. Sometimes I dreamed about that, too.

Doolittle froze for a painful second. His voice was quiet. "Was I that easy to read?"

"You had just come back from death," I said.

"I meant no offense. When I spoke about going too far, I meant that your urge to protect sometimes ends with you being hurt. You take on too much. But we might as well get this out in the open. I appreciate everything you're willing to do, but I won't live as anyone's slave. My family has been legally free since 1865 and I won't surrender my freedom no matter how benevolent of a master I'll get. I would rather be dead."

"I understand," I told him.

We sat quietly for a few long moments.

Doolittle reached over and touched my hand. "Your brand of magic is . . ."

"Evil?"

"I was going to say frightening. I don't fear you. I don't fear who you want to be. I do fear who you might become in spite of yourself. But you don't need to be defined by your magic or an old man's fears. There is a good word for the kind of person you are—honorable. It might be old-fashioned, but it fits. I'm glad I have the privilege of knowing you."

I forced a smile. "Even if I don't follow your prescriptions and you have to drug me with your iced tea to keep me off my feet?"

Doolittle smiled. "Even so. Speaking of prescriptions, you are to stay off your feet for as long as you can."

"Absolutely." I got up. "I'll open the door for you."

Doolittle growled. "At least have the decency to wait to ignore me until I leave."

"Ehh, sorry." I held the door open for him.

"My life would be much easier without so many hard cases in it," he grumbled.

"You love us, Doc. You know you do. We keep you busy. Without us, there's no guessing what sort of trouble your idle hands would lead you into."

11

I WENT TO my room, took a shower, and lay on the ridiculously large sofa in our living room. Curran's quarters were sized to his beast form. The bed, the tub, the sofas, everything was built to accommodate an enormous prehistoric lion. But in all of our time together, I had never actually seen him use the sofa as a lion. On the rare days when he trotted into our rooms in his fur, he usually lounged about in the tub or lay on the floor, and I usually ended up on the floor with him, leaning against his side and reading a book. Maybe it was the principle of the thing.

I missed him. Still no word on whether he was dead or alive.

I glanced at the clock. Eight forty-five a.m. Three hours and fifteen minutes until Hugh's deadline.

They should've found Curran by now.

I would take Hugh apart. I would wipe that smug grin off his face. He wouldn't have a face once I was done.

But I had to wait. Wait for Double D, wait for Hugh's next move, wait for Curran to be found. I fucking hated waiting.

I forced myself off the couch. I had to get dressed and be seen. With Curran gone, the Pack would look for me. The People would be moving on us soon. I needed to check our defenses and to field questions from the Pack Council. I needed to check on Derek, Desandra, and Ascanio.

A knock sounded on my door.

"Come in."

Andrea strode in, her face hard. "You okay?"

"I'm fine."

"I came back twice earlier and your goons wouldn't let me in." Andrea landed in a chair. "I haven't heard from Raphael."

She had known I'd ask.

"Anything from Curran?"

I shook my head. "I have something to tell you and you won't like it."

I explained about Nick and the massacre at the chapterhouse.

Andrea's face turned white. She locked her hands together into a fist and bent her head toward it. Her fingers went pale from the pressure. "All of them died?"

I nodded.

"And Mauro?"

"Yes."

"Are you okay?" Andrea asked.

"I'm peachy." My voice sounded brittle and bitter.

"I thought something might happen with the Order, but not this," she said. "Not this bad."

"You thought something bad would happen?"

She grimaced as if she'd bitten into a rotten lemon. "After Erra almost took out the Atlanta chapter, Ted fell out of favor."

"Been keeping tabs?"

"Oh yes. I always keep tabs on people I may need to kill."

She sounded just like Aunt B.

"Moynohan was never one of the best knight-protectors, but he'd been with the Order since the beginning."

"A knight-founder, I know. Mauro told me."

Andrea leaned back. "I started to guess which way the wind was blowing when I found out that he had repeatedly refused efforts to increase the chapter's size."

"Why?" I'd never understood why a city the size of Atlanta had only seven knights assigned to it.

"Because a chapter of ten members or more requires a knight-diviner," Andrea said.

A knight-diviner functioned like a chaplain in regular Army units. Greg Feldman, my now-deceased guardian, had been one. He handled whatever personal issues the other knights could throw at him, and they threw quite a few.

"I spoke to a couple of the new knights who'd transferred in," Andrea continued. "Ted wasn't shy about bending the rules to get where he was going, and he wanted a group of knights loyal enough to bend the rules with him. A knight-diviner would've diluted his authority. That's one of the reasons why he let you in, by the way. He saw you as a nobody with a talent and a chip on your shoulder after your guardian died. He thought that if he gave you your big chance, you'd spend the rest of your life thanking him for it."

Well, wasn't he in for a surprise. "I bet he opened a bottle when Greg died."

"Probably." Andrea sighed. "I never thought he would retire. His ego was too big. He'd want to go out in a blaze of glory. Well, he did it, the asshole. He got his last hurrah. People died for it. God, poor Nick. He must've been through hell and Ted just burned him. That's years thrown away. I would've killed him."

"He was kicking his corpse the last I saw him."

Andrea grimaced.

"The Order isn't going to help us, is it?" I asked.

She faced me squarely. "No."

Shit. "That's what I thought." The Order didn't like the Pack or the People. It had no reason to get between them. They would come down, they would investigate, and they would hunt Hugh like a rabid dog, but counting on them to intervene for our benefit now was futile. Even if they were willing to help, they wouldn't get here in time or in large enough numbers to make a difference.

"What are you going to do?" Andrea asked.

"I don't know. Ask me after we recover Double D."

She raised her head. "Whatever it is, Clan Bouda will back you up."

"Thank you." At least my best friend was still in my corner.

"Thank you for saving Ascanio," she said.

"I didn't."

"Yes, you did." Andrea looked at me. "I should've gone to the Conclave with you."

"You went last time."

"You needed me to watch your back." She sighed. "Sarah got herself arrested up in South Carolina, and I went there personally to get her out. I should've just sent a Pack lawyer, but I went myself because I feel like Aunt B's looking over my shoulder. I feel like I have to be everywhere and do everything. I never thought I'd say this, but I miss her. I so wish she were here."

"I know the feeling."

Andrea hesitated, opened her mouth, and closed it without saying a word.

"What is it?"

"I'm pregnant."

I closed my mouth with a click. "Congratulations!"

She stared at me and spread her arms as if to say, *There it is.*

"How are you? How far along?"

"Four weeks. I'm not sick yet. I just had a feeling, so I checked."

"Are you okay?"

She leaned forward, her voice barely above a whisper. "I'm so scared."

I had no idea what to say. I'd be scared, too. "Did you tell Doolittle?"

"Not yet."

"You need to tell Doolittle. You need to take panacea." And I was pretty sure neither she nor I knew how much to take. "Does Raphael know?"

She shook her head. "I took the test yesterday."

Oh crap. We still didn't know if Curran and Raphael were even alive.

"I know exactly how Jennifer felt when Daniel died," Andrea said. "Raphael didn't even want to go. He was trying to win a bid on some building for the business, and I told him, 'Go, honey. We're brand-new alphas and this will make us look good.'"

"They'll be fine," I said.

"Of course they'll be fine."

We looked at each other and made a silent effort to believe our own bullshit.

ANDREA LEFT AND I took myself down to the medward. Desandra and Derek had been treated, given a dinner, and both were asleep.

One of Doolittle's nurses told me that Ascanio's mother was with him. They probably needed some private time, so I went into the observation hallway instead. Dim and narrow, it ran along the individual patient rooms, offering a one-way window into each. Sean, a nurse in training, nodded to me from his perch on a pillow in the corner. An intensive care unit for shapeshifters meant patients who could go loup at any minute. The rooms were reinforced and someone was keeping an eye on them 24/7 until the danger passed.

Ascanio lay under the sheets. His color was almost back to normal. His mother sat by his bed reading him a book. He said something. Judging by his grin, he thought he was funny. His mother sighed.

The door opened and Robert joined me.

"He's recovering," the alpha rat said.

"Yes."

Robert glanced at Sean. "Would you mind giving us a minute?"

Sean rose and left the room.

"I spoke to my husband," Robert said.

"This sounds ominous."

"I like you a great deal," he said. "He respects and values my opinion of you."

"But?" There was always a "but" attached.

Robert looked at the ceiling for a long moment. "I'm trying to find the right way to say this."

"Go ahead, I've braced myself."

"If Curran's death is confirmed, the question of your retaining leadership will arise. There may be a no-confidence vote."

Well, that didn't take long. "Have you heard something?"

"Yes."

That came out of nowhere. I guess I'd been too complacent and this was my wake-up call. I had no plans to lead the Pack without Curran, but it still stung. I had fought hard for them, and I thought I'd earned the Pack's respect. What else did they need from me?

Robert frowned. "I might be asked about my experience during last night. I plan to answer truthfully. I realize it's not the best timing, but I don't want you to feel stabbed in the back."

"Was there something wrong with my conduct last night?"

Robert met my gaze. "People like to assign their leaders noble qualities. Generosity, kindness, selflessness. The hard truth of it is, the best leaders are ruthless. Curran is ruthless. As long as there is a chance of him being alive, we will support you. We like you as a pair. You balance each other out."

"So you don't think I'm ruthless enough?"

Robert nodded at Ascanio. "I like the boy. He's smart and brave. Funny. But when Hugh was playing with his life, I would've let him die."

I turned to him.

"I would've mourned him with his mother," Robert said. "I would've felt terrible and grieved. But I would've let d'Ambray kill him. He's just one of the Pack's children. You're the Consort. If you had let yourself be taken by d'Ambray, we would've been leaderless. I would have to go to the Pack with the news that d'Ambray had captured you, and they would have marched on the Casino to either save you or retaliate. It would be a bloodbath. So as painful as it is, I would've let Ascanio die."

"I can't do that." I didn't want to lead, but now I was doing it and that was the only way I knew how.

"I know," Robert said. "I think it goes against your nature. It makes you a better person than many. That's what I am trying to say. We, the alphas, we're not always good people. We try to be, but there are times when there are no good choices. If my clan were running from an enemy, I would sacrifice myself for their sake in a heartbeat. But if they were running to a door only I knew how to open, I would race ahead of them even if it meant that some of those behind me might fall. We think in numbers, not individuals."

I didn't know what I would do. It depended on who was behind me.

"You saved Ascanio," Robert said. "But now Roland and d'Ambray know you have a weakness and they will use it against you. They will take someone you love and threaten to kill them, because they know you won't be able to pass up that bait. You have to prepare to sacrifice your friends."

If I had to do it over again, I would've done the same thing.

"I will stand with you for as long as I can," Robert said. "But if I am asked about what happened in the Order's chapterhouse, I will tell the Pack Council my opinion on it. No matter how I phrase it, all of them will see it in the same light Thomas and I do. I'm sorry."

"No need to apologize." I looked at him. "I respect you as a fighter and as an alpha. Without you we wouldn't have survived the night. If you ever need help, I will help you. You may want to let the Pack Council know that they may call as many votes as they want when this mess is over. However, if any of them do anything to derail my efforts to save our people by starting some sort of no-confidence vote while I'm trying to avert this war, I'll have them confined to their quarters. I'm pretty tired of being judged on every turn, and my patience is short."

Robert nodded. "Yes, Consort."

He walked out. I leaned against the wall. Just what I needed. I hadn't shown Hugh any gaps in my armor. He already knew them; he'd figured me out last summer. Now the Pack knew them as well. The Pack Council would have a field day with it when this was over.

That was fine. I failed Mauro. But Ascanio, Derek, and Desandra survived.

I was beginning to think in numbers. Well, wasn't that sad?

The door swung open and Jim loomed in the doorway. "We found Double D."

I STRODE THROUGH the hallways at a near run. "Where did you find her?"

"She was hiding at her cousin's house in the attic," Jim said.

"Have you called the alphas?"

"Yes."

"The rats, too?"

He bristled. "What about the rats?"

"They think you're hiding information from them."

"I hide information from everyone. Do they think they're special?"

I walked into the Pack Council room. A large table dominated the space, and what could be gathered of the Pack Council occupied the chairs: Robert and Thomas Lonesco; Martha, the female alpha of Clan Heavy; the betas from Clan Nimble, the female alpha of the jackals, Andrea for Clan Bouda, and Desandra, pale and bald.

"Where is the alpha of the wolves?"

George, Mahon's daughter, looked up from her spot at a small desk. "She declined to attend. She sends her apologies." She pointed at Desandra. "She's all we could scrounge up on short notice."

"Yeah," Desandra said, her voice dry. "I'm a substitute alpha."

Well, of course. Because this meeting wouldn't end well for Double D, and Jennifer didn't want to deal with the fallout. When the wolves pitched a fit and demanded to know why one of their own was sent to the People, she would tell them she had nothing to do with it. It was all Desandra's fault. Marvelous.

"I thought your teeth fell out?"

"They did." Desandra bared a new sharp set at me. "I found out I was coming to this meeting and they grew all on their own."

Someone was pissed off.

I walked to the head of the table and sat in my chair, trying to valiantly ignore the fact that Curran's chair stood empty next to me. If I let even a tiny bit of anxiety show, I would lose the Pack Council. They would begin to bicker and we wouldn't come to a decision.

"Bring her in, please," I said.

The door opened and Barabas led Dorie Davis inside. She didn't look like a bombshell. She didn't look like a streetwalker either. She looked perfectly ordinary. A woman in her early thirties, with a rounded face, blue eyes, and a shoulder-length blond bob. Not too athletic, not too curvy. Soft. The kind of woman who probably lived in the suburbs, made school lunches for her kids, and indulged in a glass of wine in the afternoon.

Barabas cleared his throat.

"Go ahead," I told him.

He turned to Dorie. "Before we start, you need to know your rights. Everyone here is either an alpha, an acting alpha, or a member of the legal department. According to state law, no alpha can be compelled to testify against a member of their pack. The State of Georgia has no jurisdiction in this room. Nothing disclosed here can be used against you in a court of law."

But it could be used against her in ours.

"Tell me what happened last night," I said.

Dorie sighed, her face defeated. "I met Mulradin at the Fox Den."

"Was he a regular client?" Robert asked.

"Yes, for the last ten months. He paid well. We had sex. He was getting ready for round two when someone busted through the door. There were six of them and they had shotguns. I was in my wolf form with a collar on and chained to the wall. One of them fired into the wall and showed the rest of the bullets to me. They were silver. The big one with dark hair told me that they would take turns shooting me. He said that I wouldn't die right away. He said they would keep shooting me until I did what they wanted me to do."

"Did you try to escape?" I asked.

"They were pointing shotguns at me."

I took that as a no. "Describe the 'big one' to me."

"In his thirties, over six feet tall. Very good shape. Muscular. Dark hair. Blue eyes."

Hugh. "What happened then?"

"He told me that I had to kill Mulradin. If I tore him up, they would let me go."

She stopped.

"So?"

"So I did." Her voice was flat. "He screamed a lot. It was horrible. Then they took off my collar and I ran."

So simple. No big mystery. Hugh had held her at gunpoint so he could manufacture this whole incident.

"Where did you go?" I asked.

"To my cousin's house. She owed me some money, and I knew she'd hide me."

"You didn't notify your clan or your alpha?" the beta of Clan Nimble asked.

"No."

"Why not?"

Dorie sighed again. "Why not, why not? Because I didn't want to be arrested. I didn't want to go to jail. I just wanted it all to go away. I wanted my life back."

"I'm sure Mulradin did, too," I said. "Did anybody see you leave the crime scene?"

"No."

I looked at Jim. "We have no witnesses and Hugh moved the body from the original scene." A good defense attorney could do wonders arguing that any evidence found on the body was contaminated.

"You're thinking surrender?" Jim's eyebrows rose an eighth of an inch.

I was thinking I wanted to avoid killing Dorie and sending her head out on a pike.

"They filmed it," Dorie said.

I turned to her. "What?"

"They filmed it," she said. "While I killed him."

Hugh had made a snuff film. Why was I not surprised?

"This alters things," Thomas Lonesco said.

I nodded to Juan, one of Jim's people standing by the door. "Put her under guard, please. Make sure she's watched."

He took her by the arm.

"What will happen to me?" Dorie asked.

"Come on." Juan pulled her.

She came to life suddenly, flailing in his arms. "I don't want to die! I don't want to die! Don't kill me!"

He picked her up and carried her out of the room.

I waited until her sobs receded and stared down the Pack Council. My memory replayed Curran's advice for dealing with the Council in my head. *I never go into the Council room without a plan. You have to give them a range of possibilities, but if they discuss them too much, they'll never make a decision. Steer them toward the right choice and don't let them derail the train.*

Steer them toward the right choice. Sure. Easy as pie. "As you know, the People intend to start a war. They are likely moving toward the Keep now. We have several courses of action opened to us. We can surrender Dorie to the People. Opinions?"

I waited.

"No," Jim said.

"We'd lose too much influence," Martha said. "Pass."

"No," Andrea said.

"No," Thomas Lonesco said.

That gave me a majority. Surrendering to the People was off the table. "Option two, we can execute Dorie and show proof of it to the People."

The pause was longer this time. They were thinking it over.

"No," Robert said.

"No," Martha agreed. "We don't kill our own without a trial."

A trial would take time. We all knew it.

Nobody else volunteered anything, so I kept going.

"Option three, we keep Dorie and tell the People to screw themselves."

"The casualties would be staggering," Thomas Lonesco said.

"If they want a fight, we can give them a fight," Desandra said. "But we're at reduced strength and it will be bloody."

"This isn't an option for me," Jim said.

"So, we don't want to execute Dorie or turn her over to the People, and we don't want to go to war," I said. "That leaves us with only one option. We can surrender her to state law enforcement."

The silence dropped on the table like a heavy brick.

Desandra frowned. "So like what, here's Dorie, here's her confession, take her off our hands?"

"Yes," I said. "Technically the murder was committed in Atlanta, which makes it the business of Atlanta's finest. If they take her into custody, the People can deal with them. Our hands would be clean. We'd remove their pretext for the war."

"We'd be abdicating control over the situation," Thomas Lonesco said. "Yes," I confirmed.

Martha turned to Barabas. "If we do this, what are her chances in court?"

Barabas grimaced. "Under Georgia law, and U.S. common law in general, duress or coercion is not a defense to homicide. The idea is that a person should not place their life above the lives of others."

"Could it be self-defense?" the beta of Clan Nimble asked.

"No," Barabas said. "Self-defense, by definition, is only applicable against the aggressor. Mulradin wasn't an aggressor, he was a victim. To impose any kind of criminal liability, one has to prove both *actus reus*, the guilty act, and the *mens rea*, the guilty mind. Dorie committed the act, and if she denied it, there is videotaped evidence. That gives us the *actus reus*. Even if everyone believes her defense, that she had to choose between her life and Mulradin's, the fact is, she made that choice, which means she meant to kill him. We now have both ingredients for a speedy conviction."

"So the death penalty?" the Jackal alpha asked.

"Not necessarily. The big question is what will the DA want to do with this. If this is malicious homicide, and they would be fools not to charge her with that, we have to fight the death penalty. We can try to negotiate it down to voluntary homicide, which is a pointless battle unless we have something to trade. It's possible they hate d'Ambray and will want her testimony if they manage to apprehend him and charge him. It's also possible that they don't want to take d'Ambray on and they would rather bury Dorie six feet under. Can we use it to our advantage? It depends on who's in charge of the prosecution. An election is coming up. Do they want to plead it out quietly or do they want to make it an election issue? If we do go to trial, can we poke holes in their evidence? We don't even know what the evidence is at this point, but the video will be difficult to circumvent. Dorie herself will be difficult. She is an unlikable defendant: she is a prostitute who engaged in bestiality with a married man."

"I'd think the married man would be more unlikable," Andrea growled.

"And you would be right, but he isn't on trial. We can put him on trial, but it's always a gamble. Who is the judge? Who are the jurors? Will attacking the victim predispose them to hate our client? Dorie is a shapeshifter,"

Barabas continued. "The general public views her as being prone to violence."

"Can you just give us a straight answer?" Jim growled.

Barabas pointed at Jim. "See? Prone to violence. And no, I can't. You gave me a client who committed a murder under duress and who will likely have to confess to it to satisfy the People and asked me a question about her chances. I'm answering."

My head was beginning to hurt. "Could you give us the idiot version, then?"

Barabas held up his hand. "Possible outcomes in order of most likely first." He bent one finger. "One, conviction for malicious homicide, life in prison without possibility of parole or death penalty before a judge or jury. Two!" He bent his second finger. "Conviction for the lesser offense of voluntary manslaughter in front of a judge or jury. Three, a plea deal for a negotiated sentence or possibly immunity depending on how much they want to get at Hugh d'Ambray. That's subject to many different factors. Four, acquittal before a judge or a jury based on reasonable doubt. Not bloody likely. Five, jury nullification. That would constitute a Hail Mary pass on our part. Jury nullification is much more rare than people think, and we would have to prove to the jury that Dorie was a victim of some great injustice. Six, we somehow blow holes in the prosecution's case and get the whole thing dismissed. The likelihood of this last one is difficult to gauge because we don't even know what evidence the prosecution has. Let me remind all of you that they may not have been notified of Mulradin's murder."

Silence claimed the table.

"If we go to the State with this," Martha said, "they'll use everything they have to smear all of us. There is a price to be paid here."

"True," the male beta of Clan Nimble said.

"We'll face restrictions again," the female alpha of Clan Jackal said.

"The alternative is worse," I said.

"Depends on how you look at it," Martha said. "No good choices, it's true."

I was losing them. My train was rapidly sliding off the rails.

Robert glanced at me and said very carefully. "What is the penalty for Dorie's actions under Pack law?"

"Death," Barabas said. "It was a malicious murder. A life for a life applies."

He was helping me. I grabbed onto the straw. It was a weak straw, but people drowning in quicksand couldn't be choosers.

"As alphas we have an obligation to our Pack members." I made a mental note to thank Barabas again for making me learn the Pack laws backward and forward. "We must ensure the overall safety of the Pack and its individual members. Our first priority is the preservation of life."

"We know, dear," Martha said. "We've read the laws."

"Barabas, what sentence would Dorie get if we gave her to the People?"

"Death," he said.

"What if we try her?"

"Death."

"What will she get if we turn her over to the State?"

"I don't know," Barabas said. "I can tell you that we will fight our hardest to keep the death penalty off the table."

"So it's a maybe?"

"It's a maybe." He nodded.

"Death, death, maybe." I looked around the Council. "I vote for maybe. Who's with me?"

Five minutes later the Council filed out of the room. Martha stopped next to me. "Nicely done."

"Not really," I said. "Have you heard from Mahon?"

She shook her head. "Don't worry. They'll show up."

I hoped she was right.

At the door Jim spoke to someone and turned to me. "I just got a phone call from the city. The People have emptied the Casino's stables. They're coming for us."

12

I STOOD ON the balcony of the main building, watching the last of the stragglers come in. They glanced at me as they arrived. I was wearing Evdokia's sweater and doing my best to broadcast confidence. It was ten eighteen. There was no sign of the People yet, but Jim's scouts reported a large number of vampires moving out of the city in the Keep's direction. The scouts estimated at least seventy. Navigators had a limited range, which meant that the People's Masters of the Dead and their journeymen had to be traveling with the undead.

This was an extremely unwise move. Somewhere en route, Ghastek was gritting his teeth. Keeping that many undead together in one place required iron control on the part of the navigators. There was a reason why the vampires spent most of their time under the Casino confined in steel cages and chained to the walls. Even a single loose bloodsucker was a disaster.

If I were ruthless, I'd take our renders, clear a path through the undead, and let my guys wipe out the People. Once the navigators were dead, the unchained vampires would swarm us. I wasn't sure how many I could handle, but I was willing to bet I could control enough to push them off us and into the wilderness. They would make their way to the city and slaughter anything that breathed. By morning Atlanta would be the city of the dead. The blame would fall on the People and we would live happily ever after, at least until my father decided to engage in revenge for the shit storm this butchery would dump on his head.

Fortunately for Atlanta, I wasn't Hugh d'Ambray. Atlanta wouldn't die today if I could help it. Once the first vampire was sighted, the gates would be barred. I would do everything in my power to reason with the navigators, but if I failed, we would not attack. Curran had built this Keep to withstand a siege. If that was the way they wanted it, so be it. A line from my favorite book came to mind. *Have fun storming the castle, Hugh.*

A woman in faded jeans and a heavy jacket strode through the Gates. A hood hid her hair. She marched through the snow like she meant business: big steps, a determined set to her shoulders, and a straight spine. A tall man wearing a black robe walked next to her, carrying a staff on his shoulder. The top of the staff was carved into the semblance of a raven's head with a vicious beak. I knew that staff. It had tried to bite me once. But then considering that its owner was a black volhv in service to an ancient Slavic god of dark and evil, ornery behavior was to be expected. I had it on very good authority that Roman also wore Eeyore pajamas, which made me reevaluate his character somewhat.

Roman was also Evdokia's son, which meant the woman with him was likely a witch. My neutral witnesses had arrived.

The woman said something to Roman. He stopped, turned to her, and shook his staff.

She crossed her arms. I couldn't see her face, but I read the body language well enough. *"I shake my magic stick at you!"* *"Let me tell you what you can do with your stick . . ."*

One of the shapeshifters, a muscular man in his forties, moved to block Roman's path. Roman pointed at me. The man turned to look at me, and I waved them in. The shapeshifter stepped aside to let Roman and the woman pass.

"Jennifer would like to speak with you," Barabas said.

I turned.

Barabas stood in the doorway of the room behind me. He hadn't slept for the last twenty-four hours, but it barely showed. His face seemed sharper than usual, and his hair had lost some of its spikiness, but other than that he was no worse for wear.

I crossed the balcony back into the room. "Have you been able to get Detective Gray on the phone?"

He shook his head. "We're still trying."

Among our contacts in the PAD, Gray was the most sympathetic to the shapeshifters. Normally he always answered the phone, but today he was proving to be elusive. I hoped it was a coincidence. If he was deliberately ducking me, I was in big trouble.

"What does Jennifer want?"

"She didn't specify. Would you like me to tell her you're busy?"

"No." Might as well get this over with.

He nodded and opened the door. "The Consort will see you."

Jennifer walked in. She looked haggard. Her sweatpants hung on her and she carried a water bottle in her hand. Judging by her eyes, there was probably something stronger than water in it. If my body processed alcohol as fast as hers, I would've found me one of those water bottles as well.

Jennifer's blond bodyguard, Brandon, the one who'd mouthed off to me on the bridge, tried to follow her. Barabas blocked his way. Brandon back-pedaled. Barabas followed him out and shut the door behind him.

"What can I do for you?"

Jennifer licked her lips. "I came to talk about Desandra."

Right. The People and Hugh d'Ambray were practically on our doorstep. Now was the perfect time to bug me about her problems. "You want to have this conversation now?"

"Yes."

I leaned against the wall. "Okay. What about Desandra?"

She swallowed. "I want you to expel her from the Pack."

Umm. "On what grounds?"

"She threatens the stability of Clan Wolf."

"Do you have evidence of this?"

Jennifer bared her teeth. "She's trying to force me out."

I sat down on a bench next to the window. "You are not synonymous with Clan Wolf. She isn't threatening the clan. She's threatening your leadership of it."

"A change of leadership right now will destabilize the clan. We're still grieving over Daniel."

Daniel had been dead for over six months now. She was still grieving and I understood that. But the clan had moved on.

"You're asking me to interfere with the selection of the alpha for an individual clan. I have no authority to do that. Not only would the other clans scream bloody murder, but even if I could somehow influence the process, I won't. It's not my place to tell your people whom they should support and choose to govern themselves."

"They support me."

"Then why are you here?"

She struggled with it for a second. "I am the alpha. She is . . ." Jennifer squeezed her hand into a fist. "She's vulgar. One of her sons is a monster."

Desandra was right. Jennifer had no intention of letting a baby lamassu grow up in her clan. If I were Desandra, wild horses wouldn't be able to drag me away from fighting Jennifer for the alpha spot.

"Desandra's child is an infant and a member of the Pack."

Jennifer kept going. "What happens when he grows up?"

"We'll burn that bridge after we cross it."

"I won't let her push me out. It's my place. I'm doing it for my child. For Daniel's child. She'll grow up to be the daughter of an alpha."

She had that half-desperate, half-determined look in her eyes. Right. No intelligent life there. "Why is it so important to be alpha? Why not just step down?"

"Because it's where I belong. Daniel chose me. He chose me out of all the other women in the Pack so I could stand by his side. Daniel didn't make mistakes. He died, and now I have to lead the Pack in his memory, because otherwise he would've died for nothing."

Oh dear God, she had deified her husband. Shapeshifters were already paranoid, but Jennifer's grief combined with her pregnancy must've catapulted her into a seriously bad place. No matter how many rational arguments I made, she wouldn't listen, because I couldn't compete with Daniel's memory.

"Someone asked Desandra the same question," I said. "She said, 'Because I can make the people in the clan safer and happier.'"

Jennifer stared at me, her eyes luminous with green. "You owe me. You killed my sister, my husband died because of the fight you dragged us into, and then you brought Desandra here. If she wins, if you can imagine it for a second, she would tell me what to do. I won't take orders from that bitch!" Her voice rose. "I won't! My child won't call that crude lowlife alpha. You made this mess; you'll fix it for me or you will regret it."

Okay, that was just about enough of that. "No."

Jennifer glared at me, her eyes blazing with green.

"Tone down your flashlights, or I'll resolve this power struggle right here and right now."

She drew back. The glow dimmed.

"Let me spell it out for you. I didn't kill your sister because I felt like it. I killed her because she had turned loup and was in pain. Ending her life was an act of mercy. Daniel didn't die so you could be an alpha. He died so fanatics wouldn't detonate a device that would've killed every shapeshifter in a ten-mile radius. You're fighting Desandra for the confidence of your clan and you're losing. The very fact that you are here now makes you weak. If I helped you, it would only make you look weaker. You have to stand on your own. No bodyguards, no Beast Lord to hide behind, just you."

She stared at me, her face completely white. I should've stopped, but in the past twelve hours I'd run around the frozen city trying to prevent a supernatural war, I'd nearly lost a child who relied on me for protection, and I'd watched Hugh d'Ambray slaughter people and hadn't been able to do a damn thing about it, and all the while, the man I loved was missing. My brakes had malfunctioned and I kept barreling on, right off the cliff.

"Explain to me why I would help you? For the entire time you've known me, you've done nothing but throw rocks at my head. Last night I had to go into the People's territory and I didn't know if we would survive. I went because the future of the entire Pack depended on it. The alpha rat volunteered to go with me. The alpha cat did, too. A member of your clan couldn't wait to join me. A child from the boudas followed me because he wanted to make a difference. They did this because they felt responsible for the safety of their friends. They did it to protect the Pack. Did you volunteer to help me?"

My voice snapped like a whip. Jennifer flinched.

"Did you come with me, Jennifer? Did you fight with me? Did you sacrifice yourself to draw off four vampires, so I could get to where I was going? Did you fight a knight with a kind of magic we've never seen before? Did you throw yourself at a fucking wendigo while poisoned and puking your guts out to save a boy? No. You sat here, plotted, and felt sorry for yourself. And less than an hour ago, when the Pack Council was trying to decide what to do with Dorie, where the bloody hell were you? You sent Desandra in, because you didn't want to face the heat."

Jennifer bared her teeth, drawing back.

"Desandra might be crude and manipulative, but you know what, she shows up. She gets into the mud and blood with the rest of us and gets her hands dirty. None of us like it, but we do it. I won't help her pull you off your alpha rock, but I won't stop her either. And after what she did, if she needs me, I'll be there to back her up, because she watched my back when it counted. You are not special. You don't get to not show up. You don't get to avoid difficult decisions. You get to climb into the muck with the rest of us. So, if you want to be in charge, fine. Reach deep down, find a backbone, and handle your own shit. Otherwise, step down and make way for someone who would actually matter."

Jennifer sat frozen, her face stunned. Her hand squeezed the water bottle.

I waited to see if she would explode.

Someone knocked and the door swung open. Barabas ducked in. "I have Gray on the phone."

Finally. I turned to Jennifer. "Are we done?"

"I can't do it," she said quietly, her voice sad. "I should do it, but I can't. It's wrong. It would be like spitting on his memory."

What was she talking about? How was fighting Desandra spitting on Daniel's memory? I didn't understand her at all. "You can step down and be a mother . . ."

She got up and fled out of the room.

. . .

BARABAS SHOWED ME to one of the conference rooms. Jim was already there, leaning against the wall, like a grim shadow, his eyes hard. Uh-oh.

"How did you get him on the phone?" I asked.

"I had two of our people walk into his office and refuse to leave," Jim said. "He was there all morning."

Gray had been ducking our calls. That was exactly what I didn't want to hear. I landed in a chair and pushed the button on speaker.

"Detective Gray."

"Hello, Kate."

"You're a hard man to find."

"What do you want?" Gray sounded tired.

"I want to surrender a suspect implicated in the murder of Mulradin Grant to your custody."

Silence.

More silence.

I imagined a hole suddenly manifesting under Gray's feet and swallowing him whole. The way my day had been going so far, I wouldn't be surprised.

"We are not aware of any murder," Gray said.

Aha. "I'm making you aware of it now. Mr. Grant is dead, he was murdered by a shapeshifter, and a member of the Pack has been implicated in this murder. I'm reaching out to you and offering to surrender her to your custody."

"This is a jurisdictional issue," Gray said. "The Keep is in DeKalb County."

Are you kidding me? "The murder was committed in Atlanta's city limits."

"The alleged murder."

Argh. I leaned closer to the phone. "We've always strived to maintain good relations with the PAD. Last year alone we've assisted you on—"

Jim raised nine fingers.

"—on nine cases. I'm asking you to help us."

Silence.

"I'm sorry," Gray said. "I can't."

The rage swelled inside me like a wave. My voice shook slightly. "I'm about to have a bloodbath on my hands."

Gray lowered his voice. "This is coming down from above. We can't get involved in a war between the Pack and the People. We don't have the numbers or the firepower. We'd be slaughtered. I'm sorry, but this is between you and them."

He wouldn't help us. "You had a chance to make a difference today and you stepped back. Your authority is only good if you do something with it, and you chose to do nothing. Do that enough times and pretty soon nobody will acknowledge it at all. The next time you need my help, don't call."

I disconnected the call.

"Diplomatic," Barabas said.

"Fuck diplomatic."

The phone rang. I picked it up.

"This is a jurisdictional issue," Gray said, his voice strained. "We have no jurisdiction over the Keep."

He hung up.

Okay. "Who has jurisdiction over us?" I asked the room.

"Most of our lands are in DeKalb County," Barabas said. "A little bit of Clayton, too."

Neither the DeKalb nor Clayton County sheriff would help us. DeKalb didn't care for us, and Clayton was severely understaffed.

"And Milton too, along the north edge," Jim said.

Wait a minute. "Milton?"

He nodded.

The last time I had occasion to travel to Milton, it was because Andrea had gotten upset over some floozy flirting with Raphael, pulled a gun, and nearly drowned her in a hot tub. Beau Clayton, the Milton County sheriff, had personally talked her off the cliff and locked everyone up until I got there.

I punched his number into the phone. "Beau?"

"Kate." A deep voice tinted with Georgia's brand of country answered.

"Funniest thing happened. One of my deputies just saw what he described as 'a whole mess of undead' moving in your general direction. Now, I am curious. Are you having a party?"

"Beau," I said. "I need your help."

I STOOD ON the wall of the Keep. The day was beautiful. The sun lit the turquoise sky, tinting it with a pale veil of gold. Before me a clear snowfield stretched to the jagged dark wall of the forest. Wind stirred a loose strand of my hair.

Behind me the Pack Council waited.

Something moved in the distance at the far-off tree line. A single skeletal shape emerged out of the brush, a dark squiggle against the white snow. The undead paused on all fours. Its magic brushed by me, revolting, like a smear of decomposing flesh on the surface of my mind.

Vampires poured out of the forest, their gaunt, grotesque bodies moving ridiculously fast. So many . . . Behind them four armored cars crept onto the field. Painted in fatigue colors and set on eight wheels, they looked like small tanks. And they were probably chock-full of navigators.

"The People got themselves some Strykers," Andrea said. "Slat armor, full hull protection. These have a layer of steel, then a layer of ceramic armor against armor-piercing rounds, then more steel and then probably reactive armor tiles. You can fire a rocket launcher at that thing and it won't even sneeze."

"How heavy are they?" Martha asked.

"Little over sixteen tons," Andrea said.

"So around thirty-three thousand pounds," Robert murmured.

Martha shrugged. "Too heavy to roll."

Prying Ghastek and his posse out of the Strykers would be a bitch.

The armored fighting vehicles rolled into position and stopped. The vampires formed around them.

Where are you, Curran? In my head I had thought he would somehow magically show up. But he wasn't here. I was on my own.

I turned to the courtyard and waved at Roman and the witch next to him.

"Is that his sister?" Andrea asked to me.

"No." I had spoken with both of them. "I'd asked her that. Her name is Alina, she isn't his sister, and she feels deeply sorry for his sisters, because if she had to put up with being in his presence for longer than a day, she would throw herself off the nearest bridge just to end the agony."

"Well," Andrea said. "Glad she cleared that up."

The dark volhv waved back at me and shouted, "Showtime!"

Alina sighed next to him. "What are you so happy about? We're going to get killed."

The two of them started toward the gates.

"It's exciting," Roman said. "Look at all of those shapeshifters and vampires. It's a historic moment and the Pack will owe us."

"How is it that you have no common sense? Were they all out when you were born?"

Roman indicated his face. "I don't need common sense. I have a double helping of charm."

"You mean a double helping of bullshit . . ."

They passed through the gates under us and Derek and two other shapeshifters barred them, lifting the enormous beam in place. The boy wonder, bald and pale, had decided that he'd had enough rest. I didn't have the energy to fight with him about it.

Roman and the witch stopped about fifty feet from the gate. A single vampire emerged from the undead horde and ran over to them. Roman spoke to it. He would be listing our conditions: we would meet two Masters of the Dead in front of the gates and discuss the murder of Mulradin. Roman and the witch would act as impartial witnesses. And if Hugh got anywhere within fifty feet of that meeting, all negotiations would cease.

The vampire returned. The witch raised her head and spread her arms. A dark green spark pulsed from her and split into a thousand narrow ribbons of green. They shot from her, falling into the snow. Steam rose as the snow melted and the green burrowed into the ground, forming a perfect ring about fifty feet in diameter. Thin green stalks sprouted from the exposed ground and stretched upward, turning into knee-high thorns.

We had our meeting.

. . .

I WALKED OUT into the snowy field next to Jim. The gates of the Keep stood closed behind us. On the wall, Andrea stood with a power crossbow. She'd brought a sniper rifle in case the magic dropped.

The sea of vampires parted and Ghastek walked out, tall, slender, wearing a long military-style white jacket and white pants, strategically broken by small irregular splotches of brown. White boots and a helmet in the same pattern completed the outfit. Apparently he intended to bury himself in the snow and snipe at us from his cover. A woman followed him. She wore an identical uniform and the helmet hid her hair, but I'd know Rowena anywhere. She was in debt to the witches and she had been secretly supplying me with vampire blood. She didn't know what I did with it, but if she ever found out, her helmet would fly right off her head because her hair would stand on end.

"What the hell are they wearing?" Jim murmured next to me.

"They're playing soldier. It probably cost them an arm and a leg."

"Still might," Jim offered.

Ghastek carefully stepped over the thorns into the circle. Rowena followed him.

The horde of undead rippled again and Hugh rode out. He wore dark leather armor and a long cloak edged with wolf fur. Nice touch. When you're going to confront a Keep full of people who turn furry, make sure you're wearing some dead animal's skin on your cloak. His enormous black horse, a massive Friesian, danced under him, long black mane flying, the black feathers on its legs raising powdery snow. Steam rose from the stallion's nostrils.

Hugh should've brought a banner with *I AM BAD* stitched on it in gold. The horse, the armor, and the fur weren't making enough of a statement.

Jim leaned forward, his gaze fixed on Hugh.

"Don't," I murmured.

Hugh guided the horse along the thorn border. The Friesian circled us, never crossing over the boundary. Hugh was clearly an "obey the letter of the agreement, not the spirit" kind of guy.

I wanted to pull him off his horse and grind his face into the dirt.

"Have you apprehended the murderer?" Ghastek asked.

"Yes." I passed him a piece of paper with Double D's handwritten confession on it. He read it and glanced at Hugh. Hugh was staring at me. *Looking is free. Try to come closer and I will cure what ails you and me both.*

Ghastek read further. Distaste twisted his face. "That is . . . unfortunate."

"I think it's tragic, personally, but we can go with unfortunate, if you want." My deadline was rapidly approaching. Beau Clayton was nowhere to be seen. Maybe he had hung me out to dry.

Ghastek folded the paper in half and passed it to Rowena. She read it and looked up. A rapid mental calculation was taking place behind Rowena's eyes. She directed the People's public relations. This whole thing was a PR nightmare for everyone involved.

"Did you read the part where d'Ambray walked in on her, held a gun to her head, and forced her to kill Mulradin, so he could manufacture this war?"

Ghastek looked like he had bitten into a peach and realized it was rotten. "I am sure she says that he did. I have not read the part where she presents evidence of this wild story. Perhaps there's a rider or an exhibit I missed?"

That's okay, I had more. "Why would she lie?"

Hugh kept circling us. A small smile curved his lips. He looked like a man who was enjoying himself. Snow, sunshine, brisk air, a fast horse . . . and impending slaughter. All the things a growing boy needs.

"To prevent this conflict. Perhaps it was a lovers' quarrel," Ghastek said. "Perhaps she wanted to rob him. I don't know, and quite frankly, I don't care at the moment. Can you prove that she is the killer and not some sacrificial lamb?"

"You're welcome to run her DNA. It will match what's on Mulradin."

"Are you prepared to turn her over to us?"

"No."

Ghastek leaned forward. "Kate, I hate to resort to threats, but there is a certain responsibility you and I both have to the people we're leading in this conflict . . ."

To the left of him, three horsemen emerged from under the trees. Beau or not Beau?

"The casualties and financial costs of war will be catastrophic," Ghastek said. "I understand that you're counting on the help of whatever navigator you hired, but I assure you, we're more than capable of neutralizing him or her."

"What navigator?"

"The one who assisted you last night at the Conclave."

What was he on about?

Oh.

Apparently I had hidden too well. For all of his intelligence, Ghastek still hadn't put two and two together. He knew with absolute certainty that I couldn't pilot vampires. He had seen me not pilot them on numerous occasions. In his mind, I couldn't possibly do it, so I had to have hired someone else and that someone must've grabbed control of the vampires at the Conclave. Right.

"We have a duty to avert this," Ghastek said.

"You're right. You should send your undead army home and we'll discuss this like reasonable people."

Ghastek sighed. "I'm a reactive party to the bloodshed."

"Ghastek, you're an intelligent man. You're standing here wearing ridiculous fatigues and getting ready to assault a place full of families and children with a horde of vampires. Does this seem right to you?"

Ghastek's face jerked. "The concepts of right or wrong are inconsequential in this case."

"The concepts of right or wrong are always consequential. It can't be situational or it's not right or wrong."

"I didn't come here to debate ethical obligations with you," Ghastek said.

"You opened the door. I just walked through it."

"You're harboring a fugitive. Deliver her to our custody."

A shout made me turn. A man jumped from the wall of the Keep and sprinted to us. Brandon, Jennifer's pet wolf. Now what? If he did anything to disrupt this, I'd break his neck.

Brandon dashed across the snow and leaped into the circle. He was clutching something in his hand.

"What the hell are you doing?" Jim snarled.

Brandon dodged him. He opened his fingers and I caught a flash of what he was holding—Jennifer's water bottle. He ripped the cap off it and hurled the liquid at me.

I moved, but not fast enough. Cold water splashed my right cheek, soaking my hair. Behind me, Ghastek threw his hands up, and what missed me landed on his fingers. The Master of the Dead stared, bewildered, water dripping from hands. His eyes bulged in angry confusion.

Jim moved. His hand closed on Brandon's wrist and twisted. Brandon dropped to his knees into the snow, his arm wrenched out of its socket.

The whole world had gone nuts on me. I couldn't even get angry anymore. I'd run out of rage.

"It's done," the blond man squeezed out. "I did it for her."

What the hell? I would kill Jennifer. I would do it myself and save Desandra the trouble.

Jim twisted his arm, bending him into a pretzel. "I'll just be a minute."

He grabbed Brandon by his collar and dragged him out of the circle toward the Keep. The gates opened just enough to let a person pass, and Derek and another shapeshifter shot out. Jim shoved Brandon in their direction, turned around, and came back into the circle.

Ghastek finally regained his ability to speak. "How dare you? Is this an insult?"

"Yes," I told him. "But to me, not to you. My deepest apologies."

Hugh chuckled.

Derek and the other shapeshifter muscled Brandon back behind the doors.

Ghastek opened his mouth. No words came out. He was obviously struggling to get himself under control.

"I'm very sorry," I repeated. Now I was apologizing to the man who was threatening to kill me. Here's hoping my arteries didn't explode from the pressure.

"This is outrageous."

"So is dropping loose vampires into the middle of a Conclave meeting."

Ghastek clamped his mouth shut.

"We will take the accused now," Rowena said.

The three riders drew closer. Sheriff hats. It had to be Beau.

"And if we give her to you? What then? A lynching? Maybe you'll burn her at the stake? Last time I checked we at least pretended we were civilized people."

Ghastek locked his teeth. He kept a pair of chains used in witch trials on the wall of his office. The reminder of witch burnings had hit home.

"She will be given every opportunity to prove her innocence," Rowena said.

"Yes, she will," Jim said. "We're turning her over to human law enforcement."

Hugh's face lost its half-smile. *Oh no. Did you find half a worm in the apple you just bit?*

"That would be extremely unwise," Ghastek said.

"Why?"

"For one, it exposes both of our factions to public scrutiny," Rowena said.

"I thought you were all about avoiding bloodshed," Jim said.

I gave Ghastek my best psycho smile. "I think we could all benefit from a little transparency."

"You're fucking up," Hugh said from his horse.

"Shut the hell up," I told him. "Nobody's talking to you."

"You're bluffing," Hugh said. "You won't find anyone to take her."

I pointed to the approaching riders.

Ghastek turned to glance over his shoulder. Beau and two deputies, a short compact man with red hair and a Hispanic woman in her forties, were closing in.

"Beau Clayton?" Ghastek dipped his head and rubbed the bridge of his nose. "He has no jurisdiction here."

"Yes he does. Those woods over there are in Milton County."

Hugh's eyes turned dark.

"He's respected and has a high profile," Ghastek called out. "If you kill him, every law enforcement agency will converge on us."

Beau was only a few yards away. Six foot six and built like one of the ancient Saxons who swung axes as tall as they were, Beau rode a dappled Percheron cross that stood about eighteen hands tall and looked strong enough to pull a semi. The two deputies rode Tennessee walkers. Three riders, three shotguns. Nothing else.

Beau came to a stop. The vampires stared at him, held in check by the navigators' minds.

"Alright," Beau boomed. "I'm Beau Clayton, lawfully elected by the people of Milton County as their sheriff. It's the duty of my office to faithfully execute all writs, warrants, precepts, and processes directed to me as sheriff of this county. I'm here to execute a warrant."

The bloodsuckers stared at him.

Hugh's stare turned calculating. He was thinking about it.

"Here's what's going to happen. I'm going to take this person into custody. You are going to turn around and go home. The lynching has been canceled. Move along. There is nothing to see here."

Hugh's stallion danced under him.

"Disperse," Beau repeated.

Hugh reached for his sword.

I raised my hand. The gates of the Keep swung open. Shapeshifters in warrior form waited in rows, filling the courtyard, their fur raised, their fangs bared. I had put every shapeshifter capable of a half-form into the courtyard. Sixty-four people. Only eighteen were combat rated, but from here, it looked like every single one was a render.

"If you assault an officer of law, the Pack will retaliate," Jim said.

"Your best people are gone," Ghastek said. "You're at half-strength at best."

I nodded. "Yes, most of our young single people have gone to hunt. You'll be facing parents whose children are in that Keep. Have you ever tried to take a cub from a wolf? You're welcome to give it a shot."

Hugh's hand was on his sword.

I reached for Slayer. Laughter bubbled up. "Go ahead, Hugh. Make my day. I'm really frustrated right now. I need to vent. Please."

He glared at me.

"You lost," I told him. "I called your bluff. Take your goons and go home."

"We have no legal standing to attack a sheriff," Ghastek said.

"You'll do what I tell you," Hugh told him.

"No, he won't," I told him. I could tell by Ghastek's eyes that he was out. Whatever Hugh decided now, I had done my job. I had stopped this war from happening.

A roar rolled through the snowy field, shaking the winter air like a sudden, terrifying clap of thunder. Hugh's Friesian jerked. The roar cascaded, frothing with menace and fury, awakening some long-forgotten instinct that severed the rational part of the brain from the body and left only three options open: fight, flight, or freeze.

Curran.

The relief drowned me, turning me weightless, and for a short blissful moment I was completely and utterly happy. Curran!

The trees at the north edge of the field shook as a flock of birds took flight. Curran leaped into the snow. He rose almost eight feet tall in warrior form, a muscled terrifying blend of a man and a predatory cat, sheathed in gray fur and armed with claws the size of my fingers. His head was pure lion. He opened his mouth and roared.

An enormous Kodiak bear emerged from the brush, shaking his big furry body. Next to him a bouda giggled. I'd never been so happy to hear that eerie hair-raising cackle in my entire life.

Shapeshifters poured out of the woods, ten, twenty, more . . . Where did he get them . . . ?

He must've gone to the Wood and pulled our people off the hunt. He'd brought an army. Yes!

Curran broke into a run. The shapeshifters followed, raising powdery snow into the air.

"We're done here." Ghastek turned to the sea of vampires. "Mission aborted. Bogey to mother."

The vampires streamed off the field.

I laughed.

Hugh turned his horse, facing me. "I tried to be nice, but I have my limits. You want to be treated like an animal, I'll treat you like one."

He opened his mouth. Magic ripped from him like a tidal wave and snapped, catching me. A power word.

The right side of my face turned hot. A pale gold light spiraled around me. Next to me, Ghastek jerked, caught in an identical glowing tornado.

On the wall behind me, Christopher screamed, "Mistress!"

Hugh smirked.

Whatever was happening, he would die before it was over. I dashed to him across the snow, sword out. The light moved with me, streaming around me in bright sunny ribbons. I leaped over the thorns.

Hugh slid off his horse.

Curran sprinted to me, his eyes pure gold.

I struck. Hugh's blade met mine. He bared his teeth at me.

The tornado of light around me pulsed with red, slicing through Slayer's blade where it touched Hugh's sword. The blade snapped in half.

No!

The field, Hugh, and Curran vanished.

13

SOMEONE JERKED THE ground from under my feet. I hurtled through empty air, weightless, my arms transparent. Bricks flashed before me. I was falling through a round shaft. Directly below me a thick metal grate blocked dark water.

I'm going to die.

I hit the grate and passed through it, as if it were air. My body plunged into the water.

Lukewarm. Wet.

My body turned solid. I kicked, surfaced, and stared at half a sword in my hand. Hugh broke my sword. He broke Slayer.

He broke my sword.

I curled into a ball around my saber, plunging into the water. I'd had Slayer since I was five. Voron gave it to me. I had slept with it under my bed almost every night for the past twenty-two years. Slayer was a part of me and now it was broken. Broken in half. It felt like someone had cut my arm off and it just kept hurting and hurting.

I would kill him. It wasn't an "if." It was a "when."

He broke Slayer.

Above me someone else was falling down, through the grate, and into the water. I choked and swam up. A moment later and Ghastek surfaced next to me with a gasp. He splashed around in panic. I gave him room. About ten seconds later, he stopped thrashing and stared at me.

"It was that water. It marked us and made us vulnerable to d'Ambray's magic."

"Yes. Hugh must have bribed one of my people. Or blackmailed them. Or threatened."

It was Jennifer. It had to be, and if that was the case, Hugh wouldn't have had to threaten very hard. She must've sat there with that bottle in her hands and tried to scrape enough courage together to throw it on me. She couldn't.

This would not break me. My sword might snap, but I couldn't. I would win. I would get out of here. I would live. I would see the people I loved again.

This wasn't my first rodeo. I slipped into a quiet, cold calm. Voron's voice murmured from my memory and I leaned on it like a crutch. *"Exits first."*

"Yes. I remember."

I bent in the water, trying to slide what was left of my sword into the sheath while staying afloat. I missed.

I fucking missed. I hadn't missed in two decades.

"You were the target," Ghastek said. "I'm an unfortunate bystander."

"It looks like that." I finally managed to slip Slayer's stump into the sheath.

"Where are we?"

"I have no idea."

"He knew we would be teleported here. He knew, and he did nothing to stop my teleportation," Ghastek said.

"It appears d'Ambray believes you're expendable."

Ghastek looked at me for a long moment. A muscle in his face jerked. With a guttural snarl, Ghastek punched the water. "That's it. That's fucking it!"

Uh-oh. In all the time I'd interacted with Ghastek, he never swore. Ever. The "premier" Master of the Dead was about to throw a tantrum. I braced myself.

"He comes into my city, he throws away my people, he orders me around like I'm his servant and now this? How dare he!"

I sighed. "How dare he!" came out. Could "Does he know who I am?" be far behind?

"I'm not some illiterate he can push around. I won't be treated this way. I worked too damn hard, for years. Years! Years of study and that fucking Neanderthal comes in and waves his arms." Ghastek skewed his face into a grimace. He was probably aiming to impersonate Hugh, but he mostly succeeded in looking extremely constipated. "Ooo, I'm Hugh d'Ambray, I'm starting a war!"

Laughing right now was a really bad idea. I had to conserve the energy.

"A war I've been trying years to avoid. Years!"

He kept saying that.

"Does he think it's easy to negotiate with violent lunatics, who can't understand elementary concepts?"

Good to know where we stood with him.

"I won't tolerate it. Landon Nez will hear about this."

Landon Nez was likely in charge of the Masters of the Dead. My father liked to divide his delegated authority. Hugh ran the Iron Dogs, the military branch. Someone had to run the People, the research branch. It was a position with a lot of turnover. Landon Nez must be the latest.

"Troglodyte. Dimwit. Degenerate!" Curses spilled out of Ghastek. "When I get out of here, I'll throw every vampire at my disposal at him until they drain him dry. Then I'll cut him to pieces and set his disemboweled body on fire!"

"You may have to get in line."

He finally remembered I was there. "What?"

"I'll give you a piece of Hugh to play with when I'm done."

He didn't appear to have heard me. "Nobody does that to me! I'll rip his heart out. Does he know who I am?"

"Okay," I told him. "Get it all out of your system."

Ghastek dissolved into a torrent of obscenities.

I turned away. We had to get out of this mess and I had to check the place for the possible exit routes.

The grate above us was a pale color that usually meant the metal contained silver. Above the grate a shaft, about twenty feet across, rose a hundred feet straight up. Blue feylanterns thrust from the walls at regular intervals, illuminating the bricks. Too sheer to climb.

The grate itself consisted of inch-wide bars set in a crisscrossed pattern. Usually grates like this had crossbars that were welded or locked in by swaging, but this one showed no seams at all. It had to have been custom made specifically for this shaft.

The ends of the bars disappeared into the wall. I kicked to propel myself up, stretched, and caught the grate with my fingers. So far so good. I brought my legs up and kicked the grate with all my strength. Not just solid. Immovable. Well, at least the holes between the bars weren't tiny.

I shrugged off my jacket, stuck one sleeve through the grate, and tied it to the other sleeve. Good enough.

I took a deep breath and dove into the murky water. Not cold, but not especially warm either. Evdokia's sweater would buy me some time. Wool kept you warm even when wet. I swam down along the wall. Darkness and bricks. No secret passages, no tunnels, no pipes with covers that could be pried loose.

Blood pounded in my ears. I had to turn back or I'd run out of air. I did a one-eighty and kicked for the surface. Above me the liquid sky promised light and air. I kicked harder. My lungs screamed for oxygen.

I broke the surface and gulped down air.

"... does he think he is?"

This was a prison cell meant to hold a shapeshifter. The silver in the bars would keep them from screwing with it. The water was too deep to kick off the bottom and try to ram the grate. Even if I somehow managed to pry the bars of the grate loose, which wasn't bloody likely, the grate would fall on us and its sheer weight would drown us. My mind served a nightmarish view of the grate landing on me and pushing me deep into the dark water. No thanks.

The lanterns just added insult to injury. You could see exactly how hopeless the situation was.

You want to be treated like an animal, I'll treat you like one. Thanks, Hugh. So glad to know you care.

I could do this. I'd trained all my life for it.

Ghastek had fallen silent.

"I don't suppose that fancy uniform comes with a flotation device?"

"Don't be ridiculous."

"A girl can hope." I dove down and untied the laces on my left boot. The right boot followed. I surfaced to grab some air.

"What are you doing?" Ghastek asked.

"Lightening the load." I dove, carefully pulled off my left boot, surfaced, caught the grate, and looped the shoelaces over the bar. I tied a knot and left the boot suspended, then did the same with the right boot. "I'll get tired in an hour or two and I'll need the shoes if we get out of here."

I pulled off my belt, threaded it through the bars, and locked it into a loop. Ghastek raised his eyebrows. I thrust my arm through the loop and held on to the grate. The belt kept me in place without treading water.

Ghastek's face fell. "How long do you think he'll keep us here?"

"I have no idea."

He sighed and began stripping off his boots.

I HUNG MOTIONLESS in the water. Time crawled by. I had no idea how long we'd been here. We had taken turns diving to search our surroundings but found no exit. Eventually we stopped. Sometime while we were diving, the magic wave ended. Now four dim electric lamps lit the shaft. The light, dim and watery, felt oppressive, just another form of torture.

We'd used Ghastek's jacket and his belt to fashion two loops to hold him upright. With two supports each, we would be able to sleep. Small comfort, but it was something.

A while ago my mouth had gone dry and I had drunk a little from my canteen and passed it to Ghastek.

"Do you always carry a canteen?"

"It's force of habit." You could survive many things as long as you had a canteen and a knife.

He had taken a swallow and passed it back. "What happens when we run out of water?"

"We drink this." I'd nodded at the dark water flooding the shaft.

"It doesn't seem clean, and even if it is, it won't stay that way for long."

"People dying of thirst can't be choosers."

We hung in the water.

"What did you do with Nataraja?" I asked.

Ghastek blinked, startled.

"I was always curious. He just kind of disappeared."

Ghastek sighed.

"We're not going anywhere for a while," I told him.

He raised his gaze to the ceiling, pondered it, and shrugged. "Why not? Nataraja was always fond of hands-off management. I never understood why he was placed in charge in the first place. He looked impressive but had very little to do with the actual function of the office. I oversaw research and development, and Mulradin handled the financial aspects. A year ago Nataraja's behavior became increasingly erratic. He wandered around, mumbling to himself. He killed that monstrosity he kept as a pet."

"Wiggles? His giant snake?"

"Yes. A journeyman found sections of her strewn throughout the upper floor. A report was made to the main office. A high-ranking member of the Golden Legion arrived and conducted some interviews. Nataraja disappeared. We were told he was recalled."

"Do you think he was recalled?"

Ghastek shrugged. "What's the point of speculating? Mulradin and I were left jointly in charge of the office until either one of us 'distinguished' ourselves or a replacement was assigned. I suppose now the question of distinction is moot. He's dead and I'm here." He spat the last word.

Now he had gone to sleep. It was best I slept, too. I closed my eyes and imagined being on the beach with Curran. It was such a pleasant dream . . .

OUR CANTEEN HAD gone dry. It held enough water for over two days if carefully rationed, and we'd split it in half. We'd been imprisoned here for more than twenty-four hours. Probably closer to forty-eight. We had begun drinking the water around us and it didn't sit so well in my stomach.

The water in the shaft had turned colder some hours ago. The temperature hadn't actually changed, but water sapped body heat about twenty-five times faster than air. We'd been soaking long enough to really feel it.

I was starving. My stomach was a bottomless pit filled with ache. I'd kick myself for not gorging on something delicious while I was in the Keep that morning, but it would waste too much energy. I had to conserve every drop. Hang in the water. Last. Survive.

When the cold got to me, I untangled myself from my belt and swam. The exertion burned through what meager supplies of energy I had left, but it made me feel warmer. Until the shivering started again.

"We're going to die here," Ghastek said.

"No," I told him.

"What makes you say that?"

"Curran will come for me."

Ghastek laughed, a brittle sour sound. "You don't even know where we are. We could be halfway across the country."

"It doesn't matter. He'll come for me." He would turn the planet inside out until he found me—and I'd do the same for him.

Ghastek shook his head.

"You have to will yourself to survive," I told him.

He didn't look at me.

"I'm not dying in this hole. Curran will come for me and we'll get out of here. This isn't how it ends. Hugh doesn't get to win. We'll survive this. One day I'm going to ram my broken sword right through his throat."

Ghastek peered at me. His voice was hoarse. "Let me reiterate. We've been teleported to some unknown place probably thousands of miles away from everyone you know, possibly on another continent. The man who put us here likely teleported as well, taking the knowledge of our location with him, so nobody we know has even an infinitesimal idea of where we might be. We have no way to communicate with the outside world. Even if we could communicate by some magical means with those we know, we would be of no assistance, because we don't know where we are. We're floating in cold murky water."

"It's pretty warm, actually."

He raised his finger. "I haven't finished. We have no food. We have been here for at least forty-eight hours, because the hunger pangs I'm feeling are now less intense. Right now our bodies are burning through what meager fat reserves we have, which will result in severe ketosis, which in turn will lead to blood acidosis, bringing with it nausea and diarrhea. Soon faintness, weakness, and vertigo will follow. As our brains are deprived of the necessary nutrients, we'll begin to hallucinate, and then we'll suffer catastrophic organ damage, until finally we will die of cardiac arrest. It's a brutal and torturous death. Mahatma Gandhi survived for twenty-one days when campaigning for India's independence, but considering that we're in the water and our bodies are going through nutrients at an accelerated rate, I give us two weeks, maximum."

"If you ever decide on a career change, I'd avoid motivational speaking."

"Don't you understand? The only person who knows where we are is d'Ambray, and he put us here to slowly starve to death. Even if he changes his mind and decides to pull you out, since he has some strange fascination with you, he has no such relationship with me. I'm disposable. What few dealings I had with this man were abrupt to the point of rudeness. He clearly has no regard for me."

"I promise you now that we went in here together and we're leaving together. Curran will get me out and I won't leave you behind."

"To expect that Curran will somehow come and rescue you before we die is absurd."

"You don't know him like I do."

"Kate! You are delusional!"

"This isn't my first time trapped without food," I said. "I used to have to do this frequently. We have water, which is a huge advantage. We're not dead yet."

He stared at me.

"I've survived the Arizona desert. I've survived in a forest scorched by fires. I've been starved, drowned, frozen, but I'm still here. The key to survival is to not give up. You have to fight for your life. You have to have hope. If you let go of hope, it's over. Giving up is dying quietly with your hands bound in a hut where the man who tied you up threw you. Hope is kicking your way out and running ten miles across snow and forest against all odds."

Ghastek blinked. "Did you actually do this?"

"Yes."

"Who put you in the hut?"

"My father."

Ghastek opened his mouth. "Why? What kind of a father does that to a child?"

"The only one I had. Don't give up. Don't let the troglodyte win, Ghastek."

He shook his head.

His brain was too loud. He needed to stop thinking, because his mind kept running in circles, driving him deeper into despair. Despair was the kiss of death.

We needed to conserve energy, but if I didn't distract him, he would fold on me. "You keep analyzing the situation and the more you dissect it, the more hopeless it seems. Try not to think about it. Talk to me instead."

"About what?"

"I don't know. Why did you decide to become a navigator? Did you always want to pilot the undead? Why didn't you strike out on your own? Why the People?" There, that ought to keep him occupied.

He hung motionless in the water. "Ghastek isn't my real name. I grew up in Massachusetts, near Andover. I was smart and poor. Not crushingly poor. I've known children who were poorer. Poverty is when your parents get home from the first job and hurry up to eat their mac and cheese, because in five hours they have to get up for their second job and they want to catch some sleep. We weren't quite that poor. We had food. We owned a house. I saw both of my parents at the dinner table at the same time.

"In eighth grade, there was a science tournament between the local schools. The local private preparatory academy was participating, primarily to demonstrate the vast superiority of its education over the public system. I won. The academy gave me a scholarship. I remember how happy my parents were for me. It was a Yale feeder school and they thought I now had a future. So the next school year, I started at the prep school. It was a forty-five-minute drive and every day my father would take me there in his work van. My father repaired gas lines. The van had a logo on it, written in large yellow letters: GasTek. The name of the company. Nobody was interested in learning my name. I became that Gastek kid, then Gastek, and then one of the class clowns thought it would be hilarious to slip an *h* in there. Ghastek. A not-so-subtle association with 'ghastly.' Ghastek or sometimes simply 'the Creep.' By the end of the year even the teachers didn't call me by my name."

I could hear the old bitterness in his voice. He'd come to terms with it, and it no longer hurt, but it was still there.

"I realized in that first year that I would never be accepted. It was understood by all that no matter how hard I tried, no matter how I brilliant I was, the best I could hope for was to work for one of my dumber classmates when we grew up. They would be the owners. I would be an employee. You see, it's not enough to be smart. If you're handsome or a good athlete, they might grant you some degree of acceptance, because adolescents are shallow. You might become a trophy for one of them, if you let yourself be used, but I was neither. Being rich would open the door a crack, but they would never let you in the whole way. They'll spend your money and laugh at you behind your back. I've seen it. You see, money, brains, looks, none of it is enough. There is this thing called legacy. It wasn't just about where you went to school or who with. It was about where your grandfather went to school and who his best friends were."

"I take it the school wasn't your favorite place."

"I fucking hated it. Then the People's recruiter came in when I was a junior. They brought in a caged vampire and let us try one by one. The feeling when I first realized I could control it . . . I can't describe it. It was right. For the first time in my life, something felt right. I made the undead unlock the door of the cage and then I chased my darling classmates with it. The recruiter wasn't strong enough to take it away from me. They ran from me. It didn't matter how rich they were. It didn't matter what their name was. Their august grandparents couldn't save them, because if they had been there, they would've run from me, too."

Ghastek smiled, a bright happy smile. "Some of them begged me to stop."

He looked so happy I tried my best to scoot a little farther away from him in my restraints.

"They expelled me within the hour." He laughed. "By the end of the day, the People brought my parents a check totaling more than they'd made together in the previous three years. A hardship fee to make their lives a little easier if I chose to leave home and study with the People. But my parents didn't want to let me go. The money made no difference to them."

"They loved you," I guessed.

He nodded. "They did. I put the check in their hands and walked out of the house. I wanted the power. I wanted respect and money too, but most of all I wanted power. You asked me why I'm a navigator. Because I love it. I love when my magic makes that first connection. I love the precision of it, the subtlety, the art of it. If you could pilot, you'd understand."

Oh, if he only knew.

"It's like being connected to a spring of pure power. It nourishes you. I have risen so far. I'm now ranked seventeenth in the Golden Legion."

The Legions were Roland's top Masters of the Dead. Gold was the top fifty, and Silver was the next fifty. "I thought it was the Gold Legion."

"They changed it last year," Ghastek said. "'Golden' sounds better. Navigation is like anything else. It takes practice and discipline and eventually the hard work pays off. Every year my power is increasing. I could be in the top ten, but I choose to not make the bid for that spot."

"Why not?"

"You wouldn't understand," Ghastek said.

"Try me."

"No. Enough to say that I worked for years and now all of my efforts have brought me here. To this . . . hole in the ground. I'm going to rest now. I've talked enough for today."

Ghastek grew quiet. Minutes passed. His head dropped.

I could picture him in the yard of the school, a skinny kid in cheap clothes sending an undead after the people who looked down on him. Who knew?

I closed my eyes. It was all I could do.

We would get out of here.

Curran would come for me. Of course he would.

A FIREPLACE LIT the room, and warmth flowed from it, so luxuriously hot and soft that for a long moment I simply basked in it. I was warm and dry. The savory scent of seared meat floated through the air. Food. This was heaven.

"Hey, baby," Hugh said.

Heaven just got canceled.

I turned. He was sprawled in a large wooden chair, leaning against the back, big legs in blue jeans stretched out in front of him. His shirt was off and the firelight played over the sharply defined muscles of his chest and arms. A small pendant hung around his neck on a plain steel chain. I liked how he was sitting, all loose and relaxed. It would make it harder for him to dodge and there was a lovely heavy chair next to me.

I grabbed the chair.

Except I didn't move.

And I didn't have any arms or legs either. Awesome.

Hugh chuckled.

"Let me guess, this is one of those special dreams." At least my mouth still worked.

"Something like that. It's a projection."

"Aha. But the magic is down."

"Nope. Came back about fifteen minutes ago. You'll feel it when you wake up."

"How long have I been in your little prison cell?" Might as well get whatever information I could.

"Three days."

That long. Hell.

"How's the water?" Hugh asked. "Getting cold yet?"

Asshole. "So that's how you teleported out of the burning castle? Did you have water on you somewhere?"

He touched the pendant hanging from his neck and lifted it. The light of the fire played on the glass of the bullet-shaped pendant. Water sloshed inside.

"I always have one on me. It takes a second to crush. Once the water touches you, a power word pulls you through to the source of the water."

So the water Jennifer dumped on me had come from the shaft where my body was currently floating.

"Teleporting is a last resort," Hugh said. "It takes a few seconds for the transfer depending on the distance. If tech hits while you're in transit, you're dead. But you left me no choice."

"What did you promise Jennifer to betray me?"

"Power," he said. "She was supposed to drench you in private, so nobody would suspect her once I triggered the teleportation. You would disappear and she'd use the time while everyone was running around looking for you to solidify her hold on the clan. In a week or two one of my people would take out Desandra for her, which would've made things easier. Except she fucked up, and then her boy screwed the pooch even further. I imagine they're fitting the stone on her grave about now. I told you before: shape-shifters are difficult to train. You've got to get them young."

"You're a sick fuck."

"I know." Hugh nodded at the table next to him. "Hungry?"

Food covered the table. Fresh bread, still warm and crusty from the oven waited on a cutting board. A rib eye roast, the fat crisped and melting, lorded over a bowl of soup, a tub of golden butter, and a dish of mashed potatoes. The air smelled of seared meat, roasted garlic, and fresh bread.

My mouth watered, while my stomach clenched in pain. How come I didn't have arms to throw a chair at him, but I still had a mouth and a stomach? The Universe wasn't fair.

"I'm an hour away," Hugh said. "If you ask me, I'll come and fish you out and all this will be yours. All you have to do is say, 'Hugh, please.'"

"Stick a thumb up your ass and twirl on it."

He smiled, cut a piece of bread, and spread butter on it. I watched the butter slide over the slice. He bit into it and chewed.

Bastard.

"Are you done with your food porn show? I have a cold wet hellhole I need to get back to."

"Sooner or later you'll break," he said.

"Keep hoping."

"You're a survivor. Voron put you on the edge of that cliff again and again until he conditioned you to claw onto life. You'll do whatever you have to do to survive, and I'm your only chance of getting out. At first you'll balk, but with every passing hour my offer will look better and better. You'll convince yourself that dying will accomplish nothing and you should at least go out with a bang. You'll tell yourself that you're accepting my offer just so you can stick that broken sword into my chest and feel it cut through my heart. Even if you die afterward, the fact that I'll stop breathing makes your death mean something. So you'll call me. And you'll try to kill me. Except you've gone three days without food, and that body . . ." He tilted his head and looked me over slowly. "That body burns through calories like fire goes through gasoline. You're running out of reserves. I can put you down with one hit."

"You're right about the sword. You broke mine. I owe you one."

He tapped his naked chest over his heart. "This is the spot. Give it a shot, Kate. Let's see what happens."

"What is it you want from me, Hugh?"

"Short term, I'd like you to say my name with a please attached to it. I'd like to walk into Jester Park with you on my arm."

Jester Park, Iowa. Once a park in Des Moines, and now one of my father's retreats.

"Long term, I want to win. And I will win, Kate. You'll put up a good fight, but eventually you'll be sleeping in my bed and fighting with me back to back. We'll be good together. I promise you."

"What part of no don't you understand?"

"The part where I don't get what I want. You need to be taught your place. It's not at the Keep."

Something inside me snapped. "And you're going to teach me where my place is?"

"Yes."

Time for a reality check, Hugh. "You have what you have only because my father mixed your blood with his. Everything you do and everything you are, you owe to someone else and when he's done using you, he'll toss you aside."

Hugh's eyebrows came together.

I kept going. "I've carved my own life out of this world. You try getting by without Roland's help and then come back and lecture me. Oh wait, you did, and first I kicked your ass, then Curran broke your spine and threw you into a fire. How does that feel, Hugh? To know you're second best?"

"You're pushing it," he told me.

"You're hired help. You can't even tell Roland no. So how about you shut up and go back to what you do best. Roland's boots need cleaning."

"Suit yourself." He put his hands behind his head and smiled. "I have nothing but time."

I jerked awake. The cold water washed over me. Ghastek stared at me, bleary-eyed.

"Curran will come for me," I told him.

MY LEGS WERE cramping. The cramps came with sickening frequency, twisting me, so painful I would've screamed if I hadn't been so weak. We had gone through four magic waves now. During the third, Ghastek spoke to the wall begging his mother not to die. We were on our fourth wave now and he had fallen silent hours ago.

I'd tried using power words, but none of them worked. They just bounced off the walls of the shaft. Hugh must've warded it.

I tried to sleep as much as I could. When I couldn't, I counted the bricks. Lately they had turned blurry and out of focus, as if I were looking at them through hot air rising from the pavement. I was no longer Kate. I was a thing. Cold. Exhausted. Starving. Filthy.

I don't want to die in this dark hole. I don't want to die!

I just want to see the sun. I want to hug Julie one more time. I want to kiss Curran.

Maybe I was wrong.

Maybe he wouldn't find me in time.

WARM. DRY. FOOD. Hugh.

"Five days in. It's an anniversary. I thought I'd check on you. The offer is still open."

"Fuck you."

"Okay then."

Cold, wet darkness. Ghastek convulsing in his restraints. Holding his head above water. *Don't die. We will make it. We have to make it.*

THE WATER SPLASHES me. I no longer know if it's warm or cold.

The wall of the shaft falls apart. Curran looks at me. I see him. I see his gray eyes. I hear his voice. "I'm coming, baby. Hold on. Just hold on for me."

He's come for me! He's come to get me out. "I love you so much . . ."

I just want to touch him, but I can't get through. Something is blocking me. He is right there. I can see him *right there.* I can't . . .

"Kate! Kate!" Something is trying to hold me back, but I have to get to Curran. I have to get out.

"It's not real." Ghastek's voice. "It's not real. See?"

Curran fades. There are only the stones, the dark cold stones and smears of my blood, where I'd clawed at them.

SIX MAGIC WAVES. I float in a lake of blood. I'm hallucinating, but I can taste it on my lips, the salty hot flavor of a human life.

It will pass. It's just the hunger.

Ghastek, blurry, his face out of focus, floating in the blood next to me. "I'm afraid."

Have to keep him alive. "We'll make it."

"I just wanted life," he whispers. "I watched my mother die. She suffered. She suffered so much. I can't do that. I can't. I'm too afraid. I did all this because I wanted the Builder's gift. I wanted him to make me immortal."

He stares at me with deranged eyes. He doesn't really see me.

"Ghastek?"

"My name is Matthew." His voice is a feverish whisper. "If the Builder cares about you, if he needs you, he'll let you live forever. He won't let you die."

"I care about you, Matthew. Hold my hand. I won't let you die."

SEVEN MAGIC WAVES.

Curran stands on the grate above me and I talk to him. I say, *I love you all. This is not the end. I won't roll over and die.*

I wish I had been a better person. I wish things had been different.

This place won't kill me. I will survive. I won't break.

Curran smiles at me. He's holding his hand out. I know he'll come for me.

He'll come for me. He just might be too late.

NOISE. LOW RHYTHMIC noise, like the pounding of some giant heart.

It keeps getting louder.

It keeps coming.

I'm hallucinating again.

Pain.

My left hand is gripping the grate. There is a chunk of brick on the other side of the grate next to it.

There is a chunk of a *brick*.

My mind started working slowly, like a rusty engine trying to will itself back to life.

Thud! Something hit the wall above us.

Another brick bounced off the grate.

I reached over and shook Ghastek. He hung motionless in his restraints. I could barely move him.

Thud!

"Ghastek," I whispered. "Ghastek . . ."

His eyes opened slowly.

Thud.

Bricks showered the grate. In the dim light of the electric lamps, the shaft wavered, blurry, but I saw the hole about twenty feet up. Another thud. More bricks plunged down, bouncing off the metal. Someone moved at the top of the hole, leaped, and landed on the grate. Gray eyes looked at me.

Curran.

Please let it be real.

He stared at me. His eyes were horrified. "Kate? Jesus Christ."

My lips moved. "Please be real."

He pulled a metal hacksaw out of his backpack and started slicing through the grate. "Stay with me, baby."

This was a dream. Another hallucination. Or Hugh screwing with my head. I braced myself. I would wake up and he would disappear.

Two others landed on the grate. Jim. Thomas, the rat alpha.

Jim saw me and swore.

"Get me out," Ghastek whispered. "Please."

"I should leave you in there, you sonovabitch," Curran snarled. "Cut him out."

Jim pulled out another saw.

The blade sliced through the bars above me. Back and forth. Back and forth.

Please be real. I reached through the bars and touched his fingers in cutoff gloves. His hand was warm.

"Hold on, baby. I've got you."

A creature tumbled out of the hole and landed on the grate. Hairless and muscled, it crouched on all fours as if it had never walked upright. Thick curved talons crowned the toes of its feet. Its chest was wide, its hindquarters muscled like those of a boxer dog. A bone ridge protruded from its spine. The massive jaws unhinged and finger-sized fangs pierced the air. Its eyes, deep set and bright red, burned with hunger.

A vampire. An ancient vampire, so old it sent a shiver down my spine.

Curran whipped around. The vamp leaped. Curran's right hand closed on the vamp's throat. He spun, oblivious to the talons ripping at his jacket, and drove the undead's head into the wall. The vamp's skull bounced off the brick. Curran bared his teeth and smashed it into the wall again and again, his face savage.

The bones cracked. Undead blood splashed the bricks. Curran ran the bloodsucker into the brick one last time, and twisted its head off like he was wringing out the laundry. The vamp body fell one way, the head went the other.

"Show-off," I whispered.

"Hold on. Almost through."

He gripped the grate. The skin of his fingers turned gray—the silver burning him. Curran strained. His legs shook under the pressure. The last two bars bent, and he pushed part of the grate aside like a lid on a can. He dropped to his knees and reached for me. I slid out of my restraints. Someone must've turned my legs to lead, because they pulled me down like an anchor. I sank. The water rose over my neck and my mouth . . . He grabbed my arm, pulled me up through the grate, out into the air, and hugged me to him.

He smelled like Curran. He felt like him. I buried my face in the bend of his neck. His skin was so hot, it burned.

"Don't die on me." He kissed my face, pulling off his jacket. "Don't die on me."

I couldn't stand. I just slumped there on top of the grate, holding on to him.

He wrapped me in his jacket, closed his arms around me, and jumped. Then we were in a narrow hallway. He carried me through it.

"I love you," I told him.

"I love you, too." His voice was raw. "Stay alive, Kate."

"Ghastek . . ."

"They'll get him. Don't worry. Stay with me."

"Where would I go?"

He squeezed me to him. "I'm going to kill that fucker."

"Dibs," I told him. "He broke my sword."

"Fuck the sword. I almost lost you." He kicked a door open and lowered me to a fire built on the concrete floor. "Andrea, clothes! Quickly."

Curran ripped my shirt in half. My pants came off—someone was pulling off my sodden clothes. The heat of the fire swirled around me. Christopher swung into my view, his hair snow white, and held a thermos to my lips. "Drink, mistress."

I sipped. Chicken broth. I drank again and he pulled it back. "Not so fast. You'll get sick."

"Hang on," Andrea told me, and slipped socks on my feet. "Don't ever pull this shit again, you hear me?"

"Sure," I whispered.

"Here." Robert handed Curran a shirt.

"What are all of you doing here?" I whispered, as Curran put it on me.

"We came to save you." Christopher smiled. "Even me. I didn't want to come back to this place, but I had to. I couldn't leave you in a cage."

He gave me more broth. I drank. Curran hugged me to him.

We were in some sort of large room. A fire burned in the center, eating the remains of office furniture. A pile of cubicle partitions rested against one wall. There were windows in the ceiling. The room looked like it was on its side. That made no sense.

"Where are we?" I whispered.

"You don't know?" Christopher's blue eyes widened. "We're in Mishmar."

Roland's tower prison. I only knew what Voron told me of it. When the business district of Omaha fell, my father had bought the rubble from the impoverished city. He had taken colossal chunks of fallen skyscrapers, two, three, four stories tall, pulled them into a remote field somewhere in Iowa, and piled them onto each other into a huge tower, held together by magic and encircled by a wall. It was a vicious place, an ever-changing labyrinth, where exits sealed themselves and walls took on new shapes. Feral vampires roamed here. Things for which nobody had any name because they had no right to exist hunted here. There was no escape from Mishmar. Nobody ever got out.

"You came into Mishmar for me?"

Curran hugged me to him, cradling me like I was a child. "Of course I did."

I loved him so much. "You're a fucking idiot." My voice was hoarse. "What the hell did you do that for?"

"Because I love you. Give her more broth. She's coming around."

"We have to get out of here," I said. "Hugh checks up on me in my dreams."

Curran's eyes went gold. "Let him come."

"A vampire!" Andrea shouted.

The window above and to the left of us broke. Shards of glass and wood cascaded to the floor. A vampire fell into the room, its mind a hot spark in front of me. It landed on all fours, old, gaunt, and inhuman. A sharp bone crest protruded from its back. Another ancient one.

The vamp shot forward and then stopped abruptly.

"I'm still . . . a Master of the Dead," Ghastek said from a blanket on the floor. "Kill it before I lose consciousness."

14

I OPENED MY eyes. I lay on a blanket, wrapped in several layers of clothing. I couldn't see Curran. He'd been holding me for what felt like hours. Every time I woke up, he was there, but not now. Anxiety spiked.

Okay, I had to snap out of it. He wasn't going to evaporate. He wasn't a hallucination. He was here . . . somewhere.

Above me small hateful points of magic moved back and forth. Vampires. One, two . . . Nine. I pushed back the blankets. The room was mostly empty. Christopher napped, leaning against the wall. To my left Ghastek lay on his blankets. Robert, the alpha rat, sat next to him. No Curran or Jim. I also thought I saw Andrea, but that couldn't be right. Andrea couldn't be here. She was pregnant. She wouldn't risk the baby.

A brown-eyed woman knelt by me. She was my age, with dark hair, a full mouth, and brown skin. She wore a black loose abaya, an Islamic-style robe, and a matching hijab, a wide scarf, draped over her head. She looked Arabic to me. I'd seen her before among Doolittle's staff.

"Who are you?"

"My name is Nasrin." She gently touched my face, examining my eyes. "I'm here to heal you."

"Where's Curran?"

"He's checking the barricade," Nasrin said. "Jim and others are standing guard there. How do you feel?"

What barricade? "The room isn't blurry anymore."

She smiled. "That's good. We've had a short magic wave, and I've worked on you a little."

"I think I remember."

I had passed out at some point, but Curran woke me up every five minutes to eat. At first it was broth, which I vomited once or twice. I vaguely remembered Andrea passing me a wet rag to clean my face and Nasrin murmuring something and holding a canteen to my lips. Whatever I'd drunk had made me feel better. Then I was given some mysterious concoction Doolittle had made up and sent with them especially in case we had been starved. I asked what was in it, and Christopher very seriously told me, "Forty-two percent dried skimmed milk, thirty-two percent edible oil, and twenty-five percent honey." I was afraid to ask about the other one percent and I had trouble keeping it down. Then a magic wave came and someone chanted over me, and suddenly I was ravenous. I had gone through two quart containers of the stuff and my stomach wanted more, but I had passed out. It seemed like that whole sequence happened more than once, but I couldn't be sure.

"What was in the bottle you gave me?" I asked.

She smiled. She didn't look a thing like Doolittle, but something about her communicated that same soothing confidence. "The water of Zamzam."

"The blessed water from Mecca?"

"Yes." She nodded with a small smile and held a bottle to my lips. "Drink now."

I took a sip.

"When Prophet Ibrahim cast Hajar and their infant son, Ismail, out into the barren wilderness of Makkah, he left them there with only a bag of dates and a leather bag of water." Nasrin touched my forehead. "No fever. That is good. When all the water was gone, Ismail cried for he was thirsty, and Hajar began to search for water. She climbed the mountains and walked the valleys, but the land was barren. Any dizziness?"

"No."

"That's good also. Finally at Mount al-Marwah Hajar thought she heard a voice and called out to it, begging for help. Angel Jibril descended to the ground, brushed it with his wing, and the spring of Zamzam poured forth. Its water satisfies both thirst and hunger." Nasrin smiled again. "We brought some of it home with us when my family went on a holy pilgrimage. My medmagic encourages the body to heal itself by making it metabolize food at an accelerated rate. You had no wounds, so as your body absorbed the nutrients, they all went directly to where they were supposed to go and the water sped up the process even further. If we can keep this up, you'll be walking soon. Not too bad for thirty-six hours of treatment, and it looks like we might have avoided refeeding syndrome. Without magic, restoring your strength would take a few weeks."

I glanced at Ghastek.

"He's recovering slower," Nasrin said. "But you were in better shape to begin with and you had more reserves than he did. Don't worry. I'll get you back to fighting weight. That's my specialty. I'm the head of the Keep's recovery unit. We suspected you might become malnourished, so Dr. Doolittle and I agreed that I would be the most effective."

"Thank you."

"You're welcome."

I tried to lift my head up. "You said there was a barricade. Where is it?"

"It's at both ends of the hallway." Nasrin looked up. "The floor above us is infested with feral vampires. Ghastek tried to count them at some point and mentioned four once and six two hours later. We killed a couple, but they're warped. This place isn't healthy for vampires either."

There were nine vampires now. They could sense us somehow, and they'd keep aggregating. We had to nuke them or move.

"They're feeding on each other," Ghastek said. He turned to lie on his side, facing me. His eyes had sunk in their sockets. He looked like a ghost of himself.

"I've never heard of undead doing that," I said.

"There have been cases," he said. "It involves severe starvation or controlled feeding. I've been able to reproduce it before in a laboratory environment. There are"—he yawned—"many variables. A vampire who feeds on other undead undergoes morphological changes. It must be done very carefully, or the vampire may die. Some undead . . ." He yawned again. "A consistent diet of other vampires over time . . . What was I saying?"

I had trouble concentrating, too. "Something about vampires feeding on other vampires."

"It makes them feel older, more powerful to us," Ghastek said. "The navigators can feel an undead's age, and a diet of other undead makes a vampire feel older."

I had met vampires that felt old enough to be pre-Shift before and I never could get over it. It should've been an impossibility. Before the Shift, the magic was so weak, it was barely there. The Immortuus pathogen didn't manifest until after the first catastrophic magic wave. Now I knew. They weren't really old. They were cannibals.

"Older how? By decades?"

"Yes." Ghastek yawned. "Unless you just want an overpowered specimen, it's not cost-effective to continue to feed a vampire other undead over time. The procurement of vampires is expensive. It's really a waste." He yawned again. "You have to tell your lion to avoid killing them. Cannibalistic vampires target the weaker of their species and they react to undead blood. Kill one, and a swarm will converge on the corpse."

He closed his eyes.

"How many vampires are in Mishmar?" Robert asked.

Ghastek opened his eyes. "I've been here only once, five years ago. I had to take a test to be admitted to the Golden Legion. You must walk into Mishmar and bring out a vampire. Back then, I felt hundreds."

Hundreds. We had to go. The faster we got out of here, the better our chances of survival. Ghastek and I were keeping us anchored here. I needed to get mobile fast.

I reached over for the container and began to eat more of Doolittle's paste.

"Thank you," Ghastek said.

"For what?"

"For keeping me alive." He closed his eyes and fell asleep.

Curran pushed through the door. His blond hair looked longer than it had before he left for North Carolina. Heavy stubble sheathed his jaw. He also hadn't shaved in a couple of weeks. Blood splattered his clothes, some of it old, some new.

He landed next to me. I put my arms around him and kissed him. The taste of him against my tongue was magic. He kissed me back and held me against him. "Did you eat?"

"I did. It tastes much better than the feast Hugh was offering."

"I'll break his neck," Curran whispered, his voice vibrating with so much menace that I almost winced. The muscles on Curran's arms hardened with tension. He was probably picturing killing Hugh in his head. I wouldn't want to be Hugh d'Ambray at this point. Between me and Curran, his prognosis for a long life didn't look good.

"Ghastek says the vampires here are feeding on each other. If you kill one, they'll swarm. How's the barricade?" I asked.

"It will hold for a couple more hours." He stroked my shoulder and kissed my hair. I leaned against him. It felt so good just to know he was here.

"You can have one more nap and then I'll carry you," he said.

"I might manage a walk."

"That would be good, but if not, I've got you."

I wrapped my arms around him again. There were things I wanted to say, but I didn't know how. He'd crossed half of the country, broken into an impenetrable prison, and found me against all odds. There were no words to explain to him how I felt about that.

"I love you," I told him. There. Nice and simple. "I knew you would find me."

He smiled at me. "I would never stop looking."

And he wouldn't. He would've kept going until he found me. I had no doubt of that.

He reached into his jacket and handed me something wrapped in a rag. I unfolded the fabric. Slayer's other half. I imagined sliding it into Hugh's eye. It was that or start crying, and I would not cry in Mishmar.

"Can it be repaired?" Curran asked quietly.

"No." I'd broken the tip off before, once, and Slayer regrew it, but this break was right in the middle. My saber was done. An old friend had died.

Thinking about it made me cringe. I stroked the blade. It was like a part of me had been cut off. I felt . . . naked. "Even if I managed to fix it somehow, the blade would always have a weak spot."

"I'm sorry."

"Thank you. Hugh got under my skin and I got careless."

"Don't worry, I plan to get under his skin, too." He curled his fingers as he did when he had claws. "He won't like it."

We sat quietly for a long minute.

"I brought your other saber," he said.

"The Cherkassy?"

Curran nodded.

"Can I have it?"

He reached over and pulled it from the pile of backpacks. I drew the slightly curved metal blade from the sheath and ran my fingers along it. Not the same.

Curran nudged the container of food toward me. "Eat."

"Feeding me again, Your Furriness?"

"Of course," he said. "I love you."

It made me feel warm all over.

"I figured out how Hugh teleports," I said between bites. "He wears an emergency vial of water around his neck. He breaks it and the water wets his skin, he says a power word, and it teleports him to the water's source. Once the process begins, you go ethereal for a few seconds from start to finish. He teleports only as a last resort—if the tech hits during transit, he's toast."

"Good to know."

"Was Gene's invitation a setup?"

Curran shrugged. "I don't know. But when we get back, I'm planning on asking him. He is our guest at the Keep." The way he said "guest" didn't bode well for Gene.

"What happened after I left?"

Curran leaned against an overturned chair. "I chased Hugh across the field, but he teleported before I could get to him. I got his horse. You want it?"

"His Friesian? No thanks. It looks pretty, but they don't make the best riding horses. Did they tell you I rode a giant donkey?"

He blinked. "You what?"

"A giant black-and-white donkey. She was like twelve feet tall and bad tempered. I left her in the Keep's stables. I'd rented her from a livery stable, so we may have to buy her now, because of all the time that's passed. Her name is Cuddles."

He struggled with it for a minute. "Sometimes hunger has strange side effects . . ."

"No, I was there," Robert said, his eyes still closed. "I've seen Cuddles. Long ears."

Curran's eyes widened.

"If we get out of here, I'd like to keep her," I told him.

"If you finish eating this food, I'll get you a whole herd of giant donkeys."

"That's the strangest bribe I've ever heard of," Robert said.

"I don't want a herd. I just want one." I ate more of Doolittle's paste. "What are you going to do with Hugh's Friesian?"

"I don't know. Hell, I might keep it. I'll walk it around like a dog on a leash."

I laughed. "You hate horses."

"No," Curran said. "I don't trust them. There's a difference."

"So what else happened after I went poof?"

"Then I had a problem," he said. "You were gone, Hugh had disappeared, and Ghastek vanished, too. The People were screaming bloody murder and running back and forth. Jim told me about Brandon and his water trick. I needed more information and I wanted to know what inside Brandon made him so stupid that he would do this, so I opened Brandon's stomach and pulled his guts out while Jennifer watched. I told her that if she moved an inch, I would do things to her that would make what I was doing to Brandon seem civilized and kind."

He lost control. I could count on the fingers of one hand the times Curran had let himself go, and they were branded in my memory. He prided himself on always being in control. I finally did it. I had driven the Beast Lord crazy. He must've been either really scared for me or angry, or both. I knew exactly how he felt. I couldn't roar, but if he'd been teleported off that field, I'd make the entire Pack cringe and wet themselves.

"Did Jennifer move?" I asked.

"No. Stood there quietly as he screamed. Brandon didn't give me anything constructive. It was Barabas who remembered that Jennifer had walked into your meeting with that bottle."

"She couldn't do it," I told him. "I think she went into the meeting planning on it, but she backed out at the last minute."

"Since Brandon wasn't helping, I gave what was left of him to Mahon and told Jennifer it was her turn. She said I wouldn't dare. I assured her I would. I grabbed her by her throat and shook her a little. I may have roared."

Robert sighed. "He was in half-form. He'd grown claws the size of walrus tusks and they were wet with Brandon's blood. His fur stood on end, his mouth was this big"—Robert held his hands about two feet apart—"he'd sprouted an extra set of fangs, and his eyes looked on fire. He was roaring so loud the windows in the Keep vibrated, and when he spoke, he sounded like a demon from hell. I would've told him anything."

I brushed my fingers along his stubbled cheek gently. "Did you have a failure of control, Your Furriness?"

"No," Curran said. "I was perfectly in control."

Across the room, Robert shook his head. "He was holding Jennifer up a foot off the ground the whole time he questioned her."

"Did you strangle the wolf alpha?" Not that she didn't deserve it.

Curran grimaced. "Of course not. I needed information. After I put her face in my mouth, we agreed that it was in her best interests to tell me what I wanted to know. Then the floodgates opened and all sorts of interesting things fell out. She had been approached five months ago, just after Daniel died. A man met her in a restaurant and told her that he was from Ice Fury, and that they wanted inside information. At first she told them to take a hike, but then paranoia set in. When we left for Europe, they offered her panacea. She took it."

She was pregnant, alone, and afraid. Her baby was also Daniel's baby, and she would do anything to keep her child from going loup. But to betray everyone in the Pack . . .

"She started feeding them intel about us," Curran continued. "In return, they supplied her with panacea and other favors. Do you remember when Foster and Kara's business burned down?"

Foster and Kara Hudson served as Jennifer's betas for a while. She'd inherited them from Daniel. They had owned a small textile mill and clothes shop until it burned to the ground while we were gone on our "let's get panacea" trip. "Arson? Against her own betas?"

Curran nodded. "For a while it looked like Foster might challenge Jennifer, but after the fire, he took a loan from the Pack and both he and Kara stepped down from the beta spot to focus on rebuilding. Jim had thought it smelled bad so he checked it out, but neither Jennifer nor anybody else from Clan Wolf was anywhere near the fire at the time."

Wow. I didn't think she'd sink that low. Kate Daniels, brilliant judge of character. Not.

"Then we came back with Desandra, she took the beta spot, and things got worse and worse, until Jennifer demanded they make her go away. Before the Conclave, Jennifer was given the bottle and told that either she dumped it on you in the morning and Desandra would be taken care of, or evidence of her betrayal would be presented to the Pack."

"You can have everything you want if you do what we say, or we'll take away everything you have?"

"Yes. According to her, she couldn't do it, so Brandon did it for her. She didn't ask him. He volunteered." Curran grimaced.

Robert shrugged. "I can't decide if her failure to completely betray us was to her credit, because she still had some scruples, or if it was the ultimate sign of her cowardice, because she'd manipulated someone else into doing it."

"I don't care," Curran said.

"What happened next?" I asked.

"Next I dropped Jennifer down and told Desandra that if she wanted to lead the wolves, now was a good time. To her credit, she didn't drag it out. Jennifer put up a good fight, but in the end it was a quick kill."

I should've hated Jennifer. If she had somehow escaped discovery, I would've killed her when I returned, not because I disliked her, but because she was a traitor and a liability. I should've been angry, but Hugh had a monopoly on all of my anger lately. All I felt for Jennifer was sadness. Two years ago everything was great for her. She had a husband who loved her and a job that fulfilled her. They were planning on having children. Her life held so much promise. Instead it all went sideways and ended in a tragedy.

"What happens to the baby?" I asked.

"Winona took her," Curran said.

One of Jennifer's sisters. She had five. "Are they going to cause a problem?"

"I don't give a flying fuck," Curran said. "If they decide to cause a problem, I'll cull them down until they stop being a problem."

Okay then. "How did you find me?"

"I found Nick first," Curran said.

Oh boy. "Please don't tell me you opened up the crusader's stomach to see if he had something stupid in him, too."

"I didn't have to. He told me where you were." Curran waved his hand at the grimy office. "This was Hugh's backup plan. If he didn't get his way, you would end up in Mishmar. I went back to the Keep and asked for volunteers to come with me. We had to move fast. Christopher showed up with your hair and said he could track you with it."

"You brought Jim." I smiled.

Curran rolled his eyes. "I wasn't planning on it. Then Jim and I snarled at each other for half an hour, and Raphael and Mahon decided that this time they could stay behind. I had Jim and Christopher. Derek wanted to come, but he wasn't at one hundred percent, so I wouldn't take him. Robert and Thomas volunteered. Andrea, too."

Oh, you bloody idiot. She shouldn't have come. I'd give her shit for it when we got out. I glanced at Robert. "Why?"

He sighed. "Because I understand. If my mate were gone, I would find him. No matter what it took. He would do the same for me. Where one of us goes, the other follows."

"Thank you," I said.

"You're welcome."

"With the two of them, we had enough, but we needed a medmage.

Doolittle couldn't go, but he asked for volunteers." Curran nodded at Nasrin.

The medmage shrugged. "I go where I'm needed."

"Then I had to make fucking arrangements to make sure the Pack didn't fall apart while we were gone. The Council pitched a fit. We didn't set out until the next morning."

The way he said that didn't bode well for the Council. "They didn't want you to go."

"Somebody got excited and told me that I couldn't go since it wasn't in the best interests of the Pack," Curran said.

Figured. No matter how well I served the Pack, my life wasn't worth risking Curran or the other alphas. It should've hurt, but I was used to it by now.

"They were panicked," Robert said.

"What did you do?" I asked Curran.

He shrugged. "I reminded them that I was the one who decided things."

"It took us two days to get here," Robert said. "There is a really fast ley line coming back from here that starts around St. Louis, but there's almost nothing going northwest."

"The roads are shit," Curran said. "We didn't exactly know where Mishmar was in the first place, and when we finally got here it took another day to find a way in. But the real issue was that we couldn't move during tech. Christopher suspended your hair in some solution and we used it as a compass, but it only worked while the magic was up. I had to sit on my hands and wait half of the time. We've been wandering through the damn place for days."

Poor Christopher. *I'll follow you to the ends of the earth, but not there. I cannot go there again.* But he did. He came to Mishmar for me. If we got out of here alive, I would find a way to repay him.

"Did Christopher tell you to bring the saws?"

Curran nodded. "He said there were prison cells . . ."

Curran raised his head. Robert turned toward the doorway.

A rhythmic staccato of shots was coming from somewhere down the hallway. Ten to one, it was Andrea.

Thomas stuck his head into the doorway. "We have to move."

.   .   .

WE RAN THROUGH the narrow hallway. Well, I wasn't really running. I was dragging myself forward.

Curran leaned toward me. "Are you going to be a hardass about this?"

"What do you think?" We were already down by one, because Ghastek couldn't walk and Jim decided to carry him. I wouldn't tie up Curran's hands by making him carry me, too.

"If you say you got it, you got it. But if you fall down, I'll pick you up."

"Deal."

Falling didn't seem like such a bad idea now.

The narrow hallway kept going, its plain brown walls punctuated by doorways that opened into offices filled with filthy shattered furniture. The two wererats led the way, both in half-form, lean, shaggy, and fast. Nasrin followed, then Curran and I, Jim with Ghastek, and Christopher and Andrea bringing up the rear. Behind us, the vampires dashed through Mishmar. I could feel their minds. There were close to twenty now, six directly behind us and the rest above and on the sides. It felt like they were moving through the walls.

Thomas, the larger of the two wererats, made a sharp turn. I followed just in time to see him jump through a jagged hole in the floor. I ran after him and looked through the hole. A nine-foot drop. Sure, why not. I climbed into the hole. Ow. I stumbled. Okay, this wasn't a good idea. Curran dropped down after me.

"Got it, baby?" he asked quietly.

"Piece of cake."

Nasrin was already jumping through another hole a few feet to the right. I checked the height. More like twenty-five feet this time and too narrow for me and Curran to go through at once. "I'll take that help."

Curran jumped in and landed down below. "Go."

I dropped into the hole. He caught me and lowered me to the floor. "Good?"

"Good."

"Necro in the hole," Jim called from above. I looked up in time to see Ghastek falling out of the ceiling. Curran caught him.

"This is ridiculous," Ghastek said.

Jim jumped down. Curran handed Ghastek off and we were on our way. The room we were in now was wide and stretched for hundreds of feet. It resembled a hotel lobby: tall gray columns of natural stone, textured ceiling, steps with some glossy black finish, dusty elaborate chandeliers that had somehow survived the disaster . . .

The magic rolled over us like a viscous invisible wave.

Black stalks spiraled out of the ground.

Curran and I moved at the same time. He scooped me up just as I jumped in his arms and then he sprinted across the room like a bat out of hell. When a magic wave hits and something weird pops out of the ground, you don't wait to find out what it is. You put some distance between you and whatever the hell that thing is.

Behind us, Andrea barked. "Run, Christopher!"

All around us the stalks split, their offshoots widening into triangular leaves.

Curran flew across the room. Ahead of us a wall loomed, with a wide stone staircase leading upward. The steps were flower-free. Nasrin was already there, waving.

The stalks sprouted fat black bulbs.

Undead magic smeared my mind. I glanced back over Curran's shoulder. Andrea had locked Christopher's arm in a death grip and was pulling him across the floor. Behind them a vampire fell through the hole in the ceiling and charged after us.

Curran leaped and landed on the stairs. Jim with Ghastek was only a step behind.

The flowers opened, releasing a dense corona of thin filaments glowing with pale purple, as if someone had taken the fringes from several passionflowers and strung them together on the same stem.

Andrea reached the stairs, dragged Christopher a few steps up, and let him go. He collapsed.

The vampire glided among the blossoms, silent and quick.

"Don't kill it," Ghastek murmured. "I need a ride."

The flowers shivered. A cream-colored shimmering mist rose from their petals. The vampire stumbled, reared back in complete silence, and collapsed.

"Damn it," Ghastek swore.

The stalks rustled. Black hairy roots stretched over to the bloodsucker's body.

"Beautiful," Christopher whispered. *"Mortem germinabit."*

"Come on, Christopher. We have to go." Andrea hauled him upright and we climbed the stairs.

"I know we've been following our own scent trail, but I don't remember any of this," Jim said.

"That's because we didn't come this way," Robert said.

"But I remember the two holes we climbed out of on the way up," Andrea said. "I smelled us. This lobby or whatever it is wasn't supposed to be here. This should have been a hallway. Are you saying the room moved?"

"We don't know," Thomas said.

The stairs ended in another door. Robert eased it open. A typical hotel hallway rolled out before us, complete with long red carpet and numbers on the doors.

"So we have no idea where we're going?" Nasrin asked.

"We're going down," Curran told her. "Unless this place develops its own gravity, the direction shouldn't be that hard."

I wouldn't bet on that.

FOUR FLOORS LATER the section of Mishmar that was lifted from a hotel ended. We took the stairs, squeezed through a gap in the wall and suddenly the carpeted hotel hallway was gone, replaced by the hardwood floors and open plan of a modern apartment. The walls changed from beige to polished glossy red, rich like the color of arterial blood. The dark gray furniture stood intact, the couch and chairs arranged as if waiting for a party to begin. Even the pots still hung from a baker's rack above the range. Now how did my father manage that? How does one pick a chunk of a building and set it on top of other buildings without the furniture sliding around? Maybe someone put it all back together after it became a part of Mishmar?

I tried not to think about the sheer power required to sever several floors of a building and lift them hundreds of feet in the air without disturbing the contents. It broke my mind.

We tiptoed across the hardwood. Modern art hung on the walls, a collection of strategically placed streaks of red and white. An open suitcase, half filled with men's shirts, lay in the middle of the floor, just by where the door should be. A long brown streak stretched across the polished wood toward the missing door. Dried blood.

The wererats checked the hallway beyond, slinking forward.

"Clear," Thomas called.

"Not exactly," Ghastek murmured.

I felt them too, behind us, above us, to the right . . . More than twenty now. The vampire horde kept growing, like a snowball as it rolled down a snowy hill. I didn't know if these were new vampires or if the ones we left behind somehow found a way around the deadly flowers. I didn't even care. I just wanted out of Mishmar.

We pushed on into the hallway. Fatigue was slowing me down and I dragged myself forward, each step an effort as if an anchor was chained to my legs. I wanted to lie down, but taking a nap wasn't an option.

"An elevator shaft would be nice right about now," Jim said.

"Keep dreaming," Curran told him.

A wide gap severed the floor of the hallway. Robert dropped to all fours and stuck his head into it, bending down so much that half of his body disappeared. By all rights, he should've tipped over. "I don't see anything moving."

"Any undead?" Curran asked Ghastek.

The Master of the Dead looked at him. "Pick a direction, I'll tell you how many."

"Is there a direction in which there aren't vampires?" Andrea asked.

"No."

Curran glanced at me.

"Down is as good as any," I said, and pulled my saber out. It didn't feel like Slayer, probably because it wasn't Slayer. Slayer lay broken in Curran's pack.

"Down it is."

The two wererats dropped into the gap, and Curran followed. I jumped after him, and he leaped up to meet me, caught me in the air, and landed on soft feet.

"Fancy," I told him, scanning one end of the room, while he peered at the other. This floor appeared to be a high-end gym, filled with rows of ellipticals and treadmills.

"Trying to impress, baby." Curran set me on my feet, caught Ghastek, and handed him off to Jim none too gently. We started moving. The machines stood in a single row to the left and in another two rows with a path between them to the right. Above them flat screens, now dull and dusty, mourned the passing of the tech age on their swivel mounts.

The multiple points of undead magic shifted, streaming toward us.

"Incoming," Ghastek said. "Moving fast. They probably found a point of entry to this floor."

We backed away.

A gaunt, skeletal shape squeezed through a crack in the wall near the ceiling and sat there, fastened to the wall with huge talons, the two red eyes like burning coals.

"Above and to the right," I murmured.

"I see him," Curran answered.

Another undead squeezed out of the gap and crawled next to the first one. This one was clearly older. The ridge of bony protrusions along his spine rose at least three inches, and his jaws looked like a bear trap. Across from us a third vampire crawled out of a dark crack in the other wall. This one felt old, too. A long ragged scar marked its face, trailing down over its chest past the point I could see. A cannibal vampire. The two words didn't even go together. What's next, zombie pirate Viking ghosts?

A shape flickered across the corner of my eye, dashing behind the treadmills. Another moved in the corner. Six vampires had entered the room, and they were stalking us. This wouldn't be pretty.

"There are many vampires," Christopher reported.

"Shhh," I told him. "Keep moving."

Vampires reacted to prey that ran, so we didn't run. We moved quietly and steadily toward the back of the room.

The ancient vampire on the right wall slunk down. Behind us, an undead leaped onto the treadmill and perched there, like some mutated hairless cat. More undead eyes glared at us through the gaps in the machines.

Not good.

Something clanged ahead. I glanced that way. Thomas had found a huge metal door.

"Locked," he called out quietly.

Nice. Beating on it would definitely provoke the vampires.

The undead moved toward us, two on the ground, two on the walls, one across the tops of the treadmills. I braced myself. If I had to kill them, so be it.

Andrea raised her crossbow.

The leading undead leaped. The ancient bloodsucker with the scar dashed across the gym and disemboweled the first vampire in midleap. Undead blood hit the floor, and Scar jerked a chunk of vampiric spine out of its opponent. The injured bloodsucker dropped like a stone. Scar leaped, spinning like a corkscrew, its talons opened wide, and sliced two other vampires, carving their flesh down to the bone. Two clumps of spongy dry lungs with bloated hearts hit the floor.

I closed my mouth.

The three remaining vampires, two old and one with its spinal ridge just beginning to develop, trotted over to us, crossing each other's paths, their heads down.

I turned. Ghastek stood on his own feet, his face pale, his eyes determined. The younger vampire twisted upright and picked up the Master of the Dead. The two ancients perched on the floor, Scar on the left and the other, large vamp, so pale it looked completely white, on the right, moving in perfect unison.

"You may want to break the door down," Ghastek said from four mouths, three vamps' and one his own, in the familiar dry voice I remembered. "The rest of the undead will smell their blood. We don't have much time."

== CHAPTER ==
15

THE DOOR OF the gym opened to a half-ruined restaurant. Then followed a room with vampires and Ghastek got to use his new undead, while I got to use my substitute saber. It still wasn't Slayer, but it did okay enough to get me from one end of the room to another. We slammed the door shut and had ourselves a run across another hallway to a staircase. Down we went.

Filthy rooms, crumbling chairs, floors that made no sense, one moment a luxury high-rise, the next a ruin, then a hospital . . . Sometimes icy cold, sometimes sweltering hot. One room housed a pile of rotting corpses slithering with huge snakes. Another had an imaginary floor. The floor was there, we could see it, but when Thomas stepped on it, he went completely through. Robert caught him and pulled him out, but not before the rat alpha got a glimpse of what was under the floor. He wouldn't say what it was. He just had this wild look on his half-rat, half-human face, backed away, and took off in the same direction we had come from. It took us ten minutes to catch up with him.

At one point we'd reached a hole in the side of the building and one by one stuck our heads out of it. The breath of cold, fresh air was like manna from heaven. We were high above the ground. I saw a piece of a sky, a distant field of snow, and then a giant reptilian-looking bird swooped down and tried to claw my face off with its talons. Thanks, Roland. Much appreciated.

Curran pounded on the wall for a few minutes trying to break us free. The wall held, but even if we did manage to break through and start climbing down, the birds would pluck us off.

We'd clustered around that hole for a while, not wanting to leave, but eventually we had to move. Down and down, picking up more stray vampires as escort. They were everywhere now, a constellation of filthy magic sparks moving along with us, always trying to close the distance.

"Maybe this hellhole has no end," Andrea growled, as we opened yet another door.

"No." Christopher gave her a smile as he walked through the doorway. "It ends. It is finite . . ." He stopped.

We stood in a prison block. In front of us two rows of cells stretched forward, and in the distance I saw a section of a familiar circular clearing. I had seen this exact setup underneath the Casino. Rows of cells radiated from the central circle like spokes from a wheel, except the Casino's cells held vampires. These cells held corpses.

"No," Christopher whispered. His legs crumpled under him. He dropped to the floor and pulled the hood over his face, squeezing his slender body into a small ball. "No, no, no . . ."

Bodies filled the cells. Some skeletal, grasping at the bars with fingers that used to have flesh. Others fresher, with rotting muscle still clinging to their bones. A few didn't look human. One of these cells must've been Christopher's. He had sat here, in a cage, dying slowly and watching the dead around him fall apart.

"How horrible . . ." Nasrin whispered.

I knelt by Christopher and put my arms around him.

"No . . ." he moaned.

Nasrin crouched by me, her voice calming. "It will be fine, Christopher."

"We're not staying," I told him. "You are not in a cage. You are free."

He tried to rock back and forth. He couldn't even hear me.

Behind us, the vampiric horde swelled somewhere in the walls, like an avalanche ready to break and bury us whole.

"We can't linger," Ghastek said, shifting in the vampire's arms. His other two bloodsuckers halted.

"No . . ." Christopher murmured.

"Shhh," I told him. "Look at me. Look at my eyes."

I let my magical defenses slip a little. My power curled around Christopher. He raised his head and looked at me. "Mistress . . ."

"I won't let anything bad happen to you." I was getting very good at making promises I couldn't keep. "I won't let you get stuck here in a cage. Come on."

I pulled him to his feet.

Curran looked at Nasrin. "Carry him if you have to. We need to go."

Nasrin took Christopher's hand. "Here, hold on to me. It's okay. It will be fine."

We began jogging past the cells. Corpses watched us pass with empty orbs. The putrid smell choked me. Dear God. So many people.

"Child!" a female voice called.

I stopped in midstep. I knew that voice.

An arm in a dark sleeve thrust between the bars, above a rotting corpse pressed against the iron. A woman looked at me from inside the nearest cell. The last time I saw her she had been middle-aged, with a stocky powerful build and a face the color of walnut. She looked decades older now. Her cheeks sank into her skull, hollow and withdrawn. Her skin hung off her bones. Dirt and dry blood stained the indigo mesh veil covering her dark hair and forehead. She was a ghost of her former self.

"Naeemah."

"Child."

She came from an ancient family of shapeshifters who served as bodyguards. Months ago Hugh had hired her to guard me, though not out of the goodness of his heart. He had begun to suspect that there was something off about me, but Roland sent him on another assignment, so he instructed her to watch over me and keep me alive until he could come back and pick up where he'd left off. My aunt had chosen that particular time to waltz into town. Without Naeemah's help, I would've been dead.

I turned to Curran. "We have to get her out."

He grabbed the bars and let go. "Silver. I need the saws."

"We're short on time," Jim said.

"I'm not moving until she's out," I said.

Jim gave me a hard look.

"She said she wants her out," Andrea told him. "Don't give her any crap."

"Take your time," Ghastek said. His vampires moved to cover the way we had come. "Nobody should starve to death in a cell."

Jim pulled out the saws and he and Curran began slicing through the bars. Metal screeched.

Naeemah watched me with feverish eyes.

"What are you doing here? Did Hugh put you here?"

"Yes. For helping you," she said. "And for my son."

"What happened to your son?"

"He refused a job for d'Ambray. I'm a lesson he wants to teach my children."

I added one more item to my "Reasons to Kill Hugh" list. It was getting long.

One cell bar hit the floor.

A vampire shot into the passageway. Ghastek's ancients moved like the two blades of a pair of scissors. Two coordinated slices of their talons and the invader's head rolled to the floor.

I hadn't realized how tired I was while I was moving. I was standing still now and the exhaustion was trying to pull me to the ground. And once I landed, I would stay there.

The second bar dropped down. One more and the gap would be wide enough for her to get out.

The avalanche of vampiric minds was getting closer.

Third bar. Naeemah squeezed through the opening.

"We need to run now," Ghastek said, his voice very calm.

"Which way?" Curran asked.

"This way." Naeemah ran down the hallway. "I know the way out."

"Do you trust her?" Jim asked.

"Yes!" I ran after her, stumbling.

We dashed across the room. Behind us the door shuddered—the undead were trying to break through. My legs decided this would be an awesome time to stop supporting my weight. Curran grabbed my arm, steadying me.

A dark hole gaped in the wall in front of us. Naeemah dove into it. The wererats followed her.

A vampire fell from the ceiling, cutting off Nasrin and Christopher. The healer reared back and slapped the undead upside the head, ramming it against the cell on the left. The vampire's skull broke like an egg dropped on the pavement. I turned to Curran. "What is she . . . ?"

"Iranian lion." He pointed at the hole. "Go!"

I reached the hole and looked down. All I could see was a shaft leading down at a sharp angle. *Here goes nothing.* I jumped in legs first and slid down on my ass, rolling through complete darkness. My butt hit something wet. I smelled algae. My hands slid over slime. I hurtled down through the tunnel. If there was a concrete floor waiting for me below, I'd make a lovely splat.

Light flared ahead. I planted my boots into the bottom of the tunnel, but the slick, algae-coated stone offered no resistance. If this had been a movie, this would be the part where I was supposed to yank a knife out and dig it into the stone to slow myself down. Except I'd break my nonexistent knife, hurt my arm, and still end up as a wet human pancake.

The tunnel ended. I went airborne for two terrifying seconds and plunged down into warm water. Yay, survival. I kicked up to the surface and swam away from the hole in the ceiling.

A huge room spread before me. Above, an ornate yellow ceiling, beautiful and gilded, soared in elegant arches, as if someone had opened a portal in time and Renaissance glamour spilled out. The golden swirls glowed, bright enough to bathe the entire chamber in soothing light. An enormous dusty chandelier hung from the circular recess in the ceiling, like a collection of crystals suspended from the roof of a cave. The remnants of red curtains sagged on both sides of me. Beyond them the room widened, its bottom flooded with emerald-green water. Plants covered the water's surface. Cream and ivory lotuses, the tips of their petals touched with pink, floated next to larger bright yellow lotus blossoms. Star-shaped lilies bloomed among wide leaves, some lavender, some scarlet, some with petals of light orange darkening to copper-red near the center. Ten feet above the water a balcony, cushioned in greenery, dripped vermilion and moss-green vines.

What the hell?

Curran swam up next to me.

"Are you seeing this?" I asked.

"Yep."

"So I'm not hallucinating?"

"Nope."

"Think if we crawl on that balcony, those plants will eat us?"

"If they try, I'll eat them first."

Naeemah climbed up the side wall and jumped onto the balcony, disappearing behind the plant growth. Thomas and Robert followed.

"We're in the Orpheum Theater," Ghastek said behind me.

"You've been here?" I asked.

"No, but I've seen the photographs, when I studied for my trip to Mishmar. This is Slosburg Hall, one of Omaha's historic buildings. It was among the structures Roland had bought."

I swam through the water. It was so warm and I was so tired.

"Are you okay?" Curran asked.

"If I pass out face down in this water, will you fish me out?"

"Will you promise to call me Your Majesty?"

"Hell no."

"Then I'll have to think about it."

Ghastek and his trio of vampires swam past us. This water would never end. The place was getting hazy, and I knew I'd run myself dry. My body had nothing left.

My fingers touched the wall. I gripped the gouge in the stone, trying to pull myself up, and then Curran put his hand under my foot and lifted me up, out of the water. I climbed the wall, grabbed Robert's hand, and made it onto the ledge. The balcony rose in terraces, each terrace filled with soil. Here and there, the tops of red chairs poked through the moist ground. Flowers filled the terraces: roses, tulips, poppies, daisies, and odd but strikingly beautiful blossoms that looked like a cluster of inverted tulips hanging in an umbrella arrangement from a single purplish stem. Breathtaking . . . A strange serenity came over me.

"Safe here," Naeemah said. "Vampires do not come here."

I sank to the ground and closed my eyes, and the world disappeared.

"WHAT THE FUCK were you thinking?" Curran growled.

I rolled to my feet. Slayer felt wrong in my hand. The weight was off.

Reality hit me like a brick in the face. Oh. That's right. It wasn't Slayer. Damn it.

A sour smell hit my nostrils. To the side Andrea bent over and vomited into the grass. She wiped her mouth and straightened. "I was thinking that my best friend was stuck in Mishmar and she would need my help getting out."

"I meant to talk to you about that," I said.

"I'm all ears," Andrea said.

"This is a suicide mission and you're pregnant. What the fuck were you thinking?"

"He already said that. You guys are no fun. How about 'I'm happy for you' or 'How far along are you' instead?"

"You're a moron," I told her.

"They needed a shooter and someone who knows something about Roland and Mishmar besides Christopher."

"You're pregnant," I told her.

"You'd do it for me," she said. "Now excuse me, I'm going to go pee and puke some more." She wandered off and disappeared behind the greenery.

Curran shook his head and held out a container of Doolittle's wonder food for me. I took it and began eating. "How long was I out?"

"Two hours."

"No vampires?"

"No."

I looked around. Curran, Christopher, Nasrin, Jim, Andrea, and Ghastek, bleary-eyed. That's right. He had to stay awake. If he fell asleep now, his vampires would rip into us. "Where is everyone else?"

"The rats and Naeemah went ahead to scout the way," Curran said.

I reached out with my magic. Constellations of vampires surrounded us. Some above, some to the sides . . . Their numbers had swelled while I slept. Fifty . . . Sixty? If they jumped us now, even with my help, we might not survive. I asked Curran for Slayer's pieces and tucked them away into my clothes. It was broken, but it made me feel better. I'd crushed vampire minds before, when trapped in Hugh's castle. I could kill some off, but making their heads blow up took a big chunk of magic out of me.

Ten minutes later, I was about halfway through eating the food when Thomas, Robert, and Naeemah came through the door in the back of the garden.

"Do you want bad news or bad news?" Thomas said.

Curran sighed. "Give me the bad news."

"There's only one way out of here," Robert said. "Directly behind that door is a huge round room, extremely deep. There's a metal bridge that controls the only access to the other side."

"Is it broken?" I guessed.

"No, it's retracted. From the other side."

"If it's retracted, there must be a mechanism to extend it," Ghastek said.

Thomas grimaced. "That's the other bad news."

WHEN IT CAME to size, huge could be an understatement. I stood on a narrow ledge. A cavernous chamber lay open in front of me, molded together from the walls and stones of a hundred different buildings. Shaped like an egg set on its wide end, it stretched up and down for at least a hundred feet. A narrow spire of concrete blocks, chunks of brickwork, and steel beams, cemented together by hardened soil, sprouted from the center of the chamber. An identical but inverted spire stretched from the ceiling. They met in the center, clamping between them a rectangular box of solid rock about the size of a large two-story house. A narrow doorway allowed a glimpse inside the room. Whatever was in there glowed with pale purple, as if the room were a geode containing a treasure within.

A metal breezeway circled the rectangular box. A metal bridge led from the ledge where I stood to the breezeway. I could see a large door in the opposite wall, slightly to the left. Another bridge led from that door to the breezeway. But it fell short, the last two-thirds of it retracted.

"Too far to jump," Robert assessed.

"What about down?" Andrea asked.

I looked down. Steam slunk along the bottom of the chamber. Odd shapes protruded from it. I looked closer. Vampire bones, half sunken in the reddish goo. As I watched, a bloodsucker moved slowly through the goo, oblivious to us.

"That would be a very bad idea," Ghastek said.

No shit.

"There's a wheel inside the room," Naeemah said. "If we turn the wheel, the far bridge will extend and we can cross."

"So what's the problem?" Curran asked. "We go in and turn the wheel."

"Try it," Thomas told him.

Curran started down the bridge. A third of the way down, he stopped and gripped the rails. The muscles on his arms bulged. His face changed, reshaping itself into a leonine muzzle. His hair stood on end. He snarled, like a pissed-off cat.

"Honey?" I called out.

"Well, he got farther than I did," Thomas said.

Curran's body shook. He was straining but making no progress.

"Curran!" I called.

He turned around and shook himself. His face reshaped itself back into a human. He spat a single word out. "Magic."

"Alright," Ghastek said. "My turn."

The ancient vampire with the scar scuttled forward onto the bridge. Curran leaned to one side, letting the bloodsucker pass. The vampire made it about six feet past Curran and stopped. Ghastek planted his feet, his eyes fixed on the room, and slowly extended his right arm forward. The vampire shivered and hugged the bridge. A vein on the side of Ghastek's face pulsed. The vampire didn't move an inch.

"If your head explodes, can I have your stuff?" I asked.

"My head won't explode," Ghastek said, his voice dry, and strode toward the bridge. "May I pass, please?"

"Knock yourself out." Curran came back and stepped off the bridge onto the ledge.

Ghastek began walking across the bridge.

"This will be interesting," Robert said.

Ghastek slowed, then stopped a few feet behind the vampire. He stared at the glowing room in the heart of the chamber for a long second, his spine rigid, and spoke, his voice too muffled to make out the words.

"What is he saying?" I asked.

"*I can't,*" Curran said. "*Power. Darkness* . . . I think he's losing it."

Ghastek sank to his knees.

"You might want to go and get him," I murmured to Curran.

"Can't we just leave him there?"

"No, we can't."

Curran walked along the bridge, touched Ghastek's shoulder, and pulled him to his feet. The Master of the Dead turned around. His eyes were wide under furrowed eyebrows, his mouth slack. I knew this emotion very well. Something had terrified Ghastek out of his wits. He returned to the ledge, his vampire and Curran following him.

"What was it?" Andrea asked.

Ghastek took a deep breath.

"I think he needs a minute," I said.

Slowly Ghastek's face relaxed. "Power," he said finally. "Incomprehensible power. We're in the very center of Mishmar, and that room is its heart. Everything you saw, all of the magic you felt, that room is the source of it all. I can't enter. I tried. I just can't."

"We could wait until the tech hits," Andrea said.

Naeemah shook her head. "Magic never goes away here."

Curran looked at me, his gray eyes calm. "Baby?"

"Don't," Ghastek warned me. "You have no idea what it's like to feel the weight of it on your mind. It will burn you. It's darkness in the primordial sense of the word."

It probably was darkness, but it was my kind of darkness. It spawned me and its magic ran in my blood. I stepped onto the bridge. Magic brushed against me, thin like gossamer but saturated with power. Wow.

"At least tie a rope to her so she doesn't fall," Ghastek called out.

I took another step. The gossamer magic thickened, sliding against me, guiding me, its touch soft against my skin but not against my mind. There the magic surged, overwhelming, terrifying, and potent. It offered no resistance. It just watched me, waiting, aware and alive, so strong that if I made one misstep it would choke the life out of me.

"That's not a bad idea," Curran said. "Kate?"

The gossamer veils pierced my mind, sliding through me in a flash of blinding pain.

"Kate?"

The magic moved around me, unimaginably ancient. I could see it now. It swirled with blue and gold, flowing into silver and then into deep red, a diaphanous light, its own aurora borealis spilling out in front of me, and beyond it an ancient heartless power that watched me.

"Get her off that bridge!" Ghastek yelled.

The magic beckoned me. To refuse was to die. I strode across the bridge and walked into the stone room.

Plain walls greeted me, devoid of any ornament or decoration. The room was just a hollow box of stone with a simple stone platform at the far end. But on the floor, in the center of the room, something magic waited. It started as a long pale mass rooted to the floor, and like a coral spreading from a common root and splitting into dozens of branches, it too spread out, growing out into a forest of pale protrusions. They glowed pale blue and purple, some as tall as me, some short, the size of my hand, but all sharp and dripping magic that swirled like tendrils of smoke. This looked so familiar . . .

The magic pulled me forward. I followed it, circling the mass, toward a platform at the far wall. I walked up five stone stairs, each a foot tall, and turned. The odd magic coral lay below me on the floor. In my head, I cleaned the main mass of protrusions, trying to see the form beneath.

Magic swirled at the other end of the coral.

The contours of what lay on the floor suddenly made sense.

A skeleton.

An enormous skeleton, at least nine feet tall. Its ribs curved up, its bones stretched, distorted, each bearing branching antlers of pale metal, but it was a human skeleton.

The magic snapped and shone like a length of silver silk suddenly stretched taut. A woman appeared above the skeleton, a translucent shape hovering above the bones level with me. She had dusky skin and big brown eyes. Gold colored her full lips and dusted her eyelashes. Blue-black hair cascaded down her back in soft curls. She wore a diadem of thin gold, so light and intricate, it looked spun rather than forged. Two golden winged serpents, crafted with meticulous detail wound around her arms, their spiderweb-thin wings cradling her wrists.

She looked like me.

No, wait. That was wrong. I looked like her.

Pressure ground on me. The magic of Mishmar waited like a colossal hammer poised above my head. If it fell on me, it would crush every bone in my body.

The magic drove me down. I sank to my knees.

I reached into my clothes and pulled out pieces of broken Slayer wrapped in a cloth. They matched the skeleton below perfectly. Same pale substance, neither metal nor bone, but both. A pale purple radiance emanated from Slayer's blade, matching the bones below.

The magic ground against my mind and I heard the same word whispered over and over in my head.

"Z'emir-amit. Z'emir-amit. Z'emir-amit."

Oh my God. I knew that name. I read about her. I studied her legends, but I never thought I would come across anything of hers because she had been dead for thousands of years. Dead and buried in distant Iraq, somewhere on the east bank of the Tigris River. That name belonged to the bones in front of me. I could feel it. I knew this magic.

I was looking at the corpse of my grandmother.

She wanted me to say her name. She wanted to know that I understood.

I opened my mouth and said it out loud. "Semiramis."

Her magic drenched me, not the blow of a hammer, but a cascade of power, pouring onto me as if I stood under a waterfall.

Z'emir-amit. The Branch Bearer. The Shield of Assyria. The Great Queen Semiramis. A line from Sarchedon floated up from my memory. *When she turns her eyes on you, it is like the golden lustre of noon-day; and her smile is brighter and more glorious than sunset in the desert . . . To look on her face unveiled is to be the Great Queen's slave for ever more.*

She had ruled ancient Mesopotamia. The gates of Babylon bore her name, but through the centuries she had returned to her beloved Assyria again and again. She built the walls of its cities, she led its armies, and she breathed life into its first hanging gardens.

I had carried a piece of her with me all these years and never knew it. Did Voron even know where Slayer came from, when he gave it to me? If he knew, then he must've wanted me to murder Roland with a blade made of his mother's bones. How poetic.

The image of Semiramis floated forward. The magic clamped me in its jaws and lifted me into the air. I rose above the platform, held so tight I couldn't even breathe.

Semiramis reached me. Her dark eyes looked into mine. I stared into the depth of her brown irises and saw the abyss. Time disappeared. Power battered me, crashing against my mind again and again. The first wave cracked my defenses, the second shattered it, and the third set my mind on fire. All of my secrets, fears, and worries lay before her and she drank them in like a starved vampire. It was like being thrown into the heart of the sun and feeling its raging fire consume you.

Her fury saturated me. My father had taken the bones of my grandmother from her resting place in Iraq and brought them here. She hated it. Her magic, her anger, and her grief permeated every inch of Mishmar and twisted it into hell on earth.

Hot tears bathed my cheeks. I was weeping.

She recognized me. She knew who I was. It was as if I were the grandchild of a devastating hurricane or an insane monster that had crushed and destroyed for so long, it no longer remembered how to nurture its young, but it still recognized its own blood and it tried to be gentle and to keep its own wrath from destroying me.

The magic released me. I floated down to the floor, landing on my feet, the translucent image of Semiramis looming before me. A single bone blade slid off the skeleton and landed before my feet.

A gift.

Slayer clattered on the floor before me. The hilt fell apart, releasing the broken blade. I slid the new blade into it, and the hilt sealed itself, binding to the new sword as if forged together. I picked it up. It wasn't Slayer. It was a quarter of an inch longer and slightly heavier, but it felt *right*. I knew exactly what I would call it.

I raised my head. My grandmother was gone, her magic withdrawn. It hadn't disappeared. It had just pulled back, waiting. She would let our party pass as long as they didn't disturb her.

I walked back to the doorway. A metal wheel thrust from the wall by the exit. I turned it and heard the clang of a metal bridge sliding into place. I stepped onto the breezeway and saw Curran running up the bridge. The rest of our people waited on the ledge, looking at us. "You okay?"

I swallowed and nodded. "Don't go into the room. She'll kill you. As long as nobody enters, we can pass to the other side."

"She who? What the hell was in there?" Curran asked.

"The bones of my grandmother."

Curran opened his mouth, closed it, and finally said, "Your grandmother is the magic of Mishmar?"

"She wants to go back to the Tigris. She hates it here." I slid Sarrat a little out of its sheath. "Look, she gave me a new sword."

Curran peered at it. "It looks like Slayer."

"That's because they're both made of her bones."

"Your sword is made out of your grandmother's bones?"

"Okay, I see how it sounds weird when you say it in that tone of voice . . ."

Curran grabbed my hand. "I'm not even going to say anything else. Let's just get out of here."

CHAPTER

16

I HAD STOOD in the doorway of my grandmother's tomb, blocking access to the inside, until the last of our party made it across. She let us go. When I got to the other side, nobody spoke. They just looked at me, their faces freaked out.

"Keep moving," Curran growled.

We ran through the twisted hallways of Mishmar. We'd been going for the better part of an hour now. I was so damn tired.

"Break," Curran called.

I almost ran into him, but at the last moment, I twisted away and sagged against the wall. Kate Daniels, the picture of grace.

Ghastek paused in front of me, still in the arms of his vampire. "I demand an explanation."

Bite me. How about that for an explanation?

"Let me know how that goes for you," Robert told him. "I've been demanding explanations for the last two weeks."

"You're not in a position to demand anything," Jim said.

"Me?" Robert turned to Jim.

"No, him." Jim nodded at Ghastek.

"Clearly, I haven't been made aware of certain things, and considering that I'm an innocent bystander to this entire sordid affair, I deserve to know what's going on," Ghastek said.

Curran turned. His voice dropped into the flat tone that usually meant he was half a second from erupting into violence. "You and your undead brood came to my house and threatened my people and my mate. I have a strong urge to crush your neck between my teeth. Now, so far I've been resisting this urge because Kate is fond of you—why, I can't understand. But my patience is wearing thin."

"You wouldn't dare," Ghastek told him.

Curran glanced at Jim. "Would I dare?"

Jim chuckled. "You would. In fact, I can't understand why you haven't dared yet. Mulradin is already dead. If Ghastek doesn't make it out, the People will experience a power vacuum. Either they'll fight it out or they'll get a new boss from above who doesn't know anything about Atlanta. Either way it's a win for us."

"We don't really have to kill you," Thomas said. "It can be a happy accident. You could step into a dark hole and break your neck. Or you and Jim could linger behind for a moment or two, and then you'll slip and fall."

"On my claws," Jim added. "Very unfortunate."

"Or I could accidentally shoot you," Andrea offered from behind. "It was dark, I saw something move. Everybody knows I'm a terrible shot."

"Ha-ha," I told her.

"We'd get back," Robert said. "And the People would ask us 'Where is Ghastek?' and we'd say 'Terribly sorry, couldn't find him. Mishmar is a big place, you know.'"

"I feel like I've been captured by a horde of savages," Ghastek said dryly.

"You are a man who pilots monsters," Nasrin said. "We *are* monsters. We look after our own. You are not one of our own."

"I would like to go on record now: we should kill him," Jim said. "We'll be kicking ourselves in the ass if we don't."

"Yes, Curran," Andrea said. "After all, how mad would Kate really be? She loves you. She'll kick you a couple of times and then she'll forgive you."

"You guys are a riot," I said. I didn't hold Ghastek's head above the water for hours so they could bump him off. "I promised him he would get out of here. You're not killing him."

A flood of undead magic rushed at us, as hundreds of bloodsuckers surged toward us somewhere above. The vampires must have found a way around Semiramis's chamber.

"Run!" Ghastek screamed.

We sprinted through the hallway. Turn, another turn . . . The hallway opened into what must've been at one point a lobby. Giant double doors blocked our way and in between the doors, a narrow, hair-thin gap glowed weakly. Sunlight. We'd found the exit. I almost couldn't believe it.

Robert slammed into the door. "Locked from the outside. I can see the bar."

"Stand back." Curran took a running start and rammed the door. It shuddered. He rammed it again. Wood splintered, the doors burst open, and we shot out into blinding daylight. The fresh air tasted so good. I stumbled, blinking, trying to get used to the glare.

A bridge melded together from sections of a concrete overpass stretched before us, covered with snow and chunks of ice. It spanned a gap at least two hundred yards deep and about a hundred yards wide. An enormous sheer wall encircled the gap. The bridge ran directly into the wall and in the place where they met, a large steel door marked the exit.

In the middle of the bridge stood Hugh d'Ambray.

Adrenaline surged through me. My heart hammered. The world slid into sharp focus. I saw it all at the same time in half a second: the six people in the familiar black tactical gear of the Iron Dogs behind Hugh; the E-50, an enhanced heavy machine gun that spat bullets so fast, they cut through steel like a can opener, mounted on a swivel platform to the left; the two gunners half-hidden behind the gun's blast shield; Hugh himself, huge, wearing dark armor; and the door behind him. He stood between us and freedom. Hugh in front of us, the undead horde behind us. We had to go through him or die.

"Bar the door, please," Ghastek said. "Also, just in case you're wondering, I have no idea how to open that outer gate."

"We'll deal with it when we get there," Jim snarled.

Thomas picked up the broken wooden bar and slid it back into the rungs. It wouldn't hold for long, but anything was better than nothing.

Hugh's face was grim. His cloak was black. His armor was black, too.

Clearly he had a theme going. The armor didn't look like either modern tactical gear or medieval plate. It looked woven, as if tiny metal threads had been somehow made pliant, painstakingly crafted together into a fabric, and molded to Hugh's muscular frame. The fabric thickened into dense plates, mimicking the large muscles on his chest, stomach, and arms, and flowing over limbs and midway up Hugh's thick neck. Part of my aunt's blood armor looked like that, except hers was red. It looked like something my father would make, which meant claws, fangs, and blades wouldn't cut through it.

I unsheathed Sarrat. It fit perfectly into my hands.

Where to strike? Back of the arm, covered. Inner thigh, covered. Mid-section, covered. His face was about the only thing not protected, but he wasn't going to just stand there and let me take a shot at it. I wasn't at a hundred percent either. I had a hard time standing.

Hugh's eyes promised death, but he wasn't looking at me. He was look-ing to the right of me. At Curran.

Curran snarled. His irises went gold. All rational thought fled from his face. His expression turned savage. He grinned, baring his teeth.

Holy shit. Apparently they were happy to see each other.

Hugh reached behind his back and pulled out two short black axes. He pointed one at Curran and roared, "Lennart!"

It was the kind of roar that would cut straight through the chaotic noise of battle. It bounced off Mishmar behind us, and far above the giant birds screeched in alarm.

"Come on!" Hugh screamed.

"Curran?" I asked.

Curran didn't even hear me. He had already started forward, pulling off his jacket as he moved. The jacket fell on the bridge. Muscles on his back and shoulders bulged under the dark shirt. He broke into a run. Curran was gone. Only the Beast Lord remained.

Hugh gripped his axes. He must've decided swords couldn't do enough damage to Curran, so he went for something that could cleave a limb off in one blow.

"Why isn't the Beast Lord shifting?" Nasrin murmured next to me.

"No point," I told her. Curran had fought my aunt with me. He would remember the armor. "Claws won't penetrate that armor."

"Shoot anyone who interferes!" Hugh roared and charged.

They tore toward each other. There wasn't a force on the planet that could stop them from colliding. Here's hoping the world didn't end when they hit each other.

I wanted to cut Hugh into pieces. I owed him for Mauro, my broken sword, and seven days in the hole. But Curran owed him for seeing me disappear, for finding out where I went, for running after me across half the country not knowing if I was still alive, and then for fighting his way to Mishmar only to find me half-dead. Curran had a much bigger score to settle.

Blood rushed through my veins. I could hear my own heartbeat. The familiar metallic taste of adrenaline coated my tongue. *Come on, Curran. Hit him hard.* At least the magic was down.

"Can you take out the gunners?" Thomas asked Andrea next to me.

"No," she said. "Not while they're hiding behind the blast shield. I could get one, maybe."

The two men collided.

Hugh spun the axes as if they weighed nothing and chopped with the right axe straight down, putting all of his power into the swing. Curran blocked the haft with his forearm, but Hugh's left axe was already moving. The axe head bit into Curran's stomach and sliced sideways right to left.

No!

The world slowed. I saw the bloody blade of the axe slide free, flinging the fine mist of Curran's blood into the air. My heart was beating too loud in my head.

Curran dropped his guard. Hugh continued the stroke with his left axe, bringing it up and cleaving with dizzying speed. Curran knocked Hugh's arm aside before Hugh could bury his right axe head in Curran's side. Instead, the blade grazed Curran's side. *Move faster, baby. Move. Move!*

Curran leaped back. His left side bled. The cut on his stomach couldn't have been deep, but it bled, too.

Hugh flicked his axes and flung the blood at Curran. Red spray splashed over Curran's neck and chest. He'd flicked Curran's own blood at him.

Asshole. Hugh smiled. Curran stepped forward, his hands raised, aiming for Hugh's face. Hugh spun, picking up momentum, and sliced at Curran's midsection in a horizontal cut with his right axe, leaving his face wide open. *It's a trap, Curran. Don't!*

Curran dodged and rammed his forearm into Hugh's jaw. *No.*

Hugh staggered back, leaning back, turning the energy of the impact into his own blow, and chopped at Curran's left side. The axe bit into flesh at least two inches deep. Damn it all to hell!

Curran danced back. Hugh lunged forward, slicing at Curran's leading leg. Curran dodged left, jerked his fists up, and brought them down like a hammer toward Hugh's head.

What was he doing? I kicked the snow. Curran was better than this. I fought him every day in our gym. He was better than this.

Hugh jerked his axes up, hafts crossed, caught Curran's arms, and pulled the axes apart, letting Curran's blow slide off. Curran kicked with his left leg, sweeping Hugh's leading leg out from under him. D'Ambray rolled on the ground and sprang back up. Curran chased him. They moved across the overpass, cutting and blocking, each blow fast and hard enough to knock most fighters out of the fight.

The undead horde behind us was growing closer and closer.

Curran was cut in four places. His blood was all over the overpass. Hugh favored his right leg, but he showed no signs of tiring. His axes cleaved, chopped, and carved, one second aiming to sever an arm, the next threatening Curran's chest. I began to pace back and forth. It was that or I'd explode.

Another graze of the axe. Another open wound. More blood.

Curran was taking too much damage, even for a shapeshifter. I wouldn't lose him on this stupid bridge. This wasn't the way it ended. It couldn't be. Hugh would not take him from me.

The door behind us shuddered under the press of undead bodies. *Finish it. Finish it, Curran.*

Hugh reversed the blow and rammed the top of his right axe head into Curran's midsection. Curran staggered and Hugh smashed the haft of his left axe into Curran's skull.

My heart clenched into a painful hard ball.

Curran bent forward, dazed.

D'Ambray smiled, his grin demonic, and swung the two axes at once. Stupid flashy move. In my mind the blades connected, like razor-sharp scissors slicing closed. Curran's head slid off his shoulders . . . My throat closed. I couldn't take a single breath.

Curran surged up, grabbed Hugh's wrists, planted his foot into the left side of Hugh's stomach, and fell back. Hugh tumbled forward, pulled by Curran's weight. Curran swung his right leg over Hugh's neck. Hugh crashed to the ground on his back and Curran rolled up on top of him, Hugh's arm clamped in his hands, one leg over Hugh's throat, the other over his chest. Juji Gatame, the most powerful armlock in judo.

Curran bent back and pulled the arm. Hugh screamed as his shoulder joint came apart. His rotator cuff must've torn. Triceps too, probably. Curran arched his hips. Hugh's elbow joint popped like a chopstick snapping. Yes! *Heal that, you sonovabitch.*

Hugh roared and tried to chop at Curran with his remaining axe.

Curran rolled clear.

Hugh staggered to his feet. His left arm hung useless. It was over now. Curran would take him apart piece by piece. Hugh's face was ashen. He was beaten and he knew it.

Hugh swung his axe. Curran leaned out of the way and hammered a quick punch into Hugh's face. Ooo, broken nose. Curran spun and kicked him in the chest. Bone crunched. Hugh flew back and crashed into the snow.

The door creaked. In my mind, the space behind the door was just a wall of undeath.

"Shoot the left gunner," Ghastek said quietly.

Andrea blinked.

The two gunners stood together, the right hidden by the blast shield, the left standing so just the top of his face protruded above the shield as he craned his neck to watch the fight. It was an impossible shot. We were too far away and the target was about the size of a large matchbox.

"Shoot. The left. Gunner," Ghastek repeated, pronouncing each word exactly.

Andrea snapped her rifle up and fired.

The bullet punched the left gunner right between the eyes.

Ghastek's scarred vampire shot out from under the bridge and knocked the remaining gunner off his feet. His second vampire leaped onto the Iron Dogs from the other side. Ha! He must've sent them under the bridge while we were watching the fight. They had crawled on the bridge's sides out of sight, and now Hugh had no gun.

Hugh rolled to his feet.

Curran pounced on Hugh. The preceptor of the Order of Iron Dogs tried to kick him. Curran grabbed Hugh's foot and kicked at the leading leg. Hugh's knee popped.

In front of me, two of the four remaining Iron Dogs jerked their guns up. Andrea's rifle barked twice, the shots so close they were almost one sound, and Hugh's people fell.

The door creaked and groaned under the press of the vampires. We were out of time.

I sprinted to Curran and Hugh.

Curran knocked Hugh off his feet and ground his face into the bridge. I grabbed Curran's arm. "We have to go."

He bared his teeth.

"Now!"

Christopher, the two wererats, Nasrin, Naeemah, Ghastek, and Andrea dashed by. Behind us the door burst. An avalanche of vampires poured out onto the overpass. They tumbled over each other, a single huge mass of writhing undead flesh.

Jim landed next to me, his eyes pure green. "Come on!"

We ran.

The undead avalanche rolled over the overpass, dropping loose vampires. Hugh tried to rise. He got to his knees, saw the vampires, and froze. The undead wave crested and swallowed him whole. *Bye, Hugh. Have fun with my father's vampires. It was nice knowing you.*

Andrea dropped into the E-50's gunner seat. Jim landed next to her. The rest of us ran by the gun. I looked over my shoulder. The E-50 whirled and spat a steady stream of bullets, ripping the front line of undead into mush. But the undead horde itself hadn't even slowed.

I reached behind me with my magic, trying to hold back the horde. It was like trying to block a tide with my fingers. There were too many, and their magic blended them into an unstoppable cataclysmic force.

"Fuck it!" Andrea leaped out of the gunner seat. Jim followed her, abandoning the gun.

Curran grabbed my arm and hauled me forward. I didn't run, I flew, the air turning into fire in my lungs.

A door to the outside loomed before us, the only break in the sheer wall. We were about to run out of the bridge.

Christopher reached the door and screamed something. Robert dashed to the left, to the other side of the door, and grabbed a lever protruding from the wall. A square section of the wall, about a foot wide, slid open next to Christopher, revealing a complex mechanism of gears and metal dials. Christopher began to turn the dials.

We crashed into the gate. I vomited on the ground.

The mechanism next to Christopher clicked. The door swung open, revealing a narrow stone passageway. An identical door blocked it just twenty feet ahead.

"Hold the lever," Christopher yelled. "Turn the right gear on your side when I tell you. If you let go, all doors close. They'll be trapped."

Robert leaned on the lever. I had no idea how Christopher knew the combination to the gates of Mishmar, but if we survived, I would find out.

Christopher turned the dials.

The second gate opened.

The vampires were almost on us. They swelled behind us, climbing on top of each other, biting, fighting. If they could run, we'd be dead already, but there were too many of them and they trampled each other.

"Go!" Christopher yelled. "Go!"

We wouldn't make it. I halted by them and pushed the undead horde back. It was like trying to hold back a train. The writhing mass slowed, but it still kept rolling. Curran stopped by me.

Nasrin ran past us. Thomas and Naeemah followed. Jim and Andrea dashed by. Ghastek, his face a mask of complete concentration, moved back slowly.

The pressure on my mind ground me. I shook. I couldn't hold them. There were too many. Even if we made it through the gates, the horde would chase us. We couldn't kill them all.

"Go now, mistress!" Christopher yelled.

In my mind, I saw Aunt B standing in front of the gate. *No. Not today. Nobody is sacrificing themselves on my account today.* I couldn't go through that again.

Curran pulled my arm. I pulled back. "I'm not going without them."

The undead minds blended into a single red fire. My mental defenses broke. I staggered back.

Curran swept me off my feet and ran through the passageway.

"Put me down," I snarled.

"No." Curran clamped me tighter. "I'm not losing you."

The third gate opened ahead of us. Beyond, a wide, snow-covered field stretched. Curran carried me outside, dropped me to my feet, and clamped me to him.

"Robert!" Thomas screamed.

Robert leaned into the doorway. I saw Christopher next to him. The slight blond man smiled, his face mournful. Behind them the vampire wave crested, feet away.

No! No, not again, no, no!

Robert looked over his shoulder at the undead horde, then back at Thomas.

Don't do it.

"Don't!" Thomas screamed.

"I love you," Robert said, and let go of the lever.

The gates crashed into place, blocking the undead avalanche. Thomas howled. It was a scream of pure pain, made of grief and despair.

Not again. Everything I kept inside in the deep dark place I had stuffed it so I could function tore out of me. Aunt B's sacrifice, Mauro dying, Robert, Christopher, all of it spilled out of me in a torrent of helpless grief and I couldn't hold it back.

I was still screaming when Curran carried me away from Mishmar into the winter.

I SAT WRAPPED in a blanket by a fire built in the remains of a crumbled gas station. The roof and most of the walls were gone, but a corner of it still stood and shielded the fire from the wind.

Andrea, Jim, Nasrin, and Naeemah had fallen asleep. Even Ghastek gave up and passed out, but not before we had found a huge chain to tether his two ancient vampires to a tree. He'd killed the third. It was too taxing to control all of them and he was tired.

Thomas had gone into the night. He wanted to be alone. So did I.

Curran sat next to me. "They knew what they signed up for."

"They're dead, because of me." My voice sounded hollow. "They came on this mission to rescue me and now they're dead. Christopher wasn't even in his right mind. He tried to warn me. He was trying to describe Mishmar to me. His voice was shaking. Going back there terrified him out of his mind, but he did it anyway and now he's been ripped apart by undead. I promised him I would get him out alive. I gave my word. He trusted me. It wasn't supposed to be like this. I can't do this. I save people. Not the other way around."

"Sometimes it is," Curran said.

My whole chest hurt, as if someone had removed my insides and replaced them with a clump of icy needles. "I just wonder who'll be next. Who is Roland going to go after next? Julie? Derek?"

"Don't do this to yourself," he said. "It's a cycle, Kate. We fight for the Pack, they fight for us. We bleed, they bleed. Sometimes people die. Everyone who came with me came of their own free will. They knew where we were going. They all knew there was a good chance that not everybody would make it out. This isn't the first fight or the last. People will sacrifice themselves for us again, and we'll do the same. I don't know how bad the future will be, but I promise you, we'll deal with it. You and I. Together."

I curled into a ball under the blankets. He wrapped his arm around me.

The hollow feeling in my stomach wouldn't go away. My memory served up Robert's face and then the look on Thomas's when the gates had slammed shut. It made my chest hurt.

I had gotten out of Mishmar. I had kept Ghastek alive. But Christopher and Robert had traded their lives for ours. I didn't want that trade.

I couldn't bear it.

I CROUCHED ON top of Hugh's castle, with fire raging all around me. Smoke filled my lungs. Below, Aunt B roared, pinned down by silver chains protruding from the body of a mage. The Iron Dogs shot her, again and again, each arrow puncturing her body. Hibla stepped forward and swung her sword. The metal gleamed in the light of the fire and Aunt B's head rolled down off her shoulders. It rolled to my feet, looked at me with Christopher's blue eyes, and said in Robert's voice, "You have to prepare to sacrifice your friends."

A foreign presence brushed against my mind. My eyes snapped open.

I raised my head. Curran was holding me. Everyone was asleep, except for Jim, who sat on top of the ruined wall keeping watch. He nodded at me, his eyes catching the light of the flames. A log popped, sending sparks into the cold.

Sleeping was overrated.

There it was again, a gentle nudge of foreign magic. It seemed to emanate from the tree where the vampires sat tethered. I reached toward it. The two vampiric minds glowed weakly. Behind them in the field a third undead mind waited, motionless. Now what?

I slipped out of Curran's arms. He opened his eyes.

"I'll be back," I told him. "Bathroom."

I rose and walked off toward the tree, the snow crunching under my feet. The sky was moonless, but the snow made the night seem lighter. Both vampires sat very still. They'd been straining at their chains after Ghastek fell asleep, but now they didn't move a muscle. Something wasn't right.

I passed the vampires. Their eyes were dull, a sure indication that someone held their minds in a steel grip. It wasn't Ghastek—he was out like a light. The third undead mind was right in front of me, in the field, about two hundred yards downwind.

I walked past the bloodsuckers and leaned on the other side of the tree. Whoever held the third vampire probably held these two, and I wasn't going into that field alone.

"What do you want?" I whispered.

"Your friends are alive," a quiet male voice said.

Hope fluttered through me. I caught it and choked it to death. He was lying. Nobody could've escaped that horde. The sheer number of undead had been too much for anyone to hold back, except possibly my father.

"There is an undead directly south of you in the field," the quiet male voice said. "I'm about to let him go. Please take hold of it."

The third vampire's mind flared and I clamped down on it with my magic.

"I'm waiting for you two miles south. We can speak there in some privacy."

I pushed the vampire south. It ran through the snow, the feedback from its mind overlaying mine, as if I were watching what it saw on a translucent screen. Another minute or two and Curran would come looking for me. I walked back to Jim.

"I can't sleep. Let me take the watch."

Jim peered at me. "You sure?"

"Sure," I said. "I'm going to sit on that log and think things through." I pointed to a log about a hundred yards out. If I kept my voice down, they wouldn't hear me.

"Want me to come with you?" Curran asked.

"No. I'd like some alone time."

He opened his mouth and closed it. "As you wish."

I love you, too.

I went and sat on the log. Jim lay down. Curran was lying down too, but I was pretty sure he was watching me. If we had traded places, I'd be watching him.

I sat quietly with my back to Curran as my vampire dashed across the snow. It cleared the open field, then the brush, the strip of woods . . . I glanced back at the camp. Curran was lying on his back. Awake. He usually turned on his side to sleep unless I was lying next to him, my head resting on his chest.

The woods ended. The vampire shot into the open onto the crest of a gently rising hill. A man stood there wrapped in a scarlet-red cloak, frayed and torn at the edges. His long dark hair fell loose around his face. Tall forehead, high sculpted cheekbones, strong square chin, dark eyes, handsome and fit, judging by the way he stood. A Native American, not young, but ageless in the same way Hugh was ageless, stuck forever somewhere around thirty.

The man inclined his head. *"Sharrim."*

It was an Akkadian word. It meant "of the king." My voice came out of the vampire's mouth effortlessly. "Don't call me that."

"As you wish."

I almost told him not to say that either, but the explanation would take too long.

"Look below," the man invited.

I brought the vampire to the edge of the hill. Below me the ground rolled down to another field. Vampires filled it. They sat in neat rows, held in formation by navigators' minds. There had to be upward of two hundred and probably at least half as many navigators. Too many for me. Holding back the undead horde had given me some perspective. If I grabbed all of the undead in that valley, I could possibly hold them long enough for the rest of our party to make a run for it, but my control over them would be measured in seconds.

"My name is Landon Nez," the man standing next to me said. "I serve your father."

Right to the point. Apparently, I could stop pretending not to be related to Roland.

"Hugh d'Ambray is the preceptor of the Order of Iron Dogs. I'm the Legatus of the Golden Legion. Do you know what that means?"

It meant we were all in deep trouble. I knew exactly zip about Landon Nez. The Legati didn't last long, because Roland was demanding and didn't tolerate mistakes. The last Legatus my adoptive father had known, Melissa

Rand, died about two years after Voron did. "It means you're in charge of the Masters of the Dead, you answer directly to Roland, and your life expectancy is rather short."

"In a manner of speaking. Your father chooses the People's policies and I implement them. I'm the brain to d'Ambray's brawn."

"Did Hugh survive?"

"Yes."

How . . . ?

"Does that distress you?" Landon asked.

"No, I'm just wondering what it is I have to do to kill him."

Landon raised his eyebrows an eighth of an inch. "I've often wondered the same thing. I'm positive that if I set him on fire and spread the ashes into the wind, he wouldn't regenerate."

"Have you tried it?"

"Not yet. But I've imagined doing it many times."

The enemy of my enemy is not my friend. Not even a little bit. "What do you want?"

"Hugh had his shot. He failed. It's my turn. I've been authorized to offer you this."

He held up a photograph. On it, Christopher and Robert sat next to each other at a table. Robert's smart eyes were blank. Wet tracks marked Christopher's face, and his eyes were red. He had wept. He was back in the hands of the man who'd broken his mind. I would walk on crushed glass barefoot to get him out and my father knew it. Now, he was using it against me.

"They are unhurt," Landon said. "His offer is as follows: if you can walk into Jester Park, take them by the hand, and walk them out, all three of you will be granted safe passage out of his territory. You must come alone. Whether you succeed or fail, the people who are waiting for you by the fire will be permitted to return to Atlanta unmolested."

"And if I refuse?"

Landon turned to the vampires. "He wants to see you. If you choose to ignore his invitation, the two men will die and I will unleash what you see here on your camp. He has no doubt that you will survive the massacre.

Perhaps the werelion may survive as well. The rest won't be so lucky. The choice is yours."

The werelion would not survive. We both knew it.

Robert's words came back to me. *But now they know you have a weakness and they will use it against you. They will take someone you love and threaten to kill them, because they know you won't pass up that bait. I know it, they know it, and now you must understand it. You have to prepare to sacrifice your friends.*

I couldn't do it. It wasn't in me. I couldn't sacrifice the people who had risked everything to keep me breathing. I couldn't let Curran or anyone else by that fire die here in this nameless field.

I looked at the Golden Legion waiting below. It was only a small fraction of what Roland could bring out, and I knew my father wouldn't stop. He would keep culling my friends one by one, until I stood alone. Everyone I cared about had become a target. I'd known it would happen. Voron had warned me about this. He had taught me that friends made you vulnerable. I ignored his warning. I started it all with my eyes open and chose to let people into my life, knowing I would have to one day face the consequences. Now it was my responsibility to keep them safe.

It had to end. I had to end it now. I had to face my father.

If I did this on Roland's terms, Curran and I would be over. I had promised Curran that when the time came, we would face Roland together. He loved me, but if I told him that he had to sit on his hands while I went to my death, he would leave me. He would forgive me almost anything else, but not that. But if we went there together, it would be double suicide.

"How did Hugh and my people survive?" I asked.

"Your father was watching. He held the undead and my people went down to retrieve the two men and the preceptor."

If he wasn't lying, it meant my father stopped that entire undead mob with a single effort of his will. The scope of that power was staggering. Curran and I wouldn't get out alive.

"Tell me why I should trust you."

"A fair question." Landon tilted his head. "If your father simply wanted to capture or kill you, he could've done it a number of times. That is one of the reasons d'Ambray is out of favor. Teleportation is too unpredictable for anything but escape from certain death. He took an unnecessary risk with his life and with yours. The relevant question is why d'Ambray did it. Why imprison you inside Mishmar when he could've simply teleported you to Jester Park or dragged you there in handcuffs? The instruction given to d'Ambray was exactly the same as the one given to me."

"And that is?"

"Persuade you to come to Jester Park of your own free will."

"Why?"

"Your father has his reasons. He chose not to share them with me. But you should know that when he gives his word, he doesn't lie."

I laughed under my breath. Walk into my parlor, said the spider to the fly.

"Yes or no?" Landon asked quietly.

If I went, Curran would try to come with me and we both would probably die. If I told Curran no, we would be over and I would probably die. If I told Landon no, everybody would die. No good choices.

It was my turn to make sure the person I loved made it out of Mishmar alive. I could just sneak out in the middle of the night. Or lock Curran in a blood ward as soon as the magic wave came. Even if he broke through the ward, it would take the wind out of his sails and he couldn't follow me.

Except I loved him. After our last fight, he promised me he would always be honest with me. I had promised him the same thing, and now I had to play by the rules.

"I'll tell you in the morning."

"I need an answer," Landon said.

I stared at him. He didn't look fazed.

It took me a full ten seconds to realize he couldn't see my psycho stare through the vampire's eyes. Nice going there, champ. "You'll get your answer in the morning. If you did your homework, you know that I think logic and restraint are overrated. If you push me, I'll get my people and see how many of this famed Golden Legion I can kill."

"You'll lose," Landon said.

"Yes, but I'll have a great time and take a hell of a lot of you with me. In the past few days, I've been threatened, teleported, drowned, starved, and locked in a cage while being forced to watch as people I care about died. I have so much rage in me, I'm having trouble keeping it inside. If you push me, you have my word that I'll make it my personal mission to find you in the melee and slice your head from your body. I'd enjoy it. It would be fun for me. If you somehow manage to survive, you'll have to go back to my father and explain how you had me in your grasp, but you were too clumsy and you failed, just like Hugh, and now a lot of vampires and I are dead. Somehow I doubt he would accept my head as a consolation prize. You'll have my answer in the morning."

I let go of the vampire's mind, got up, and moved over to the fire. Curran still lay on his back.

"I know you're awake." I lay down next to him.

He opened his gray eyes and looked at me. I loved him so much, it hurt. I loved everything about him. The way his eyes lightened when he laughed. The way they shone with little gold sparks when he wanted me. The way his thick eyebrows came together when he was pissed off. I loved his nose that never healed right. I loved the stubble on his cheeks and the hard line of his jaw. I loved that he called me on my bullshit. I laughed at his jokes and I loved that he laughed at mine. I loved that no matter where I was he would come for me. That he would always be there, helping me cut my way through the mess that was life.

I leaned over to him and kissed him. I kissed him, trying to tell him all of the things I couldn't put into words. I tried to tell him that I loved him, that he meant everything to me, and that I would fight for him. Nobody would take him away from me, because if they tried, I would carve a path right through them. He kissed me back, and tasting him was heaven. He was right here, alive, warm, and mine—but only until tomorrow. I held on to him. I'd just gotten him back. I couldn't lose him. Not now.

"I love you," I told him.

"I love you, too." His gray eyes searched my face. "Something happened and it's bad."

"Yep. I got a visit from Landon Nez."

"Who is he?"

"The Legatus of the Golden Legion. Hugh oversees the Iron Dogs; he's Roland's brute strength. Landon leads the Masters of the Dead. He is Ghastek's boss."

Curran's face slid into a neutral mask. "What did he want?"

"He showed me a photograph of Robert and Christopher. They are alive. My father watched your duel with Hugh and then plucked Christopher and Robert out of Mishmar and took them to Jester Park."

"Could the photograph be a fake?" Curran asked.

"Roland wouldn't bother," I told him. "My father is waiting in Jester Park. He wants to see me. I'm to come alone. If I can walk into Jester Park and claim our people, we can all go home. If not, Landon has about two hundred vampires parked two miles south of us."

Curran's face was impenetrable. I knew exactly what he was thinking, though. I could tell by the way he sat, very still, and by his eyes. They had iced over.

"Do you think your father is lying?" Curran asked.

"No."

"We have two options," he said, his voice quiet and calm. "Option one, you tell them no and we fight our way out. But we can't win in a straight fight."

"I agree. I could possibly kill some bloodsuckers, but all of them will be controlled by Masters of the Dead at least of Ghastek's level. Before killing any of the vampires, I would have to wrestle all these navigators for control of their minds. It takes effort and time."

"We'd be overrun." Curran pondered the flames. "We could split now and run. There's a chance they'll come at us in smaller groups. It takes time and maneuvering to get two hundred vampires moving. But as soon as we stopped to fight one group, the rest would catch up."

"Also, Robert and Christopher die."

We looked at the fire. "This is one hell of a date," I said.

"Trapped by a horde of vampires in the middle of a snow-covered field, huddling around a tiny fire on thin blankets," Curran said. "Drink it in, baby. All this luxury just for you."

"At least it's not raining."

We both looked up just in case a freak downpour decided to drench us, but the night sky was clear. Nothing but stars and desperation.

I didn't want to die.

"If we make it too expensive for the Golden Legion, would they cut their losses?" Curran asked.

"No. I think Roland has made up his mind. As long as Landon has a single vampire left, he will try to get me." Our options were shrinking with every word. I leaned against him. "Robert told me that if you didn't come back and the question of my leadership of the Pack came up, some alphas might vote no confidence."

Curran growled low under his breath. "Robert says a lot of things."

"Ted had locked us in a cage at the chapterhouse and Hugh had killed all of the knights. He got a hold of Ascanio and threatened to kill him. He was healing him and then unhealing, back and forth, and I told him if he saved the boy, I would come out of the cage."

"Sounds like you."

"Robert thought that I lacked the ruthlessness to be in charge. I should've let Ascanio die, because Hugh getting his hands on me would've been a disaster for the Pack."

"He was right," Curran said.

"I agree. But I can't do it. I can't turn my back on Robert and Christopher. I just can't. It's not in me."

"I know," he said. "That's who you are. But I'm ruthless enough for both of us. Roland thinks you might be his daughter. He wants you to come to him. He wants a big show. Either you're an impostor and you'll die in front of an audience, or you're real and he gets to show you off. Even if you walk out of there, there will be no more hiding. That's why you're not going."

"I have to go and see him, Curran. If it's not Christopher and Robert, then the next time it will be Julie, or Derek, or you in the photograph. I can't keep doing this."

He faced me, his eyes hard. "No."

"Yes."

His eyes sparked with gold. I looked into his irises. The urge to freeze gripped me. There it was, the Beast Lord's famous alpha glare. I hadn't seen it for a while.

His voice came out deep and ragged, as if the leonine snarl cut the words to pieces as they tried to break out of his mouth. "Kate, no. You're not going. I mean it."

I had to convince him or this thing between us would be over. I racked my brain trying to scrounge up smart, persuasive words, the right words, but I had nothing.

He was still staring at me, waiting.

Fuck it. "I love you. I don't want to fight. I don't want to argue. I have to do this, because like you said, this is who I am. I don't abandon the people who fought for me. If I compromise on this, soon I'll compromise on other things and then I won't be me anymore. I can't let my father bend me into something I'm not. I won't. I know it's stupid and reckless, but I have to at least try, Curran. I have to try and I'm afraid."

The alpha stare died.

"I won't ask you to stand with me," I said. "I don't want you to come, because he's forcing me to challenge him and if you come with me, you would be challenging him, too. I'm not sure I'll come through this alive and even if I do, he'll come after me with everything he has. I want you to live and be happy, Curran. I want you to survive. I want to marry you and have your children, but if I die, I want you to marry and have kids with someone who would make you happy. I want you to live. All I ask is that you let me have what's left of this night with you. Don't leave me now over this and don't fight with me about it. I need you. Please."

Curran pulled me to him. His arms closed around me and for a moment I felt safe. It was an illusion, but I didn't care.

"We go together," he said.

"No."

"I don't tell you what battles to fight. Don't tell me when to fight mine."

"Curran, there is no turning back after this . . ."

He shook his head. "I love you. We go together."

"But . . ."

"No," he said. "Not up for discussion."

Oh, you stupid idiot. "You're crazy, you know that?"

"Yes. But I'm a demon in the sack."

I laughed. "Okay then. That fixes everything."

"That's right, it does."

I fell asleep in his arms by the slowly dying fire in the cold snowed-in field. I wouldn't have traded it for the most luxurious palace.

THE MORNING BROUGHT a magic wave and even harsher cold. I opened my eyes. The sky above me was crystalline blue. I pulled back the blanket, leaving the warmth Curran and I had shared through the night, and sat up. Pure white snow stretched as far as I could see, sparkling in the morning sun like crushed crystal.

Beautiful day.

Curran jumped to his feet. I rolled one blanket up, he rolled the other, and we checked the backpacks.

Andrea watched us. "Both of you have your business faces on."

"We have someplace to be," I said.

"Rise and shine," Curran called out.

The rest of the group awoke instantly, all except Ghastek, who seemed dead to the world. One, two, three . . . Naeemah was missing. Well, we rescued her, she helped us get out of Mishmar. I suppose that made us even. Hopefully Landon's vampires had let her pass.

Andrea was on her feet. "What are you doing?"

"I have to visit Roland," I told her. "He has Robert and Christopher."

"Robert is dead," Thomas said, his voice raw.

"There is a possibility he isn't," Curran said.

Thomas froze. A muscle in his face jerked. "Then I'm coming with you." Thomas grabbed his pack.

"You can't go," Curran said, his voice calm. "If you go, he dies. Roland's condition, not ours."

Thomas dropped the bag and moved forward, the line of his shoulders set. His eyes turned green. His nostrils flared.

Curran blocked his way.

For a second I thought Thomas would collide with him, but the alpha rat stopped an inch from Curran. The two men squared off. Thomas was six three and built like he could push trucks over, but in a fight Curran would break him.

Gold drowned Curran's irises. "Look at me. This is a direct order. Stay put. If you go, you go through me."

The two of them stared at each other for a long moment.

"Stand down," Curran said, his voice quiet.

Thomas turned on his heel and swore.

"There are vampires south of us," I said. "I'm going to set a blood ward. It will protect you as long as the magic holds. Jester Park is less than two hours away by car. Stay put. We will be back."

Ghastek sat up on his blanket. "What's going on?"

"And if you don't come back?" Andrea asked me.

"Then you may have to fight your way out," Curran said. "Roland's people promised us safe passage, but I don't trust them and you shouldn't either."

"How many vampires?" Jim asked.

"About two hundred." I pulled Sarrat out of its sheath, cut my arm, and began making a circle around them in the snow.

The color drained from Andrea's face. "Two hundred. Piece of cake."

"Will someone tell me what's going on?" Ghastek demanded.

The last drops of blood connected with the first. The magic stretched from me, pooling over the circle of blood. I severed the tie. A wall of red shot up and vanished. The blood ward was set.

Behind me the snow crunched. I turned. Landon strode toward me, his tattered red cloak like a ragged red wound against the snow.

Ghastek opened his mouth and closed it again.

Landon stopped a few feet away. The wind tugged on his cloak and long dark hair.

"I'm coming with her," Curran said.

"That's not possible," Landon said.

Curran grinned and I felt an urge to step back. "Is Roland afraid of what I might do? Am I that scary?"

"Baiting me or him will accomplish nothing," Landon said.

"Tell him that if he ever loved my mother, he will understand," I said.

Landon murmured something under his breath. We waited. The wind bit at us with icy fangs. When they described dramatic standoffs in the snow in stories, nobody ever mentioned freezing your ass off. I hopped up and down, trying to warm up. If this got any more dramatic, pieces of me would start falling off.

"He'll see you," Landon said.

Ghastek rose.

"Mr. Stefanoff," Landon said to him. "Your services and conduct during these events are greatly appreciated. Once the magic is down, a car will come to retrieve you."

The familiar roar of an enchanted engine rocked through the plain. A silver Land Rover slid from behind the distant trees, heading for us. Curran and I began walking toward it. Landon caught up.

"You've used Kalina's name," Landon said. "For your sake, I hope you're the real thing."

17

L ANDON DROVE. I rode in the front passenger seat, and Curran took the back. If things went sour, I'd get Landon's attention and Curran would rip out his throat.

The sun had risen, setting the snow aglow. The ruins of another gas station slid past us, iced by the winter. Heat swirled inside the Land Rover. I had shrugged off my jacket before I got in and I rode in comfort, with Sarrat in her sheath across my lap. This would be my special present for my father. If I got a shot at him.

Thinking about our impending meeting set my teeth on edge. The pressure was almost too much. I wanted Landon to stop the car so I could run in circles through the snow as fast as I could just to burn some energy off. I settled for stroking Sarrat's sheath.

I couldn't win against my father. I knew it now. The problem was, I had no idea what choice that left me.

"Has he claimed Atlanta?" I asked.

"No," Landon said.

So the claiming hadn't come to pass. That meant I still had to somehow prevent it.

An old sign slid by. I-80 East.

Landon glanced at me. His smart eyes lingered on my face.

"Are you Apache?" Curran asked from the backseat.

"Navajo," Landon said.

"I thought the tribes discouraged necromancy," Curran said.

"They do. They didn't like what I was doing, so I found someone who does."

As Hugh once put it, that was my father's greatest power. Outcasts and misfits flocked to him. He found a perfect place for each one and inspired them to greatness. Except his kind of greatness resulted in death, misery, and tyranny.

Landon was looking at me. If he kept staring, I would have to do a trick or something. "Yes?"

"You're not what I expected," he said.

"Who did you expect?" I asked.

"Someone with more . . . presence. You seem ordinary."

"I'm sorry, was I supposed to arrive in a black SUV, wear a two-thousand-dollar pantsuit, and set my sword on fire for the encore?"

"You look terrible, which is to be expected after Mishmar," Landon said. "But you're simply not like him. There is a lot of resemblance in the face, but that could be coincidental. With him, when you're in his presence and he's happy with you, it's like standing in sunshine. Your entire being is lifted. When he's displeased with you, it's like being in a blizzard. He freezes you out and there's nothing worse. With you"—Landon moved his hand in front of me—"I get nothing."

Good to know all of my magical shields were still holding.

"That's the point," Curran said. "You're supposed to get nothing. Give her a chance to use her sword, and you'll change your mind."

Landon glanced in the rearview mirror. "You, on the other hand, are exactly what I had expected."

"And what would that be?" Curran asked.

"An uncomplicated man who thinks that everything can be solved with a sword."

"I think you've been insulted," I said.

Curran smiled. "I'm crushed. I don't even use swords."

Landon ignored him and faced me for a brief moment. "If you are who he thinks you are, you change everything. If you are genuine, your presence alters the power structure of the entire continent. What can you do? What are you capable of? There hasn't been another one like you for thousands of years. Are you going to support him or oppose him? Who will follow the daughter of the Builder of Towers? Am I driving a pretender to the throne or should I kneel? D'Ambray must've thought you were the real McCoy. I couldn't understand the motivation behind his odd political machinations in Europe over the spring and summer, but now I see—he was building a trap, which apparently failed. But Atlanta? What he did in Atlanta was rash even for him. Contrary to all of his chuckling and 'aw, shucks, I'm just a simple soldier' declarations, d'Ambray is intelligent and ruthless. Something must've happened between him and Roland to push him into . . ."

"Do you call him Roland?" I asked.

Landon's eyes narrowed. "I'll answer one of your questions if you answer one of mine."

I'd played this game before. It never turned out well. But why not. "Fine. Do you call him Roland to his face?"

"I call him Sharrum."

King. Well, that wasn't exactly surprising.

"But yes, in public, I refer to him as Lord Roland. That's the name he has chosen for this age." Landon's eyes lit up. "My turn. Do you carry Voron's sword?"

"No."

The excitement died in Landon's eyes.

"Hugh broke Slayer," I told him. "I loved that sword. It was a part of me for over twenty years."

"A convenient excuse," Landon murmured.

Oh screw it. "I mourn my sword, but that's alright. Grandmother gave me another one." I pulled Sarrat out of its sheath.

Landon spun the wheel. The Land Rover nearly careened, turning off the road. Landon parked and bolted out of the car, slapping the driver's door closed behind him.

Awesome. I'd terrified the Legatus of the Golden Legion just by showing him my sword. If I waved it around, he'd probably explode.

Sarrat smoked on my lap. Its magic wasn't subtle, like Slayer's. No, this sword emanated power. It coiled around me. It liked me.

Landon paced back and forth, his eyes a little wild.

"Well, he took it worse than I did," Curran said.

"I don't see what the big deal is."

"It's a sword made out of your grandmother's bones, Kate."

I shrugged.

Landon stared at me through the windshield, turned around, paced back and forth, and stared at me again.

"Do you know what most people have from their grandmother? A tea set. Or a quilt." Curran smiled. "If your family had a quilt, it would be made out of chimera skin and stuffed with feathers from dead angels."

"Are we talking Judeo-Christian angels, because those don't exist, or pagan angels like Teddy Jo?"

"Kate," Curran said.

"Hey, I warned you from the start it would be weird. I sat in that bathtub with you and told you that this was a really bad idea. You said you loved me and stayed in the tub. As far as I'm concerned, you've made your bed. You have to lie in it."

"I'll lie in any bed as long as you're in it, but this is still weird."

I turned back to look at him. "We're going to see my dad, who'll probably crush me like a gnat, and you're weirded out by my sword?"

Curran nodded at Landon. "I'm not the only one."

Landon peered at me again.

"Did you name it yet?" Curran asked.

"Yes. Sarrat Irkalli. It means Great Queen of Irkalla, the Land of the Dead. My grandmother was occasionally confused with her, and now that she's dead, it's fitting."

Curran spread his arms. "I rest my case."

This was ridiculous. I leaned over the driver's side, swung the door open, and yelled at the top of my lungs, trying to outscream the enchanted water engine. "Are you done?"

"What?" Landon said.

"Are! You! Done?! If you want, you can stay here. Just point us where to go, and we'll drive ourselves!"

Landon slid back into the driver's seat and pointed at my saber. "Put it away."

"Say the magic word."

"Please," Landon squeezed out.

I slid the blade back into the sheath and petted it. "It's okay, Sarrat. If he insults you, I'll cut his head off and you can drink his blood."

Landon shut his eyes for a long moment, exhaled, and steered the Land Rover back onto the highway.

Trees slid past my window, draped in snow and ice. Inside the heavily insulated SUV the world was quiet save for the low hum of the engine. Landon watched the road. Some complicated calculations were no doubt taking place in his head. Probably trying to figure out how my presence affected his little kingdom within Roland's empire.

The road wove its way through the woods. The snow ended and asphalt began, seeded with large stone blocks. "Why the stone?"

"His magic degrades modern roads," Landon said.

The woods continued. The trees grew thicker and taller, spreading their mighty branches to the sun. The snow sparkled in the weak winter light, pure white in the sun, blue in the shadows. The magic must've fed this park the way it fed the parks in Atlanta, and what began as a carefully managed spot of green had rioted and turned into a dense old forest. How odd it must've been for my father to go from ancient Mesopotamia to this winter wonderland.

Voron had dedicated his life to bringing me to this point. If he were still alive, he would know I was riding to my death. I now realized that he never expected me to win. All of his plans always ended with me confronting Roland. There was never any discussion of what to do after. He didn't expect me to have an after.

The woods parted. A building loomed in the distance, surrounded by the spiral of a wide iced-over moat, curving around the structure like a snake of frosted glass. The building rose, all but floating, above the snow-covered lawn, oblong, its walls a gathering of delicate white panels that looked suspiciously like giant feathers. They thrust from the main mass in perfect imitation of a bird. The road turned, circling the building, and I saw the whole structure.

A swan.

The building was constructed in the shape of a giant swan, its tail sitting on the ground, its chest caught in the ice of the lake, while its proud neck curved five stories above the water. The sun bathed it and it glowed slightly, as if the entire palace had been painstakingly carved by a genius sculptor out of an enormous block of glossy alabaster. Each feather stood out, distinct, its vanes and shaft clearly visible. The swan looked ready to push off from the shore and swim out onto the lake. If it had been life-sized, I would've thought it was real. The beauty of it took my breath away.

How could the man who'd built Mishmar build this?

"Why a swan?" Curran asked.

"He's fond of them," Landon said, bringing the car to a stop. "We get out here."

He stepped out of the car. Curran and I followed him toward three ornate bridges. One after the other, we walked across them and through the concentric rings of the moat. Snow crunched under my feet.

I was walking into the heart of my father's power, while the magic was up. This wasn't how I had pictured confronting him. But at least Curran was with me. So we could die heroically together. Okay, that wasn't the best thought to have right about now.

It didn't matter. I would walk in there and I would walk back out with Christopher and Robert. Or at the very least, I would see Roland's blood on my new sword before he crushed me.

Maybe I should just stop thinking altogether.

The bridges ended. I wasn't ready.

Curran paused and examined the swan. "What the hell . . ."

"Just go with it," I told him.

A wide arched door waited for me in the swan's side, right where the legs would've been tucked under the body. A stairway of white marble stairs led to the door.

He'd killed my mother. He was going to claim the city I called home. He'd stopped a horde of undead vampires in Mishmar.

This was happening.

Every nerve in my body tensed. My breathing deepened. My muscles became loose and pliant, like I had spent half an hour warming up before a big fight. It felt like my blood was boiling. Next to me Curran rolled his head, stretching his neck and loosening his shoulders.

The stairs ended. The arched door swung open. I walked through the open doors into my father's palace.

I HAD EXPECTED a sterile monochromatic space. I couldn't have been more wrong. Warm, sand-colored tiles lined the floor. An indoor garden, lush with green plants, spread on both sides of me in curved, raised beds, bordered by a gently winding pond, where fat lazy koi floated under the lily pads. The air smelled of lotus and roses. Tiny insects, blue and green and ruby-red, floated between the flowers, like a scattering of weightless jewels carelessly flung by the handful into the air.

In the center of the garden, a round mechanism of golden and silver gears rotated, balanced on a thin spike. Hair-thin wire rings wrapped around the mass of gears. The rings spun and turned, hypnotic in their beauty. Magic emanated around it. Was this an atomic model of some sort?

I made my mouth move. "What does it do?"

"I don't know," Landon said. "He built it one afternoon on a whim."

A giant door waited at the other end of the room.

I reached forward with my senses. Vampires.

My hands were trembling. Hell no. I'd had twenty-seven years to prepare. I wouldn't lose it now. I inhaled the air, letting it out slowly. My hands steadied. My pulse slowed.

"You can't go any farther than that door," Landon said to Curran.

"Fine," he said. "I'll wait in the doorway."

We passed between the flowers, circled the mechanism, and stopped before the door. I touched it and it swung open. A long room stretched before me, its white marble walls soaring up. I stood on a raised walkway.

Twenty feet wide, it spanned the length of the room, running from the door all the way to the opposite wall. A trench bordered both sides of the walkway, filled with vampires. Past the trenches, on the sides, men and women waited, standing quietly. My father's court.

The walkway ended in a raised dais. In the very center of it, on a throne formed by the bodies of serpents carved from glossy white stone, sat my father. He wore white.

I looked at his face.

He looked back at me.

The instant I saw his eyes, I knew why my mother loved him. His skin was a deep even bronze, saturated with the sun's warmth. His nose was straight with a sloping tip, his cheekbones carved with careful attention, his jawline strong and masculine. A length of white cloth tossed over his head covered most of his hair. A short beard with a touch of silver traced his jaw, but the eyebrows above it were black, and his eyes were young and full of life. He could've been Arabic or Jewish, Hindu or Hispanic. Had he been twenty years younger, he could silence a room full of women simply by walking in. But he chose to appear older. When orphans dreamed of being adopted, this was the kind of father they pictured. His eyes radiated wisdom and kindness, intelligence, and calm surety, born of age and confidence in his own power. He could've been an ancient king, a great prophet, or a revered teacher. He had killed my mother. I hated him. Yet when he looked on me now, I wanted to stand taller. It was like being in the light of the morning sun. When the power of those eyes shone on my mother, she had no chance.

What little doubts I had evaporated. He really had meant to kill me in the womb, because nothing short of complete desperation would've torn my mother from his side.

Next to me Curran paused, ready, like a lion before a strike. His face iced over. Muscles bulged on his legs, stretching the jeans. His eyes had turned completely gold. He lost all expression and slid into that perfect calm of a predator focused on his prey. He was treating my dad to an alpha stare.

For some dumb reason, nervous laughter bubbled up inside me. My father and Curran were glaring at each other. Maybe if I whistled and waited long enough, a tumbleweed would roll by.

The stone serpents slid against each other. Their heads rose above my father's shoulders and they looked at me with crimson eyes. Here he was inside a swan palace, a marvel of delicate beauty, sitting upon a throne of massive stone snakes. My father knew he was a bastard. He was the venomous serpent in a bed of roses. Apparently, he didn't just acknowledge that fact, he beat people over the head with it. All that was missing was a neon sign that read EVIL AND CONFLICTED ABOUT IT with a flashing arrow pointing at his head.

Hugh d'Ambray stood to the right of the throne and a couple of steps below it. His face looked like he had to be physically restrained from losing his shit and slaughtering everything he saw. His gaze snagged on something over my right shoulder. Landon. A muscle jerked in Hugh's face. Oh noes, someone didn't like being upstaged.

Our gazes met. I winked at him. *Your turn to be in the cage. It has no bars, but it's still a cage.*

On the other side of the throne, on a small bench, Robert and Christopher sat in identical poses, their spines rigid, their knees together. They stared straight at me with glazed-over eyes. They probably couldn't even see me.

"It's stasis," Landon whispered behind me. "It will wear off with distance and time."

The vampires and Roland's court stared at me.

"You can do this, baby," Curran said quietly, his gaze fixed on Roland. "Go in, get them, kill anything that gets in the way. You are coming out alive. I promise you that."

I raised my head. My voice rang through the room, too loud. "I've come for my people."

Roland leaned forward slightly and the snakes slid, adjusting themselves to the change in his posture. His voice resonated through the room, deep and saturated with power. "If they are yours, come and claim them."

Okay. That can be arranged.

I started down the walkway. Two vampires vaulted out of the trenches in front of me, fangs bared. *Oh look, it's a party and everybody is invited.* Good. I liked parties.

I unsheathed Sarrat. The blade sang as it sliced through the air. It slid through vampire flesh like a knife through a crisp apple. The first vampiric head rolled off the stump of its neck. I buried my sword inside the second vampire's heart, ripped it with my blade, and freed Sarrat.

Four vampires leaped onto the walkway. This was a test. He wanted a show of my power. I had no choice about it.

The vampires charged.

Four was too many.

I dropped my magic shield and grasped the four undead minds. The minds of their navigators tried to hold on, but I tore them away from their navigators. The effort hurt, but it was the most efficient way. I grasped the four undead minds and squeezed. Four skulls exploded, spilling the red mist of their blood onto the pale floor. Someone gasped. I kept walking, crushing the undead minds in front of me like peanut shells crunching under my boot. My magic churned and boiled around me. If it had a voice, it would be roaring.

The bloodsuckers leaped at me from the trenches and fell back, broken and twisted. The trenches ran with red. The stench of undead blood saturated the air. I felt the navigators bailing, disconnecting half a second before I reached for their undead.

The last vampire fell onto the floor. I stepped over it and kept walking.

A woman leaped onto the walkway from the trenches. She had a strong, harsh face and dark hair, and wore dark brown leather with a dagger on her waist and a katana in her hands. Hibla.

In my mind I saw Aunt B snarling in pain and Hibla's sword severing her neck.

Hey, Aunt B, look what I found. I smiled. I couldn't help myself. There was nothing holding me back and there were so many things we needed to discuss. I had a score to settle and if I lived, I would tell Aunt B's gravestone all about it. Hell, if I could, I'd bring her Hibla's head.

Hibla bared her teeth. She was some sort of shapeshifter. She claimed to be a jackal but nothing that came out of her mouth could be believed.

Enhanced strength, supernatural speed, and judging by the way she held her sword, a great deal of training.

On my list of people to kill, Hugh occupied spot number two and Hibla took up spot number three. My father wasn't willing to throw away Hugh, but Hibla was expendable. He wanted a demonstration of what I could do with the sword, and he must've known I couldn't resist this bait. Very well. I would oblige.

Hibla raised her katana.

I charged. She struck from above, and I caught her blade with Sarrat. She pushed, trying to bring my sword down. Shapeshifter strength. How fun. The pressure of Hibla's katana ground on Sarrat. I dropped my guard, she jerked her sword up to cleave my neck, and I sliced across her chest. My blade came away bloody. The blood soaked into the pale bone-metal. Thin tendrils of smoke rose from Sarrat, which was fed by my rage. My sword was furious and hungry.

Hibla stumbled back, her eyes wide. *Hurts, doesn't it?*

She lunged at me, her blade fast like a striking snake. I blocked, letting her sword slide off the flat of mine. She pushed me back across the walkway, each blow hard. I would tire out before she did, but she had no idea how much anger I was carrying inside.

Strike, strike, strike. She lunged at my leading foot with hers. I shifted my balance, knocked her blade aside and smashed the heel of my left palm into her nose. Cartilage crunched. Blood gushed over her lips.

She punched me. No time to dodge. I turned into it, ducking, and took the hit on the shoulder. My left arm went numb. I kicked out at her knee. It crunched. I spun and kicked her in the head. The kick took her off her feet. She rolled back, shook her head, jumped up, and I slid Sarrat between her six and seventh ribs. My saber's tip scratched Hibla's heart. Not yet. No, not yet. I pulled the blade back.

She kicked at my stomach. I saw it coming and tensed, and her foot smashed against the shield of muscle. The blow knocked me backward. It felt like someone had slapped my gut with a burning hot iron. I grunted and straightened, and Hibla raised her sword. She was good and fast. But I was better.

"I'll kill you and bring your head to Hugh," Hibla ground out.

Not in your wildest dreams. "You're good, but not my level of good. If you trained all your life, you still wouldn't be good enough, because I really want to kill you. You murdered Aunt B. She was my friend."

Hibla attacked. I blocked and sliced across her chest from left to right. She whipped about, thrusting, and I sliced her arm, severing the muscle and tendon. Hibla screamed.

"You didn't have the decency to face her or to give her a quick death."

I reversed the blade and stabbed her in the stomach. Hibla gurgled blood.

"She died in agony. I cared for her."

Her leather armor was in my way, so I cut a piece of it off and tossed it aside.

"This won't be quick. This will be painful for you. But if you ask me now, I'll end this fast."

"I'll rip your heart out and eat it while you die." She stabbed at me. Her sword grazed my side.

"Cute." I drove her back across the walkway, slicing bloody chunks of leather off her. "I want you to understand me."

I thrust. She moved to block but missed, and I slid the blade of my saber against her inner thigh, cutting through her femoral vein.

Her sword grazed my side and I drove Sarrat's pommel into her face, gouging her left eye. The eyeball burst and the white of Hibla's eye slipped onto her cheek. She stumbled and I pulled her dagger out of its sheath on her belt. *Oh look, I have two blades now. The better to hurt you with.*

"This isn't vengeance."

She shuddered and dropped her sword. Flesh spiraled up her bone. She was trying to shift. I lunged forward and sliced across her midsection, one, two, three. Her flesh smoked. Hibla's top half careened.

"This is punishment."

They said you couldn't bleed a shapeshifter to death. They didn't say anything about cutting her apart.

She lunged at me, a huge hulking monstrosity with her claws out. I ducked between them and slid Slayer through the bottom of her chin up into her deformed muzzle. Talons raked me, but I didn't care. I plunged Hibla's dagger into her lower abdomen, jerked it out, and broke free. She roared, baring her teeth. I swung my saber and sank into a smooth easy rhythm. The world narrowed to my blade and my target in front of it. A cut. Hibla's hand slid off. Another cut. Another piece of flesh. She backed away, and I followed her, relentless, precise, paying her back for Aunt B, who would never see her grandchildren; for Andrea and Raphael, who had to watch her die; for Andrea's unborn baby, who would never know his or her grandmother; for my fucked-up nightmares . . .

A cut. A cut. A cut.

Do you want to see how cruel I can be? I will show you.

Hibla fell before me, a stump of a creature. She was done.

A man lunged onto the walkway, tall and thin, the magic flowing to him. I had felt that same magic before, just before three silver chains shot out of him and pinned Aunt B to the ground. I dragged Hibla's dagger against my bleeding side and hurled it at the mage. It bit into his throat. I sparked the magic in my blood and the blade erupted into a dozen sharp spikes, puncturing the mage's throat from within. His eyes rolled back into his skull. He crashed down.

I looked back at the bleeding piece of meat that used to be Hibla. She couldn't hurt any more than she hurt already. I swung my sword and watched her head topple off her shoulders. I should've just left her there to suffer, but I had things to do.

I could feel Curran watching me from the doorway. I wasn't alone. He was there with me, like a rock I could lean on. I leaned on that stare and looked up.

The dais was almost in front of me. I wiped Sarrat on my jeans and took a step forward. A wall of red pulsed in front of me. A blood ward. My father had sealed the dais with his blood. If I broke it, no person in this room would have any doubt I was his daughter.

My father's gaze fixed on me.

It was too late to turn back. I had a sword and he was feet away. My entire life had been spent working up to this moment. I could do this. I was the daughter of Nimrod, the Great Hunter, the Builder of Towers, Hero of

His People and Scourge of His Enemies. My father's kingdom and those like it had brought about the cataclysm that purged magic from the world.

I thrust my bloody hand into the ward. It shuddered like a living thing caught in convulsions and solidified into a translucent wall of red. The people behind me screamed. The wall cracked and shattered into chunks. The pieces of the ward rained down, melting into thin air.

It didn't hurt. It didn't hurt at all.

Magic spread from my father. It rose behind him like wings, like a hurricane pulled apart into shreds that could condense into a devastating storm at any second. The barrier of the blood ward had been containing it, but now the ward was broken and I felt every iota of Nimrod's power. I forgot to breathe.

My grandmother was not completely dead, but she wasn't alive, not in the true sense of the word. My father was alive. Semiramis's magic had terrified me to the bone, but against this storm, her power was a mere shadow, a candle caught in the blinding glow of an industrial floodlight. It was the kind of power that could pick up chunks of skyscrapers and fuse them into Mishmar.

If that power turned against me, it would destroy me. He would simply will me out of existence and I would disappear.

So this was what Hugh meant when he said I couldn't win.

I had no chance. No chance at all. If I lunged at him now and tried to bury Sarrat in his heart, I would simply stop being, as if I had never existed. I felt it with complete certainty, the same certainty I'd feel if I stood on the roof of a high building and looked at the hard pavement below. To jump was to die.

Christopher and Robert would die a second or two after me, Curran would never leave this place, and Atlanta would fall.

"Do it!" Voron screamed at me in my mind. *"Do it! Kill him!"*

I felt no fear, just an utter calm. Things became really simple. If I tried to kill my real father, everyone else, especially the man I loved, would pay the price. I could feel Curran's gaze on me. There were people waiting for me to protect them from Roland in Atlanta, I couldn't throw my life away. It wasn't completely my own anymore.

I stopped and stood still. It took all of my will.

My father was looking at me and his eyes told me he knew what I was thinking.

"Do it!" the ghost of Voron roared. *"This is what you worked for. This is why I trained you!"*

Something fluttered inside me and I realized it was hope. I wanted to live. I wanted Curran to survive this. I thought of him. I thought of Julie. Of Derek and Ascanio. Of Andrea and Raphael. Of Jim. I wanted to bring Robert back to Thomas. I wanted Christopher to smile again and tell me he was trying to remember how to fly.

Death is forever. Death is nothing. But to save a life, that's everything. My mother understood this and now I finally did, too.

Voron had a purpose for me, but it was his purpose, not mine. I loved him, I still mourned his death on his birthday, and I was grateful because he made me what I was. But I was done living for someone else's purpose. I had to live for mine. I had people to protect. Curran had sacrificed everything to save me from Mishmar. Now I would sacrifice my vengeance to save him from the Swan Palace.

I walked up the dais and put my hand on Robert's shoulder. "I claim them."

My father nodded slowly. "Take them."

The two men rose, their eyes still glassy. I turned and walked back along the gore-splattered walkway. They followed me, two androids on autopilot. At the doorway Curran looked at my father one last time.

"I'll see you both in Atlanta," my father said.

Curran smiled, his eyes like two burning moons. "If you want a war, we'll give you one."

I passed him and kept walking, out of the room, out of the garden, into the winter, Christopher and Robert following me and Curran guarding our backs. Nobody stopped us.

I MARCHED ALONG the cobbled road, Robert and Christopher following me. They still wore the warm clothes they had brought to break me out of

Mishmar, but I had left my jacket in Landon's car. The cold was scraping the flesh off my bones.

I had met my father. I had met him and survived.

I'd failed Voron. I should've killed Roland, but I had walked away and I'd done it deliberately. I'd betrayed Voron's memory. And I didn't care. I lived. We all lived.

I felt free.

"We survived," I whispered. The words tasted strange. "We survived."

Curran picked me up and kissed me, his lips burning mine.

"I killed Hibla," I told him.

"I saw," he said. "Do you feel better?"

"Yes."

"We're going to have a nice dinner with Martina when we get back," he said. "I think that would be a really good idea."

Ahead a steady pounding of hooves announced an approaching horse. A cart rolled into view, pulled by a roan horse. Naeemah held the reins. I sped up.

"Get in!" she called.

Shit. "What are you doing here? You shouldn't have come."

"I went to get a cart."

Oh no. I turned back to look at the palace. "She didn't know she couldn't come with us."

Silence reigned.

"She didn't know."

No answer. Somehow I didn't think it would matter.

"Get in," Naeemah called.

"Climb in," I told Christopher and Robert. The two men didn't move.

Curran picked them up and set them into the cart one by one. Naeemah pulled a blanket out and threw it at me. "Here. Come before Roland changes his mind."

Curran climbed up next to her. I sat in the cart with the two men. They lay stiff like two wooden statues. Naeemah turned the cart and the horse clopped its way down the road, heading out of Jester Park.

"Well?" she asked. "How did it go?"

"I had a shot and I didn't take it."

"You chose to live. Smart choice. Life, it should mean something. A death is just a death. If you died there, what would your death mean? Nothing. You would stop nothing. You would change nothing." She blew on her fingers and waved them at the road. "A bug under a shoe. But you lived. And now they live, too."

"Damn right," Curran said.

"I killed Hibla," I said.

"Did she need killing?"

"Yes."

"It wasn't exactly a killing," Curran said. "It was more like punishment piece by piece."

Naeemah looked at him. "And you? Did you roar at the wizard?"

"No," Curran said. "I'll roar at him if he comes to Atlanta."

"See, you both did good. You accomplished things and got out alive. Best behavior."

The laughter finally broke free and I laughed, gulping in the cold air.

THE MAGIC WAVE receded three hours after we had left the Swan Palace. Twenty minutes later a lone figure dotted the field ahead of us.

"God damn it," Curran swore.

The dot grew at an alarming rate until it finally became Thomas, running full speed over the snow. He sprinted to us, leaped into the cart, and hugged Robert to him.

"It will wear off," I told him before he could freak out over Robert's stasis. "The more distance between us and Roland, the better."

Thomas turned to me. "Make her go faster, Consort."

We found the rest of our people waiting where we had left them. We loaded up our gear and headed toward Atlanta.

At some point I climbed into the back of the cart and fell asleep. I dreamed of Christmas and garlands. They wrapped around me in long shiny strands.

I kept trying to break free, while Jim was reassuring me that I was a lovely Christmas tree and the Pack was appreciating my efforts on its behalf.

Another magic wave hit closer to the morning. I felt the moment we passed out of Roland's territory. It was like hitting a speed bump in the road. I lay there with my eyes open and took a deep breath.

He'd let us go.

We weren't done. He said he would see us in Atlanta. Things would only get worse from here. Not only that, but both Naeemah and Thomas had disobeyed. It was a partial disobedience—Naeemah had left to get the cart before I announced that they had to stay put, and Thomas ran to us after we had left the Swan Palace—but still, there was a price to be paid. I half expected their eyes to melt from their sockets.

"Incoming," Curran said.

I raised my head. A swirling clump of darkness appeared on the road in front of me. The tightly wound whirlwind of dark twine, snakes, and feathers spun on its end, stretching to seven feet high.

"What the hell now?" Curran growled.

"No clue," I told him.

The clump broke open and spat a person onto the road. He or she wore pants and a tunic of animal hide with patches of fur sewn onto it at seemingly random places. Pale paint covered the person's hands and face, with two scarlet vertical lines stretching from the hairline on both sides of his or her nose down to the lips. Three scarlet lines curved from those two, tracing the cheekbones. A pair of longhorn's horns, painted with bands of red and white, rested on top of the person's head, positioned so the tips pointed downward.

The person shook a staff at us. "Daughter of Nimrod!"

A man.

"I cast my eye upon you!"

The man threw something to the ground. Red smoke exploded. The wind cleared it, and the man had vanished.

Shaman ninjas. Perfect. Now my life was complete.

Curran looked at me.

"I've blown my cover," I told him. "Now every weirdo with a drop of power will be coming over to investigate."

"It's like you had a coming-out party," Andrea said. "You've been presented to polite society, except now everybody wants to kill you."

"Spare me."

"Kate Daniels, a debutante." Andrea grinned.

"It's not funny."

"It's hilarious." The smile slid off Andrea's face and she vomited on the snow.

"Karma," I told her.

"Daughter of Nimrod?" Curran asked quietly.

"Nimr Rad, if you want to get technical about it. He who subdues leopards. The great hunter."

"Nimrod like in the Bible?" Curran asked. "The one who built the Tower of Babel?"

"It's an allegory," I said. "My father and his contemporaries built a civilization of magic. It was great and mighty, like a tall tower. But they made the magic too strong and the Universe compensated by starting the first Shift. Technology began to flood the world in waves, and their civilization crumbled like the tower. The language of power words was lost."

"How old is your dad, exactly?"

"A little over five thousand years old."

"Why does he build towers?"

"I don't know. He has a thing for them, I guess. I think they might help him with the claiming of his territory."

"The claiming?"

I explained what the witches had told me about the genocide of the Native tribes and the lack of natural protection for the land, and the Witch Oracle's vision of Roland claiming Atlanta.

Curran stared straight ahead, his expression grim.

"Are we okay?" I asked.

"Yeah. We're okay," he said. "I just need some time to process."

It was one thing to know that you were sleeping with Roland's daughter. It was a completely different thing to have met Roland. And to have challenged him. "Why the hell did you invite him to start a war?"

"He needed to know. We're ready and we won't roll over for him. It had to happen sooner or later. We knew he was coming and we've known for a while. If he shows up, we'll deal with it. We've dealt with Hugh and Erra; we'll deal with him as well."

An hour later Robert began to cry. He didn't say anything. He made no noise. He just rode in the cart, tears rolling down his face. Thomas talked to him, saying quiet soothing words. Eventually Robert stopped, and then Christopher began to weep.

Half an hour later Robert cleared his throat. "Tom?"

"Yes?" Thomas bent to him.

"If Roland tries to capture me again . . ."

"He won't."

"If he tries, kill me."

BY NOON WE reached the ley line point and the two Pack Jeeps they had parked there. Naeemah told me she wouldn't go any farther.

"Thank you," I told her.

"I will see you," she said.

We boarded the Jeeps and steered them into the ley line. The magic current grabbed the vehicles and dragged them southeast. We rode the ley line for hours. I slept. I was so tired. Sometimes I would wake up and hear Jim and Curran discussing war plans or see Christopher asleep next to me with a small smile on his face, or hear Andrea vomit into a paper bag. At some point Jim asked her how she could possibly have anything left to throw up and she threatened to shoot him.

Finally the magic squeezed the Jeep, compacting us inside it, as if some unseen force somehow moved our atoms closer together. The pressure vanished and the ley line spat us out onto solid ground. I opened my eyes. "Where are we?"

"Cumberland." Curran was looking at something ahead.

Northwest end of the city. We were home.

I raised my head and looked in the direction Curran was looking. Barabas stood on the sidewalk.

"How did he know we were coming?"

"He didn't," Curran said.

We got out of the car and Barabas trotted to us. "I'm so glad you're alive!"

"We're glad, too," I said. "What are you doing here?"

"The People notified us that you would be coming in at this ley point. Actually they gave us the exact time you would arrive, which is odd."

Not odd at all. Apparently my father had us watched.

"The People want to have a Conclave meeting tonight, and they requested the presence of both of you and the Pack Council. They said they want to bury the hatchet. It's in two hours."

"Tell them no," Curran said.

"I tried," Barabas said. "They said, quote, 'Sharrim's presence is requested.' Does that mean anything to you?"

Curran swore.

"I've sent our guys to sweep the location and establish our presence," Barabas said. "They're reporting that the People are already in place. The Pack Council is on standby. Do you want me to cancel?"

"If we don't go, it will make things worse," I said. "Roland's giving us the time and place. If we ignore him, he can hit us at the Keep, and the loss of life will be greater."

Curran put his arm around me. "It's your call."

I was as ready as I was going to be for now. Another few days or even a few more weeks wouldn't make a difference. I would've taken a century or two if it was offered, but it wasn't on the table. "Screw it. I'm tired of waiting. Let's get it over with."

Curran looked at Barabas. "Call the Council. The Pack will make a stand."

CHAPTER
18

T HE RUINED CITY slid by outside the Jeep. Atlanta. Ugly and beautiful, decaying and rising, life and death at the same time. Home. For better or worse, home. The sun was just beginning to set and the sky burned with a riot of orange and red. Curran drove, his face somber.

"This isn't the way to Bernard's."

"The Conclave isn't being held at Bernard's," Barabas said from the backseat. "We're going to Lakeside."

"What's Lakeside?" I asked.

"It's a new development where North Atlanta High School used to be."

"The one that was overrun by boars with steel quills?" I remembered that. Took the city two years to boar-proof the area.

"Yes. Supposedly it's been constructed by the same firm that made Champion Heights."

Champion Heights was the only surviving high-rise in Atlanta. "It's a tower?"

"Twelve floors."

I laughed. What else was there to do?

"Did I miss something?" Barabas asked.

"You should drop me off and bail," I told Curran.

"What, and miss the fun? Not a chance. We'll pound him into the ground."

We couldn't win. I knew it. He knew it. But I loved him so much for those words, he didn't even know.

We turned onto Northside Parkway. The ground rose, forming a hill, and on top of it a tower perched above a long, narrow lake. Built with yellow rock and turquoise glass, it faced the setting sun and the sky set its windows on fire.

Curran parked in front of the tower near a row of black SUVs that probably belonged to the People. A row of Pack Jeeps sat at the opposite end of the parking lot. The party was all here. Now I just had to bring the entertainment.

"Who is running security?" Curran asked.

"Derek," Barabas answered.

Well, the place would be secure. Also, Derek would probably die. I needed to get him and our people out of the building.

The second Jeep parked next to us and spat out Jim, Andrea, Thomas, and Robert. When I tried to suggest Robert should stay behind, both were-rats acted mortally offended. I let it go. I was tired of trying to talk people out of this mass suicide.

We walked through the double doors, manned by two guards. The taller of the men on the right stepped forward. Curran looked at him for a second and the two guards turned around and decided to look somewhere else.

We crossed the lobby.

"The elevator doesn't work yet," Barabas informed me. "The bottom floors aren't finished. Only the top three are."

"That's fine. We'll take the stairs," Curran said.

We climbed the steps. I knew stairs would be the death of me one day.

Twelve floors went by fast. I opened the door and we stepped into a wide hallway lined with green carpet. Six journeymen stood on the left, six vampires sitting by their feet. Across from them Derek and five of our combat-grade people stood on the right. Derek saw us and pushed himself from the wall.

If I knew anything at all about Derek, this wasn't the totality of the Pack's forces in the building. They would have people stashed on the roof, on the floor below, in the parking lot.

"No need for everyone to die," I murmured.

Curran nodded at Derek. "Clear the building. Take our people out." He didn't even blink. "Yes, Lord."

"Everyone, Derek," I added. "A complete recall."

"Yes, Consort." He turned to the shapeshifters. "Full evac."

They turned and took off toward the stairs. He followed them, his voice raised, talking to people with supernatural hearing above and below us. "Full evac. I repeat, full evac. Clear the building."

The journeymen looked at each other. One of them, a young girl with red hair, barely a woman, ran toward the door at the far end of the hallway. Curran and I followed. We weren't in a hurry. We wanted to give our people enough time to leave Lakeside.

The hallway ended. Curran pushed the door open and walked into the room. A hundred feet long and about half as wide, the room housed two long tables, one at the left wall and the other at the right, each covered with a tablecloth, the floor between them empty. The alphas of the Pack Council sat on the right. The People sat on the left. I saw familiar faces, Mahon and Martha, Raphael, Desandra . . . Everyone was here.

We took our seats. I reached under the table and squeezed Curran's hand. He squeezed back.

"We're about to be attacked," Curran said.

"We know," Mahon said.

Across the room, the seven Masters of the Dead gaped at me, each holding two vampires arranged in a precise line against the wall behind them. Six familiar faces, and one new, an older man with gray hair. The red-headed journeyman was whispering to Ghastek. He glared at us and waved her off. "I don't care who Lennart pulled out of the building."

The gray-haired man rose, walked over, and knelt on the floor directly across from me. Oops. Looks like I sat down too soon.

"Sharrim."

I'd heard his voice before. When we tried to escape Hugh's burning castle, before Aunt B died, Hugh had sent vampires after me. I had slaughtered the undead, ruining the minds of the navigators who had piloted them, but I left one alive. When that vampire had spoken to me, it spoke in this man's voice.

The People stared at us. Rowena was blinking rapidly, stunned. Ghastek leaned forward, focused on me with a laser's precision. I wondered what Landon had told him. Maybe nothing. Wouldn't that be funny?

"Sharrim," the man repeated.

Showtime. I got up and walked over to him. He looked up at me, his hands folded on his lap.

"You are young," the Master of the Dead said. "You have the power, but lack control. Think of all the things he could teach you. Think of the secrets that would open to you."

I felt a power gathering beyond the walls of Lakeside, like a distant storm flashing with lightning on the horizon. The windows didn't permit me a view of the sky, but I bet it churned with storm clouds. My father was coming.

"Think of what you could become."

Oh, I was thinking about it. I did nothing but think about it the whole time it took me to get from Jester Park to Atlanta.

The arcane storm drew closer, terrible, swirling with power currents.

There were twenty-two vampires in the immediate vicinity. Six in the hallway, twelve in the room, and four in the adjacent room.

It would have to be enough. There was one power I didn't demonstrate to my father. It was about time.

"There is no need to fight a battle that can't be won."

The storm swelled just outside the building, about to break on us.

"Think of who you are."

The hurricane of magic burst. Lightning flashed outside the narrow windows and smashed into the wall in front of me. The stone cracked. I grabbed the vampires and pulled them to me. The navigators' minds kicked and bucked like runaway horses. Rowena cried out. The Masters of the Dead pulled back, struggling to keep control.

I opened my mouth. *"Hesaad."* Mine.

The power word tore from me, cracking like a whip. The navigators' resistance vanished. The Master of the Dead in front of me got to his feet and pressed himself flat against the left wall. The vampires streamed to me.

The wall in front of me split open. Chunks of stone moved back, away from me, held apart, hung in the air for a long moment, and plunged down. The sky was black and gray with the full fury of a storm, and below the clouds, the sunset bled onto the sky. Icy wind bathed me, tugged my hair.

The mass of vampires circled me, forming an undead maelstrom around my feet.

Golden light burst into the space where the wall had been. Tendrils of pale smoke rose from it. The wall of light shimmered with yellow and white as if someone had ripped away a chunk of the sun's corona and thrust it into Lakeside. My father's face filled it, enormous, his eyes blazing with power.

His voice shook the tower. **"DAUGHTER."**

I looked into the power roaring into my face. "Father."

"Father?" someone squeaked to the left. Ghastek might have just had a heart attack.

Power reverberated through Lakeside, shaking the stone. **"COME TO ME. STAND BY MY SIDE."**

The light and flame surged forth and I saw myself wearing crimson armor. A golden crown rested on my head. I looked like my grandmother.

I pushed with my power and the vampiric heads surrounding me exploded. Undead blood flooded the floor. I raised my left arm and sliced across it with Sarrat. My blood streamed down, mixing with the dark ruby liquid by my feet. My magic shot through the undead blood like fire down a detonation cord. The undead blood streamed to me, pliant and obedient. It curved around my feet, coating my clothes, slid over my arms, and drained down Sarrat, widening the blade as it coated the saber in crimson.

"TAKE YOUR PLACE."

"No."

The blood armor surged up, sheathing my body. The image of me wearing a crown burst and shattered.

I raised my head. "This is my city. Get out."

The coronal fire in front of me swelled. A spear shot out, colossal, forged of golden light and power, aiming at me. The claiming.

I lunged, swinging my new blood sword. Sarrat connected with the spear.

Magic revolted, bursting and screaming around me. The impact nearly took me off my feet. It was like playing tug-of-war with a tornado. The blade shook and shuddered in my hands.

The spear of power pushed. The enormity of my father's magic pressed on me, crushing me, grinding my bones into dust. Pain started from the tips of my fingers and washed down over me. I burned. From the top of my head to the soles of my feet, I burned. My eyes couldn't see any damage, but my senses screamed that my skin was bubbling from the heat.

If I gave up now, Roland would claim Atlanta. I couldn't let that happen. He would not take this city. People I knew, people I loved, wouldn't bow and kneel to him as long as I stood.

"Amehe," I whispered to my blade. *"Amehe. Amehe."* Obey. Obey. Obey.

My bones cried out. In my head my muscles began to unravel, fiber by fiber, frayed nerves shaking in the raging wind. But I would not move.

I would not move.

"This is my city. These are my people."

I tasted the sharp bite of my magic on my lips. My nose was bleeding. Tiny red drops rose from my cheeks and floated to join the blood coating Sarrat. My eyes were bleeding, too.

My arms shook. My feet slid back half an inch. Another half an inch.

A muscular arm wrapped around my stomach. Another closed over my chest. A deafening lion roar, proud and furious, thundered over my shoulders. Curran braced me. His magic mixed with mine.

My feet stopped moving.

My father pushed and we pushed back.

Thin, painfully bright cracks appeared in the spear where it met my blade.

The strain was ripping my body apart. I poured even more of my magic into the force of my strike. I thought I had given it all I could, but it kept coming and coming, fountaining from inside me.

The cracks widened.

Just a little more . . .

The spear shattered.

I tried to pull back, but I couldn't. The magic continued to rush out of me, as unstoppable as a flood, more, more, *more* . . . I struggled to contain it, but it refused to stop. It ripped me out of Curran's arms and jerked me off my feet into the air. My blood armor crumbled into dust. Words appeared on my hands and arms, strange words written in dark ink. The air around me turned red. The ceiling above me exploded. My body bent back, my arms opened wide, my back arched. The building swayed, shaking. Below me, people crouched by the walls, trying to hide from my power.

The magic inside me erupted. My voice rolled like the sound of an enormous bell.

"HESAAD." MINE.

A pulse of pure red shot out of me, spreading in a ring over Atlanta. The blast wave rolled with a sound like thunder. I felt it slide over the city all the way past the outskirts, past the Keep until finally it dissipated. The magic soaked into the ground and it responded, sending a surge of magic back to me.

Oh no.

I had claimed the city. I had marked Atlanta as my dominion.

My father smiled and disappeared.

I plunged down and landed on the hard floor in front of Curran, still in his warrior form. The two of us looked at each other. Chunks of something that probably used to be the roof rained down around us.

Curran unhinged his monstrous jaws. I braced myself.

"Show-off."

I just stared at him. My brain couldn't string any words together.

He grinned at me. "Come on, baby. We're going home."

WALKING DOWN TO the bottom floor of Lakeside and then to the Pack Jeep was a lot harder than anticipated. Someone had already started the enchanted water engine for us. I got in on the passenger side. I was so numb. I just kept moving forward on autopilot. I should've felt something.

Relief, fear, some sort of human emotion, but there was nothing there. Only cold detachment.

Curran pulled a spare set of sweats from the back of the Jeep Wrangler, shifted into human form, put them on, and slid into the driver's seat. He shifted the Jeep out of park and steered it onto the street. A caravan of Pack Jeeps joined us.

The storm clouds had long since dissipated. The sunset had burned itself out, leaving a mere smudge of red in the sky, a distant memory of its dying. The sky above us turned a deep purple.

My mouth finally moved. "Don't."

Curran looked at me.

"Don't take me back to the Keep. They'll want an explanation. I can't do it right now."

Curran made a sharp right turn into a snowed-in lot between an office building and a ruin. The car screeched to a stop.

Behind us the caravan of vehicles stopped. The leading vehicle's door opened and Jim trotted out and to our car. Curran rolled down the window, letting the earsplitting noise of the enchanted water engine into the vehicle.

"What's the problem?" Jim yelled over the noise of the motor.

"No problem," Curran yelled back. "Go ahead without us."

"What?"

"Go ahead without us!"

"Why?"

"Because I want to spend some time with my wife in peace!" Curran roared.

Jim nodded, gave us a thumbs-up, and went back to his Jeep.

Curran rolled the window up. "It's like living in a fucking fishbowl."

The Pack vehicles passed us. Curran turned the Jeep and drove in the opposite direction, southwest.

"Where are we going?"

"You'll see."

The city slid by the window, the dark silhouettes of buildings, some crumbling, some sturdy and new, highlighted by the blue glow of feylanterns. It was my city now. Truly mine. I'd claimed it and now I was responsible for it.

"I claimed the city," I told Curran.

"Would you like me to build you an office?"

What? I stared at him.

"You could have a little plaque with your name on it. Kate Daniels, City Owner."

"It's not funny."

"We can get you one of those bank line setups with stanchions and velvet rope and a little pillow in the front, so people can form a line and kneel before you in humble supplication . . ."

"Will you stop?"

"We can get Derek one of those dark suits and aviator shades. He can look menacing and give out numbers. 'You are seventh in line to bow before Kate Daniels.'"

"I'm going to punch you in the arm," I growled.

"We can get you a throne with snakes. I'll stand next to you and roar at anybody who fails to grovel. Fear Kate Daniels. She is a mighty and terrible ruler. Grendel can anoint the petitioners with his vomit. It'll be great . . ."

Oh God. I put my hands over my face.

"Come on, baby," he said. "I'm just trying to cheer you up."

"I claimed territory that my father wanted. He'll lose his shit completely now. Not only that, but every ambitious idiot with a drop of magical power will know that this area is claimed and will look for whoever claimed it. Not to mention that right now the Witch Oracle, the neo-pagans, and the People are all having a fit of apoplexy. I was supposed to prevent the claiming, not take the city. The Pack Council will be having kittens."

"The Witch Oracle and the neo-pagans can bite me," Curran said. "They'll get over it. If anybody comes to challenge you, we'll kick their ass. We'll find a way to handle Roland. And if the Pack Council produces any kittens, we'll give them to Jim to raise. He needs to mellow out anyway."

I looked at him.

He took his hands off the wheel and held them apart about six inches. "Cute fluffy kittens. Just sitting on Jim's lap."

I pictured Jim with his badass-chief-of-security expression covered in small fluffy kittens. It was too much. The numbness inside me broke, like a dam. I giggled and laughed. Curran laughed, too.

"Cute kittens, meow-meow," I managed. In my head, Jim held up his finger and sternly lectured a pack of kittens. Oh God. "He'd make them all hard-core."

"He'd take them to the Wood to hunt deer," Curran said between the bouts of laughter. "They'd . . . pounce."

I would've doubled over if the seat belt had let me.

We were still laughing like two idiots when he pulled into a parking lot before a dark apartment building. The place looked familiar. Oh. This was my old apartment building. I had inherited an apartment from my guardian, Greg Feldman, and made it my own during the time I worked for the Order. But my aunt had gutted it. The last time I saw the place, it was completely destroyed.

"There's nothing there," I told him.

"Let's go see anyway," he said.

Why not?

I got out of the car. Surprisingly my legs held me. We went up the stairs together. A new door barred the access to my apartment. A mechanical combination door lock secured the door. A column of numbers, one through five, each with a button by it, waited above the lock.

"Four, four, one, two, three," Curran said.

I pressed the buttons in order. The lock clicked. I swung the door open.

A clean, furnished apartment looked back at me. The floor in the hallway was wood. I could see a little bit of the kitchen through the doorway, backlit by feylanterns. New oak cabinets had replaced the broken wrecks of the old ones. I stepped inside. On the left, the living room, which I had used as a bedroom, stood perfectly intact. The walls had been repaired and painted in soothing blue-green. A queen-sized bed with a dark, soft comforter stood against the wall. Another feylantern hung above it. A plush beige rug lay on the floor. Across the room, by the window, a flat TV set was mounted on the wall, next to bookcases filled with books. Gray curtains matching the comforter framed the window. Outside the glass windows, steel and silver bars glowed weakly, reacting with magic and the light of the rising moon.

I moved through the living room and glanced into the small room that Greg had used as his bedroom and I had turned into a library. Bookcases lined the walls, waiting for books to be put in them.

"I know it's not an exact duplicate," Curran said, turning the valve on the radiator. He'd had a radiator installed. Wow. The super must've finally caved and fixed the damn boiler. "But I thought you might want to come back here one day."

It wasn't an exact duplicate. It looked like a brand-new apartment and that was so much better. Too many memories had been tied to the old one.

Curran strode through the room, coming closer. He moved with a kind of smooth contained power. His gray eyes focused on me. He looked at me as if I wore nothing.

We were alone. In an apartment. The door was locked.

I unbuckled the belt that kept Sarrat's sheath on my back, slipped out of it, and put it on the night table.

He closed the distance between us. His arms closed around me, one across my back, the other pressing in on the curve just above my butt. He pulled me to him. My breasts brushed against his muscular chest, my legs bumped against his hard thighs, and the rigid length of him pressed against my stomach. I was caught in his arms. He had collected me and trapped me. His body caged me. I could barely move.

My survival instinct kicked in, screaming at me to escape. My eyes widened. My breath quickened, each rise of my chest pushing my nipples against him. My body tightened, as if before a fight, the muscles gathering themselves in anticipation. I breathed in his scent, familiar and tempting. It said Curran. Male. Sex. Lust flared inside me like a well-laid-out fire.

He stroked my ass, pressing me closer against him. A narrow predatory smile lit his face. He caught me. I was his and he was determined to enjoy every second. A tiny spark of instinctual alarm flared in me and mixed with an overwhelming need to have him, like spice adding a punch of heat to a dish. A needy warmth spread through me, turning into liquid heat between my legs.

"Mmm," he said. "Kate Daniels, the great and powerful."

I raised my chin. My voice was a challenge. "What can I do for you, Your Majesty?"

He grinned a crazy feral smile and kissed me. His mouth sealed on mine, his lips hot, capturing my breath. We connected and the pure exhilaration of that contact resonated through me in an electrifying rush. The dread of the claiming's consequences and the memories of Mishmar that hung around me like a dark tattered shroud vanished, annihilated in a rush of lust, need, and love.

He buried his hand in my hair, pulling me closer. My body snapped to attention as if I had been asleep for ages and suddenly woke up. I loved the way he kissed me. I loved how he tasted. His tongue thrust into my mouth, possessing, seducing, enticing, pulling me in, deeper and deeper. I loved him so much. I loved him more than I could say. I locked my arms around him and kissed him back. *I love you. I want you.*

We broke apart. He made a low masculine noise, halfway between the happy half-growl of a predator catching his prey and the deep chuckle of a man confident he was about to get laid.

"I'll tell you what you can do for me," he growled. "Better, I'll show you."

My breath was coming in ragged gasps. My nipples tightened. I wanted him in me now. "Decided to do some claiming of your own?"

"Yes." His eyes shone with gold. "Mine."

He pounced on me, trapping me again, and kissed me. His hands roamed my body, caressing my back and my butt. It wasn't a kiss; it was an assault. If I had put up any defenses, he would've demolished them, but I offered none. I just let him ravage my mouth and I reveled in it. He tasted male, hot, and eager. He tasted like Curran, my Curran. If someone threw a mountain between us now, he would rip right through it just to get to me and I loved it.

I slid my hand into his sweatpants, found the hard length of his cock, and ran my hand up and down its shaft.

He pulled my shirt off me, tore off my bra, and sucked at my nipple, grazing it with his teeth. An electric burst of pleasure radiated from my breast all through me. I shivered. I sank my fingers into his hair. He pulled my jeans open and slid his hand inside, sliding it against the short curls of hair, over the sensitive folds, and dipped his fingers into me. I gasped. He dragged the slick liquid warmth up and stroked my clitoris. Bursts of pleasure rocked me, sliding through my body, turning it pliant, flexible, and hot. I ground against his fingers, lost in chasing the ecstasy, wanting more. More . . .

He tripped me onto the bed. I fell onto the comforter. My boots went flying. He pulled off my jeans. I was naked, gloriously unashamedly naked. I raised my arms, inviting him in. He pulled off his shirt and paused for a tiny moment, nude, powerful, muscular, long, and mine. All mine. His eyes glowed, drowned with gold. His muscles tightened on his frame, like steel under the heated silk of skin. I knew every harsh edge of that body and the sheer overwhelming strength of it. Curran's body made me drunk from lust, his eyes seduced me, but the stubborn unbending will that drove it made me love him.

He knelt on the bed, slid his hands under my butt, and lifted me up. His tongue licked the sensitive bundle of nerves.

Oh my God. The wave of pleasure hit me and dragged me under. I cried out.

Each strumming of his tongue stoked the tension inside me. I was burning up and I was moaning his name over and over. My body tightened in anticipation, each caress winding me a little more, until I could no longer stand it.

"I want to come with you inside me."

"That can be arranged."

He mounted me and thrust himself inside me. The hard length of his shaft filled me. He pulled back and thrust inside me again, and I arched my back, grinding against him, faster and faster. I kissed his neck, my tongue sliding over sharp stubble. I opened my eyes and saw him, above me. Sweat slicked me.

"Harder!" I whispered.

He sped up, his pace frenetic, rocking me with every thrust. I gripped his back, desperate, wanting to be one, and matching his pace. It felt so right. This was what heaven had to be like . . . My body clamped around him. The tension was too much, almost a pain. Suddenly it crested and broke in quick contractions full of pure bliss. I cried out. Curran's body shook, tense, muscles taut.

It felt like I was flying . . .

He growled and emptied himself inside me.

We floated through the world, spent and happy. One.

METAL RATTLED. AGAIN.

Curran raised his head and swore.

I raised my head. Once the afterglow wore off, we both realized that the apartment could be a lot warmer. We had pulled the comforter and sheets over us. Curran held me and I had just begun to slip into soft comfortable sleep.

Another rattling. It came from the window.

God, what was it now? Could we not have a few minutes of peace?

"I'm going to twist someone's head off." Curran rolled out of the bed and strode to the window. He was still nude. Well, at least I got a little thrill out of it.

I sat up with the sheet around me.

He pulled the drapes aside and swore again.

"What?"

He stepped aside. A vampire sat outside our window, banging on the bars with his fist. How the hell was he doing this with the wards active? Oh wait, my aunt had broken all my wards. If we kept this place, I'd have to redo them. That would be a pain.

Curran looked at the vampire. "What do you want?"

The vampire's mouth moved, but I couldn't hear it.

"No," Curran said.

The vampire said something.

Curran's eyebrows came together. "Ghastek, if you don't go away, I'll rip that thing's head off and shove it up its ass."

The vampire launched into a long tirade.

I didn't want to talk. I wanted to sleep. But Ghastek was now in charge of the People. I so didn't want to go back to being the Consort. Just for one night, I wanted to be Kate.

Ghastek kept talking. He wouldn't go away. He would keep on and on. I surrendered to my fate. "Let him in. The sooner he gets it off his chest, the faster we can go back to sleep."

Curran slid the window up and unlocked the metal grate. The vampire slipped in and strode toward me on its hind legs. "His daughter!"

"Was that a question?"

"His daughter! The lost child. The Sharrim!" The vampire scuttled forward and pointed a finger at me. "You didn't tell me! We were dying and you didn't tell me!"

I shrugged. "I can't help it if you're the last person to figure it out."

"Who else knew?"

"I've known for a while." Curran picked up his sweatpants and put them on. "Jim knew before me. Mahon. Aunt B. Doolittle. Andrea. Barabas. The Witch Oracle knows. Saiman at least suspects. Obviously Hugh d'Ambray figured it out."

The vampire ran to one side of the room, turned, and ran to the other. Ghastek must've been pacing back and forth and so caught up in his own thoughts, that he subconsciously pushed the vampire to do the same.

"It's basic intelligence work," Curran said. "You should've put it together. The pieces were there. You need to invest in information gathering. I get that you concentrate on research and development, but you can't run the People without a solid intelligence network in place. If you can't do it, get someone who can. I don't even know why I'm telling you this, because really, your ignorance is my bliss."

The vampire stopped and stared at Curran.

"You didn't even know your rival had a bestiality fetish," Curran said. "You were fighting him for the top spot. You needed leverage. If you had known about his trips to the hit-'n'-split, you could've gathered evidence. You could've publicly embarrassed him, you could've sent the evidence to his wife and destroyed his marriage, you could've packaged it and sent it to HQ informing them that you had a potential security breach, you could've blackmailed him, you could've sat him down in private and told him that you have this evidence, but you know how important his family is to him and you'll destroy it out of solidarity, so he would be eating out of your hand. That's how you control the situation, Ghastek. You didn't control it, because you didn't know."

And there it was, the Beast Lord in all his glory.

"Are you done?" Ghastek asked.

"You deserve it," I told him. "You come here demanding to know why you weren't told. People don't tell you their secrets, Ghastek. You have to find them out."

The vampire spun to me. "Do you even realize the enormity of what you've done?"

"Yes, I do. That's why the man I love and I came here to have quiet time before the storm hits. And you're interrupting it."

"You challenged him. He can't let it go unanswered."

"I know."

"He'll come here and scorch this place."

"I know, Ghastek. I'm his daughter. I know him better than you do."

The vampire opened his mouth.

"Stop," I told him.

The vampire stopped, silhouetted against a window. "Do you have it?"

"Have what?" Curran said.

He was asking if I had the Gift. The promise of immortality that kept people like him anchored to my father. I looked at the vampire. "You're alive, are you not?"

The vampire froze, his mouth slack.

The door fell off its hinges and four shapeshifters tore into the room, Myles the wolf render in the lead.

Curran spun on his foot and roared, "Stop!"

They froze.

Curran in sweatpants, me in a sheet, obviously naked under it, a vampire in the middle of the floor and four combat-rated shapeshifters. I put my hand over my face.

Curran's face was terrible. "Explain."

"We were instructed to provide necessary assistance," Myles said.

"By whom?"

"Jim."

Great. Jim had us followed.

"We saw an undead enter the room," Myles said.

Curran's eyes blazed with gold. His expression turned flat. His anger had imploded. He'd taken his towering rage and distilled it to cold precision. The shapeshifters didn't move a muscle.

"Did the vampire break down the door?" I asked. "Or did it knock and was let in?"

The shapeshifters stayed perfectly still.

Curran spoke slowly, pronouncing each word exactly. "What made you think that the two of us together couldn't handle a single vampire?"

Myles swallowed. "It was my call. I take full responsibility."

"Go back to the Keep," Curran said, his voice eerily calm.

The shapeshifters turned around and fled.

Ghastek's vampire slipped out the window. Curran and I looked at each other.

They'd broken the door to the apartment he'd made for me. For some reason that hit me harder than knowing the Pack Council didn't want him to come and rescue me.

"I'll have it repaired," he said.

They would break it down again the next time. "It's okay," I said. "It's just a door. We might as well go back to the Keep."

"I'm sorry," he said.

I smiled at him. "I knew what I signed up for."

He was worth it.

WE TOOK OUR time. By the time we rolled into the Keep's courtyard, the night was in full swing. We trudged up the stairs, while Derek trailed after us and spit out facts: triple patrols, Keep on high alert, blah-blah-blah-blah-blah . . . I stopped listening. The last drops of my patience had evaporated long ago.

We went straight to our rooms. Curran shut the door. I landed on our couch. Outside the large living room window the night reigned, Atlanta a distant smudge of deeper darkness studded with pale blue feylantern lights.

Home . . .

The door swung open. Barabas stepped inside, his face serious, his eyes slightly distant, as if he were looking at something far away. Something was wrong. He always knocked.

"The visitor you were waiting for is here," Barabas said.

He stepped aside and held the door open. A person wrapped in a plain brown cloak with a deep hood walked in. Barabas bowed a little, walked out, and shut the door behind him. The figure pulled back the hood, revealing my father's face.

Why me?

Curran started toward Roland. His eyes were on fire.

I shot between them and blocked him with my body. "Stop."

"Move, Kate," Curran said, his voice calm.

Roland smiled. "I mean no harm. I just came to see my daughter. No audience, no need for any grand gestures. I simply wish to talk."

I turned my back to him so I could see Curran's face. "Please, stop."

He finally looked at me.

"Stop," I asked him.

He took a step back, leaned against the couch's side, and crossed his arms. "Touch her, and I'll end you."

"May I sit down?" Roland asked me.

His magic wrapped around him like a mantle, muted. I still felt it, but he seemed much more human now. This must've been his version of traveling incognito. Nobody would ever know. Yeah, right.

I sat on the couch. "Sure."

"Thank you." He sat in the soft chair across from me.

Roland had walked past our tripled patrols like they were nothing and then compelled Barabas to let him in. All of the defenses we'd built, all the walls and gates and safeguards, meant diddly-squat. He could just walk into the Keep at any time. *He could walk in and sit by Julie's bed and I would never know it.*

Curran's face turned expressionless. He pulled his Beast Lord's face on like a mask. He must've come to the same conclusion. Whatever little illusions of safety we'd had just turned to ashes.

Roland sat. "It's a well-made fortress. Considerably more comfortable on the inside than it appears from the outside."

Lovely paintings you have here on the walls. Don't mind me, I'm just making small talk. "Did you hurt anybody on the way up?" I asked.

"No. I came to talk, and if I had hurt one of your people, you wouldn't speak to me." Roland glanced at the sword hilt protruding over my shoulder. "You visited your grandmother."

I pulled Sarrat out and showed it to him. He passed his hand over the blade, his face mournful.

"I wish you hadn't gone to see her. She's dangerous."

Yes, she is. Legend said she'd murdered my grandfather. All things considered, he probably deserved it. "It wasn't by choice."

"That was an unfortunate turn of events," he said.

"You shouldn't have taken her bones out of Persia. She misses it."

Roland sighed. "Persia is a challenging place right now. Old powers are awakening. Those who had slept, those who were dead or perhaps not quite dead. Mishmar is the safest place for her right now."

"Close enough so you can crush her if she tries to rise?"

"Exactly."

This was a surreal conversation.

"How's the child?" Roland asked.

What?

"The young girl whose blood you purified. How is she?"

I leaned forward. "Leave her out of this. Don't talk to her, don't haunt her dreams, or I swear, I'll finish what my mother started. Was it the left eye or the right? Tell me, so I'll know which to target."

"The left." Roland tapped his cheek below the left eye. "You're so very like your mother. She was fierce, too."

"You killed her."

"Yes," he said. "Not a day goes by that I don't mourn her death."

"And you tried to murder me before I was born."

"Yes."

"And you sent your warlord to hunt down and kill the man who raised me."

"Yes."

"And now you wish to have a conversation."

Roland's eyes turned warm. "I loved your mother. I loved your mother so much that when she wanted a child, I promised her I would give her the kind of child this world hasn't seen for thousands of years." He reached over and held out his hand.

Curran stepped forward.

I put my hand into Roland's palm. His touch was warm. Magic slid against my skin.

"I poured my magic into you from the day you were conceived."

Words appeared on my hand, turning dark and then melting back into nothing.

"I inscribed the language of power on your body while you were still in the womb. You were to be my crowning achievement, my gift to Kalina. I was in love and I was blind. Then I foresaw what I had made. Your aunt was the City Eater, your grandmother was the Scourge of Babylon, and you . . . You would destroy nations. If I let you live, if I raised you with your mother, like Kali's fury, your rage would devour all. I tried to tell your mother. I tried to explain, but she didn't want to listen. You were her baby, her precious one. You weren't even born and she loved you so much. So yes. I planned to kill you in the womb. I planned to do it gently."

"Oh well, then it's perfectly fine," Curran said. "As long as you choked the life out of her gently, I guess there's no hard feelings."

I leaned forward. "How did I turn out? Are you proud of the monster you made?"

Roland smiled. Hugh and Landon were right. It was like the sun had risen. Like digging a hole in your backyard and finding a glittering jewel in the dirt.

"Child, my dangerous one, my beautiful one. You've claimed your city. You shouldn't have been able to do that for another hundred years. I'm so proud that my pride could topple mountains. If you let me, I would show you to the world. I would show the world to you."

"So I could see it through your eyes?"

"So you could see it through your own."

I leaned forward. "From the time I could walk till I was fifteen years old, every memory I have is about you. If I wasn't studying about you, your children, and your kingdom, I was training to kill you or hiding from you. I was never afraid of monsters in my closet or under my bed. I was afraid you would find me. The entire purpose of my existence was so I could one day murder you."

"Here I am. You have a sword. Why don't you use it?"

I met his gaze. There was no point in lying. "Because I'm done living my life according to Voron's expectations. I don't know you. I know only what I was told. If you threaten Curran or anyone else I love, if you try to destroy this city, I'll do everything in my power to kill you, no matter how futile it is. But I won't do it because a dead man told me so."

He leaned back and laughed softly. "You truly are my daughter."

"That's not a compliment."

He smiled at me the way one would smile at a talented but naive child. I pictured kicking him in the head. I'd die a second later, but it would be so satisfying.

"Shall we bargain for the future of the city you love?" he asked.

"That is why you came here, isn't it?"

He rubbed his hands, his eyes bright. He looked . . . happy. "Very well. Do you know what you did?"

"I've blocked your claim on Atlanta and claimed it instead."

"Anyone crossing into Atlanta now will feel the borders of your territory. They won't necessarily know the territory is yours, which will give you the element of surprise. A territory claimed is a challenge. It will be answered, if not by me, then by others."

"I realize that."

"For my part, I can't allow you to remain in a position of visible power. You and I are invaders in this land. Our magic wasn't born here." Roland nodded to Curran. "Your magic was. Somewhere back in the mists of time your ancestors made a pact with a creature of this land. The blood might have been diluted through generations and mixed with that of the newcomers, but not enough to matter. You pose a threat."

"Which is why you've been trying to destroy the Pack," Curran said.

"To be fair, I haven't really tried," Roland said.

"The rakshasas," I said.

"They were more of a nuisance than a real threat. They sought an alliance with me. I found them annoying, so I gave them a target as a condition of the alliance. They failed as brilliantly as I had expected."

"And my aunt?"

My father leaned forward. "Eahrratim." He said her name with grief as if something of great beauty had been lost forever. "Your aunt didn't want to wake up. She did in spite of herself and when she rose, she was a mere shadow of herself. She didn't like this new world. She was going through the motions of living, but she couldn't permit herself to give up on life. We were taught from the earliest age that life is precious. Death must truly mean something. I wish you could've seen her at the height of her power. She was a force. Erra wanted something to do. I told her of the Pack. She thought it over for a few weeks and one day she told me she would go and see if she could find anything of amusement in Atlanta. She must've been so thrilled to have found you, her niece, in this distant age. You look like her."

"I know," I said. I had looked so much like her, it was eerie. Except she was more. Larger, stronger, faster, with magic that made whatever I could do pathetic. Killing her was the hardest thing I had ever done and it took both Curran and me to do it. I nearly lost Curran because of her. He'd spent eleven days in a coma.

"She could pass the torch and finally let go. There is no shame in being killed by one of your own bloodline. The night before you fought, she called me." His eyes clouded. "She wanted to talk about the Water Gardens. In the palace where we grew up, there had been water gardens, acres and acres of shallow water, crossed by narrow pathways. It was a beautiful place, of sand and warm water, where flowers bloomed and small fishes darted back and forth. We used to splash through it for hours. My fondest memories had been born there. I knew when she spoke of it, I wouldn't see her again. I felt the moment she surrendered her life and then I understood that you were still alive. She was the City Eater. You must've realized her death came too easily."

I nearly choked.

Roland sighed. "I suppose we should return to the business at hand. You can't fight me. I can sear the walls of this Keep until they melt with everyone inside it. In a day, everything you've built and everyone you serve will be gone. The city will do nothing about it, for such is the nature of human prejudice."

"He won't do it," I told Curran. "When he decides to do away with us, he'll do something elaborate, like send us magic seeds, which will sprout beautiful flowers with poisonous pollen. The pollen will root through our veins, we'll die in agony, but our corpses will be covered in gorgeous blooms. If he's feeling like making a statement, the flowers will drip blood just for fun."

Roland smiled. "Death should have a terrible beauty to it, don't you think?"

"What is it you want from us?" I asked.

"I want to know you. You are precious to me, as your mother was before you. But I can't let you lead the Pack." He looked at Curran. "You alone are enough of a threat. The two of you together at the helm of that many shapeshifters is too clear a statement for me to ignore. You'll be seen as actively opposing me."

"And?" Curran asked.

Roland looked at me. "I want you to leave the Pack."

My heartbeat sped up. Curran would never walk away from the Pack. He was the Beast Lord. He'd hammered it together; he gave it laws and structure, he lived and breathed it. The shapeshifters were his people. If I stayed with him, I would be Consort, even if I refused to have anything to do with the Pack. It would never work and my father knew it. The only way I could step down would be to leave Curran.

"In return, I'll let you keep your claimed territory," Roland said. "And your city."

"Not good enough," Curran said.

He was actually thinking about it. It made sense. We would avoid a bloody war. We could keep so many lives safe . . .

"Very well, let's put a number on it. I promise to take no direct action personally, nor instruct my people to take any action against anyone within the territory my daughter has claimed, for the next hundred years. Should any of my people challenge you, they would do so without my permission and incur my wrath. I will, however, keep the installation of the People in Atlanta and their business will proceed as usual."

My mind started working. "I want more. I want you to promise that neither you nor your people acting on your orders will ever harm Curran or Julie, in my territory or outside of it."

"I'm being rather generous. It's already a good trade," Roland said to me. "You wish to protect your people. I'm the biggest threat you face. Eliminate me as a danger. If you refuse, blossom of my heart, I will come to Atlanta and I will bring fire and ruin to it. I will purge the Keep the way I purged Omaha."

The earthquakes of Omaha had killed thousands. But they had always been viewed as a freak cataclysm brought on by a flare, a massive magic wave.

"You . . . ?"

He nodded.

"Why?"

"There was a Native power that chose to oppose me," Roland said. "I didn't strike the first blow. I merely retaliated. Is that disturbing to you?"

"Yes."

"You will understand eventually. No challenge, no matter how insignificant, can be left unanswered. Even a cry in the wilderness must be acknowledged, because someone might have heard it." Roland smiled. "I'm fortunate you survived. It will be so interesting to watch you grow. We have nothing but time on our hands."

"You're telling me to give up the man I love," I said.

"I can't say I approve of your choice. He's powerful, but also paranoid and xenophobic. He will be difficult to bend."

"Oh that's rich," Curran said.

I unclenched my teeth. "I can go years without worrying if you approve of me. And I have no interest in bending him. I like him the way he is. You have no right to comment on my relationships."

"I'm your father. That's the great privilege of parenthood; we can comment on whatever we want."

"I don't want you to be my father."

"Of course you do," Roland said. "You want to be loved, just like all of us want to be loved by our parents. Don't you want to know about your mother? What she was like? About our family?"

"Our family consists of monsters."

"Yes. But we are great and powerful monsters. Love demands sacrifices. When you love something, the way you love your people, Blossom, you must pay for it. Besides, I'm not forcing you to leave him, only the position of power that comes with him."

"How exactly does this get around me challenging you?"

"You claimed a territory. I made you step down in retaliation. This demonstrates to those who are watching that I have power over you and our relationship is much more complex than the simple rebellion of you against me."

"You are incredibly powerful," I told him. "But I'm your daughter. If you hurt Curran or Julie, I will hunt you. I will dedicate every waking moment of my life to killing you, and I will succeed. Maybe not now. Maybe in another century or two. But I will never give up. Your powers work half of the time, when the magic is up. My sword works always. Promise me, Father. Promise it."

Roland looked at Curran. "So be it. But this is the last concession I'm willing to make."

"We have a deal," Curran said. My heart broke into small jagged pieces.

Roland smiled again. "I always gave my children what I thought they wanted. Usually they wanted power. I am giving you what you need instead. Consider it an early wedding gift."

There wouldn't be a wedding. The Beast Lord and the Pack were one and the same. Even if we tried to make it work, we'd fail. The Pack would pull and pressure him to spend time at the Keep, where I couldn't be, while I would pull and pressure him to stay with me.

Roland rose. "The two of you have some choices to make. I shall leave you to it. Oh, and I would like to be invited to the wedding."

"No," Curran and I said at the same time.

Roland paused by the door, his face wise, his eyes timeless. "I've often asked myself why I could never raise my children to be the people I envisioned them being. I believe it was because they were with me. Power corrupts, it is true, but none succumb to its rot as readily as the young. You don't see it this way, but what I am giving you now is a blessing. You will understand in time."

He put his hand on the door handle. "Almost forgot. Teleportation by water requires an incantation and the ignorance or agreement of the one being teleported. *Aar natale*."

The words clicked in my mind, their meaning clear. "Interrupt?"

My father nodded. "That's all you have to say to stop a teleportation incantation."

He walked out.

If I stayed with Curran, Atlanta would burn and the Pack would die. I could do nothing to stop it.

"Fighting him will be difficult," Curran said.

"Yes." Understatement of the year.

"Do you like being the Consort?" he asked.

"You're kidding me, right?"

He came over, crouched by me, and took my hands into his. "Kate, do you like being the Consort?"

I couldn't ask him to give up the Pack for me. But I couldn't lie to him either. "No. I never wanted to be the Consort. I just wanted you."

"Then problem solved. Barabas!" Curran called.

The door opened and Barabas stepped inside, his face puzzled. "I just saw a man leave. I've been at the guard station since we got here. I'm positive he didn't come in. Unless I'm insane, none of us let him in."

"I want you to release a general announcement to the Pack," Curran said.

"Should I get a pen and paper?"

"No, it will be short."

"I'm ready," Barabas said.

Curran looked at me. "Effective tomorrow, we are retired. Jim has our blessing."

What?

Barabas opened his mouth. Nothing came out.

"Take your time," Curran said.

"You what?"

"We are stepping down," Curran said.

"You can't!"

"We just did."

"But—"

"We'll talk about the details in the morning."

"But what do I tell them?"

Curran sighed. "Which them?"

"Them!" Barabas waved his arms. "Everybody."

"Tell them we quit. Thank you, Barabas. That will be all."

Barabas blinked several times, turned around, and left the room. The door behind him closed.

"You're leaving the Pack?" I couldn't believe it.

"No, *we* are leaving. Together. It's freedom, Kate. Freedom from paperwork, freedom from sorting through petitions. We can have a day off whenever we want. We can have sex whenever we want. You can run Cutting Edge, I'll help you apprehend bunnycats, we can go to Julie's plays or whatever the hell she does, without having to make excuses . . ."

I put my hand on his lips. "But you're the Beast Lord."

He kissed my fingers and took my hand off his mouth. "I haven't liked being the Beast Lord for a while now. I built all this so my family—so you—would be protected. Then I almost had to kill my own Council so that I could leave to save my mate. In the end, Roland just walked past all of my defenses. Screw this. I'm done with it. This is the best way to protect you and Julie for now."

"You created all of this. I can't ask you to give up your life for me."

He smiled. "I know. You did it for me. You moved into the Keep with me. My turn."

Words came running out of me, one over the other. "You realize that my father won't leave us alone? He can't help himself. He meddles. He won't attack us directly. Instead, he'll find some ancient god with an axe to grind and suggest to him that Atlanta might be a nice place to put down roots, just so he can watch us take him down. Didn't you see him? He was so happy I passed his little test. He's already thinking of ways he can manipulate and use me and you."

"That's fine," Curran said. "He'll meddle with us instead of the Pack and we'll deal with it. The real question is, will you still love me if I'm not Beast Lord?"

I put my arms around him. "Of course I'll still love you, you stupid idiot. The Beast Lord is an arrogant jerk. I never wanted him. I only wanted Curran."

"Stay with me," he said.

"Always," I told him.

EPILOGUE

"I LIKE THIS one," Julie announced.

I surveyed the three-story house. Solid, with thick walls and grates over the windows, it was built post-Shift from hard brown stone. Curran tilted his head. The announcement of our retirement had hit the Pack first thing in the morning and spawned a shit storm of enormous proportions. We were supposed to be attending an emergency Pack Council session, except the three of us sneaked out of the Keep instead. We had breakfast at a small mom-and-pop joint and then stopped by a Pack real estate office. Once Nina, the real estate agent, a red-haired woman in her forties, regained her ability to speak, she sprang into action. This was the third house we had seen and I really liked it. It sat by itself on a five-acre lot on the outskirts of Atlanta, only three miles from Cutting Edge. Peach trees grew in the back, but the house itself sat in the middle of what would be a grassy lawn in the spring. Julie circled around and reported the presence of a pool in the backyard.

"All of this used to be office buildings." Nina waved her arm at the street. "Once it was cleared, they decided to subdivide it into five-acre lots. You have neighbors on the left and on the right, but across from you there's only about a hundred yards of trees and then Lake Smallish. Pool and stables for six mounts are in the back. This is a relatively safe area as far as northern Atlanta goes."

"Safe isn't a problem," Curran said. "I'll make it safe."

"It's only half an hour from my school," Julie said. "That cuts my commute in half."

"You might have to ride a horse," I told her. "Jezebel won't be able to take you back and forth anymore." Jezebel worked for the Pack and we were severing ties.

Julie's eyes lit up. "Can I ride Hugh's horse?"

"I'll think about it," Curran said.

I thought she'd be upset about leaving the Keep. Instead, she'd shrugged and announced that as long as she could go to the same school, she didn't care.

"Shall we go in?" Nina unlocked the door.

Julie went inside.

"It's kind of big," I said.

Curran grinned. I tapped him on the arm.

"That's good. Plenty of privacy."

"Can we afford this?" I asked Curran. It had to cost an arm and a leg.

"Yes," he said. "I'm loaded."

"Well, aren't we smug, Your Furriness."

"Technically, you can't call me that anymore."

"I'll call you whatever I like."

We stepped inside. Sand-colored tile lined the floor. The house was bright and open. Light streamed through the windows. The air smelled like freshly baked cookies. Here we go. It felt so comfortable here. And the office was less than twenty minutes away by horse. It was like it was tailor made for us.

"Four thousand square feet. Open floor plan," Nina rattled off. "Tile on the first floor, hardwood on the two top floors. Beautiful windows throughout, state-of-the-art grates with high silver content . . ."

We followed her into the kitchen. It was almost as big as my old apartment. A platter of cookies waited for us on the counter with a small white note.

"The cookies are a nice touch," Curran said.

Nina paused. "I didn't do that. I had no idea I was going to show this one today."

I plucked the note from the counter.

I like this one. Plenty of room for the grandchildren and a sizable guest suite.

PS. The wards on the north side need to be reinforced.

~R

MAGIC TESTS

A Short Story in the World of Kate Daniels

Ilona Andrews

SOMETIMES BEING A kid is very difficult. The adults are supposed to feed you and keep you safe, but they want you to deal with the world according to their views and not your own. They encourage you to have opinions, and if you express them, they will listen but they won't hear. And when they give you a choice, it's a selection of handpicked possibilities they have prescreened. No matter what you decide, the core choice has already been made, and you weren't involved in it.

That's how Kate and I ended up in the office of the director of Seven Stars Academy. I said I didn't want to go to school. She gave me a list of ten schools and said to pick one. I wrote the names of the schools on little bits of paper, pinned them to the corkboard, and threw my knife at them for a while. After half an hour, Seven Stars was the only name I could still read. Choice made.

Now we were sitting in soft chairs in a nice office, waiting for the school director, and Kate was exercising her willpower. Before I met Kate, I had heard people say it, but I didn't know what it meant. Now I knew. Kate was the Beast Lord's mate, which meant that Curran and she were in charge of Atlanta's giant shapeshifter pack. It was so huge, people actually called it the Pack. Shapeshifters were kind of like bombs: things frequently set them off and they exploded with violent force. To keep from exploding, they made up elaborate rules and Kate had to exercise her willpower a lot.

She was doing it now; from outside she looked very calm and composed, but I could tell she was doing it by the way she sat. When Kate was relaxed, she fidgeted. She'd shift in her chair, throw one leg over the other, lean to the side, then lean back. She was very still now, legs in jeans together, holding Slayer, her magic saber, on her lap, one hand on the hilt, the other on the scabbard. Her face was relaxed, almost serene. I could totally picture her leaping straight onto the table from the chair and slicing the director's head off with her saber.

Kate usually dealt with things by talking, and when that didn't work, by chopping obstacles into tiny pieces and frying them with magic so they didn't get back up. The sword was her talisman, because she believed in it. She held it like some people held crosses or the star-and-crescent. Her philosophy was, if it had a pulse, it could be killed. I didn't really have a philosophy, but I could see how talking with the school director would be difficult for her. If he said something she didn't like, chopping him to tiny pieces wouldn't exactly help me get into the school.

"What if when the director comes in, I take my underwear off, put them on my head, and dance around? Do you think it would help?"

Kate looked at me. It was her hard-ass stare. Kate could be really scary.

"That doesn't work on me," I told her. "I know you won't hurt me."

"If you want to prance around with panties on your head, I won't stop you," she said. "It's your basic human right to make a fool of yourself."

"I don't want to go to school." Spending all my time in a place where I was the poor rat adopted by a merc and a shapeshifter, while spoiled little rich girls jeered when I walked by and stuck-up teachers put me in remedial courses? No thanks.

Kate exercised her will some more. "You need an education, Julie."

"You can teach me."

"I do and I'll continue to do so. But you need to know other things, besides the ones I can teach. You need a well-rounded education."

"I don't like education. I like working at the office. I want to do what you and Andrea do."

Kate and Andrea ran Cutting Edge, a small firm that helped people with their magic hazmat issues. It was a dangerous job, but I liked it.

Besides, I was pretty messed up. Normal things like going to school and getting a regular job didn't hold any interest for me. I couldn't even picture myself doing that.

"Andrea went to the Order's Academy for six years and I've trained since I could walk."

"I'm willing to train."

My body tensed, as if an invisible hand had squeezed my insides into a clump. I held my breath . . .

Magic flooded the world in an invisible wave. The phantom hand let go, and the world shimmered with hues of every color as my sensate vision kicked in. Magic came and went as it pleased. Some older people still remembered the time when technology was always in control and magic didn't exist. But that was long ago. Now magic and technology kept trading places, like two toddlers playing musical chairs. Sometimes magic ruled, and cars and guns didn't work. Sometimes technology was in charge, and magic spells fizzled out. I preferred the magic myself, because unlike ninety-nine point nine-nine-nine-whatever percent of people I could see it.

I looked at Kate, using a tiny drop of my power. It was kind of like flexing a muscle, a conscious effort to look the right way at something. One moment Kate sat there, all normal, or as normal as Kate could be, the next she was wrapped in a translucent glow. Most people's magic glowed in one color. Humans radiated blue, shapeshifters green, vampires gave off a purple-red . . . Kate's magic shifted colors. It was blue and deep purple, and pale pearl-like gold streaked through with tendrils of red. It was the weirdest thing I had ever seen. The first time I saw it, it freaked me out.

"You have to keep going to school," freaky Kate said.

I leaned back and hung my head over the chair's back. "Why?"

"Because I can't teach you everything, and shapeshifters shouldn't be your only source of education. You may not always want to be affiliated with shapeshifters. Down the road, you may want to make your own choices."

I pushed against the floor with my feet, rocking a little in my chair.

"I'm trying to make my own choice, but you won't let me."

"That's right," Kate said. "I'm older, wiser, and I know better. Deal with it."

Parenting, kick-ass Kate Daniels's style. Do what I say. There wasn't even an *or* attached to it. *Or* didn't exist.

I rocked back and forth some more. "Do you think I'm your punishment from God?"

"No. I'd like to think that God, if he exists, is kind, not vengeful."

The door of the office opened and a man walked in. He was older than Kate, bald, with Asian features, dark eyes, and a big smile. "It's a view I share."

I sat up straight. Kate got up and offered her hand. "Mr. Dargye?"

The man shook her hand. "Please call me Gendun. I much prefer it."

They shook and sat down. Adult rituals. My history teacher from the old school once told us that shaking hands was a gesture of peace—it demonstrated that you had no weapon. Since now we had magic, shaking hands was more a leap of faith. Do I shake this weirdo's hand and run the risk that he will infect me with a magic plague or shoot lightning into my skin or do I step back and be rude? Hmm. Maybe handshakes would go away in the future.

Gendun was looking at me. He had sucker eyes. Back when I lived on the street, we used to mob people like him, because they were kind and soft-hearted and you could always count on some sort of handout. They weren't naive bleeding hearts—they knew that while you cried in front of them and clutched your tummy, your friends were stealing their wallets, but they would feed you anyway. That's just the way they moved through the world.

I squinted, bringing the color of his magic into focus. Pale blue, almost silver. Divine magic, born of faith. Mister Gendun was a priest of some sort.

"What god do you believe in?" I asked. When you're a kid, they let you get away with being direct.

"I'm a Buddhist." Gendun smiled. "I believe in human potential for understanding and compassion. The existence of an omnipotent God is possible, but so far I have seen no evidence that he exists. What god do you believe in?"

"None." I met a goddess once. It didn't turn out well for everyone involved. Gods used faith the way a car used gas; it was the supply from which they drew their power. I refused to fuel any of their motors.

Gendun smiled. "Thank you for responding to my request so promptly."

Request? What request?

"Two of the Pack's children attend your school," Kate said. "The Pack will do everything in our power to offer you assistance."

Huh? Wait a minute. I thought this was about me. Nobody said anything about the school requesting our assistance.

"This is Ms. Olsen," Kate said.

I smiled at Gendun. "Please call me Julie. I much prefer it." Technically my name was now Julie Lennart-Daniels-Olsen, which was silly. If Kate and Curran got married, I'd be down to Lennart-Olsen. Until then, I decided Olsen was good enough.

"It is nice to meet you, Julie." Gendun smiled and nodded at me. He had this really strange calming thing about him. He was very . . . balanced somehow. Reminded me of the Pack's medmage, Dr. Doolittle.

"There are many schools in the city for the children of exceptional parents," Gendun said. "Seven Stars is a school for exceptional children. Our methods are unorthodox and our students are unique."

Woo, a school of special snowflakes. Or monster children. Depending on how you chose to look at it.

Magic didn't affect just our environment. All sorts of people who once had been normal and ordinary were discovering new and sometimes unwelcome things about themselves. Some could freeze things. Some grew claws and fur. And some saw magic.

"Discretion is of utmost importance to us," Gendun said.

"Despite her age, Ms. Olsen is an experienced operative," Kate said.

I am?

"She understands the need for discretion."

I do?

"She has a particular talent that will make her very effective in this case," Kate said.

Gendun opened a folder, took out a picture, and slid it across the table to me. A girl. She had a pretty heart-shaped face framed by spirals of red hair. Her eyes were green and her long eyelashes curled out until they almost touched her eyebrows. She looked so pretty, like a little doll.

"This is Ashlyn," Gendun said. "She is a freshman at this school. A very good student. Two days ago she disappeared. The location spell indicates she is alive and that she hasn't left the grounds. We've attempted to notify her parents, but they are traveling at the moment and are out of reach, as are her emergency contacts. You have twenty-four hours to find her."

"What happens after twenty-four hours?"

"We will have to notify the authorities," Gendun said. "Her parents had given us a lot of latitude in regard to Ashlyn. She is a sensitive child and her behavior is often driven by that sensitivity. But in this case our hands are tied. If a student is missing, we are legally bound to report it after seventy-two hours."

Report it to Paranormal Activity Division of Atlanta's police force, no doubt. PAD was about as subtle as a runaway bulldozer. They would take this school apart and grill all of their special snowflakes until they melted into goo in their interrogation rooms. How many would fold and confess to something they had not done?

I looked at Kate.

She arched an eyebrow at me. "Interested?"

"We would give you a visitor pass," Gendun said. "I will speak to the teachers, so you can conduct your investigation quietly. We have guest students who tour the school before attending, so you wouldn't draw any attention and the disruption to the other children will be minimal."

This was some sort of Kate trick of getting me into this school. I looked at the picture again. Trick or not, a girl was hiding somewhere. She could be hiding because she was playing some sort of a joke, but it was highly unlikely. Mostly people hid because they were scared. I could relate. I'd been scared before. It wasn't fun.

Someone had to find her. Someone had to care about what happened.

I pulled the picture closer. "I'll do it."

MY STUDENT GUIDE was a tall dark-haired girl named Brook. She had skinny legs, bony arms, and wore round glasses that constantly slid down her nose. She kept pushing them up with her middle finger, so it looked as if she was shooting the bird at the entire world every five minutes. Her magic was a strong simple blue, the color of human abilities. We met in the front office, where they outfitted me with a white armband. Apparently they marked their visitors. If there was any trouble, we'd be easy to shoot.

"Okay, you follow me and don't touch things," Brook informed me. "Stuff here is randomly warded. Also Barka has been leaving little tiny charges of magic all around the school. You touch it, it zaps you. Then your fingers hurt for an hour."

"Is Barka a student?"

"Barka is a pisshead," Brook told me and pushed her glasses up. "Come on."

We walked up the stairs. The bell rang and the staircase filled with kids.

"Four floors," Brook told me. "The school is a big square, with the garden slash courtyard in the center. All the fields, like for soccer and football, are outside of the square. First floor is the gymnasium, pool, dance studio, auditorium, and cafeteria. Second floor, humanities: literature, history, sociology, anthropology, Latin—"

"Did you know Ashlyn?" I asked.

Brook paused, momentarily knocked off her course by the interruption. "She did not take Latin."

"But did you know her?"

"Yes."

"What kind of a student was she?"

Brook shrugged. "Quiet. We have an algebra class together, fourth period. I thought she might be competition at first. You have to watch out for the quiet ones."

"Was she?"

"Naaah." Brook grimaced. "Progress reports came out last week. Her math grade was seventeen. One seven. She only does well in one class, botany. You could give her a broom and she'll stick it in the ground and grow you an apple tree. I took botany last semester and she beat my grade by two points. She has a perfect hundred. There's got to be a trick to it." Brook squared her shoulders. "That's okay. I am taking AP botany next year. I'll take her down."

"You're a little bit crazy, you know that?"

Brook shrugged and pushed her glasses up at me. "Third floor, magic: alchemy, magic theory—"

"Did Ashlyn seem upset over the seventeen in math?" Maybe she was hiding because of her grades.

Brook paused. "No."

"She wasn't worried about her parents?" When I got a bad grade in my old boarding school, Kate would make a trip to the school to chew me out. When I got homesick, I'd flunk a grade on purpose. Sometimes she came by herself. Sometimes with other people. Boy kind of people. Of whom I promised myself I wouldn't be thinking about, because they were idiots.

"I met her parents on family day. I was in charge of Hospitality Committee. They are really into nurture and all that," Brook said. "They wouldn't be upset with her. Fourth floor: science and technology—"

"Do you have lockers?"

"No. We have storage in our desks in the homerooms."

"Can we go to see Ashlyn's homeroom?"

Brook stared at me. "Look you, I'm assigned to do this stupid tour with you. I can't do the tour if you keep interrupting."

"How many tours have you done so far?"

Brook peered at me. "Eleven."

"Aren't you tired of doing them?"

"That's irrelevant. It's good for my record."

Right. "If you don't do the tour this time, I won't tell anyone."

Brook frowned. That line of thought obviously stumped her. I worked my iron while it was hot. "I'm here undercover investigating Ashlyn's disappearance. If you help me, I'll mention it to Gendun."

Brook puzzled it over.

Come on, Brook. You know you want to.

"Fine," she said. "But you'll tell Master Gendun that I helped."

"Invaluable assistance," I said.

Brook nodded. "Come on. Ashlyn's homeroom is on the second floor."

ASHLYN'S HOMEROOM WAS in the geography class. Maps hung on the walls: world, Americas, U.S., and the biggest map of all, the new magic-screwed-up map of Atlanta, complete with all the new additions and warped, dangerous neighborhoods.

A few people occupied the classroom, milling in little clumps. I took a second to look around and closed my eyes. Nine people in all, two girls to my right, three boys farther on, a girl sitting by herself by the window, two guys discussing something, and a blond kid sitting by himself at the back of the class. I opened my eyes. Missed the dark-haired boy in the corner. Oh well, at least I was getting better at it.

Brook stopped by a wooden desk. It was nice, large and polished, the sealed wood stained the color of amber. Pretty. None of the places I ever studied at were this nice.

"This is her desk," Brook said.

I sat down into Ashlyn's chair. The desk had one wide drawer running the entire length of it. I tried it gently. Locked. No big. I pulled a lockpick out of the leather bracelet on my left wrist and slid it into the lock.

The blond kid from the back sauntered over and leaned on the desk. His magic was dark, intense indigo. Probably an elemental mage. He had sharp features and blue eyes that said he was up to no good. My kind of people.

"Hi. What are you doing?"

"Go away, Barka," Brook said.

"I wasn't talking to you." The kid looked at me. "Whatcha doing?"

"I'm dancing." I told him. Ask a dumb question . . .

"You're breaking into Ashlyn's desk."

"See, I knew you were smart and you'd figure it out." I winked at him.

Barka made big eyes at Brook. "And what if I tell Walton you're doing that? That would be a spot on your perfect record."

"Mind your own business," Brook snapped.

"He won't," I told her. "He wants to see what's inside the desk."

Barka grinned.

The lock clicked and the drawer slid open. Rows of apples filled it. Large Red Delicious, Golden Delicious, green Granny Smith and every color and shape in between, each with a tiny sticker announcing its name. Even a handful of red crab apples the size of large cherries, stuck between Cortland and Crimson Gold. I had no idea so many varieties of apple even existed. None of them showed any signs of rotting either. They looked crisp and fresh.

I concentrated. My sensate vision kicked in. The apples glowed with bright green. Now that was a first. A healthy hunter green usually meant a shapeshifter. Human magic came in various shades of blue. Animal magic was typically too weak to be picked up by any of the machines, but I saw it just fine—it was yellow. Together blue and yellow made green. This particular green had too much yellow to belong to a regular shapeshifter.

Most shapeshifters were infected with Lyc-V virus, which let them turn into animals. Sometimes it happened the other way and animals turned into humans. The human-weres were really rare, but I've met one, and the color wasn't right for them either. Human-weres were a drab olive, but this, this was a vivid spring green.

"What kind of magic did Ashlyn have?"

Brook and Barka looked at each other. "I don't know," Barka said. "I never asked."

Whatever she was, she didn't advertise it. Totally understandable. Seeing the color of magic was an invaluable tool for law enforcement, for mages, basically for anyone who dealt with it, so much so that people actually made a magic machine, called an m-scanner, to imitate it. My magic wasn't just rare, it was exceptional. I was a hundred times more precise than any existing m-scanner. But in a fight, being a sensate didn't do me any good at all. If I walked around telling everyone about it, sooner or later someone would try to use me and I had to use other means than my sensate ability to protect myself. It was easier to just keep my mouth shut.

Ashlyn could be that kind of magic user, something rare but not useful in combat.

Still didn't explain her obsession with apples, though. Maybe she was using them to bribe her teachers. But then her grades would be better.

The shorter of the three girls to our left glared at me. Her magic, a solid indigo when I came in, now developed streaks of pale celery green. Normally the magic signature didn't change. Ever. Except for Kate.

Hello, clue.

I pretended to look at the apples. "Did Ashlyn have any enemies?"

Barka picked up a pen and rolled it between his fingers. "Not that I noticed. She was quiet. A looker, but no personality."

Brook pushed her glasses up at him. "Pervert."

The girl took a step toward us. "What are you doing?"

"Dancing!" Barka said.

Brook didn't even look in her direction. "Mind your own business, Lisa."

Lisa skewed her mouth into a disapproving thin line, which was quite a fit because she had one of those pouty-lip mouths. Eyebrows plucked into two narrow lines, unnaturally straight hair, carefully parted, pink shiny on those big lips . . . Lisa was clearly the Take-Care-of-Myself type. Good clothes, too. Girls like that made my life miserable at the old school. I was never put together enough, my clothes were never expensive enough, and I didn't stroll the halls broadcasting to everyone who cared that I was much better than they were.

But we weren't at my old school, and a lot has changed since. Besides, she could be a perfectly nice person. Although somehow I doubted it.

"You shouldn't be doing that," Lisa said, entirely too loudly.

If I poked her, would her magic get even veinier? Was *veinier* even a word? "I'm looking for Ashlyn," I told her.

"She's dead," Lisa announced and checked the room out of the corner of her eye.

Don't worry, you have everyone's attention.

"Here we go," Brook muttered.

"How do you know that? Did you kill her?" Poke-poke-poke.

Lisa raised her chin. "I know because I spoke to her spirit."

"Her spirit?" I asked.

"Yes, her spirit. Her ghost."

That was nice, but there was no such thing as ghosts. Even Kate had never run across one. I never saw any ghost magic and I had seen a lot of messed-up things.

"Did her ghost tell you who killed her?" I asked.

"She took her own life," Lisa declared.

Brook pushed her glasses up. "Don't be ridiculous. This whole 'I see spirits' thing is getting old."

Lisa rocked back on her heels. Her face turned serious. "Ashlyn! Show yourself, spirit."

"This is stupid," Barka said.

"Show your presence!" Lisa called.

Yellow-green veins shot through her magic, sparking with flashes of dandelion yellow. Whoa.

The desk shuddered under my fingertips. The chairs around me rattled. Brook took a step back.

The desk danced, jumping up and down. The two chairs on both sides of me shot to the ceiling, hovered there for a tense second, and crashed down.

Nice.

Lisa leveled her stare at me. "Ashlyn is dead. I don't know who you are, but you should leave. You disturb her."

I laughed.

Lisa turned on her heel and walked out.

"So Lisa is a telekinetic?" I asked.

Brook shrugged. "A little. Nothing like this. The chair-flying thing is new. Usually she has to sweat to push a pen across the desk."

And this new power wouldn't have anything to do with those lovely yellow-green streaks in her magic, would it? Like Ashlyn's apples, yellow green, but not the same shade. Two weird magic colors in one day. That was a hell of a thing, as Kate would say.

"You're not leaving?" Barka asked me.

"Of course she isn't leaving," Brook told him. "I haven't finished the tour."

"When people tell me to leave, it's the right time to stick around," I told him. "Did Lisa have any problems with Ashlyn?"

"Lisa has problems with everyone," Brook said. "People like her like to pick on you if you have any weakness to make themselves feel better."

"She's a dud," Barka added. "Well, she was a dud, apparently. Her parents are both professors at the Mage Academy. When she was first admitted, she made a big deal out of all this major magic that she supposedly had."

"I remember that." Brook grimaced. "Every time she opened her mouth, it was all 'at the Mage Academy where my father works' or 'when I visited my mother's laboratory at the Mage Academy.' Ugh."

"She claimed to have tons of power," Barka added, "but she couldn't do anything with it, except some minor telekinesis."

"Let me guess, people made fun of her?" I asked.

"She brought a lot of it on herself," Brook told me. "Not everybody here has super-awesome magic."

"Like Sam." Barka shrugged. "If you give him a clear piece of glass, he can etch it with his magic so it looks frosted. It's cool the first time you see it, but it's pretty useless and he can't control it very well either. He doesn't make a big deal out of it."

"It's in Lisa's head that she is super-special," Brook said. "She feels entitled, like we're all peons here and she is a higher being. Nobody likes being treated that way."

"Does she get picked on?" I asked.

Barka shrugged again. "Nothing too bad. She doesn't get invited to hang out. Nobody wants to sit with her at lunch. But that's just pure self-defense, because she doesn't listen to whatever you have to say. She just waits to tell you about her special parents. I guess she finally got her powers."

"Did she get them about the time Ashlyn disappeared?"

"Yeah." Barka grimaced. "Then she started sensing Ashlyn's presence everywhere. Who knows, maybe Ashlyn is really dead."

"Location spell says she is alive. Besides, there is no such thing as ghosts," I told them.

"And you're an authority on ghosts?" Brook asked.

"Trust me on this."

Ghosts might be better. I had this sick little feeling in my stomach that said this was something bad. Something really bad.

I could call Kate and ask her what would cause the magic of two different colors to show up. The colors weren't blended or flowing into one another the way Kate's colors did. They were distinct. Separate. Together but not mixing.

Ehhh. There was some sort of answer at the end of that thought, but I couldn't figure it out.

Calling Kate wouldn't be happening. This was my little mission and I would get it done on my own.

I tried to think like Kate. She always said that people were the key to any mystery. Someone somehow did something that caused Ashlyn to hide and Lisa really didn't want me to keep looking for her. "Did Ashlyn have a best friend?"

Brook paused. "She and Sheila hung out sometimes, but mostly she kept to herself."

"Can we go talk to Sheila?"

Brook heaved a long-suffering sigh. "Sure."

"You're leaving? In that case, Brook, hold this for me for a second." Barka stuck the pen he'd been rolling between his fingers at Brook. She took it. Bright light sparked and Brook dropped the pen and shook her hand.

Barka guffawed.

"Moron!" Brook's eyes shone with a dangerous glint behind her glasses. She marched out of the class. I followed her.

We went down the hallway toward the staircase.

"He likes you," I said.

"Yeah, sure," Brook growled.

Sheila turned out to be the exact opposite of Ashlyn. Where Ashlyn's picture showed a petite cutesy girly-girl, Sheila was muscular. Not manly, but really cut. We caught her in the locker room, just as she was going out to play volleyball. It's not often you see a girl with a six-pack.

She sat on a wooden bench by the small wooden room inside the locker room that said *sauna* on it. I wondered what the heck *sauna* meant. It was a first-class locker room; the floor was tile, three showers, two bathrooms, "sauna," large lockers. The clean tile smelled faintly of pine. Special locker room for special snowflakes.

"I don't know why Ashlyn pulled this stunt." Sheila pulled on her left sock.

"Was she worried about anything?"

"She did seem kind of jumpy."

"Did she have a problem with Lisa?"

Sheila paused with the shoe on one foot. "Lisa the Dud?"

Okay, so I didn't like Lisa. But if they called me that, I'd get pissed off really quick, too. "Lisa who senses Ashlyn's 'presence.'"

"Not really." Sheila shook her head. "One time someone left a paw print on Ashlyn's desk. She got really upset."

"What kind of paw print?"

"Wolf," Brook said. "I remember that. She scrubbed her desk for ten minutes."

"How big was the print and when did this happen?"

"Big," Sheila said. "Like bowl-sized. It was about a week ago or so."

Prints that large could indicate a shapeshifter, a werewolf, possibly a werejackal or a werecoyote.

"If anybody had a problem with her, it would be Yu Fong," Sheila said.

"He is the only eighteen-year-old sophomore we have," Brook said. "He's this odd Chinese guy."

"Odd how?"

"He's an orphan," Sheila said. "His parents were murdered."

"I thought they died in a car accident," Brook said.

"Well, whatever happened, happened," Sheila told me. "For some reason he didn't go to school. I heard he was in prison, but whatever. Anyway, he showed up one day, talked to Master Gendun, and got himself admitted as a student. He tested out of enough credits to start as a sophomore. He's dangerous."

"Very powerful," Brook said.

"Uber-magic," Sheila said. "You can feel it coming off of him sometimes. Makes my skin itch."

Brook nodded. "Not sure exactly what sort of magic he has, but whatever it is, it's significant. There are three other Chinese kids in school and they follow Yu Fong around like bodyguards. You can't even talk to him."

"And Ashlyn had a problem with him?" Somehow I couldn't picture Ashlyn deliberately picking a fight with this guy.

"She was terrified of him," Sheila said. "One time he tried to talk to her and she freaked out and ran off."

Okay, then. Next target—the mysterious Yu Fong.

THE SEARCH FOR the "odd Chinese guy" took us to the cafeteria, where according to Brook, this uber-magic user had second-shift lunch. Brook led the way. I followed her through the double doors and paused. A large skylight poured sunshine into the huge room, filled with round metal tables and ornate chairs. At the far wall, the buffet table stretched, manned by several servers in white. Fancy.

The students picked up their plates and carried them to different tables. Some sat, talking. To the right, several voices laughed in unison.

To the left, a wide doorway allowed a glimpse of a smaller sunroom. In its center, right under the skylight, grew a small tree with red leaves, all but glowing in the sunshine. A table stood by the tree and a young guy sat in a chair, leaning on the table, reading a book. He was too old to be called a boy, but too young to be called a man, and his face was inhumanly beautiful.

I stood and stared.

I'd seen some handsome guys before. This guy . . . he was magic. His dark hair was brushed away from his high forehead, falling back without a trace of a curl. His features were flawlessly perfect, his face strong and masculine, with a contoured jaw, a tiny cleft in the chin, full lips, and high cheekbones. His eyebrows, dark and wide, bent to shield his eyes, large, beautiful, and very, very dark. Not black, but solid brown.

I blinked, and my power kicked in. The guy was wrapped in pale blue. Not quite silver, but with enough of it to dilute the color to a shimmering blue gray. Divinity. He was either a priest or an object of worship, and looking at him, I was betting on the latter. Glowing like this, he reminded me of one of those celestial beings of Chinese mythology they made me learn about in my old school. He looked like a god.

"That's him," Brook said. "And his guards."

Two boys sat at a second table a few feet away. "I thought you said there were three," I murmured.

"There are—Hui has algebra right now."

I scanned the two guys sitting next to Yu Fong—plain blue—and let go of my sensate vision. His face was distracting enough. I didn't need the glow.

"I'll go ask him if he'll talk to you," Brook said.

"Why don't we go together?" They took the pecking order really seriously in this place.

Brook compressed her lips. "No, they know me."

She made it about two-thirds of the way and then one of Yu Fong's guards peeled himself from the chair and blocked her way. Brook said something, he shook his head, and she turned around and came back to me.

Of course, it was a no. And now they knew I was coming.

Well, you have to work with what you've got.

I raised my hands and wiggled my fingers at the uber-magic guy. He continued reading his book. I waved again and started toward him, a nice big smile on my face. I've seen Kate do this, and if I didn't screw it up, it would work.

The first guard stepped forward, blocking my path. I gave him my cute smile, looked past him, and pointed to myself, as if I was being summoned over and couldn't believe it. He glanced over his shoulder to check Yu Fong's face. I drove my fist hard into his gut. The boy folded around my fist with a surprised gasp. I slammed my hand onto his head, driving his head down. Face meet knee. Boom! The impact reverberated through my leg.

I shoved him aside and kept moving. The second bodyguard jumped to his feet. I swiped the nearest chair, swung it, and hit him with it just as he was coming up.

The chair connected to the side of his head with a solid crunch. I let go and he stumbled back with the chair on top of him. I stepped past him and landed in the spare chair at the table.

The uber-guy slowly raised his gaze from his book and looked at me. Whoa.

There was a kind of serious arrogance in his eyes, a searing intensity and determination. Living on the street gives you a sixth sense about those things. You learn to read people. Reading him was easy: He was powerful and arrogant, and he imposed control on everything he saw, including himself. He had been through life's vicious grinder and had come out stronger for it. He would never let you know what he was thinking and you would always be on thin ice.

I touched the surface of the table with the tip of my finger. "Safe."

There was some scrambling behind me. Yu Fong made a small motion with his hand and the noises stopped. I'd won the right to an audience. Wheee!

He tilted his head and studied me with those dark eyes.

I smelled incense. Yep, definitely incense, a strong, slightly sweet smoke. "I always wondered, how would one address an object of worship? Should I call you 'the lord of ten thousand years,' 'the holy one,' or the 'son of heaven'?" Dali, one of the shapeshifters, was teaching me the beginnings of Asian mythologies. Unfortunately, that's as far as we got, since I only just started.

"I am not an object." His voice was slightly accented. "You may call me Yu."

Simple enough.

"Is there something you want?" he asked.

"My name is Julie Lennart." Might as well go with the big gun. Most people didn't know the Beast Lord's last name so if he recognized it, it would be a good indication that he was some sort of magic heavyweight.

"It is a weighty name for someone so small." Yu Fong smiled a nice easy smile. He would smile like that while he watched a cute puppy play with a butterfly or while his flunkies were torturing his enemy. Take your pick. "The Beast Lord commands fifteen hundred shapeshifters."

"More or less." It was more, but he didn't need to know that.

His dark eyes fixed on me. "One day my kingdom will be greater."

Ha-ha! Yeah, right. "I'm here with Master Gendun's knowledge and at his request."

He didn't say anything. The metal table under my fingers felt warm. I rested more of my hand on it. Definitely warm. The cafeteria was air-conditioned and even now, with magic up, the air stayed pretty cool, which meant the metal table should've been cold.

"A girl disappeared. She was a small girl. Shy. Her name is Ashlyn."

No reaction. The table was definitely getting warmer.

"She was scared of you."

"I don't kill little girls."

"What makes you think she was killed? I didn't say anything about her being killed."

He leaned forward slightly. "If I take notice of something that offends me, I choose to ignore it or kill it. I ignored her."

Boy, this dude was conceited. "Why did she offend you?"

"I've never threatened her. She had no reason to cringe in my presence. I don't expect you to understand."

I thought hard on why he would find an obvious display of fear offensive.

"When she cringed, you felt insulted. You had no intention of hurting her, so by showing fear, she implied that your control over your power was imperfect."

Yu's eyes widened slightly.

"I'm the ward of the Beast Lord," I told him. "I spend a lot of time with arrogant control freaks."

The table under my hand was almost too hot to keep touching it. I held on. "Ashlyn annoyed you. You said you ignored her. You didn't say anything about your bodyguards. Did they do something to Ashlyn to make her disappear?"

His face was the picture of disdain, which was just a polite way of saying that he would've liked to sneer at me but it was beneath him. I've seen this precise look on the Beast Lord's face. If he and Curran ever got into the same room, Kate's head would explode.

I waited but he didn't say anything. Apparently Yu decided not to dignify it with an answer.

Thin tendrils of smoke escaped from his book. The table near him must have been much hotter than on my end. That had to be something because the metal was now hurting my fingers.

"If I find out that you hurt Ashlyn, I'll hurt you back," I said.

"I'll keep that in mind."

"Do. Your book is smoking."

He picked it up. I slowly raised my hand, blew on my skin, and got up to leave.

"Why do you care?" he asked.

"Because none of you do. Look around you—a girl is missing. A girl you saw in class every day got so scared by something, she had to hide from it. Nobody is looking for her. All of you are just going on with your business as usual. You have all this power and you didn't lift a finger to help her. You just sit there, reading your book, comfy behind your bodyguards, and demonstrate how awesome your magic is by heating up your table. Somebody has to find her. I decided to be that somebody."

I couldn't tell if any of this was sinking in.

"True strength isn't in killing—or ignoring—your opponent, it's in having the will to shield those who need your protection."

He raised his eyebrows slightly. "Who said that?"

"I did." I walked away.

Brook was staring at me.

"Come on," I told her, loud enough for him to hear the derision in my voice. "We're done here."

IN THE HALLWAY I walked to the window and exhaled. The nerve. All that power, all that magic boiling in him, and he just sat there. Didn't do a thing to help Ashlyn. He didn't care.

Brook cleared her throat behind me.

"I just need a minute."

I looked outside at the courtyard, enclosed by the square building of the school. It was a really large courtyard. No place to hide, though: benches, flowers, twisted stone paths. A single tree rose toward the northern end of it, surrounded by a maze of concentric flower beds, spreading from it like one of those little handheld puzzle games where you have to roll the ball into a hole through a plastic labyrinth.

"You're wrong," Brook said behind me. "You know what, we all got problems. Just because I didn't look for Ashlyn doesn't make me a bad person. Do you have any idea how competitive the Mage Academy exams are? Getting the right credit is taking up all my time. And I don't even know you! Why do I have to justify myself to you?"

The flowers were in full bloom. Blue asters, delicate bearded irises, cream and yellow, purplish spiderwort—I had a lot of herbology in my old school. Normal for early June. The tree had tiny little buds just beginning to unfurl into gauzy white and pink petals.

"It's not like I even knew her that well. I don't see why I should be held accountable for whatever problem made her hide. If she'd come to me and said, 'Brook, I'm in trouble,' I would've helped her."

"What is that tree?"

"What?"

"The tree down in the yard." I pointed to it. "What kind of tree is it?"

Brook blinked. "I don't know. It's the dead tree. You can't get to it now anyway, not with the magic up, because the flower garden is warded. Listen, I'm not proud that I didn't look for Ashlyn. All I am saying is that maybe I didn't look for her and I probably should have, but I was busy."

I bet it was an apple tree. Some apple trees bloomed late, but most of them flowered in April and May. It was June now.

"How long has that tree been dead?"

"As long as I can remember. I've been in this school for three years and it was always dead. I don't know why they don't cut it down. Are you listening to me?"

"It's flowering."

Brook blinked. "What?"

"The tree is blooming. Look."

Brook looked at the window. "Huh."

Perfect hundred in botany. Apples in the drawer. Wolf print on the desk. Terrified of a boy who creates heat, because where there is smoke, there is fire. Blooming apple tree that has been dead for years.

It all lined up in my head into a perfect arrow pointing to the tree.

"Can we get down there?"

Brook was staring at the tree. "Yes."

Two minutes later I marched out of the side door into the inner yard and down the curved stone path. I was fifty feet from the tree when I sensed magic in front of me. I stopped and snapped into the sensate vision. A wall of magic rose in front of me, glowing lightly with pale silver. A ward, a defensive spell designed to keep out intruders. Currents of power coursed through it.

Some wards glowed with translucent color, both a barrier and a warning that the barrier existed, and walking into it would hurt. This one was invisible to someone without my vision. And judging by the intensity of the magic, touching it would hurt you bad enough to leave you writhing in pain for a few minutes or knock you out completely.

I turned and walked along the ward, with Brook following me. The spell followed the curved flower bed.

"What's the point of the ward?"

"Nobody knows," Brook said.

"Did you ever ask Gendun?"

"I have, actually. He just smiled."

Great.

Ahead, a two-foot-wide gap severed the circle of the ward. I stopped by it, looked through, and saw another ward. This was a magic maze, with rings inside rings of wards and in the center of it all was the apple tree.

"She's watching us," Brook hissed.

"What?"

"Second-floor window, on the left."

I looked up and saw Lisa looking at us. Our stares connected. Lisa's face had this strange mix of emotions, part realization, part fear. She had figured me out. She understood that I saw the ward somehow and I knew about the apple tree, and she was afraid now. It couldn't be me she was scared of. I wasn't that scary. Was she scared that I would find Ashlyn?

A bright green glow burst from Lisa's back. It snapped into the silhouette of an eight-foot-tall wolf. The beast stared at me with eyes of fire.

My heart fluttered in my chest like a scared little bird. Something ancient looked at me through that fire. Something unimaginably old and selfish.

The wolf jerked and vanished. If I had blinked, I would've missed it.

"Did you see that?"

"See what?" Brook asked.

So I had seen it with my sensate vision.

Lisa turned away and walked off. My forehead felt iced over. I swiped the cold sheen off my skin and saw sweat on my hand. Ew.

Things were making more and more sense. I turned to Brook. "Do you have a library?"

She gave me a look like I was stupid. "Really? Do you really need to ask that question?"

"Lead the way!"

Brook headed to the door. Just as she reached for it, the door swung open and Barka blocked the way. "Hey!"

Brook pushed past him and marched down the hall, clenching her teeth, looking like she would mow down whoever got in her way. I followed her.

Barka caught up with me. "Where are we all going so fast?"

"To the library."

"Is it on fire and they need us to put it out?"

"No."

Barka must've run out of witty things to say, because he shut up and followed us.

The library occupied a vast room. Shelves lined the walls. With magic coming and going like the tide, the e-readers were no longer reliable, but the library stocked them, too. If you needed to find something in a hurry, the e-readers were your best bet. You just had to wait until the magic ebbed and the technology took over again.

Sadly the magic showed no signs of ebbing.

I walked through the library, checking labels on the shelves. Philosophy, psychology . . .

"What are you looking for?" Brook snapped. "I'll find it faster."

"Greek and Roman mythology."

"Two ninety-two." Brook turned and ducked between the bookshelves. "Here."

I scanned the titles. *Encyclopedia of Greek and Roman Myths.* Score!

Brook's eyes lit up. "Shit! Of course. The apples. It's so plain, I could slap myself for being so stupid."

"You got it." I yanked the book from the shelf and carried it to the nearest desk, flipping the pages to get to the letter *E.*

"What's going on?" Barka asked.

"She found Ashlyn. She is in a tree," Brook told him.

"Why?"

"Because she is an Epimeliad," I murmured, looking for the right listing.

"She is a what?"

"An apple dryad, you dimwit," Brook growled.

Barka raised his hand. "Easy! Greek and Roman was three semesters ago."

"Epimeliads are the dryads of apple trees and guardians of sheep," I explained.

Barka leaned against the desk. "That's a bit random."

"Their name comes from Greek *melas,* which means both apples and sheep," Brook said.

"This explains why she's scared of Yu Fong," I said. "He's all about heat and fire. Fire and trees don't play well together."

"And someone left a wolf print on her desk. Wolves are the natural enemies of sheep," Barka said.

"Someone was trying to terrorize her." Brook dropped into the chair, as if suddenly exhausted. "And none of us ever paid attention long enough to see it."

"It was Lisa." I scanned the entry for the dryad. Shy, reclusive, blah-blah-blah . . . No natural enemies. No mention of any mythological wolves.

"How do you know?"

"She has a wolf inside her. I saw it. That's why her powers are stronger. I think she made a deal with something and I think that something wants Ashlyn."

They looked at each other.

"Just what kind of magic do you have, exactly?" Barka asked.

"The right kind." I pulled a chair out and sat down next to Brook. "If

Lisa had made a deal with a three-headed demon or some sort of chimera, I could narrow it down, but a wolf, that could be . . ."

"Anything," Brook finished. "Almost any mythology with a forest has a *canid*. It could be French or Celtic or English or Russian or anything."

"Can any of you remember her saying anything about a wolf? Maybe there's a record of books she checked out?"

"I'll find out." Brook got up and made a beeline to the library desk.

I flipped through the book some more. Dryads weren't too well-known. They were just supposed to be these flighty creatures, easily spooked, pretty. Basically sex objects. I guess Ancient Greeks didn't really have a lot of access to porn so it must've been fun to imagine that every tree hid a meek girl with big boobies.

Somehow I had to untangle Ashlyn, and not just from that apple tree, but from this entire situation. I didn't know for sure if Lisa had made some sort of deal with the creature. I could be wrong—it could be forcing her. The only thing I knew for sure was that I alone didn't have the strength to take it on in a fight. My magic wasn't the combat kind and that thing . . . well, from the intensity of the wolf's magic, it would give even the Pack's fighters pause.

Sometimes I wished I had been born a shapeshifter. If I was Curran, I'd just bite that wolf's head off.

Curran. Hmm. Now there was a smart thought. I pulled a piece of scratch paper from the stack on the library desk, wrote a note, and read it. He would do it. After I pointed out all of his shortcomings, he would do it just to prove me wrong. I felt all happy with myself.

Brook came back with a disgusted expression on her face. "Apple trees. She checked out books on apple trees."

"That's okay. Barka, can you take this note to Yu Fong?"

He shrugged. "Sure. I like to live dangerously." He took the note out of my fingers. "Later!" He winked at Brook and took off.

"You're going to fight the wolf," Brook said. "You are the stupidest person I've ever met. We need to take this to adults now."

"I think Gendun already knows what's going on. He wouldn't have

missed the tree coming to life. He didn't seem frantic about Ashlyn's disappearance and he said that the locating spell indicated she was on the
grounds. I think that I'm meant to solve this one myself."

"He would be putting your life in danger." Brook shoved her glasses
back up her nose. "And Ashlyn's."

"I can't explain it. I just know that I'm trusted to do this on my own."
Maybe it was something only I could do. Maybe Ashlyn would trust another
girl her age, but not an adult. Maybe Gendun was just clueless. I had no
idea. I just had to get Ashlyn out of that tree.

When I was stuck in my old school, there were times I would've hid in
a tree if I could have. I knew Kate and Curran and even Derek, the dimwit,
would come to rescue me. But I knew none of my school friends would.
Sometimes you just want a kid like you to care. Well, I was that kid.

"I'm coming with you," Brook announced.

"I don't think this is a good idea," I told her.

She pushed her glasses up at me.

"Fine." I grinned. "Get yourself killed."

I WAITED IN the courtyard on one of the little benches on the edge of the
wards, reading my little book in plain view. I'd borrowed it from Brook. It
was explaining how the universe started with a giant explosion. I understood about two words in it, and those were *the* and *and*.

The day was dying down. Most students were long gone and those who
lived in the dormitory had left campus, too. Strangely, no teachers came up
and interrogated me or demanded to know when I was planning on leaving.
That only confirmed my suspicion that Gendun knew all along what I was
up to. Maybe he had some sort of secret adult reason for handling this
problem through me. Maybe it was a test. I didn't really care. I just waited
and hoped the magic would hold.

The dusk had arrived on the wings of a night moth, silent and soft. The
sky above me darkened to a deep, beautiful purple. Stars glowed high above,
and below them, as if inspired by their light, tiny fireflies awoke and crawled
from their shelter in the leaves. Late enough.

I put my book on the bench and started toward the wards. The magic still held, and when I focused, using my sensate vision, the glowing walls of the wards shimmered slightly. I walked along the first gap and paused. I was pretty sure I'd be followed. Lisa alone might not be capable of remembering all the gaps in the invisible fence, but a wolf would follow his nose and my scent.

I'd have to ask people in the Pack how to make my scent signature stronger. If I had had dandruff, I'd scratch my head, but I didn't. I dragged my hand through my blond hair anyway and moved on, walking along the next ward to the narrow gap.

I weaved my way through the rings of defensive spells, taking my time, pausing at the gaps, until finally I emerged in the clear space around the tree. Blossoms sheathed the branches. Delicate flowers with white petals blushing with faint pink bloomed between tiny pink buds.

I hoped I was doing the right thing. Sometimes it's really hard to figure out what the right thing is. You do something, and you wish you could go back in time for five seconds and undo it or unsay it, but life doesn't work that way.

Nothing ventured, nothing gained.

I pulled a Red Delicious apple from my pocket. The skin of the fruit was so red, it was almost purple. I crouched and rolled the apple gently to the tree's roots. It came to rest against the trunk.

The bark of the tree shifted, crawled . . . A bark-sheathed leg separated from the trunk and stepped into the grass around the tree. The toes touched the grass and the bark melted into human skin. A moment, and a short petite girl crouched in the grass. I caught my breath. Ashlyn's hair had gone completely white. Not just blond or platinum. White.

She picked up the apple. "Red Delicious."

"Hi, Ashlyn."

She glanced at me with green eyes. "Hi. So you found me."

"It wasn't very hard."

A spark of magic flared beyond the wards. Ashlyn cringed, her eyes wide. "It's coming!"

"It will be okay."

"No, you don't understand! The wolf is coming."

Lisa walked up to the outer ward.

"She's here!" Ashlyn squeaked. "Go away! You'll get hurt."

"Trust me."

Lisa dashed through the wards, running fast, following my trail. I stepped in front of Ashlyn.

Lisa burst out of the ward maze and stopped. "Thank you for showing me the way."

I kept myself between her and Ashlyn. As long as Lisa concentrated on me, she wouldn't look behind her to see who was following her through the ward. "What is the wolf?"

"You saw him?"

"Yep."

Lisa sighed. "It's a forest spirit. It's called Leshii."

"It's a creature of the forest?" Ashlyn gripped my arm. "But why does it want to hurt me? It's like me."

"It wants your blood," Lisa said. "It's weak, and your blood would make it stronger."

"It wants to eat me?" Ashlyn whispered.

"Pretty much. Look, I never had a problem with you. I'm just tired of being Lisa the Dud."

"How did you make the deal?" I asked her.

"I let it out of the Mage Academy," Lisa said. "My dad showed it to me. The mages trapped it during the last magic wave and gave it some trees, to keep it alive while they studied it, but the trees weren't enough. It wants a forest and I want people to take me seriously. It's a win-win."

"Except for Ashlyn, who will be eaten alive. No biggie," I said. Bitch.

"What am I supposed to do?" Lisa's voice went up really high and I saw that same fear I glimpsed earlier. Except now it was in her eyes and written all over her face. "I didn't know what it wanted when I took it out. The deal was, I carry it out inside me and it gives me powers. I didn't know it was going to kill her!"

"Are you a total moron? That's the first thing they teach you in any school," I growled. "Never make deals with magic creatures. It's a spirit of the damn forest! Do you know how powerful it is? What the fuck did you think would happen?"

"I'm tired of listening to you," Lisa snarled. "This is over. Nobody asked you to stick your nose where it didn't belong. I told you to leave and you didn't listen. You can't fight it. And now you're both going to die, so who is a moron now, huh?"

"You're a terrible person," Ashlyn told her.

"Whatever . . ." Lisa's arms snapped up and out, as if she was trying to keep from falling. A scream filled with pain and terror ripped out of her. A phantom wolf burst out of her chest, huge, shaggy, glowing with green magic. It landed on the grass, towering over us. Its fur turned gray. The wolf's cavernous mouth gaped open, suddenly solid. Monstrous fangs rent the air.

"Now!" I yelled.

Yu Fong stepped through the ward into the clearing. His irises glowed with orange and in their depth I saw tiny spirals of flames.

The wolf spun to face him.

Magic unfurled from Yu Fong like petals of a fiery flower. It shone with scarlet and beautiful gold and shaped itself into an outline of a translucent beast. It stood on four muscular, strong legs, arms with huge claws rippling with flames. Scales covered its body. Its head belonged to a meld of Chinese dragon and lion, and long whiskers of pure red streamed on both sides of its jaws. Spikes bristled among its crimson mane and its eyes were pure molten lava. Within this beast Yu Fong smiled, a magic wind tugging at his hair.

Wow. He was a dragon.

The wolf charged, aiming for Lisa. Yu Fong stepped into its path, knocking Lisa out of the way. She fell on the grass. The dragon opened its mouth. Flame burst with a roar, like a tornado. The fire engulfed the wolf, and the shaggy beast screamed, opening its mouth, but no sound came.

The wolf lunged at Yu Fong, biting at the dragon with its enormous teeth. Yu Fong clenched his fists. A wall of towering flames shot out from the dragon and wrapped itself around the wolf.

Heat burned my skin.

The wolf writhed in the cocoon of flame, biting and clawing to get free. Yu Fong's face was serene. He leaned back, laughed softly within the beast, and the fire exploded with pure white heat, singeing my hair.

Ashlyn hid her face in her hands.

The wolf burned, crackling and sparking. I watched it burn until nothing was left except for a pile of ashes.

The dragon melted back into Yu Fong. He stepped to the pile of flames and passed his hand over it, so elegant and beautiful, he seemed unreal. The ashes rose in a flurry of sparks, up into the sky, and rained on the courtyard beyond the wards, settling to the ground like beautiful fireflies.

"Well, that's that," Brook said, at the outer ward. "Ashlyn, I have this blanket here for you."

Yu Fong stepped toward us, and Ashlyn took a step toward the tree.

"Don't be afraid. I won't hurt you," he said, his voice soothing. "Come, let's get you dressed."

Around us, the world clenched. The magic vanished, abruptly, like the flame of a candle being blown out by a sudden draft. The wards disappeared. The garden seemed suddenly mundane.

Well. How about that?

Yu Fong escorted Ashlyn away from the tree, guiding her toward Brook.

Lisa got up. Her legs shook. She shuddered and limped away, into the courtyard. I didn't chase her. What was the point?

Brook draped the blanket over Ashlyn's shoulders and gently led her away. I sat down on the grass and leaned against the trunk of the apple tree. I was suddenly very tired.

Yu Fong walked over and looked at me. "Happy, Julie Lennart?"

"It's Olsen," I told him. "I only pull Lennart out of my pocket for special occasions."

"I see."

"Thank you for saving Ashlyn."

Yu Fong reached for the nearest apple branch and gently pulled it down, studying the fragile blossoms, his inhumanly beautiful face framed by the blooms. Somebody should have taken a picture. It was too pretty.

"Of course, now you owe me a favor," he said.

Jerk. No, you know what, forget it. He wasn't pretty. In fact, I've never seen an uglier guy in my whole life.

"The satisfaction of knowing you saved Ashlyn's life should be enough."

"But I didn't just save her life. I saved yours, too," Yu Fong said.

"I would've handled it."

The look he gave me said loud and clear that he thought I was full of it. "I expect to collect this favor one day."

"Don't hold your breath."

"I imagine I'll have plenty of opportunities, since you will be spending a lot of time here," he said.

"What makes you think I'll be studying here?"

"You've made friends," he said. "You will be worried about them." He let go of the branch and walked away. "I'll see you tomorrow, Julie Olsen."

"Maybe!" I called. "I haven't decided yet!"

He kept walking.

I sat under the apple tree. Somehow leaving Ashlyn and Brook to his tender mercy didn't give me a warm and fuzzy feeling.

I was pretty sure I could get admitted into this school. It wouldn't be that hard.

I was right. Kate had set me up.

But then again, maybe it wasn't such a bad thing.